PENGUIN BOOKS

Never Kiss your Roommate

D0756619

Never Kiss your Roommate

Philline Harms

PENGUIN BOOKS

Content Warning: sex, bullying, assault, kidnapping

PENGUIN BOOKS

UK | USA | Canada | Ireland | Australia
India | New Zealand | South Africa

Penguin Books is part of the Penguin Random House group of companies
whose addresses can be found at global.penguinrandomhouse.com.

www.penguin.co.uk   www.puffin.co.uk   www.ladybird.co.uk

Penguin
Random House
UK

Published in Great Britain by Penguin Books in association
with Wattpad Books, a division of Wattpad Corp., 2021

004

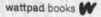

wattpad books

www.wattpad.com

Printed and bound in Great Britain by Clays Ltd, Elcograf S.p.A.

The authorized representative in the EEA is Penguin Random House Ireland,
Morrison Chambers, 32 Nassau Street, Dublin D02 YH68

A CIP catalogue record for this book is available from the British Library

ISBN: 978-0-241-51645-4

All correspondence to:
Penguin Books, Penguin Random House Children's
One Embassy Gardens, 8 Viaduct Gardens
London SW11 7BW

To my readers; this book wouldn't exist without you.

1

Evelyn

Long train rides, to me, had always felt a little bit like slipping out of reality.

There was something about the smooth glide of the wheels on the rails and the monotonous hum of the engine, the way there was nothing interesting to focus on except the landscape outside and the bored faces of other passengers, that made it so easy to get lost in my fantasy.

All I had to do was close my eyes and I was in another time, another place, another one of those lives I had lived vicariously through the pages of some tattered paperback. I could be a young farm girl on her way into the city for the first time. Or maybe a detective on his way to a small town where he would investigate a mysterious murder. Or maybe some aristocrat's daughter sent off to marry an unknown spouse—a noble*woman*, of course, because although I had a vivid imagination, it wasn't *that* creative—the ambient noise of the train morphing into the rattling of a carriage across cobblestones in my mind.

It was all there, a whole world inside my head in which to immerse myself, and once I got bored of it, I could simply dive into the next one.

That was, unless the train came to a stop.

Right now, it stood in a train station somewhere in the middle of nowhere, the doors open to spit out people whose travel ended here. I blinked open my eyes and stifled a yawn behind my hand as I looked out at the platform, watching as people kissed their loved ones good-bye or hello while others strolled off alone.

Not many passengers were left around me and the announcement about the train's departure that crackled through the speakers led me to the conclusion that no one else would be getting on—until a boy suddenly skidded inside, his large suitcase almost getting stuck between the closing doors.

He turned around, swearing under his breath when the duffel bag he had slung across his shoulder got caught on one of the seats. After heaving his suitcase into the overhead carrier, he slumped down on a seat on the left-hand side, level with where I was sitting. His third piece of luggage, a large backpack that looked like it was stuffed full to the very top, he placed on the seat next to him. Only then did he release a relieved exhale, one hand coming up to brush aside the strands of unruly brown hair that had fallen into his eyes. After what I assumed had to be an impressive sprint to the train platform, there was a bright flush that spread from his pale cheeks all the way to the tips of his ears.

The train left the station with a steadily increasing rumbling sound, the landscape outside turning into a blur of browns and greens once again, the sky a steely gray that promised rain. I hoped that it would wait until I reached my destination.

My destination. So far, I had managed to distract myself from the looming unknown, but now, with nightfall fast approaching and only a few stations left until the train would reach it, an anticipatory shiver ran down my spine.

Luckily, a loud rustling sound ripped me out of my thoughts before panic truly set in. In the reflection of the window, I could see the boy digging around in his backpack until he finally pulled out a paperback book. A quiet gasp tore free from my throat when I recognized the cover: a train driving down snowy train tracks, headlights cutting through the night.

In the deserted carriage, the noise was loud enough to make the boy look up, shooting me a confused glance. His bewilderment seemed to ease when his eyes drifted down to the book I was balancing in my lap, my train ticket serving as a bookmark after I had put it down an hour ago—a similarly tattered copy of Agatha Christie's *Murder on the Orient Express*.

His lips quirked into the hint of a smile. "Good book, huh?"

"It's one of my favorites," I said. I was silent for a moment but then, because I hadn't had anyone to talk to in over five hours, much less anyone my age who also happened to read, I asked, "What chapter are you on?"

"Chapter five. But I've already read it a hundred times, so . . ."

"Me too."

His smile widened. "Nice." He hesitated for a moment before he lifted his backpack, previously acting as a barricade between us, and slid over to the seat closer to the aisle. "So . . . is this your first year at Seven Hills?"

My heart skipped a beat at the name I had previously tried to block out. "How do you know I'm going there?"

"You look about seventeen, meaning you're the right age to be a student. You're carrying a lot of luggage, indicating you might have packed for a pretty long stay." He pointed up at the two suitcases occupying the overhead carriers. "And finally, there are only two more stops. The next one is in some small village, so it's unlikely that you'll get off there. That leaves only the last stop, which happens to be within walking distance of the school."

"All right, Sherlock," I laughed. "You're right, it's my first year. What about you?"

"Me too."

I was more relieved than I cared to show. The prospect of having to enter the school all alone had been terrifying, to say the least, so this was a lovely turn of events.

Leaning into the aisle, I stretched out a hand. "I'm Evelyn."

He shook my hand with a grin, blowing a strand of hair out of his eyes. "Seth. Seth Williams."

"You're not from around here, are you?"

It took no deduction skill to be able to tell that; his thick Northern accent was hard to mistake.

"No," he laughed. "I'm from Manchester. You?"

"Leicester."

Outside a light drizzle had begun, raindrops trailing down the windows and blurring the landscape behind them. The carriage's overhead lights flickered a little.

Seth was still studying me, his head cocked slightly to the side. "Why did your parents want to get rid of you?"

"They didn't want to *get rid of me*." In fact, that had been exactly what my mom had said: *Sweetheart, it's not like we want*

to get rid of you. We just think that a change of scenery would be nice, don't you think? "I didn't exactly like my last school."

"I see," he said slowly. "No heart-wrenching sob story there? You just wanted to go?"

"Yes." I changed the subject. "Why do you ask? Are your parents forcing you?"

"They got divorced over the summer and didn't know what to do with me. Said that I could come back around Christmas if everything is *sorted out* by then." The dark expression clouding his face mirrored the gloomy weather outside. "It's a bloody shit show, the whole thing."

"I'm sorry."

Seth shrugged, but there was a tension in his shoulders that contradicted the casual gesture. "It's not your fault. Just sucks that I'm away from my sister."

"Is she too young to go to Seven Hills?"

"No, we're twins. But I got held back in primary school, so she's going to uni already." He was silent for a moment, chewing on his thumb. Finally, he looked at me again and asked, "Did you visit Seven Hills beforehand?"

I nodded. "They had an open house earlier this summer that my parents and I went to. Why, have you not been there before?"

"No. Everything was pretty . . . spontaneous," he murmured.

In hopes of calming him, I said, "I was only there for an hour, but it looked nice. The castle is lovely, and the teachers seemed really friendly."

Seth didn't seem convinced, his expression only darkening when a female voice announced the train's final destination, Gloomswick, just then. With a groan, he shoved his copy of *Murder on the Orient Express* into his backpack.

While carefully storing mine away, I said, "Maybe it won't be so bad. Who knows, Seven Hills might even be fun?"

Seth's snort gave away his opinion on that statement. "Right. I'm sure everyone at this posh private boarding school is going to be dead funny. I'm buzzing for it."

The train rocked to a stop before I could reply. After Seth helped me get my luggage from the overhead carrier (this boy was *tall*), we stepped out onto the platform. He swore quietly when a cold gust of wind took a hold of us, tearing at our clothes and whipping rain into our faces.

Gripping tighter onto my suitcases, I glanced around the train station. It consisted of nothing but the platform we were standing on and a small brick building where you could purchase tickets during the day, with a map of Gloomswick mounted on the wall next to the door. The small town slumbered at the feet of the hills that gave the school its name, but covered in a blanket of woods and with night falling, it was hard to see all seven.

Together, we left the train station and took off on a road that led right into the woods. Streetlamps stood every few yards or so, illuminating the road but not the forest, which seemed to edge closer to us from both sides. I kept throwing wary glances into the woods every time I heard a creak or a snap, but there was nothing to be seen except shadows and even darker shadows.

"You would think this rich-ass school would have some sort of shuttle to get us there," Seth grumbled.

"Probably part of the *discipline* thing they're all about," I chuckled. We were walking uphill, and I was out of breath already. "This is just the first endurance test."

Seth's only response was a stream of colorful swear words as he pulled his hood farther over his face. Keeping my head down,

I dragged my two suitcases along with me. My left shoulder was hurting from the heavy bag slung over it, the strap digging into it, and the rain was soaking through my clothes to the point where they clung to my body like a second skin.

Lightning flickered across the sky, followed by deafening thunder that made us both jump. The rain fell even heavier now and I dimly worried about the books in my backpack, when Seth suddenly let out an incredulous laugh.

"Are these the gates of heaven?"

Blinking against the rain clinging to my eyelashes, I raised my head enough to see what he was talking about. Seven Hills was an old castle with protruding alcoves and sprawling turrets that reached into the night sky, the windows in them a hundred unblinking eyes watching us warily as we neared the entrance. On the mild summer day I had come here with my parents, the building had looked enchanted with its arched doorway and the ivy climbing its stone facade; however, with the thunder roaring in the distance and lightning tearing through the sky behind it, right now it just looked haunted.

"*Lovely*, you said?" Seth grimaced. "This looks a little less Hogwarts and a lot more *Dracula* than I expected."

"Let's just go inside," I said, my teeth chattering.

"Do you want to go first, or . . . ?"

"Oh, I'm good."

With a sigh, Seth reluctantly walked up the steps leading up to the front door and pushed down on the handle. He made a surprised noise when it swung open just like that, luckily without the scary creaking sound I had already braced myself for.

Instead of the gloomy vault the outside of the castle suggested, the hall in front of us was drenched in the warm glow of a chandelier hanging overhead. The stone walls were covered in certificates from several sports tournaments Seven Hills had won and photos hung in golden frames, each one showing widely grinning teenagers from all different decades. There were large doors on each end of the hall that led to the different wings of the building, and then there were two flights of stairs leading to the first floor.

I nudged Seth when I spotted the figure descending the stairs on the left, but he had already seen her. With ginger hair that shone like copper in the chandelier's light, the girl was hard not to notice.

"There you finally are!" she said as she reached the end of the stairs. "Mrs. Whitworth was already worried you'd gotten lost on the way."

The way she carried herself, with an air of confidence and authority that was almost tangible, contradicted the look of her face, which, with soft features and a splatter of freckles, seemed no older than seventeen. Her gray eyes studied us appraisingly when she came to a stop in front of us.

"Sorry to keep you waiting," I said apologetically. "Are you supposed to give us the tour?"

"Yes, I am," she said. "My name is Amelia Campbell, head of the student council, and captain of our cheerleading team. First of all: Welcome to *Seven Hills International School for Boys and Girls*. We are happy to welcome you to our community."

She paused for a second as if waiting for an answer but continued before either of us could open our mouths. "Community is the most valued thing at this school, as you probably gathered from our website. You two are welcome, and even encouraged, to join one of our clubs or sports teams. It is important to get involved and contribute to our school's success and reputation."

Seth shot me a pained look that echoed his earlier statement about the *dead funny* private school students.

"With that said, let's get into the rules." Amelia flipped through the papers on her clipboard. "You are not allowed to leave school grounds without notifying a teacher. You must wear your school uniform and stick to the dress code. This is just another factor in establishing a community. Boys are not allowed to be in the girls' wing and vice versa. Intimate relationships are not encouraged."

"Bit heteronormative, isn't it?" Seth said, quiet enough that only I could hear him.

Amelia continued without taking notice. "You need to attend every meal in the cafeteria. If you are ill, you must see the nurse and either go to classes or remain in bed according to her judgment. Bedtime is at ten o'clock to ensure peak performance."

There was a meaningful pause. "Any breaches of these rules will be punished with community service at our school or, in the worst case, expulsion. Are there any questions?"

"What are we actually allowed to do?" Seth asked.

"You are allowed to study and serve the school's community, as I previously stated. That is the sole purpose of Seven Hills, and hopefully the reason you are here."

"Um . . . sure."

"Fantastic," Amelia replied and handed us a few papers. "Here is some information regarding the dress code and possible clubs or teams you might consider joining. Now, I will take you, Evelyn, to your room in the girls' wing. Seth, you will wait here—your roommate, Gabe, should be here at any moment to bring you to your room and help you settle in."

Seth didn't look happy at the prospect of being left alone here, but nodded.

I reached out and lightly squeezed his arm. "See you at breakfast tomorrow?"

His expression brightened a little bit at that. "It's a date."

"Hurry, Evelyn!" Amelia called, already climbing the stairs. "Bedtime is less than twenty minutes away, and we still need to get you settled in. You do not want to break the rules your first night here, do you?"

"Of course not," I murmured. Seth chuckled quietly behind me.

Amelia either didn't hear me or didn't pick up on the sarcasm. Instead, she wordlessly led me up the stairs and down a narrow corridor with tall windows that looked out onto the front yard, the thick red carpet swallowing the sound of our footsteps. Glancing over my shoulder, I could see the wet footprints I was leaving behind and hoped that Amelia didn't notice them. She seemed like the kind of person who would notice if anything was out of step, maybe fine me for an infraction I didn't even know existed.

At the end of that corridor, we climbed another flight of stairs where I struggled with all my luggage.

When Amelia suddenly spoke, it wasn't to offer help, but to say, "Evelyn, I do have to warn you about something."

"What is it?" I asked, almost tripping over my suitcases as I tried to keep up with her.

"Your roommate . . . let me phrase it like this: she is not easy."

"What do you mean?"

"She is impossibly rude and does not care about anyone else other than herself and that boy, Jasper, that she's always with.

Fact is, all of the girls she's shared a room with moved out within a few weeks. But I am sure you will last longer than that," she said. "Let us hope so, at least. There is no other girl at this school that would volunteer to move in with Noelle Daniels. Everyone is rather . . . intimidated by her."

"*Intimidated*?" I laughed. "I'm sure she can't be that bad."

Amelia spared me another, almost pitying look before she said, "See for yourself. This is your room."

With that, she pushed a key into my palm and pointed at the door at the end of the corridor. I hesitantly closed my fingers around the cool metal and walked past her, raising a hand to knock. When a few seconds had passed and no answer came, I inserted the key and turned it slowly, surprised when the lock only opened with a *click* after a second turn.

The room behind the door was almost exactly like I had imagined. The walls were bare stone, the floor a dark wood marred with scratches and dents left there by decades of girls. Two beds, two drawers, and two desks with one chair each occupied the two halves of the room. The left side was obviously taken by the other girl, books and magazines scattered all over her desk and clothes lying on the unmade bed.

Only after I had taken all of this in did my eyes fall on her. Noelle Daniels was sitting in the window, one foot standing on the sill, the other dangling outside like she had a death wish.

Her skin was a rich brown that, illuminated by the lamp on her desk, glowed golden, but that was all I could tell about her: the springy dark curls falling into her face made it impossible for me to see her features as she lifted the cigarette between her fingers to her lips, and she didn't react to the door opening. Sitting by the open window with lightning flashing and rain pouring behind her, unimpressed and unblinking, she looked like an avenging angel.

Only when Amelia cleared her throat behind me did Noelle turn her head. In a voice that was deeper than I had expected, she said, "What is it, Amanda?"

"Amelia. My name is Amelia. You know that," Amelia hissed and pushed past me. "Oh my God, is that a *cigarette*?"

"No, Amanda. Why would you think that?" Noelle flicked ashes onto the windowsill.

"Put that out right this second, Daniels. Your new roommate is here. Can't you at least *pretend* to be interested?"

"I suppose I could, couldn't I?" she mused, glancing my way. Suddenly overly conscious of my soaked state, I crossed my arms in front of my chest, aware that my hair was matted across my forehead and I was dripping onto the hardwood floor. In anyone else's face, Noelle's chocolate brown eyes, framed by long lashes, would have looked warm and comforting; however, as they slowly raked me up and down, a shiver that had nothing to do with the gust of cold air blowing through the open window ran down my spine.

Surprisingly, Noelle was the first one to look away, but the expression on her face made it clear the reason wasn't that I had beat her in the staring contest—she had simply lost interest. Lazily waving a hand in my direction, she said, "You know, there *is* a question I have. What the fuck is *she* doing here?"

"She lives here with you now. Didn't you hear me?"

"Not what I meant, Amanda. I remember clearly telling Whitworth not to bring another girl in here. So: What. Is. She. Doing. Here?"

"Evelyn will be living here," Amelia repeated. "Your hissy fits won't change that."

Noelle took another long drag from her cigarette before stubbing it out on the windowsill and tossing it outside. "We'll see about that."

"A map of the school grounds and additional information are on your bed, Evelyn," Amelia curtly said, fed up with the pointless discussion. "Breakfast begins at seven. Good luck with her."

I gave an uncertain nod, fighting the childish urge to cling onto her sleeve and beg her not to leave. When the door had fallen shut behind her and I turned back around, Noelle was sliding off the windowsill, not even looking at me anymore.

"I'm Evelyn," I said after a few tense seconds of silence. "Do you know where I can get a towel? I'd like to dry off."

Noelle lit another cigarette. I tried not to wrinkle my nose as the smell spread through the room.

"Noelle? I know you don't want me to be here, but maybe we can get along? I'll try not to be too annoying—"

At that, she finally turned around and walked up to me, not stopping until we were almost touching, and I could smell not only the cigarette smoke but also her perfume. "Try harder."

Breathing suddenly felt like a Herculean task. Noelle waited a few seconds, slowly exhaling the smoke from her nose. When I didn't say anything, she laughed—a short, raspy sound that made the blood in my veins freeze—and disappeared through the door that Amelia had left open. Looking after her, I realized that Noelle *was* as intimidating as Amelia had said. Almost as intimidating as she was beautiful.

And right now I wasn't sure which was worse.

2

Evelyn

Noelle didn't sleep in our room that night. When I had gone to bed, I had half expected to be woken up by her returning, but instead I awoke to the sound of my phone's alarm and the morning sun streaming through the window.

Breathing in the scent of an unfamiliar washing powder that clung to the bedsheets, I noted the room seemed bigger in the daylight, though that might have also been owed to Noelle's absence. I dimly wondered where she might have spent the night, but decided I didn't want to know.

At least her disappearing act had allowed me to take my time unpacking most of my luggage last night without feeling like I was bothering her. With a stack of my favorite books on the bedside table and a picture of my parents next to it, the space already felt more like home.

Looking at it, I remembered with a start that I hadn't texted my parents last night. I quickly scrambled for my phone, opening it to three worried messages from my mom.

How was the train ride? :)

Did you get there okay? I saw online that it was raining! Did you pack your raincoat?

I'm going to bed now. Please text me back when you read this! Have a good first day and call if anything happens, all right? Love, Mom xx

Guilt reared its head inside my chest as I quickly typed: *Sorry for not responding last night. The train ride was good, I met a boy who's also going to Seven Hills so I didn't have to walk there alone. Everyone's really nice so far.* A lie, but one that I knew would calm her. *Maybe I'll call you after class. Love you loads!!*

Finally, I dragged myself out of bed, showered, did my hair and makeup, and then tackled my uniform. It lay neatly folded in my unzipped suitcase, a pristine white button-down shirt that peeked out from under a dark navy sweater and a blue tie with stripes in a lighter shade. Additionally, there was a black skirt and white socks that almost went up to my knees.

The tie turned out to be a particular problem since I'd never worn one before; the fact that my hands were shaking a little with nerves for what lay ahead of me didn't help. Once I had accomplished something that at least approximated a knot, I gave up trying to make it any better.

My first day.

The mantra I had been telling myself in bed every night over the past few weeks echoed through my head again: *A new school, a new chance.* Studying myself in the mirror, I tried to imagine how the other students might view me. With my blond hair in a neat braid, a splatter of freckles from the summer that my makeup couldn't quite conceal, and my eyes slightly widened in apprehension, I looked . . . innocent? Inconspicuous? Hopefully enough of the latter to not get ripped to shreds on my first day here, I thought, flashing back to my former school, and gave my reflection a shaky smile.

Slinging my bag over my shoulder, I stepped out into the corridor. The building had an entirely different atmosphere by day: sunlight poured through the high windows and the hallways were bustling with students, laughter and the scent of perfume and hair products filling the air while a steady stream of girls was rushing down the stairs to breakfast.

I was about to fall in step with my new classmates when I felt a hand on my arm.

"Evelyn!" Amelia said. "I was just about to come to your room to see if you needed any help."

I stepped aside to let a pair of girls pass. "I'm fine, but thank you. That's really sweet."

"What in heaven's name did you do with that tie?"

"I've never tied one." I shrugged sheepishly.

Amelia shook her head with a quiet *tsk* sound and stepped closer. Within seconds, she had undone the knot and rearranged it neatly, so my tie matched her own. "There," she said, taking a step back. "Try and do it like this tomorrow."

I was almost 100 percent certain I would not be able to accomplish anything remotely similar, but said, "Thanks."

"Come along then. We don't want to be late."

I tried to hide my surprise when she looped her arm through mine, and I let her drag me along. Like last night, she was walking like she was late to an appointment, even though I had a feeling

Never Kiss
your Roommate

that she had not once been tardy to anything in her life. She ground to a halt only when we reached the top of the stairs; I was about to ask why, when my eyes found the reason for the disruption.

Noelle Daniels.

She was jogging up the stairs, pushing through a group of younger girls who readily made way for her. Instead of the school uniform everyone else was wearing, she was in a pair of black tracksuit bottoms and a matching top, both of which bore Seven Hills' emblem. Some stray curls had escaped her ponytail and were sticking to the thin sheen of sweat on her skin, and her earphones were blasting music loudly enough for me to faintly hear it as she neared us. I expected her to simply ignore me again; instead, Noelle gave us a sneer as she pushed past us towards our room.

Shaking her head, Amelia tightened her grip on my arm and tugged me along. "Pay no attention to her. The more you do, the worse she'll get, trust me. She probably made your first night here a living hell, didn't she?"

"Oh, it was all right," I murmured.

"Anyway, since she probably won't even talk to you, I suppose I should tell you that Noelle is on Seven Hills' basketball team. In fact, she is the first female captain the team has ever had."

Impressed by how quickly she had gotten the conversation back to after-school activities and *companionship*, I asked, "Basketball team?"

"Yes. Since this is an international boarding school and we have students from all over the world, we offer a wide variety of sports. I, myself, am the captain of the cheerleading squad. If you are interested in joining, you can visit our practice some time."

"Maybe, if I have the time," I lied.

A moment later, we arrived at the entrance hall where Amelia had picked Seth and me up yesterday. There, she led me towards a door between the two flights of stairs that I hadn't noticed last night because it had been shut. As we neared it, I could hear the clattering of tableware and loud voices.

"The Great Hall," Amelia commented. "We have all our meals here."

Behind the door lay a huge hall with long rows of tables and benches. Banners in black, white, and navy—the colors of Seven Hills—adorned the stone walls and were wrapped around the tall pillars that held up the arched ceiling. Nearing the buffet in the back of the room where the students queued to get breakfast, I was engulfed in the smell of pancakes and toast, sausages and scrambled eggs.

When it was our turn, Amelia said, "I recommend the whole grain bread and some fruit."

Pretending not to hear her over the racket, I loaded my plate with a chocolate croissant and a fruit yogurt. Amelia eyed my choice with disdain but took off towards the tables without commenting.

As we crossed the hall, I was glad to have Amelia with me. Most of the tables were already occupied by different groups that seemed like they were formed based on age, with the year-nine students at one end and students who seemed to be our age at the other. However, there were also other distinctions, as one table seemed to be made up of athletes in tracksuits like Noelle's worn over their uniforms while another group looked like it consisted of theater kids. I didn't know where I fit into the ecosystem yet, so I happily followed Amelia as she hunted down an empty table close to the entrance.

I was even happier when Seth made his way towards us. The tray he was carrying had two plates overflowing with food and clattered loudly against the table when he slammed it down.

"Are you all right?" I asked, scooting a little to the side to make room for him as he slumped down next to me.

Seth's answer was a groan and a shake of his head. Up close, I could see the dark circles under his eyes, his skin even paler than it had looked yesterday.

"Didn't sleep well?"

He stared darkly into his coffee. "It's bloody Gabe."

"Who's Gabe?"

"My roommate." Looking up at Amelia with a pleading expression, he asked, "There's no way I can change rooms, is there?"

Amelia gave a brusque shake of her head. "We cannot please everyone. Consider it a lesson to improve your social skills."

Seth looked like he was about to chuck his cup of coffee at her face, but instead he only took an angry sip. "God, you should see our room. If you can call it that. *Rubbish tip* is more accurate. How can one person alone make such a mess over the course of the two days he's been here? And the *smell*."

"Are you sure you're not exaggerating?" I laughed.

"*Yes.* I'm not the most organized person, either, but Gabe . . . I went in and I swear I couldn't even see my bed under all the trash he'd thrown on it. I literally had to *shovel* empty cans and crisp bags *off my sheets*."

"You are being overdramatic," Amelia stated. "There are worse people to room with. Just ask Evelyn."

Seth looked over at me in surprise. "Why, what happened?"

"Nothing happened," I quickly said. "Noelle is just a little . . ."

"Deranged?" Amelia threw in.

I frowned. "Harsh."

"What'd she do?" Seth asked. Bracing his elbows on the table, he suddenly seemed much more awake.

"Nothing, it's fine," I said before Amelia could answer. "She's just not very happy to have me as her roommate, is all. I'm sure we'll get used to each other eventually."

Amelia didn't look convinced. Her expression darkened even more when she spotted something behind me. "Speak of the devil and she shall appear."

Noelle was just settling down at a table at the opposite end of the hall. While she was wearing parts of the uniform, she was breaking the dress code completely; instead of the socks, she was wearing fishnet tights, along with black boots that looked ten times more comfortable than the ballerina flats the rest of us were wearing. She had also disregarded the tie and the blue jumper and was just wearing the white button-down and the skirt instead.

Next to her was a boy who immediately caught my eye because of his unusual hair color, a bright silver. When Noelle sat down next to him, he grinned at her and pressed a kiss to her cheek.

"Who's that guy?" Seth inquired. Like me, he was also looking over his shoulder to get a better view.

"That is Jasper Des Lauriers."

"Is he Noelle's boyfriend?" I asked.

"Jasper?" Amelia asked. "No, they are friends. *Best* friends, apparently. Noelle is with a guy from year twelve. Jasper's also in year thirteen with us."

Seth considered the pair for a few more seconds before he turned back with a shrug and dug into his scrambled eggs. "She doesn't seem that bad."

"That's because she probably isn't," I said.

Amelia raised an eyebrow. A moment later, she checked her watch and got to her feet. "Class is about to begin. I have to make some copies for the student council first, do you think you will find your way there yourselves?"

"I'm sure we'll manage," Seth said.

"All right. Don't forget the assembly later today! Mrs. Whitworth is going to welcome all the new students and give you a tour."

Seth waited until she was out of earshot before he said, "Bit strange, that one. And proper posh."

I nodded, watching as she disappeared through the door. "She definitely likes her rules."

"God, she *got off* on them when she read them to us last night," Seth snorted. "It's all a bit much though, isn't it? Especially the whole *no girls in the boys' wing and vice versa* thing to prevent *intimate relations*." He shook his head with a crooked grin. "Fools. I'm bisexual, these rules can't stop me."

I was silent for a moment, taken off guard by how casually the words rolled off his tongue. Before I could stop myself, I said, "I'm—I like girls."

"Sick. We're really conquering the system, huh?"

"Looks like it," I laughed, almost incredulous at how easy that had been before I suddenly realized that the hall was almost empty. "And we're also late."

Seth immediately got to his feet. "Shit. What class do we even have?"

"English Lit, I believe."

Seth groaned. "The name makes it sound like so much fun but once you need to interpret poems, nothing's *lit* anymore."

"You don't like English?" I asked in surprise while we crossed the entrance hall. Using the map of the castle that had waited on my bed along with a bunch of other pamphlets last night, I managed to lead us to the hallway with the classrooms that were located in the west wing.

"I like reading, but I don't like writing. Technology, maths, physics, that's the kind of stuff I understand."

"At least I know who can help me with my homework now."

"Only if you write my essays."

"Deal."

Seth wrapped an arm around my shoulders. "You know, Eve, I can already tell that this is the beginning of a beautiful friendship."

I couldn't help the smile that spread on my face at his words. With Seth, it all seemed so easy; we had met reading the same book and naturally started talking, came out to each other in a joking conversation, and now he considered me his friend. He embodied everything I had wished for when I had agreed to my parents' idea of going to a boarding school.

However, before I could express any of this, a thin voice sounded from my left. "Excuse me? Excuse me, children?"

Seth let go of me as we turned around to look at the short woman trying to get past us. She appeared to be about sixty years old, with gray curly hair that spilled out from underneath a big purple hat. "You two must be new here!" she chirped. "Are you in my English class?"

"I think we are?" I answered.

"Fantastic!" the woman said, clapping her hands in excitement before she walked off in the direction of her classroom. "Follow me, follow me! Oh, it's so good to see new faces! We will

Never Kiss your Roommate

have so much fun together! The lectures this year . . . Children, you are going to have a lark with them, I will make sure of that. Have either of you read *Wuthering Heights*?"

"I have," I said.

"Magnificent! I will make sure to have you read some of your analyses to the class this year. There's nothing I love more than teaching children who are truly interested in literature. Oh dearie me, I forgot to introduce myself again, didn't I? My name is Miss Pepperman, teacher for English Literature and Seven Hills' librarian. I'm also the boarding parent for the girls, so if you ever encounter any lady problems, be sure to come by my room! I live in the tower of the girls' wing and I always have an open ear, not to mention a fantastic tea collection!"

"Nice to meet you," Seth said, looking vaguely amused. "Though I'll apologize in advance. I'm really not good at writing—"

Miss Pepperman shook her head, her curls bobbing around her round little face. "Oh, love, everyone can write! I will make sure that you pass this class with flying colors. Now, come on in!"

She ushered us into a classroom that was smaller than I had expected, or maybe it just seemed that way because of all the bookshelves lining the brick walls.

At the front of the room was the teacher's desk, which was mainly covered in papers and little porcelain figures. The blackboard behind it, which was where Miss Pepperman headed, was filled with notes in neat calligraphy. With the golden morning light streaming through the high windows, catching in the specks of dust that were lazily floating about, the room seemed much more inviting than any of the claustrophobic, dimly lit classrooms I was used to at my former public school.

Most seats were already occupied when we entered, but we were lucky to spot a free table in the back. Seth and I had to exchange only one glance before we darted towards it and sat down next to one another.

Looking around the room, I was surrounded by faces I didn't know, briefly wondering where Noelle was. Since there weren't more than thirty students in each of the four years, therefore only roughly a hundred and twenty in total, the students in each year had every lesson together. In the end, she and her best friend arrived only a few seconds before the start of the lesson, not appearing to be in any hurry as they crossed the room and took up the last free table.

"Jasper!" Miss Pepperman exclaimed as soon as she noticed them, hurrying over to him. "How lovely to see you again. I missed your essays so much over the summer, you wouldn't believe it! Have you been busy? How is your play going?"

"You know me, Miss Pepperman, I'm always busy! And the play is going *fantastic*. Rehearsals start again on Wednesday. I would love to hear your opinion on the script, especially on the third act. I took out some things to make the plot more comprehensible for the year-nine pupils, so . . ."

"I will be happy to read the script, though I doubt I will find anything to criticize," Miss Pepperman laughed.

After a bit more talk about whatever play Jasper was working on, she walked back to the front of the class and clapped her hands. "Good morning, children! This year I am happy to welcome five new students to this class. Two of you I already greeted, to the rest of you: Hello, my name is Miss Pepperman. I will be your teacher for English Literature this year."

Some mumbled responses sounded through the room.

Never Kiss your Roommate

Miss Pepperman smiled brightly at us, eyes twinkling behind her thick glasses. "I know that some of you may have reservations regarding literature, but I promise that even you will be able to find some joy in my lessons. After all, we will start this year with a lecture on *Wuthering Heights* by the exceptional Emily Brontë."

The rest of the period passed quickly as the class read the first chapter out of the worn paperback books she handed out. Whenever Miss Pepperman asked a question, Jasper was the first one to put up his hand. I was nervous to participate at first, but after Seth nudged me with his knee to say something, I followed Jasper's lead.

It was strange to see how invested he was, while Noelle sat next to him with her arms crossed stubbornly in front of her chest, not saying anything. When it was her turn to read, she simply passed the book on to Jasper, who read her part without hesitation. Miss Pepperman's only reaction was a resigned sigh, like this wasn't the first time this happened.

After seeing Noelle's behavior in English Lit, I was all the more surprised when her hand was constantly up in math class only two hours later.

In every class, I realized one thing: I needed to catch up. Amelia hadn't lied when she said the school expected peak performance and some things mentioned today I had never even heard of, like the natural logarithm or Aristotle's *Nicomachean Ethics*. While I assumed I could read up on the latter, the former seemed impossible to teach myself, especially considering my rather slender grasp on all things mathematical.

I would have asked Amelia, but she had a student council meeting that afternoon, and Seth had seemed just as lost as I was. So, when I came back to my room after the assembly and the tour across the castle grounds, I was determined instead to ask Noelle for help. She was good at school, and excellent at math, so I was confident she could help me. All I needed to do was get her to talk to me. And that couldn't be so hard now, could it?

At least that was what I thought until I unlocked the door to our room and Noelle was nowhere to be seen. Unsure of what to do next, I took a tentative step towards her desk, which, just as I had expected, was covered in notes.

I knew that it was probably a bad idea—the worst idea ever— to touch her stuff, especially in her absence, but they were just school notes; surely she wouldn't mind. After glancing at the closed door once more, I reached out and blindly took one of the pages.

I was still trying to decipher her handwriting and figure out which notes belonged to which class when the door suddenly flew open and I whirled around, my back pressed against the edge of the table.

I knew the second her eyes fell on me that I had made a mistake, my heart fluttering like a panicked bird in my chest as Noelle stomped towards me and snatched the piece of paper out of my grip.

"Have you read any of this?" she asked in a dangerously low voice.

"No," I breathed. "Noelle, I'm sorry if I overstepped, I didn't think—"

Noelle looked at me for what felt like hours with an expression I couldn't read, her hand rumpling the paper in her hand with how hard she was clutching it. Finally, she said, "Don't *ever* touch my things again."

"I won't," I said. "I'm so—"

Noelle cut me off with a low *don't*. I didn't dare move as she slid the paper under one of the magazines on her desk and grabbed a duffel bag from her bed.

A moment later, the door slammed shut behind her and I slumped back against the desk, releasing a shaky breath. If I had had any chance of getting Noelle to like me, or even stand to have me around, I'd just ruined it.

3

Seth

I was starting to understand why the people in the novels I read became murderers.

It had been only a few days since I had arrived at Seven Hills, but I already felt one minor inconvenience away from snapping.

Reason number one: the fact that I had been sent here in the first place. It was all right that my parents were divorcing; after all, it had been a long time coming, and in the end, it was their decision to make. When they had sat me down at the kitchen table, apologetic smiles pasted over obvious discomfort, I had even been relieved for a split second to know that this was it—the storm cloud that had been building up under the roof of the house, growing darker and more threatening with every year that went by, charging the air with so much tension that my hair stood on end every time I came through the door, was finally

Never Kiss
your Roommate

erupting and it wasn't as loud as I had feared. No earthshaking thunder or blinding flashes, just a sheepish apology for the way things had been lately and an earnest *This has nothing to do with you, we both love you so much*. None of that would have been a bad thing in itself. It was only when my dad slid his phone over to me, the words *Seven Hills International Boarding School for Boys and Girls* written in an elegant font at the top of the website he had pulled up, that I realized I had let my guard down too soon. This was absolutely fucking terrible, but not in any of the ways I had anticipated.

Reason number two: Seven Hills was just as god-awful as I had thought it was going to be. Surrounded by the thick castle walls in the middle of bloody nowhere, I was a fish out of water. While things had come easily to me at home, I suddenly had to fight tooth and nail not to fall behind in all of my classes and spent the afternoons wading through a flood of homework that inched higher every day. Every bit of fun that might have remained was prevented by the thousands of rules that Amelia was all too glad to remind me of on a daily basis. Around her and all the other stone-faced boarders in their pristine uniforms, with shiny cars financed with their daddy's money parked behind the castle, I felt out of place and overly conscious of my ill-fitting blazer and scuffed-up shoes. Most of the time, I tried my best not to be seen; I simply sidestepped and ducked and blended into the brick walls whenever someone passed me by.

The only exception was Evelyn. Without her, I was sure I would have gone insane already, maybe turned into some kind of madman that had to be locked away in the attic like a character in some Gothic novel and whose wailing could be heard around the castle halls at night.

The third reason for my misery: *Gabe*.

Rooming with a complete stranger was anything but comfortable as it was; rooming with a complete stranger whose goal seemed to be to drive me mad was almost unbearable.

Every time I entered our room, it looked worse. Now it wasn't just empty food packaging and school stuff that were scattered all across the room, but also clothes, most of them dirty, and not only in his half of the room but in mine as well.

The cause of all the chaos was lying on his bed in nothing but boxers, playing something on his laptop. He wasn't wearing headphones, because that would have been too considerate, but was blasting his stupid gaming music out of the crappy speakers. To top it all off, he was eating crisps, sending crumbs flying everywhere when he yelled at his opponent.

Meanwhile, I was sitting at my desk, trying to study. "Gabe," I snapped, for probably the third time in five minutes. "Can you tone it down a little? I'm trying to do my homework."

Gabe looked at me, stuffed another handful of crisps in his mouth, and turned the sound up to its highest volume.

This little fucker.

Massaging my temples, I closed my eyes for a second. Being two years younger than I was, Gabe seemed to be intent on making up in attitude what he lost in age. It had been exactly the same the two nights before when I had tried to sleep, so this wasn't the first time we'd had this kind of argument. By now I was irritated and sleep deprived and was honestly considering throwing his damn laptop out of the window. Or him. I still had to decide.

But not right now when I had a summary of the first two chapters of *Wuthering Heights* to finish and two pages of Spanish

Never Kiss your Roommate

vocabulary to memorize. By leaving, I knew I was giving him some kind of satisfaction, but I didn't care. Focusing on schoolwork was hard enough for me as it was, and I knew I wouldn't get anything done with him in the room.

So I got up and gathered my things, only stopping in the doorway once more to say, with as much authority as I could muster, "When I come back, your things had better be on your side of the room or I swear I'll burn them."

The only answer I got was a loud burp. Clutching my books so tightly my knuckles turned white, I slammed the door shut behind me. The *looney-in-the-attic* idea was honestly starting to appeal to me. That way, I would at least have my own bloody space.

With only an hour and a half before curfew, there weren't many quiet places around here to work; the common room for boys and girls was crowded in the evenings, and the Great Hall was being cleaned after dinner. There was the library, but Miss Pepperman would be there, and I didn't want to do my English Lit homework around her, knowing that she'd probably offer help and it'd be awkward.

I ended up strolling around the castle for a bit to see if I could find a room where I'd be undisturbed. The entrance hall was as eerily silent as it had been when Evelyn and I had first arrived, my steps echoing from the walls as I walked towards the door that led to the west wing.

The corridor behind it was darker than the entrance hall, with pictures of the school's former headmasters on the walls and myriad doors on each side. The eyes of the grainy black-and-white photos followed me as I hesitantly neared the first door to my right. I didn't know what was more of a surprise: that it opened when I pushed against it, or that the room behind it was a huge auditorium.

Entering felt a little bit like I was doing something forbidden, but the ceiling lights were on, so I figured it was okay to be in there. My steps were muffled by the thick red carpet that matched the velvet of the seats that went all the way to the back of the room. At the front, there was an empty stage, only some of it visible as the curtain was drawn.

Whistling quietly to myself, I climbed up to one of the highest rows and slumped into one of the comfortable seats. I decided that I liked this room. No Gabe and no trash lying around, and instead of stinking like decay, this room only smelled faintly like dust. In the long-awaited silence, I opened my Spanish book and muttered the vocabulary out loud, but I hadn't even finished the first half of the page when the door suddenly flew open with a loud bang.

I looked up in fear of seeing a teacher or, even worse, Amelia. Instead, my eyes landed on Jasper, the chiseled-out-of-marble-by-Michelangelo-himself lad who was in all my classes and seemed to be friends with Evelyn's roommate.

He didn't look in my direction and I doubted he even noticed me as he crossed the room to lean against the stage; after a few days here, I had apparently perfected the art of being invisible. I briefly wondered what he was doing here alone, but that question was answered when, one after another, about twenty other students filed in after him.

None of them seemed to notice me sitting in the back of the room as they went to sit down in the first row. I was grateful to remain undiscovered because it gave me the chance to really look at Jasper for the first time.

I had always liked watching strangers, to try to see if I could

Never Kiss
your Roommate

deduce anything about them just by studying their clothes, their expressions, the way they carried themselves. With Jasper, it was especially interesting. There was so much to see, so much worth a second glance.

The first thing that caught my eye—the first thing I had noticed upon seeing him in the Great Hall yesterday—was his bright silver hair. It was styled in a way that seemed effortless, tousled just enough to look like he had just rolled out of bed, a few strands falling onto his forehead. I could tell that his appearance was important to him, but that he didn't want other people to think it was.

There was something intimidating about his eyes, a piercing blue that intently fixed on the kids sitting in front of him. Or maybe it was his height. I already considered myself quite tall, but Jasper easily had a few inches on me. However, when my eyes drifted down his legs, I realized that this was also owed to the shoes he was wearing; black boots with a tall platform that looked higher than anything I had ever seen my sister wearing.

Those shoes weren't the only things that broke the school's dress code: he wasn't wearing the stupid blue jumper or the tie, only the white button-down with the sleeves rolled up to his elbows. It was infuriating that the blue bowtie and suspenders he had added for some reason didn't look silly on him. With his perfect appearance and calculating gaze, he was a prime example of the type of unapproachable boarders who surrounded me.

I almost jumped when he spoke. "*Salut* everyone, welcome to the first rehearsal of the school year. We don't have much time, the premiere is in two months, that's only a few rehearsals before everything has to be perfect. I hope all of you have learned your roles over the break because today we are starting off book."

In class, he had only spoken a few short sentences at a time. Now, the French accent was unmistakable, with harsh *R*s, barely there *H*s, and sentences with a melodic rhythm, like a river flowing over stones.

"Sadly, as some of you may have noticed, Tom, the guy who did the electronic stuff, graduated this summer. So, until we find someone who's good at stuff like that, I will have to try to do the lights." He ran his fingers through his hair, grimacing a little, before he clapped his hands. "We'll start with the third scene. Into position, everyone, we don't have all night. Also, please appreciate the tower I spent the last week building with all the other early comers."

The others got up as soon as he was finished talking, rushing to stand in their positions. Two of them pushed open the curtains, revealing the stage, completely empty save for a tower made of papier-mâché and wood that stood in its center.

It had one window, and that's where the head of a boy with dark skin and even darker curls now appeared. At Jasper's signal, another guy, this one with a buzz cut, entered the stage and cautiously neared the tower. His eyes widened when he saw the boy sticking his head out of the window above, but before he could get too close, a girl wearing a scarf around her head and leaning on a walking stick shuffled across the stage.

While Buzz-cut Boy hid behind the tower, she croaked, "Rapunzel! Rapunzel, let your hair down!"

I sat up a little straighter, carefully closing my Spanish book.

Curly looked down at his mother with an exaggerated eye roll before he threw down some bedsheets that he had knotted together. "I cut my hair, Mom! Those extensions were tacky!"

The girl huffed, but grabbed the sheets and pulled herself up. Apparently, she was on the cheerleading team Amelia had talked about or something, at least I was sweating just watching her climb the tower. Once she reached the top, she sat down on the surprisingly sturdy windowsill and gave Curly's cheek an affectionate caress. "How was your day, my love?"

Curly slapped her hand away. "It sucked! Do you know how boring it is up here? You promised you'd install Wi-Fi . . ."

"Watch your tone, young man!" the girl scolded. "The last time I allowed you to be on the internet, all you did was text on Grindr! The last thing I want is to catch you up here with MuscleMan68."

"MuscleMan69," Curly corrected her.

I stifled a laugh as a few other students chuckled. A gay Rapunzel adaptation was . . . surprising, to say the least.

The girl shook her head with a dismissive wave of her hand. "Tomato, to-mah-to. I have to go now. I'll be back tomorrow."

"Whatever," Curly huffed and crossed his arms.

Seconds later, the girl was back on her feet, muttering something about how difficult teenagers were before she exited the stage.

"Say that line louder next time, Gina," Jasper said from the side.

The girl nodded and went back to her seat, slightly out of breath. On the stage, Buzz-cut Boy was rounding the tower to stand beneath the window and yelled, "Hey, Rapunzel . . . Come out!"

Curly poked his head out of the window and shouted, "Who are you? How do you know I'm gay?"

Before Buzz-cut Boy could answer, Jasper climbed onto the stage and interrupted the scene with a clap of his hands. "All right, thank you! Well done, Aiden, that was great," he said to Buzz-cut Boy. "Gina, next time I really want to hear you, but great job on climbing."

Gina giggled. "Thanks, Jasper. I worked out."

"I can tell," he said. Then he looked at Curly. "Sammy, can I talk to you for a moment? Everyone else, please prepare for the next scene."

The boy immediately turned and sauntered over to Jasper. It was hard to understand what they were saying from where I was sitting, especially as the rest of the drama club began reading their next lines out loud, but I could pick up bits of it. ". . . were so good . . . no, really, that was amazing . . . so glad that you joined the drama club . . ."

Sammy didn't seem to care about lowering his voice as he said, a sly grin on his face, "Do I get a reward for that?"

Jasper reached out to straighten Sammy's tie. "My roommate won't be back till eleven, *chéri*."

Only then did it finally click in my head and I rolled my eyes at myself. Of course they were together. How stupid to assume that someone like Jasper was single.

"That's what I like to hear." Sammy chuckled before he went back to his tower.

Meanwhile, Jasper turned on his heels and walked up the aisle between the seats. I tried my hardest to shrink back into my seat, but I shouldn't have worried. On his way to the small platform in the back of the room where the control panel for all the electronics and the spotlights was, Jasper didn't look my way once and walked right past the row where I was sitting.

"This scene once again, please!" he shouted. "I'll try to do some lights."

I watched him curiously as he stared at the control panel before him with nothing but confusion written on his face.

On stage, Aiden, the guy with the buzz cut, opened the scene. Jasper frowned as he pressed random buttons, and nothing happened. A moment later, he jumped when the ceiling lights right above him suddenly flickered on. Releasing an angry stream of French, he began hitting every button at once, only for the lights to rapidly flicker on and off.

Maybe it was pity for him, or maybe it was the fact that the way he hacked at the buttons physically hurt to watch, but whatever it was, it made my legs move almost on their own accord as they carried me up the stairs and towards Jasper.

He looked at me over his shoulder, raising one eyebrow, but took a step back to give me better access to the panel.

Without meeting his eyes, I reached around him and found the button to turn off the ceiling lights immediately. Then I turned a lever to turn on one of the spotlights and pointed the beam at the tower, following the silhouette of the girl currently climbing up the bedsheets.

Next to me, Jasper whistled quietly through his teeth. "Not bad, strange boy I didn't notice was here."

I turned to look at him but forgot what I was going to say. Up close, he was even more intimidating, especially since he was so much taller than me. I was suddenly acutely aware of the fact that my shirt was too big, the sleeves pushed up so they wouldn't fall over my wrists, and my tie wasn't knotted properly.

Jasper, amused at my prolonged silence, reached out a hand. "I'm Jasper Des Lauriers."

"I know," I said, shaking his hand—God, I hoped my palms weren't sweaty—and belatedly added, "I'm Seth. We're in the same class."

"Right. Want to do the lights today?"

The word tumbled out of my mouth before my brain could think. "Sure."

"Oh thank God," he said, the last word twisting up into a small laugh. "I probably would have caused a short circuit any second."

Some kind of short circuit had to have already happened in my brain because all I could get out was a softly echoed, "Probably."

"All right. The control board is all yours." Jasper slowly backed away. Just before he turned around, he offered me another brilliant grin. "*Merci.*"

Whatever reply I had got stuck in my throat, so I just nodded. Watched as he made his way to the front of the room. Dragged my stare back to the stage. Adjusted the spotlight so it landed on Jasper's boyfriend.

And just like that, homework was suddenly my smallest concern.

4
Evelyn

It was around nine in the evening when I heaved myself up the stairs to the girls' wing on Thursday.

Life at a boarding school had proven to be much more tiring than I had expected; being surrounded by other students at all times wore on me, as I usually preferred to have some time to myself. But rooming with Noelle was harder than everything else—getting to know all the other students and teachers; trying to keep up with the lessons; and hiding from Amelia, who seemed to have a penchant for following me around—combined.

Since the incident with me trying to read her notes, Noelle hadn't said a single word to me. She didn't even look at me when we were alone, which was impressive considering we had every single class together and lived only a few inches apart.

The only relief in the tension between us came when she spent the night somewhere else. I still wasn't sure where she slept, but Amelia had implied she was with her boyfriend.

Though, as Amelia had been quick to correct me, *boyfriend* wasn't really the right term, as they probably only had a sexual relationship. I tried not to think too much about it.

After finally making my way up the last staircase, I hesitated at our door for a second. I thought I had heard a noise inside, but then I brushed it off as Noelle was rarely there at this time. And even if she was, right now I couldn't care less. I just wanted to lie down somewhere.

With the key scraping in the lock, the door swung open with a squeak, followed by another noise. One I hadn't expected.

Cheeks burning, I immediately spun around and pulled the door shut as quietly as possible behind me so they didn't notice me, but the images were already etched in my memory, even as I tried to will them away: a pile of clothes in the middle of the room, roaming hands, Noelle's hair spilling over her shoulders as she threw her head back, someone else's blond hair and broad shoulders illuminated by the light of the bedside lamp.

I almost tumbled down the stairs in my haste to bring as much space between myself and my room as fast as possible, not sure where I was going until I slithered through the foyer and the doors of the east wing. It was dimly lit, with rooms on each side, but I barely took any notice of them. The only thing my eyes were fixed on were the huge double doors that were slightly ajar at the end of the corridor, spilling light onto the stone floor. The library.

Mrs. Whitworth had pointed it out to us during our tour on Monday, but we hadn't entered. Now, as I stepped through the threshold, I couldn't help but gasp, this time not in horror, but in awe.

The library was so much bigger than I expected. Rows and rows of bookshelves took up every wall, reaching almost to the high ceiling, each of them adorned with intricate wood carvings. Nearby, there were a few desks with old computers and some comfortable-looking red armchairs between the shelves that invited visitors to curl up with a book.

Almost in a trance, I shut the door behind me. As I walked past one of the shelves, tracing a finger along the spines of dozens of books, I felt the most at home I had felt since my arrival here on Sunday. The overwhelming scent of old paper and ink was as soothing as it was grounding, and the little lamps in every shelf drenched the library in an ethereal glow that made it seem just a little bit otherworldly.

The bookshelves standing everywhere made it impossible to see the back, so it was hard to estimate the real size of the room. To me it seemed like you could spend an eternity in here, surrounded by thousands of stories and characters, so many universes to get hopelessly, wonderfully lost in.

"Evelyn, dear!"

Miss Pepperman's voice ripped me out of my reverie. Clapping her hands in childlike excitement, she appeared from behind her desk and skipped towards me. "I was wondering all week when you would come by!"

"I would have come sooner if I had known Seven Hills had such a huge library," I said, my eyes still wide as I took in my surroundings.

Miss Pepperman blinked solemnly behind her thick glasses. Along with her hands, which were fluttering excitedly at her sides when she talked, they gave her an owl-like appearance. "Most students don't. Or they just don't care. Some evenings, not a single soul comes down here. Can you imagine? All these wonderful stories and no one cares to read them. It's a pity, really . . ."

"For what it's worth, I will come here more often from now on," I promised.

"Wonderful! Then I don't have to be all alone here! It does get quite lonely after a few years. There's only one other person who comes here regularly."

"Who is it?" I curiously asked.

"Jasper Des Lauriers, of course!" she said. "You two would get along famously, I'm sure. He had exactly the same look on his face when he came in here for the first time!"

I almost had to laugh at the thought of befriending Noelle's best friend. He seemed nice enough in class, but if he was anything like Noelle, I doubted we'd click as friends. "Perhaps."

Miss Pepperman moved her arms in an expansive gesture that seemed to encompass the entire library. "Well, go ahead, darling, take a good look at everything! And don't you leave without taking at least one book with you!"

"I won't!" I promised as she got back behind her desk. Now I could see why I hadn't noticed her at first: sitting on her chair, she was barely tall enough to look over the counter.

There were only two other girls in here, sitting at one of the computers and giggling about whatever they were seeing on the screen. As if sensing my stare, one of them, about thirteen years old, turned around to me.

"Hey, Evelyn!" she chirped.

"Hey." I blinked at her in surprise. "How do you know my name?"

"Oh, everyone knows your name," the other girl giggled. "You're on the *Who's New?* page on The Chitter Chatter!"

Never Kiss your Roommate

"The what?"

The girls exchanged an amused glance. "The Chitter Chatter, Seven Hills' gossip blog!"

"Someone . . . writes a gossip blog about the students here?"

"Yes," the other one said impatiently. "No one knows who's writing it. It's been going on for about two years now, but no one has a clue."

"There's a pretty large betting pool, so if you have an idea and it turns out to be true, you might get a few hundred pounds out of it," the other girl added.

"So . . . whoever's behind it wrote something about me?" I asked, still hung up on that part.

"Not just about *you*. At the start of each year, there's an article introducing every new student at Seven Hills."

I frowned and tried to look over her shoulder to see some of the computer screen. Noticing, she got up from her chair and said, "We're done here, so you can read through it if you want?"

"Thanks," I replied, slowly sinking into one of the chairs while they left.

At the top of the site was the name of the blog, The Chitter Chatter, written in the same style as the Seven Hills' school emblem. Below was a small section introducing the author:

> Welcome to The Chitter Chatter Blog, your source for the newest gossip and the hottest scandals at Seven Hills. You will never find out my real name, but here I will call myself The Watcher. I'm right among you, waiting to expose all your dirty little secrets. Watch out, suckers.

I snorted quietly. Whoever was writing this blog clearly had a flair for the dramatic.

The rest of the website was plain and well organized, with different categories like *Tops and Flops of the Week*, *Rankings*, *Spilling the Tea*, and *Upcoming Events*. And then there was the section that the girls had been talking about: *Who's New?*

This was the one I clicked on, already preparing for the worst. In alphabetical order, there was a photo and a few sentences about every new student.

I didn't pay any attention to the others for now and scrolled until I reached *Evelyn Greene*. I had to close my eyes to gather myself for a moment when I saw the photo below it—it was a snapshot taken during dinner, showing me in the process of eating a sandwich.

The picture was taken from across the hall, which made it look grainy and unsharp, but you could still see most of my face. I was biting into the sandwich, my braid almost undone and my blouse adorned with a bright red ketchup stain.

Couldn't get much worse, I thought, until I read what was written beneath it.

> Evelyn Greene is what one might call a complete and utter klutz. Not only does she manage to stain every shirt she owns, she also tripped down at least two stairs on only her first day here and apparently hasn't worn a skirt in her entire life (a little tip, honey: you don't sit with your legs spread wide open).
>
> Besides that, she seems like your typical

naïve schoolgirl. Perhaps not the sharpest knife in the drawer, but she's trying, guys.

She has even made two friends already! Seth Williams (also new at Seven Hills) and resident teacher's pet Amelia Campbell have taken it upon them to try and . . . I don't know, stop her from embarrassing herself too much, I guess.

There's really nothing more to say about her, except for the fact that the poor girl is Noelle Daniels' new roommate. Bets on how long she will last?

I didn't know what I had expected, but it wasn't this. The Watcher, whoever it was, was *cutthroat*.

Trying not to be too affected by the snide remarks—at least I wasn't the only one being made fun of and the person had mostly just taken shots at my appearance—I scrolled farther down and skimmed through a few more entries. One of them was Seth's, the description of him as *an oblivious, boring nerd with a sense of humor that no one but him finds funny* somehow making my blood boil more than the article about myself.

With a bitter taste in my mouth, I left the *Who's New?* category and visited the page called *Rankings* instead. There were rankings for a bunch of different things, but the first one to catch my eye was called *Hottest Students*.

In the first place was, unsurprisingly, Noelle, followed by Jasper Des Lauriers. Then came a bunch of other girls' and boys' names I didn't know. And then . . .

I squinted at the screen to make sure I wasn't seeing wrong. But there it was: my name, in eleventh place.

For just a second my previous contempt was replaced with pride at the unexpected flattery, but I quickly caught myself. Who even cared about the opinion of a superficial online blogger?

Not me, I decided as I closed the window and went back to the home page.

Still, out of sheer boredom and the fact that I couldn't return to my room yet, I decided to do some research. I made sure to look over my shoulder to see if anyone was near and could see me typing Noelle's name, but other than Miss Pepperman, who was enthralled by the book she was reading, the library was deserted.

As soon as I hit *Search,* article after article popped up until there were at least twenty search results. Clicking a random title brought me to an article from six months ago that talked about how Noelle had bullied the former captain of the basketball team out of her place. After reading the first few lines, I was convinced that The Watcher had made the story up. Even though Noelle could be intimidating and rude, I doubted that she would go to such lengths just to be captain. At least I hoped so.

The next article I selected started with a blurred picture of Noelle making out with a boy. She was sitting on the windowsill in her—now our—room, her legs wrapped around a guy with flaming red hair.

Written under the photo was:

> To absolutely no one's surprise, Noelle Daniels has yet another boy toy. This time it's fellow basketball player Tom McHardy.

Never Kiss your Roommate

> I wonder if this is the reason for Tom's per-
> formance improving on the court? I'm sure
> his captain knows how to motivate him . . .
>
> Attention, team: I would steer clear of the
> locker room for a while unless you want to
> walk in on some steamy post-game sex ;)

I grimaced as the memory of Noelle with that other guy in our room returned, but tried to shake off the thought and continued browsing the articles.

There were a bunch of similar reports, all announcing Noelle's newest relationships. With each of them, the author got snarkier, more and more spiteful as they kept track of every single boy she had been seeing since her arrival at Seven Hills about three years ago.

There was one article that stood out though: instead of talking about an established relationship and giving proof in the form of explicit photos, it merely uttered a suspicion.

Are Jasper Des Lauriers and Noelle Daniels dating?

A few photos were attached to it, images of Noelle and Jasper laughing together in the Great Hall, them sitting together on the stairs outside with Jasper's arm around her shoulders and her hand on his knee while they were looking at something on his phone, Jasper hugging her after a basketball game victory.

Even though I was pretty sure they weren't together, seeing as Noelle was currently *busy* with someone else, I could see why someone who looked at these photos might mistake their friendship for something more. Especially after reading the article that accompanied them:

> Since Noelle Daniels and Jasper Des Lauriers arrived at Seven Hills three years ago, they seem to be attached at the hip. Whenever you see one of them, you can be sure the other isn't far. Whenever they're together, there's loads of physical contact, initiated by both of them.
>
> It really wouldn't be a surprise: we all know that Noelle isn't too picky and that Jasper isn't one to decline a hookup. Could Seven Hills' two hottest students really be a thing?

Curious about Jasper, whom everybody at this school from Miss Pepperman to The Watcher seemed to talk about, I clicked the link that took me to all the articles about him.

After only a few minutes of research, I knew that Jasper had been attending Seven Hills for the past four years and had made a name for himself with several plays he had written and directed for the school's drama club.

He was from Marseilles, which explained his French accent, and according to the blog, he was *pretty damn rich* because both his parents were surgeons in France. He also had two sisters, Alice and Catherine, who were twins and had graduated from Seven Hills two years ago.

Similar to Noelle, there were a few articles about several flings he'd had at Seven Hills, though they weren't nearly as many as Noelle's and nowhere near as mean.

At the moment he was in some kind of relationship with a guy named Sam from the drama club, but according to The Watcher, it was nothing serious.

There also was an introductory article from two years ago about him, but it didn't reveal any new information besides what I had found out already.

And then there was a picture of him. It was the first photo of someone on this entire blog that looked good: Jasper was sitting on the front stairs with his head in a book, hair falling in his eyes, and a faint smile on his lips, his dark coat billowing in the wind. Either he was extremely photogenic and The Watcher hadn't managed to take a bad picture of him, or the writer had a soft spot for him and had deliberately spared him the embarrassment.

Just when I had come to the conclusion that the former was probably the case, there was a quiet chuckle next to my left ear that made me jump.

Jasper stood inches away from me, leaning down slightly so he could get a glimpse at the computer screen, his hand braced on the back of my chair.

"*Mon dieu*, look at that side profile," he commented. "If the quality was better, this would be all over my social media."

"Oh," I muttered, fighting the impulse to reach out and turn off the screen, "H-hey Jasper."

With a grin, Jasper leaned his hip against the table. "So, you found The Chitter Chatter?"

I nodded, aware that my cheeks were probably flaming red.

"Find anything interesting?"

"Not really," I lied. "I was just looking at it to get to know everyone a little better."

"M-hm. Let me guess, you looked up Noelle's name?"

My face got even hotter, which didn't go unnoticed. "Oh, no need to get all flustered, *princesse*," he chuckled. "I would want to find out as much as possible about her too. You know, to make sure she won't suffocate me with a pillow in my sleep."

"She . . . she wouldn't do that. Right?"

He shrugged nonchalantly. "Not without a good reason."

My eyes widened when I thought back to her violent reaction to me trying to read her notes. "She hates me."

"She hates everyone. Don't take it personally."

"She doesn't hate *you* though."

"She doesn't hate me as much as everyone else," he corrected me. "Either way, don't believe everything that's on The Chitter Chatter. Half of it is made up."

"Do you know who writes it?"

"No. No one does."

I hummed, intrigued. There was an element of mystery to this that I was sure Seth, with his penchant for crime novels, would appreciate when I told him about it later.

Jasper leaned forward a little. "How does it feel to be in the top twenty? Flattered?"

"You tell me," I retorted with a smile. "You're in second place."

He breathed an exaggerated sigh. "So I've been told. I can't help it, I'm just too damn attractive."

"I'd like to have your confidence," I laughed.

"Why don't you have it?" Jasper cocked his head to the side. "Open that braid and pimp the boring uniform a little and you'll make it into the top ten of The Watcher's ranking."

50

"How do you pimp a white button-down and a stupid skirt? Not to mention these ballerinas. Walking in these *hurts*."

"Just don't wear them then. Noelle wore them the first day and then never again."

"But what about—"

"Dress code? No one really cares about it, except for Amelia," he said. "Just look at me. I break pretty much every rule, and no one's suspended me from class yet."

For the first time, I really took a look at his entire appearance. He was right. If he could walk around wearing black platform shoes and a long coat instead of a blazer, then I could at least disregard the ridiculous shoes.

"Tell me if you need any help," Jasper said, pushing himself off the desk. "I'm heading back to the boys' wing; the library closes in five minutes. I think it's safe for you to go back to your room now."

Immediately, the blood returned to my cheeks. "How did you know that's why I'm here?"

"I saw you bolting through the entrance hall like you'd seen a ghost," he answered. "It's not that hard to put two and two together."

"No, I suppose not," I laughed, thinking back to the many entries about Noelle's alleged hookups. "Good night, Jasper."

"Good night." Before I knew what was happening, he leaned down and pulled me into a short hug. I was frozen in shock for a second before I returned it, a little awkwardly since he was so much taller than me.

When he pulled away, the toothy grin was back on his face. "See you around, princesse."

Still reeling from the unexpected affection, I watched him leave before I turned the computer off and got up.

Remembering Miss Pepperman's order to take a book with me, I picked out *Great Expectations* by Charles Dickens, which I had read twice already and loved both times.

Moments later, I arrived back at our room. This time, I was much more cautious when opening the door, listening carefully and pushing it open slowly.

I found the room abandoned; all that hinted at what had happened were her crumpled bedsheets and the faint smell in the air but I was too tired to care and fell asleep as soon as my head hit the pillow.

5

Evelyn

Friday evening saw Seven Hills buzzing with excitement. There was a party in Gloomswick, I had heard, where a lot of the older students were going. Seth and I weren't all that interested in getting drunk, but we also didn't want to waste our Friday night. In the end, we decided to go out for pizza together after Seth had complained that he was sick of all the healthy food the cafeteria served.

Noelle also seemed to plan on going somewhere, as she was standing in front of the mirror doing her makeup while I got ready. Since she still didn't talk to me, I didn't know where she was heading, but I also didn't think asking was worth the trouble.

I was relieved when a knock at the door cut through the silence. Because I was expecting Seth—and Noelle didn't move an inch—I was the one to get it, only to freeze when instead I found Elias, Noelle's boyfriend.

"Oh," I said, eloquent as ever, and stepped aside to let him through, trying to push away the images that popped into my head at the sight of him.

Elias winked at me, obviously mistaking my blushing for something else, and strolled past me. "Hey, baby. Lookin' good."

Noelle, who was still doing her makeup, only smirked at him through the mirror, tilting her head slightly to the side when he wrapped his arms around her waist and pressed a kiss to her neck.

I felt horribly out of place.

"What took you so long?" Noelle, finished with applying her mascara, asked and turned around to face him.

"Had to wait until my roommate left so I could get *this*"—he produced a bottle of vodka out from beneath his coat—"out from under my bed."

"I knew there was a reason I kept you around. I'll give you the money later."

Uncaring of my presence in the room, Elias pulled her in by her hips again. "You know, there are other ways to pay me back . . ."

"Getting greedy there."

"How could I not when you look like *that*?"

I couldn't help but feel with him. Noelle was wearing a tight-fitting skirt that showed off her toned legs and a white top that contrasted with her skin. In addition, she had put on a leather jacket and a pair of heavy combat boots that made her even taller than she already was. All of it had made not staring at her impossibly hard.

Noelle seemed unfazed by Elias's flirting. Stepping out of his embrace, she lifted the bottle to her mouth and took a decent swig, not even grimacing at the burn of alcohol, before she slid the bottle into her purse. As she did, she made eye contact with me for a split second, raising a brow as if to dare me to say something.

I didn't and was relieved when there was another knock at the door behind me that excused my breaking eye contact.

"G'day, milady," Seth said in an exaggerated posh accent, bracing his arm against the door frame with a grin. "I am here to escort you to your dinner."

"Why, thank you," I laughed and turned around once more to grab my bag from my bed.

Noelle didn't seem to notice me leaving, too busy pressing her boyfriend against the wall next to the bathroom.

Shutting the door with more force than necessary, I stepped back into the hallway where Seth was waiting. "How'd you get up here?"

"Took the stairs," Seth informed me. "It's not like someone's keeping watch to make sure no boy comes to the girls' wing. And I'm clearly not the only one. Just the only one who didn't come here to shag, I reckon."

I shook my head with a laugh and fell into step beside him. My mood always seemed to lighten the moment I left Noelle's proximity. With her there, it was as if there was a vacuum that sucked all of the air out of the room, making it hard to breathe. Her presence felt *heavy* in a way no one else's did.

"Is it always like that?" Seth had read my mind.

"Like what?"

"That tense."

I nodded. In front of us, two other girls stepped out into the corridor. They seemed to be a year younger than us, stifling giggles and hiding their party outfits under long coats as they scurried down the stairs.

"I wonder what Noelle's deal is," Seth mused.

"I'll let you know if I figure it out."

Seth looked like he wanted to say something else, but was beaten to it by a high-pitched voice that sounded behind us.

"What on earth is *he* doing here?"

We exchanged a pointed look before we slowly turned around.

Amelia was standing behind us with a horrified expression and a hand on her hip. "You cannot be serious, Evelyn," she exclaimed and pointed at Seth. "What are you thinking, bringing him here?"

"She didn't *bring* me here," Seth said with a frown. "Believe it or not, I am capable of making decisions for myself."

Amelia looked over her shoulder like she was expecting a teacher to come around the corner any minute. Lowering her voice, she insistently said, "You need to get out of here!"

"Yes, that's what we were about to do before you stopped us," Seth groaned.

"*We*? Did you get permission to go out?"

"No, but we figured it was okay because everyone else is going out as well—"

Amelia's horrified gaze now fixed me. "You're *sneaking out*? Do you really want to get expelled after barely two weeks of being here?"

Seth pinched the bridge of his nose. Downstairs a clock struck nine, only increasing the panicked look on Amelia's face. I could almost hear her thoughts: *only one hour until bedtime.*

Never Kiss your Roommate

"Amelia . . ." I sighed, gently putting my hands on her shoulders to make her look at me. "We're just going out to eat. We'll be back in two hours or so, all right? It's not that big a deal."

"Honestly. We want to get pizza, not commit a bloody felony."

Amelia stared at Seth like she truly didn't see the difference between the two. I expected her to continue arguing, but instead she said, "All right then, suit yourselves."

"You're not going to tell anyone though, are you?"

"Don't be ridiculous," Amelia snapped, looking insulted that I had even dared to ask. "I'm not a snitch."

Seth nodded and slowly backed away, his hands raised like he was dealing with a frightened animal. "Okay. So . . . see you at breakfast?"

"Yes," she snapped. "Now get out of here."

Seth and I didn't need to be told twice. Under Amelia's wary gaze I hurried down the stairs, Seth sliding down the banister next to me.

Once we were downstairs, he led us into the west wing. At the very end of the hallway, there was a door I hadn't yet gone behind, which led into a huge gym. There, the emergency exit that had been propped open with a brick opened out onto a football field.

It was dark outside already, the night air surprisingly chilly for September. I kept my fingers tucked deep into the pockets of my coat while Seth and I made our way down the same road we had taken when we had first come here. It was only then I realized I hadn't left the castle since arriving; without being aware of it, my entire world had condensed into one building.

After a few minutes of walking, we reached the train station and from there it was only five more minutes until we found ourselves on the outskirts of Gloomswick. The town lived up to its name: the streets were gloomy and narrow, with old houses made of coarse brick pressing in from both sides. They leaned onto each other like weary elders and as we passed between them, I swore I could hear the tired creaking of the beams, the long-suffering complaining of the roofs that had to brace against the weather. The wind blowing through the dark alleys sounded like a drawn-out sigh, enough to make the hairs at the back of my neck stand on end.

All things considered, I was relieved when we finally reached the restaurant that Seth had been talking about. It looked relatively small from the outside, but the warm light spilling out of the windows and the name of the place, Giovanni's, blinking above the entrance in red, white, and green made it much more inviting than its neighbors.

"Here we are," Seth said and opened the door for me.

I was engulfed in the heavenly smell of fresh pizza and pasta as soon as I crossed the threshold. Most seats were occupied, but Seth guided me towards a table in a less noisy corner of the restaurant. We had barely sat down when a huge guy with an even huger moustache walked up to us and slammed the menu down on the table.

"Welcome to *Giovanni's Pizzeria*," he boomed. "I'm Giovanni! Let me light you a candle for some more *romanza*."

Seth chuckled, reaching over the table to pat my hand. "Thank you, that is exactly what we need."

I pulled my hand back, unable to keep myself from laughing.

"What's so funny?" Frowning, the man pocketed his lighter.

Seth sent me a questioning look. After I gave a small nod, he explained, "She's gay. We're best friends."

"Well, that's good, *bambina*," Giovanni said, patting my head

Never Kiss
your Roommate

with one giant hand. "You're too pretty for him anyway. What are you two ordering?"

While Seth was busy gaping at him, the expression on his face somewhere between incredulous and offended, I gave Giovanni my order.

When he left to get us drinks a moment later, I said, "I wish people reacted like that every time I came out."

"By crushing my self-esteem? Wow," Seth laughed.

I couldn't help but smile as well. At the table next to us, a child knocked over a glass, making both of us look over for a second.

Meeting my eyes again, Seth was more serious. "Why didn't you tell him yourself?"

I shrugged, running my finger along a dent in the table. "I don't know, I just don't really feel comfortable saying it out loud yet. Is that bad?"

Seth hummed quietly, blowing a strand of dark hair out of his eyes. "No, it's normal. Internalized homophobia is a bitch."

"Agreed," I laughed.

I wasn't sure if it was our interaction or the fact that we had momentarily found shelter from chilly Gloomswick, but sitting here with him, a reassuring warmth had settled over me. It was nice having someone as easy to talk to, who understood the way I was feeling and could put a name to it. There was a kind of vulnerability and comfort in it that I hadn't known before, when the only people I could talk to about my sexuality had been my parents, who, even though they tried, could never understand everything I was going through.

Giovanni returned with our drinks and two plates of pizza a moment later. While I had ordered a small one, Seth had ordered one in the biggest size available.

"So," he said around a bite, "How are you liking Seven Hills so far?"

I shrugged. "Noelle is . . . you know—Noelle—but other than that it's fine. What about you?"

"Could be worse, I guess," he murmured. His feigned nonchalance wasn't very convincing.

"What's wrong?"

"I just miss home a little bit, is all."

"Have you spoken to your parents yet?"

"No. Just talked to my sister on the phone for an hour or something yesterday. She's the one I miss the most if I'm being honest."

I didn't have any siblings, but I could imagine how he was feeling. I called my parents almost daily, but I was still missing them like a phantom limb. To distract both of us, I said, "Hey, have you heard of The Chitter Chatter yet?"

"My roommate was talking about it." Seth swallowed a gigantic bite of pizza.

"No one knows who's writing it. That should be right up your lane, right? There's so much mystery around it, it's almost like one of your crime novels. Are you going to investigate the case?"

"What's there to investigate? Someone's bored and thought it would be fun to take the piss out of people. Can't blame them, to be honest; I bet we're going to be looking for anything to make us feel alive as well after a few months of private school."

"We could always join one of the clubs Amelia is so enthusiastic about," I laughed.

Looking up from his plate, Seth said, "You know . . . I may have done that already. Accidentally, kind of."

I gaped at him. We had barely spent a moment apart aside from

Never Kiss
your Roommate

the evenings, and I had expected him to be spending them lazing around in his room just like me. "What? How? Which club?"

"The drama club." Seth scratched at his neck. "I was in the auditorium on Wednesday before they came in and I helped them with the stage lights."

"Jasper directs it, right?"

"Yeah. He asked me if I wanted to come to the next practice as well. I said yes."

"I didn't know you were a technician on top of a detective," I teased.

"At my last school I was on the team that organized all the school events," he explained. "It's really not that complicated. Jasper just didn't have a clue what he was doing."

Chuckling, I went back to my pizza. While Seth had scarfed his down in record time, I couldn't finish it for the life of me. He gladly ate the rest of mine and leaned back in his chair when he was done, tomato sauce and a satisfied grin on his face. "This was so worth it. Honestly, for all I care we could get expelled for this and I wouldn't be mad."

I was about to tell him not to let Amelia hear that when Giovanni suddenly appeared at our table again. Staring at Seth's empty plate, then back at him, he said, "Bambino, how are you still a beanpole? Why don't you look like me yet?"

"Stress," Seth answered promptly.

Giovanni raised one bushy eyebrow. "Your poor mother. You probably eat her out of house and home."

"Maybe that's the reason she wanted to get rid of me, and sent me to a boarding school," Seth said. Though his tone was light, his eyes had darkened, the look in them unreadable as they mirrored the flickering candlelight.

Not noticing, Giovanni asked, "You two go to Seven Hills?"

We answered in the affirmative. "You don't seem like the other students from there," Giovanni said. "You're not snobby enough."

"It's only been two weeks," Seth said. "Next time we come here we might be."

Giovanni let out a rumbling laugh before handing us the bill.

After paying and putting our coats on, we made our way towards the door. Seth already had a hand on the door handle when, from the other end of the restaurant, Giovanni shouted, "Don't let anyone catch you! Oh, and greet Maria for me!"

Before either of us could ask who Maria was, he disappeared into the kitchen.

"Maybe his daughter?" I guessed as we stepped outside, tucking my hands into the pockets of my coat again.

"Have you met a Maria?"

"No. You?"

"Evelyn, I haven't talked to a single girl beside you."

"You've also talked to Amelia," I pointed out.

"Okay, I haven't *voluntarily* talked to a single girl beside you."

"Harsh." I chuckled, shaking my head. "She's not even that bad. Just a bit uptight."

Seth only raised an eyebrow. He was walking at a brisk speed that made it difficult to keep up with him, a chilly gust of air blowing through his hair. With his dark coat billowing behind him and his pale face briefly illuminated whenever we passed under a streetlamp, he looked a little bit like one of the detectives he adored reading about so much.

"You know," I said. "I'm sure I could introduce you to some girls."

Seth's lips quirked into an amused smile. "Thanks, but I think I'm good. I don't think a boarding school is the best place to get into a relationship."

"True," I laughed.

"And besides . . . I don't really want any of that, I think."

"Any of what?"

"A relationship. I don't know why, but I don't see myself ever fancying anyone like that, you know?"

"Maybe you're aromantic?" I suggested, trying to keep up with him as he strode down the alley. In front of us, the road back to the castle came into view.

"No, that's not what I mean—I don't know. I just don't believe that love like that really exists." He broke off. "Sorry, that was bleak."

I shook my head and quietly said, "No, it's okay."

I understood what he was trying to say, but the idea of it felt like I was a paper doll standing in front of an abyss, waiting for the next gust of wind to blow me over the edge, and so I didn't want to linger on it. Love, to me, was the thing that mattered the most. I craved it like plants craved water or my lungs craved air: the kind of heart-racing, earth-shattering, all-consuming love that I had read about thousands of times, the kind that made Darcy a better man and Orpheus turn around, the perfect kind that transformed *everything*. It simply had to exist. Otherwise what was the sense in anything?

"Did you feel that?" Seth looked up at the night sky and stretched out his hands, palms turned upward.

"Feel wha—" The raindrop that landed right on my forehead answered my question.

Seth swore under his breath and grabbed my hand, speeding

up so that I had to jog to keep up with him. "We need to get back. They'll know we were out when we come back soaking wet."

"*This was so worth it,*" I echoed his words from earlier, using an exaggerated deep voice. "*Honestly, for all I care we could get expelled for this and I wouldn't be mad.*"

Seth made a face at me but didn't stop speed walking.

The rain was pouring now, running down my face and into my collar. Neither of us had a hood, so all we could do was get back to the castle as fast as possible to avoid arriving there completely drenched.

"I'm having bloody déjà-vu," Seth said as we hurried down the same road as last time, the dark woods around us no less scary than they had been then.

It was around eleven o'clock by now, one hour after curfew, and definitely enough reason to get punished, especially since we hadn't asked a teacher for permission beforehand.

We made it back to the school by ten past eleven, out of breath and with our hair sticking to our foreheads.

"If someone sees us, we're screwed," Seth whispered as he pulled open the door to the gym and held it open for me.

I followed him, my wet shoes half slipping on the floor, and pulled the door shut behind me as silently as possible, leaving the brick to make sure the others could still enter after us.

My heart was beating out of my chest as we snuck through the abandoned hallways. While the castle had become a familiar friend over the past week, it was an entirely different entity when all the lights were out. Shadows loomed in the alcoves where we had sat and laughed just a few hours ago and the eyes of the photos on the walls seemed to follow us, some curious, some disapproving.

I almost ran into Seth when he suddenly stopped short just before we reached the entrance hall. "Why are you—" I began, but he immediately shushed me and pulled me back into the corridor.

The sound of quiet footsteps echoing from the walls made me tense, but I quickly relaxed when I looked over Seth's shoulder to see who was there. Noelle was making her way up the stairs, swaying slightly and gripping tightly onto the handrail. She was just as soaked as we were, but she had been smart enough to take off her boots to avoid leaving wet footprints. Seth and I were about to start moving again, but froze, still huddled in the hallway, when a second pair of footsteps suddenly rang out.

From our vantage point, we could see the entire hall, including the two staircases leading upstairs. That was how we spotted Mrs. Whitworth before Noelle did.

Seven Hills' headmistress was only thirty-five, a tall Black woman with a heart-shaped face and braids that were usually pulled into a strict ponytail. So far, she had worn a kind smile on her face every time I had seen her, her voice quiet yet commanding. Now, there was a displeased frown as she called out, "Noelle Daniels! Over here, right now!"

Noelle froze in her tracks and turned around agonizingly slowly.

"The school year has only just started and you're already breaking one of the biggest rules, even after we talked about all this just two months ago," Mrs. Whitworth said once Noelle had reached the bottom of the stairs.

To my surprise, Noelle didn't respond with a quip or a dismissive glare. Instead, she scuffed her socked foot against the floor and said, so softly I was barely able to hear her, "I know."

"You know what the school rules say about drinking and sneaking out. According to them, I should've expelled you the first time."

"I know," Noelle said again. "I'm sorry."

Mrs. Whitworth pressed a hand to her temple, rubbing it in circular motions as she studied Noelle's face. In the pale moonlight that filtered in through the windows, she looked tired rather than angry. "I gave you so many chances already," she sighed. "Noelle, you know I want to help you, but I don't know how if you go behind my back time and time again."

Noelle kept her eyes fixed on her feet.

"I can't do anything for you if you don't at least *try*. Now, answer me honestly for once: did you go into town alone?"

It was like a knee-jerk reaction. One moment I was cowering in the corridor with Seth, the next I stepped out into the hall, ignoring his warning hand on my sleeve, and announced, "She was with me."

Mrs. Whitworth spun around, eyes wide in surprise. "You? What's your name?"

"Evelyn." I went to stand next to Noelle. "Evelyn Greene."

Behind Mrs. Whitworth's shoulder, Seth buried his face in his hands.

"One of the new students," Mrs. Whitworth said, more to herself than to us, and took in my soaked state with a searching look.

"Yes," I confirmed. "I'm really sorry, Mrs. Whitworth. It was my idea to sneak out. I asked Noelle to show me around town and she was kind enough to do so. We didn't mean to be so late."

Noelle stared at me like she was sure I had lost my mind. Right now I wasn't sure if I had, but my mouth was talking faster than my brain could think and added, "So really, it's my fault. I should be held responsible."

Noelle opened her mouth, but I sent her a look that was sharp enough to make her shut it again.

"It honors you to be so honest, Evelyn," Mrs. Whitworth said. "And I am glad that you two have become . . . friends?"

"Yes. I'm so glad I have a roommate who I get along with so well," I said. Behind my back, I gestured for Seth to leave. "I would feel terrible if she were to receive punishment for this."

"All right," Mrs. Whitworth said, "In that case, you will receive it."

I nodded, keeping my eyes glued to her face as Seth darted up the stairs behind her back.

"Seeing as this is the first time you've broken a rule at this school I will not suspend or expel you," she said.

Next to me, Noelle let out a breath she must've been holding.

"Thank you," I whispered.

"You will, however, do community service. I think two weeks of laying the table for every meal should suffice."

"Of course. Thank you," I said hastily.

"All right." She exhaled another sigh, pulling her knit cardigan tighter around herself. "Off to bed now, girls."

Noelle and I practically raced up the stairs and to our room, Noelle still a little wobbly on her feet.

As soon as we entered our room and I had stripped off my soaking wet coat, I flopped onto my bed, one hand draped over my eyes to block out the bright ceiling light. A few feet away from me I could hear the creaking of leather as Noelle got out of her jacket, followed by footsteps as she made her way into the bathroom.

I assumed she was just going to change into her sleeping clothes. Instead, she walked back over to me, cleared her throat, and handed me a towel. Quietly, she said, "You didn't have to."

Before I could say anything, she was already turning around, avoiding my eyes, and locked the bathroom door behind her. She never thanked me, but I didn't expect her to: this was the first time she had spoken to me since the day I had touched her notes, and more than she had been willing to give me all week. Right now that seemed more than enough.

6
Evelyn

It had only been a matter of time until I had a nightmare.

Back at home, I had had them almost every night, to the point where I had dreaded falling asleep and tried to stay up as long as possible. In the two weeks I had spent at Seven Hills now, they had temporarily stopped: surrounded by new people, in a new place with new routines, I was so tired that most days I fell asleep as soon as my head hit the pillow and woke up the next morning not remembering anything I had dreamt.

However, as the days went by and I got used to my new sur-roundings, the nightmares crept back in, as stealthy and inevi-table as the cold that crept through the cracks in the castle walls at night.

I woke up with a start, the gasp that had torn from my throat still ringing in the air. My fingers were trembling when I forced myself to uncurl them from where they had been clutching at the sheets and ran them over my face instead.

I was at Seven Hills.

I was in my room.

No one else was here other than . . .

"You okay?" Noelle asked. She was sitting up in bed, legs crossed and only half her face cast in the gloomy morning light that filtered in through the curtains, making her expression unreadable to me.

"I'm fine," I rasped, my theart still racing, and pulled the blanket tighter around myself.

Noelle looked utterly unconvinced, but didn't say anything. Instead, she reached for the phone on her bedside table.

I closed my eyes, trying to rid myself of the shaky feeling to which I had already grown unaccustomed. A few deep breaths in and then out again, over and over. Grounding myself by focusing on the coarse texture of the sheets, the muffled sounds of footsteps and voices in the corridor, the by-now-familiar scent of ancient bricks and woodwork.

I was at Seven Hills.

I was in my room.

"So . . ." Noelle said. "Are you coming to the party tonight?"

Exactly a week had passed since the night I had taken the blame for her sneaking out, and since then something between us had shifted.

Noelle was spending more time in our room instead of staying the night in her boyfriend's. She had stopped smoking in our room. And, most surprisingly, she had begun actually talking to me. It wasn't like we were chatting all day long, but instead of ignoring me or pretending she didn't hear me, she now answered when I asked her something and contributed, even if only monosyllabically, to the otherwise rather one-sided conversations.

Still, hearing her question caught me off guard. Trying to hide my surprise, I asked, "What party?"

"The Welcome Back Party. It's this party in the basement to welcome everyone back and greet the new students. Happens every year."

"And the teachers allow it?"

"Not explicitly," Noelle said. "But it's the one night when the majority of the upper classes get together to get drunk, and the teachers pretend they don't know about it. Even Amelia will be there."

"I guess I have to come then."

"Would be pretty embarrassing if you didn't," Noelle said, her lips quirking into the hint of a smile. After glancing at the time on her phone, she added, "If I were you, I'd start to get ready. You've got some tables to set before breakfast if I remember correctly."

I was still too relieved about the fact that she was speaking to me to be bothered by the remark and got up without complaint, the shaky echo of the nightmare fading into nothingness.

o o o

The day passed in a blur of classes, meals in the Great Hall, and a semiproductive study session with Seth. The closer the clock hands moved to nighttime, the more charged the air became, the hallways buzzing with barely concealed excitement, all hushed murmurs and secret giggles.

It was around nine o'clock when Seth and I made our way down the stairs that led to the basement. Finding them hadn't been hard, seeing as half the students were on their way there, which further proved Noelle's thesis that the teachers were simply pretending they didn't know what was going on.

Still, there was a thrill in sneaking down the stairs, accompanied by the excited whispering of other students, the air filled with muffled music and musty basement smell.

When we reached the bottom of the stairs I unthinkingly reached out and grabbed Seth's sleeve so as not to lose him in the dark, drawing a soft laugh from him.

Finally, we reached the door at the end of the hallway.

The party was held in a large cellar, the back of which I couldn't even make out when I stepped through the threshold. Worn-down furniture, shelves filled with books, and teaching materials were pushed to the walls to make room for a dance floor in the center of the basement, the entire scene lit by some old lamps scattered around the room. The majority of the students were up and dancing or sitting on the couches with plastic cups in their hands, but I also noticed that there were a few darker, less-crowded corners that were occupied by couples.

I wasn't surprised when I spotted Noelle's curly head in one of them. She was leaning against the wall with Elias's arm slung around her shoulders, his mouth next to her ear as he whispered something to her.

"Do you want me to get you something to drink?" Seth asked over the music.

"Sure. I'll drink whatever you're drinking."

"Got it. Be right back," Seth said, saluting me with two fingers

Never Kiss your Roommate

before he made his way over to the table with drinks in the corner.

Meanwhile, I steered towards one of the tables that had been pushed aside and sat down. Nearby were a bunch of girls from my classes, but even after two weeks, I hadn't really been able to befriend any of them. I supposed it was partially because I spent most of my time with Seth, but also because they had already formed set cliques over the several years they had spent at this school. Amelia was on the other side of the room, but she was caught up in a conversation with a few members of the student council. And then there was Jasper, whose silver mop of hair stood out as always as he danced with his boyfriend.

My attention was directed elsewhere when a tall, blond guy who I was pretty sure was in year twelve made his way over to me.

"Hey," he said as he came to a stop right in front of me. "I don't think we've had the chance to talk yet. I'm Lance."

"Evelyn."

"Hm. Pretty name for a pretty girl."

My only response was a strained laugh. Craning my neck, I tried to spot Seth, but he was still standing by the table with the drinks, his back turned to me.

Lance cocked his head, his eyes slowly raking me up and down. "See, I normally don't do this, but I was wondering if you want to come up to my room with me? My roommate promised not to come back there before midnight—"

I shifted a little, my fingers gripping onto the edge of the table when he leaned in slightly. "Um . . . No, thank you. I would rather just stay here."

Instead of backing off, he only smirked even wider. I was keenly aware that I couldn't just get off the table with the way he was standing right in front of me, almost close enough for his legs to touch my knees. "Come on, don't be like that. You know you want to."

"I really don't," I firmly said.

"But—"

He was cut off when a hand suddenly grabbed the back of his shirt and yanked him away from me, abrupt enough to leave him swaying. Noelle stood behind him, one hand gripping onto his collar to pull him down to her height as she lunged out. The punch was imprecise and merely brushed his face, but it was enough to have him stumbling back.

"You better fucking listen when a girl tells you to back off," Noelle snarled and gave another push against his chest.

Lance took another staggering step back, hands raised in surrender. "Okay, okay! Jesus, chill. I was just saying—"

"I know what you were saying. Now you listen to me. You obviously don't understand the word *no*, so I will spell this out for you. If you ever talk to her like that again, I will not only kick your ass into next month but also go to Mrs. Whitworth. And I can guarantee you right now that she won't be happy about this. Got it?"

"Y-yeah."

"Good," Noelle quietly said. Her tone reminded me of the way she had spoken to me when I had looked at her notes—only then there hadn't been such a heat in her eyes, such a fierce set to her jaw. Cocking her head to indicate me, she ordered, "Apologize."

"W-what?"

"*Apologize.*"

Lance visibly gulped. Slowly turning to face me again, he muttered, "I'm sorry."

Noelle sent me a questioning look and I realized she was waiting for *me* to say something, to decide if *I'm sorry* was enough. After a second of hesitation, I gave a small nod. Lance bolted as soon as she released her grip on his shirt, the door slamming behind him. With a shake of her head, Noelle sank onto the table next to me.

"Thank you," I said. "But you didn't have to do that."

"Yes, I did. I know what it's like," Noelle said.

I stayed silent, watching as she shook her right hand. Just from looking at it, I could imagine the dull pain the impact had left behind.

"I'm serious, Noelle. You didn't have to do that. I know how to defend myself."

"Oh yeah? Didn't look like it."

"I would've done what was necessary if he had touched me," I insisted. When Noelle's only response was a disbelieving snort, I carefully reached for her hand and turned it over to inspect her knuckles. Softly, I said, "That's not how you punch someone."

"What do *you* know about punching people?"

I hesitated for a second before I said, "I used to take self-defense lessons."

"What? Why?"

Seth appeared next to us with Amelia in tow before I could respond. "Here you go," he said, handing me my drink. "It's cider."

"Thanks," I said, distracted by Noelle gliding off the table and disappearing into the crowd without another word.

"What was that about?" Amelia asked, curious as ever, and sat down in the spot that Noelle had occupied.

"Nothing," I lied.

After the incident with Lance and then the conversation with Noelle, I felt strangely off-kilter. So I did the next best thing I could think of: I drank several cups of cider and then, when I felt brave enough to do so, dragged Seth onto the dance floor.

By the time midnight rolled around, I was *proper sloshed*, as Seth had put it; the floor was a little bit wobbly and my tongue a little bit heavy when I spoke, but that was fine. I was fine, just a little bit tired, my head resting against Seth's shoulder when we sat down on one of the dusty old couches, the racket all around us softening into a pleasant background buzz.

I probably could've dozed off just like that if the music didn't suddenly get turned off. Prompted by the sudden silence, I lifted my head and forced my eyes open just as Amelia stepped into the circle that had formed in the middle of the room.

"All right, everyone, most of you will already know what is about to happen," she sighed. "You know I do not endorse this stupid tradition—which, might I remind you, breaks almost every rule we have in place—but as the head of the student council it is my duty to do this, so here it goes . . . It is time for Seven Hills' favorite party game: *Seven Minutes in Heaven*."

An anticipatory murmur went through the room as Amelia was handed a large jar filled with paper snippets, which she lifted so that everyone could see.

"In this jar I have the names of everyone in this room. I will be drawing two names, and those two pupils will get seven minutes in there"—she pointed at a large closet in the back of the room—"to do whatever they please. Any questions?"

When no one said anything, she reached her hand into the jar and slowly swirled her fingers around. Seth and I leaned forward, both equally curious.

"First up we have . . . Chelsea McDonald and Samar Khan."

Whistling and cheers filled the room as the two headed towards the closet. Chelsea, a girl from my year, pulled the door shut behind her with a giggle. As soon as she did, everyone fell deadly silent to hear as much of what was going on inside as possible.

Seth let his head roll back against the couch with a chuckle. "This is so stupid."

I nodded in agreement and took another sip from my cup.

Seven minutes went by surprisingly quickly, probably due to the fact that I was still dancing somewhere near the edge of sleep. Soon Amelia strode up to the closet and gave a demanding knock. Chelsea and Samar emerged under the mocking clapping of the others; they looked the same as they had when they had gone in, save for a faint blush on Chelsea's face and the not quite as perfectly styled state of Samar's hair.

"Seems like the seven minutes were well spent," Amelia commented, prompting another round of laughter. "Moving on . . ."

The next three pairs were all people I barely knew, making it easy for me to shut my eyes and open them only when Amelia called out the next name. Seth poked me in the ribs a few times to stop me from falling asleep, but that wasn't the thing that ultimately made me wide awake.

It was Amelia's voice as she announced, "Next pair. Here we have . . . oh. Evelyn Greene."

I sat up so abruptly I almost spilled my drink all over the couch. Amelia sent me a look that seemed to tell me to stay seated and refuse to play. But no one before me had opted out and with the alcohol in my blood, the idea of making out with a stranger suddenly didn't seem all that terrible. So I passed my cup to Seth, ignoring his hand on my sleeve trying to hold me back, and got up.

Cheers followed me as I crossed the room, hopefully not looking as unsteady on my feet as I felt, and clambered into the closet. The irony of it wasn't lost on me, and I released a soft giggle into the dark that engulfed me.

"And the second person is . . ." Amelia continued outside. "James Carter."

The mistake I had made when I'd gotten up believing I wouldn't mind kissing a random person dawned on me: I had forgotten that boys still existed. I didn't like kissing boys. But I couldn't say that now, could I?

"James? Is James here?" Amelia asked over the murmuring outside.

She waited a few seconds for an answer. Finally, she released a heavy sigh. "Fine, we will have to draw another then. Who do we have here . . ."

Silence.

Then, "It's Noelle."

My breath caught in my throat. The ground became even more unsteady to the point where I had to lean back against the wood behind me to stop my legs from giving out as I waited, not sure whether to be relieved or utterly terrified.

Heralded by loud cheers and wolf whistling, the door finally opened and a silhouette entered, making the closet feel a hundred times smaller, completely dark save for the little sliver of light that peeked in from beneath the door.

"Noelle?" I whispered. "Is that you?"

"Yeah. Give me a second," Noelle muttered. A moment later, I was blinded by her phone's flashlight.

When I opened my eyes again, Noelle had her fingers over the light so that only a faint, orange glow lit up the closet. It was only then I realized how close we were actually standing: I was pressed against the back of the closet and she was standing by the door, yet we were almost touching.

"Six minutes to go," she said, crossing her arms.

"So?" I quietly asked.

"So what?"

"Are we going to kiss?"

Noelle let out an unfamiliar sound at that, something as bright and airy as wind chimes that bounced off the closet walls; it was the first time I had heard her laugh. "Would you want that?"

I gave an emphatic nod.

"Ever kissed a girl?" she asked.

"No."

"Ever wanted to before?"

My tongue formed the words before I could think better of it. "Every time I look at you." I knew there was a reason why I wasn't allowed to say that, but it was hard to remember with her standing inches away from me, watching me with an unreadable expression.

Noelle was silent long enough for me to, in a moment of sudden clarity, realize that I would regret everything about this in the morning. However, all rational thought was erased from my brain when Noelle said, "Fine. One kiss. Come here."

After leaning against the wall for so long, I hadn't expected my walk to still be as unsteady as I pushed off the wall, swaying slightly until Noelle wrapped an arm around my waist to steady me.

She frowned. "You're drunk."

As close as we were standing, I could smell her perfume layering over the smell of dust and mothballs, the fragrance surprisingly sweet. Something flowery. With vanilla, maybe. "Only a little," I giggled and got on my tiptoes.

"Evelyn." Noelle gently pushed me back but kept her arm around me. "I'm not going to kiss you, idiot. Not when you're wasted."

I swallowed, trying hard to make it seem like that wasn't the most tragic thing I had ever heard. "But you're so pretty."

The same wind-chimes-on-a-summer-day sound tumbled from her lips again, which, now that I knew I wouldn't get a kiss, just seemed like mockery. "If I ever kiss you, I want you to be able to remember it in the morning."

"I'll remember, I promise."

"It's still no."

I wobbled backward, hitting the back wall of the closet. This was what Darcy had felt after being rejected by Elizabeth then, his pride crushed, his hopes destroyed by a few cruel words, every prospect at happiness shattered—

"Evelyn—Oh my God, are you crying?"

"No," I lied, hastily wiping over my eyes with my sleeve.

"Jesus. You're a *mess*," Noelle said without any heat.

"Sorry."

"Shut up."

Then, before I could brace myself, her hand cupped my cheek. I forgot how to breathe when I felt her lips on my skin, pressing a lingering kiss just above the corner of my mouth.

"There," she murmured, slowly leaning back. "Better?"

I nodded. Her hand still rested on my waist, the warmth of her palm seeping through my clothes before it spread into my stomach and up, until my entire chest was filled with it and I was

Never Kiss your Roommate

sure that, if I looked down, I would find golden light emanating from my rib cage.

However, before I could vocalize any of that, the door flew open and Amelia's face came into view. "Your seven minutes are up."

Noelle's hand fell from my waist and the warmth left my body at once.

She was the first one to step outside, offering me a hand to stop me from face-planting right there. Once I stood firmly on my feet again, blinking into the blinding lights, she turned to Amelia and said, "Hey Amanda. Next time make sure the people you send in there aren't drunk. They should be able to know what they're doing before they hook up with a stranger."

Her tone was unexpectedly harsh in comparison to how soft-spoken she had been just a few seconds earlier, enough so to make Amelia flinch. "Sorry, I did not know . . . she seemed fine."

"It's okay. She was with me, so nothing happened."

"I am truly sorry."

"Yeah, yeah," Noelle said, detangling our limbs from each other. "You could bring her to our room to make it up."

"Of course," Amelia immediately said, linking her arm with mine.

"Are you not coming?" I asked Noelle. In the light of the basement, I suddenly felt unbearably cold, to the point I imagined my teeth would start chattering any second. My cheek was still tingling where her lips had brushed it.

"I'll be there in a few minutes. You can wait for me, okay?"

I gave a reluctant nod, stifling a yawn behind my hand.

Amelia didn't say anything as she led me out of the room, only stopping so I could say good night to Seth, who was still sitting in the exact same spot where I had left him with our two cups in hand. It was only when we were back in my room that she asked, "So . . . how scary was being in there with her?"

"Not scary," I mumbled as I sank onto my bed, my words muffled into the pillow. "Not scary at all."

7
Seth

Uncertain what to do, I watched as Amelia led Evelyn out of the room. I briefly considered following them, but came to the conclusion that probably wasn't the best idea. Amelia had already freaked out the last time I had entered the girls' wing and I was sure that her reaction would be no different tonight.

Without Evelyn, I suddenly felt adrift amid the chaos, my only real anchor gone. I was standing somewhere between the couch where we had been sitting and the closet, my hands stuffed into my pockets to stop them from fidgeting. Earlier, I had felt good.

Good when I chugged a beer and people cheered.

Good when Evelyn took my hand and dragged me onto the dance floor.

Good when Jasper flashed me a grin in passing and his arm

brushed against mine just long enough for me to feel like I had swallowed static.

Now the drink in my veins had worn off, Evelyn was gone, and Jasper sat on one of the couches with Sammy, their legs and arms so entwined that it was hard to tell which limb belonged to whom.

I was about to leave and head up to my room when Noelle passed by me and curiosity won over the anxiety in my stomach.

"Hey, Noelle," I said, making her stop in her tracks, and gestured at the closet. "What happened in there?"

"Nothing."

Encouraged by the fact that she hadn't ripped my head off yet, I pointed out, "Seven minutes is an awfully long time to do nothing."

"We talked."

"That all?"

Noelle's eyes narrowed, but before she could respond another student council member climbed onto one of the tables and yelled, "Come on, guys, the party isn't over yet. Let's play a few more rounds."

Noelle and I groaned almost simultaneously.

"The next pair is Laura Smith and . . ." the boy began. My stomach coiled with nerves, my brain supplying nothing but a never-ending loop of *Please don't be me please don't be me please don't be me*. It wasn't, but the name he called out still made my heart stutter for a second. "None other than Jasper Des Lauriers!"

Loud cheers filled the room even before the sentence was finished. My eyes immediately found Jasper; easy, when I hadn't really looked away from him ever since I stumbled through the

Never Kiss
your Roommate

cellar door with Evelyn in tow. He looked anything but happy as he detangled from Sammy, who, to my surprise, seemed to be encouraging him.

Noelle stopped him with a hand on his arm when he passed us. "Hey, are you okay?"

Jasper nodded, even though his Adam's apple bobbed as he swallowed thickly and his face was the same color as the skeleton that was propped against the wall next to us, probably dumped there by some science teacher years ago. "Yeah. It's just seven minutes, right?"

"Jasper, you don't have to if you don't want to," Noelle insistently said. "Just say no."

Somehow I knew even before he shook his head that he wasn't going to listen. "No. I can do this."

With that, he turned around, making Noelle's hand fall away, and strode towards the closet. He hesitated for only a second before he entered, the door falling shut behind him. Like before, the room went silent as soon as the pair was inside.

"What was that about?" I whispered to Noelle.

"You ask a lot of questions."

"Sorry." I directed my eyes away from her and stared at the skeleton again. Slouched against the brick wall, with cobwebs filling the space between its ribs and glittering behind its hollow eyes, it looked decidedly unhappy.

After a few seconds of silence, she said, "He always says he hates this game. I'm not sure why—it's not like making out with strangers has ever bothered him."

I frowned but didn't say anything. Instead, I counted in my head as the seconds ticked by.

One minute.

Two minutes.

Three minutes.

Four min—

"He's freaking out!" Laura exclaimed, throwing the doors open. "We were just talking and then he suddenly freaked out—"

Noelle and I were the first ones to move.

I skidded to a halt in front of the closet to find Jasper leaning against the wall, doubled over with his hands on his knees. In the dark, I couldn't make out his face, but his ragged breathing that echoed from the walls was all I needed to know.

"Noelle, help me get him out of here," I said, stepping into the closet to wrap an arm around his middle. Noelle did the same, slinging his other arm over her shoulders.

Together, we managed to hoist him out of the closet. I could hear his choked breaths in my ear, his body shaky and limp as we struggled to hold him up.

"Out of the way, everyone!" I yelled, tightening my grip on him.

People hastily retreated, making room for us to get Jasper to the door. As they stared after us with wide eyes, I felt very much visible for the first time since I had come here, but with Jasper trembling in my arms, I didn't have time to worry about what that meant.

At the other end of the room, I almost collided with Amelia, who must have returned a few minutes ago, but she quickly jumped out of the way and held the door open for us.

Noelle and I were both breathing heavily as we guided him towards the stairs.

"Easy," I muttered. "Here, sit down."

Jasper slumped rather than sat, no trace of the grace with

Never Kiss your Roommate

which he usually moved. I crouched down in front of him, but he didn't look up at me. "You're outside, Jasper," I said, trying to make my voice as gentle as possible. For a split second, I wished that Evelyn was here to calm him down, but pushed on regardless. "You can breathe. There's enough space now."

"No, I can't—I can't breathe." A desperate hand came up to claw at his collar as if that would help.

"Noelle, get a paper bag," I said, not taking my eyes off him.

She immediately spun and ran back inside.

"It's going to be okay," I said, even though the sound of his breathing made my hairs stand on end. Jasper was still scratching at his neck, leaving behind angry red lines; I tried not to think too much about it when I caught his hand in mine and brought it down to rest on his knees instead, the pulse in his wrist a hummingbird beneath my fingertips. Usually, Jasper seemed so perfect it was hard to believe he was just a regular boy my age; this was the most alive I had ever witnessed him, and it was exhilarating and terrifying at the same time.

I let go of his hand as quickly as if I had touched a hot stove top when the door burst open again and Noelle appeared with a brown paper bag in her hand. "This is the best I could find."

I wordlessly took it from her. Under her intent gaze, I pinched the top of the bag together and sat down on the step next to Jasper. Pressing the bag over his nose and mouth, I asked, "I want you to take twelve deep breaths with me, all right? Can you do that for me?"

Jasper nodded, his eyes blinking rapidly at me. The look in them was as empty as the skeleton's had been, but I tried not to let his hollow gaze unnerve me and, taking a deep breath, said,

"Good. One. Two. Three. You're doing so well, just like that . . . Four. Five."

With each inhale, Jasper's breathing got progressively deeper and slower, his hands less shaky.

"Twelve." I took the bag away from his face. "Well done."

Jasper took a few more deep breaths before he buried his head in his hands, a tremor shaking his entire frame.

"Hey." Noelle's voice was unexpectedly soft, as was her touch when she sank onto the step on Jasper's other side and rubbed a soothing hand over his back. "You're okay."

Jasper finally raised his head, eyes glassy. "I shouldn't have agreed to do that."

"What even just happened?"

"I get claustrophobic, sometimes," Jasper said. His voice was so quiet I had to strain to understand him. "The closet was so small and I felt like I couldn't get enough air—"

Noelle shook her head in disbelief. "Why didn't you tell me?"

"I don't know. I thought it would be okay this time."

"Don't ever scare me like that again, asshole," Noelle murmured and slid a hand into his hair to ruffle the silver strands.

Jasper seemed too drained to even tell her off for ruining his hair. Instead, he turned his face to look at me, his ice-blue eyes clearer now, making me feel just for a moment that I was the one who couldn't breathe. "Thank you for snapping me out of it."

Unable to hold his gaze, I lowered my eyes to the paper bag that I had scrunched up between my hands. "Don't mention it."

"How did you know what to do, anyway?" Noelle asked.

"I used to have really bad anxiety in middle school, so . . ."

The door burst open before either of them could react.

Never Kiss
your Roommate

"What happened in there?" Sammy laughed. "You sure know how to make a scene."

Noelle shot him an icy glare. "None of your business."

"No need to be rude. I'm just worried."

"Yeah, must've been worried sick," Noelle cut him off. "Only took you ten minutes to come looking for him."

Sammy pouted at Jasper as if telling him to rein her in. When Jasper didn't react, he suddenly pointed at me and asked, "What is he even doing here?"

Jasper suddenly got to his feet. "I'm going to bed. Good night."

"Wait, I'm coming with you," Sammy said, but shut his mouth when Noelle stopped him with a firm hand on his chest.

Jasper only looked over his shoulder to mouth *Thank you* once more, then the two were gone. I was left with Sammy, who, I had a distinct feeling, wanted to sock me in the face at that very moment. Since my bone structure was one of the few things I really had going for me, I quickly pushed past him and entered the cellar again.

In there, people had begun cleaning up. I tried to make myself useful, ignoring their curious stares, but couldn't shake off the jittery feeling that had settled beneath my skin when I had been alone with Jasper. It wasn't long until I decided to go back to my room as well.

As I crossed the cellar, I passed the skeleton again. Someone had draped a string of fairy lights around its rib cage while cleaning, the battery pack dangling inside it like a wiry plastic heart. The glow of the lights extended from deep inside its chest to its skull, the dark behind its eyes lit up, almost looking alive as the skull grinned back at me. "Fuck you looking at?" I murmured under my breath before I abruptly turned around, feeling its stare following me all the way to the door.

Once I was back in the boys' wing, I got out my phone to see if there was any text from Evelyn I had missed. Instead, all that pinged were notifications for a new update on The Chitter Chatter.

To my surprise, it wasn't on Jasper's public panic attack. Instead, it was titled *Tonight's Most Noteworthy Hookups*, starting with a paragraph on Noelle and Evelyn.

> I didn't think I would witness the day that Noelle Daniels would pass on a hookup.
>
> As unbelievable as it sounds, Noelle did not make out with Evelyn Greene when the two of them got thrown together for a steamy round of Seven Minutes in Heaven.
>
> Honestly, this must've been the tamest any round involving Noelle has ever been. After all, we have proof that every other time she got picked in the last years, the game ended with more than a few hickeys and some pretty . . . flustered male partners.
>
> The reason seemed to be that Evelyn was drunk, which is why Noelle refused to do anything with her.
>
> A surprisingly honorable move for her, if you ask me.

Shaking my head, I pocketed my phone again. Maybe I would try to deduce something about The Watcher's identity from this tomorrow; now all I wanted was to go to sleep, to get the memory of Jasper's panicked pulse beneath my fingertips and Sammy's accusatory glare and the skeleton's knowing gaze out of my head.

Tonight sure had been one hell of a party.

8

Evelyn

The day after the party, I woke up with a distinct feeling of regret.

The first reason was the pounding headache that only increased when I sat up.

The second was the realization that I was still in last night's clothes and makeup, some of which had left an imprint on the pristine white pillow beneath my cheek.

The third and biggest reason was the recollection of those seven minutes in the closet. One glance at Noelle's bed—empty, thankfully, but with rumpled sheets that proved she had spent the night here—was enough to set off an avalanche of memories from last night: the furious look on her face when she had punched Lance; the sound of her laughter echoing from the closet walls; the weight of her hand on my hip. In broad daylight, all of it seemed impossible, despite the fact that I could still

Never Kiss
your Roommate

feel the phantom touch of her lips against my cheek, as soft as it had been unexpected.

Burying my face in my hands I released a quiet whimper. I had practically *begged* her to kiss me and cried when she hadn't.

I had to move out. There was no other way. I didn't think I could ever look Noelle in the eye anymore, much less share a room with her for the rest of the year.

Had she been a boy, it would not have been a big deal; I could have laughed it away and it would have been forgotten the next day. But she was a girl and I had told her I wanted to kiss her— *every time I look at you*—and the idea of the consequences was enough to make my throat feel like there was a noose around it, the loose end of it clutched in her hand with nothing I could do to get it back.

What I didn't understand was why she hadn't pushed me away. She hadn't even seemed angry; then again, maybe she was today, now that she had slept on it. Maybe the reason why she wasn't here now was that she was so disgusted with me that she didn't want to be in the same room with me or—

Forcing myself to take a deep breath, I pressed my hands over my eyes. There was no use in panicking now. What happened had happened. I couldn't spend all day overthinking it.

With this resolution, I got out of bed.

It was a Saturday, so at least I didn't have to be in any classes with her. Instead, I spent the day catching up on homework with Seth in the common room. When he had to leave for drama club rehearsal, I gathered my things and found myself a windowsill in one of the many alcoves in the girls' wing. With the rain pattering softly against the window, the wind howling around the castle, and my back against the brick wall, I quickly got immersed in the pages of *Great Expectations*, and as the scenery of bleak nineteenth-century England unfolded around me, I felt calmer than I had all day.

That was, until a pair of boots echoed down the hallway, resolute footsteps making their way closer until they came to a halt right next to me.

"You know we have a room where you can do your whole book nerd thing, right?"

I stilled, my hand frozen in the motion of flipping a page. For a second I was overcome with the childish urge to simply pretend I didn't notice her. Instead, I gathered all my courage and raised my eyes to meet her gaze. "Yes."

Noelle hummed quietly, the hint of a smile tugging at her lips. I was still trying to figure out whether it was condescending or if she was just amused when she asked, "How are you? Hungover?"

"I'm fine."

"Did you see the article on The Chitter Chatter?" Now she definitely seemed amused.

Meanwhile, my throat felt like it was closing up at her question, the noose tugging a little tighter. "Noelle, I'm sorry about what happened in that closet. I didn't mean to come on to you or anything. I was kind of out of it, so . . . I'm sorry if I made you uncomfortable."

"You didn't. It was cute." She cleared her throat, her fingers readjusting the strap of the duffel bag she had slung over her shoulder. "I mean, it was fine. We're fine."

The tension in my shoulders finally dissolved, the rope falling away from my neck. Setting the book down next to me on the windowsill, I breathed a soft, "Okay."

"Actually, there was something else I wanted to talk to you

Never Kiss your Roommate

about. Before you, you know, got wasted, you told me you used to take self-defense lessons."

"I remember."

"I was wondering if maybe you could show me?"

"You want to learn self-defense?" I asked. "Why?"

"So the next time I punch someone, I break their nose," she stated, like the answer was self-evident. "Do you have time?"

I sat up a little straighter. "Like, right now?"

Noelle shrugged and gave an absentminded little kick to the wall next to where I was sitting. "I have basketball practice later, so now would be good."

"Okay," I said before I could think better of it. "Give me five minutes."

"Nice. I'll wait for you in the gym."

I nodded and watched as she turned on her heel, heading towards the stairs with the same determination with which she had approached me. When her curly head had disappeared out of view, I quickly gathered all my things and got up.

Back in our room, I tossed my books onto my desk and changed into leggings and an oversized T-shirt.

There was a nervous flutter in my chest as I left our room and hurried through the hallways, past the weeping windows, the route to the gym familiar after my night out with Seth. Once it was in sight, I slowed my steps and tentatively pushed open the door.

According to Amelia, the gymnasium was an extension of the castle that had been added in the 1980s. Instead of majestic arches and stone walls, it consisted of simple gray bricks and maple flooring the color of honey that squeaked under the soles of my sneakers when I entered. One side of the large hall was occupied by a stand for viewers. Noelle was sitting on the bench in front of it, elbows braced on her knees and her duffel bag at her feet. While I was gone she had changed into loose sweat-pants and a tight-fitting top, her hair pulled back into a ponytail.

Upon seeing me, she got to her feet, looking inexplicably eager. "How do we start?"

"Help me get some of those gym mats?"

Noelle wordlessly walked over to the equipment room and helped me carry two thick gym mats into the center of the room.

Once we had placed them on the floor, we faced each other again, the gym mats a blue barrier between us. The pounding of my heart seemed almost deafeningly loud in the sudden silence and even though I tried, I couldn't hold Noelle's expectant gaze.

"Don't get shy on me now, Greene," she said and took a step forward onto the mats. "You said you know how to defend your-self. Prove it."

She was trying to egg me on and it worked. Raising my chin, I closed the distance between us, my sneakers sinking slightly into the mat. "First things first . . . your fighting stance," I said. Even though I was speaking in a low voice, my words rang loudly through the empty room. "It's best if you place your feet apart and squat down a little like this, one leg in front of the other so you have a strong base and aren't tackled to the ground that easily."

Noelle nodded, mirroring my posture, and waited for me to go on. I felt strangely vulnerable under her attentive eyes; after days of being ignored by her, her undivided attention wasn't something I was used to, especially not when we were all alone. It seemed harder to find the right words with her listening to my every sentence.

"What now?" she asked when I didn't continue right away.

Never Kiss
your Roommate

"Do you know how to make a fist?"

Rolling her eyes, she balled her hand into a fist and held it up for me to see.

I stepped closer, uncurling her fingers under her confused gaze. "No, not like that. You're going to break your thumb if it's tucked into your fist."

"Then where do I put it?"

"There. Lay it over your second and third small knuckles and keep it there," I said, demonstrating with my own hand. I couldn't quite hold back a smile as I did. There was something endearing about the fact that fiery-eyed, sharp-tongued Noelle, who had so readily punched a guy in the face in front of me, didn't know the most basic rules of combat sports. "Don't tuck it in or let it hang loosely. That's important, okay?"

"Yes, ma'am."

"Good. We're not getting to the punches just yet though. Maybe in a few weeks."

Noelle's half smile immediately morphed into a frown. At first, I feared it was because of my rash assumption that she wanted to go on with these lessons, but then she only said, "But that's the fun part."

"Don't worry, you'll get your chance to give me a black eye."

"Why would I want to do that?" she asked, teeth blazing as she flashed me a sudden grin. "I like your face the way it is."

My heart stuttered through a few beats. Hoping that she didn't notice the blood rushing to my cheeks, I continued, "The most vulnerable body parts are eyes, ears, neck, knees, and legs. So, you could scratch or poke your attacker's eye or strike up under their nose, for example."

"Could I also just, like, kick them in the balls?"

"Sure," I snorted. "That's always an option."

"Nice. Anything else?"

"Well, you could thrust your elbow into their throat . . . Or you could kick the side of their knee to make them lose their balance, maybe kick the front of their knees if you want to cause more serious injury." Halfway through my explanation, Noelle's eyes had glazed over, making me trail off. "What is it?"

"It's just so weird, hearing you talk about beating people up," she said, shaking her head. "You look like this innocent, delicate little thing and then you basically give me a step-by-step manual on how to beat someone to a pulp."

"That's not what I'm doing! I'm trying to teach you how to defend yourself, not purposely hurt someone."

"I know. Calm down, Greene," Noelle laughed, brushing a stray curl out of her eyes. "Go on."

I eyed her warily for a few more seconds until I continued. "I should probably tell you that all these things really are for emergencies only. Flight is better than fight, in some situations."

The face she made told me clearly that she wasn't going to listen to this particular piece of advice.

"Also, it's always good to use your voice and everything you can to seem intimidating." After looking at her, hands in the pockets of her sweatpants and an eyebrow raised, I added, "Though I think you have that part down already."

"Thanks. You don't though."

I decided not to respond to that and instead asked, "Do you want to try the first trick?"

"Bring it on," she said, ignoring the way I cringed when she cracked her knuckles.

With her watching me expectantly, I was suddenly nervous

Never Kiss
your Roommate

again. Last night in the closet, cloaked in darkness and with the liquid courage from the apple cider loosening my tongue, it had been so easy to talk to her. Now, my voice shook as I asked, "Is it okay if I touch you?"

Noelle seemed taken aback for a second, but gave a nod.

I slowly reached for her wrist, keeping eye contact as my fingers closed around it. "Try to pull your arm out of my grasp."

As I had expected, her first instinct was to try to pull it towards her body in an attempt to wrestle it out of my grip. When that didn't work, she tried to twist her wrist, but to no avail.

I held on tightly, Noelle growing more and more frustrated until she eventually stopped trying and glared at me instead. "You've had your fun, show me how to do this."

I bit back a smile and released her wrist, which she rubbed with a sour expression.

"Hold onto my arm," I ordered.

Her fingers caught my wrist without hesitation and held tightly, her eyes never leaving my face.

Before she could notice the goosebumps traveling up my skin, I leaned forward and, within seconds, freed my arm from her grip, leaving her staring at her now-empty hand in shock.

"I . . . how the hell did you do that?"

"Take my wrist again," I said. When she did, I continued, "Get into fighting stance . . . feet apart and squatting a little. Now, when someone's attacking you and grabs your arm, what'd be your first instinct?"

"To pull my arm away and run?"

"Exactly. But in this situation, you want to do the opposite. You lean forward, closer to the other person. I know that sounds stupid at first, but this is important."

Noelle nodded.

"Okay. Next, you have to bend the elbow of the arm they're holding until it touches their forearm and your knuckles touch your shoulder," I explained, showing her exactly what to do in slow motion.

A disbelieving look appeared on her face when my wrist came free from her grasp.

"Your turn."

Noelle looked almost a little nervous when my fingers clasped her wrist, her pulse thrumming beneath the pads of my fingers, eager and alive. My own heart was racing in my chest, over-whelmed at the proximity—Noelle was close enough for her hair to tickle my arm, close enough that I was sure she could hear the hitch in my breath when she leaned forward like I had shown her.

A moment later, she was triumphantly waving her hand about. "I did it!"

"You did," I said, sounding embarrassingly breathless. "Well done!"

"Can I go again?" she asked, rocking back and forth on her feet with childlike excitement.

I nodded and grabbed her arm again.

This time I didn't even have to direct her through the steps. She was just as triumphant as the first time when she got free, eyes sparkling with victory. I had never seen her this open or this radiant with joy. I had never seen her this *alive*.

The idea that I was the one who had caused that grin, the one who got to see it, made me feel just a little bit dizzy.

"I guess that's today's lesson," I softly said.

"Wait, that's it?"

I pointed at the clock that hung above the door. "Didn't you say you had basketball practice?"

"Oh. Right."

"Do you . . . have any more questions?"

Noelle seemed to think about it for a moment. "Isn't fighting also throwing people to the floor? Can you do something like that?"

"You want to get thrown to the floor?" I asked, a little bewildered.

She shrugged. "I want you to do something cool."

"Wasn't this cool enough?"

"It was, but still."

"Noelle . . ."

"Come on," she said, the teasing glimmer back in her eyes. "Are you scared? Or are you just not good enough at self-defense to—"

She was on the floor even before she could finish the sentence, an audible gasp ringing through the hall; I had kicked her feet away from underneath her.

"Was that cool enough for you?"

A smirk tugged at her lips as she propped herself up on her elbows. "Not bad, Greene."

I held my hand out to help her up. Knowing Noelle, I probably should've anticipated it. Still, I let out a startled shriek when she used her momentum to drag me to the floor, sending me crashing onto the mats next to her, all the air knocked from my lungs.

She rolled onto her side to look at me, her face only inches away from mine, laughing as I did my best to glare at her.

I swallowed hard, a little bit dazed as the familiar scent of her perfume enveloped me again, and pushed myself up. "That wasn't fair."

"I never said I played fair," Noelle pointed out and easily got to her feet.

She offered me a hand, but instead of taking it I shot her a dirty look and got up myself, which only made her laugh even harder.

After we had put away the mats, she asked, "Can we do this again sometime next week?"

"If you want," I said, still a bit cross.

"Cool." She grinned. "Now shoo, the basketball team is gonna be here any moment."

I didn't need to be told twice. As I strolled back to our room and glanced out the windows, I noticed that the rain had stopped, leaving only a few lingering raindrops to trail idly down the glass; for the first time today, the sun peeked through the blanket of clouds.

9
Seth

Since the party, something had changed. First and foremost, the (although rather one-sided) cold war that had reigned between Evelyn and Noelle in the beginning had ceased. Somehow, they had gone from avoiding each other at all costs to arriving at breakfast together in the mornings and exchanging smiles during class. I still wasn't sure what exactly had happened that had made Noelle lay down her arms—Evelyn was suspiciously quiet when it came to what had happened in that closet—but I appreciated the fact that I no longer felt like I was entering a battle zone every time I came to their room.

The second change was that, in helping Jasper, I had unintentionally stepped out of the shadows and into the spotlight. Now, people recognized me when I walked around the school, though the stories were becoming progressively more outlandish each day. I was anywhere between *the lad that helped Noelle bring Jasper outside for a bit* to *that bloke who did full-on CPR on him for half an hour, mouth-to-mouth and everything!*

All of this was to say that I hadn't become popular all of a sudden, just a little bit more known by association; not totally invisible anymore, but also still translucent enough that people didn't stop in the hallways to talk to me.

More than anyone, Jasper now saw me. Not that I cared.

The situation with Gabe hadn't changed a bit, but now I at least had other places to go when he got too much; the common room, where Evelyn and I had a regular seat by now, the auditorium, Evelyn's room, and the library.

The latter was where Evelyn and I were right now. The library was as empty as always—just us, Miss Pepperman, and a few younger students who were hogging one of the computers, their soft chatter the only sounds disturbing the silence. After about an hour of going over my politics assignment, I was unable to focus anymore. My thoughts kept wandering elsewhere and the raindrops traveling down the tall windows next to us held my attention more than John Locke's theory of *inalienable rights*, the world behind them a dreary blur.

"Seth." Evelyn's voice made me turn my head. "You're making me nervous."

I understood what she was talking about only when I followed her eyes to my left hand, which was incessantly tapping my pencil against the table.

"Sorry," I muttered and put it down.

Evelyn, with an ever-patient smile on her face, went back to her essay. Unlike me, she was actually productive, one hand

Never Kiss your Roommate

flying across the paper while the other absentmindedly toyed with the end of her braid.

Knowing that I wouldn't get any more done today, I shut my book and pulled out my phone instead. At the top were a bunch of notifications for messages from my parents—I swiped them away with a grim sense of satisfaction and clicked onto my internet browser instead. Ignoring them was a childish thing to do, but I wanted to savor the righteous anger for a little bit longer. It was an ugly emotion, but it was also the only one standing between me and the overwhelming homesickness that flashed its teeth in the back of my mind throughout the day and swallowed me whole at night.

The first site that was open was The Chitter Chatter, as always. Like everyone else at the school, I knew that it was dumb to take such an interest in the opinions of a bully who didn't even have the guts to reveal their identity, but there was a sense of morbid curiosity about it: The Chitter Chatter was like a murder scene you couldn't look away from, and the victim could be anyone.

Today, the only update was a rearrangement of the *Hottest Students* ranking. I studied it for a moment before I let out a quiet snort. "Hey, Eve, congrats."

Evelyn looked up from her paper again. "Congrats on what?"

"You've made it to fifth place on The Chitter Chatter's ranking of the hottest students now."

"Really?" she asked and leaned over the table to look at my phone screen. "Since when?"

"I don't know, I only just saw it. Seems like The Watcher has taken a liking to you."

Scrunching up her nose, Evelyn commented, "I'm not sure that's something I should be happy about."

"Bit scary to think about," I agreed.

"What place are you?"

"Eighteenth, or something."

Evelyn smiled. "Also not bad."

"Oh, sugar honey iced tea!"

My head snapped around when Miss Pepperman's voice suddenly disrupted the quiet. She was balancing on one of the ladders, struggling to put a book back onto the highest shelf. Her legs wobbled alarmingly as she stretched as far as possible, only for the book to slip out of her fingers. It landed on the wooden floorboards with a thud, spine facing up.

I immediately got up and rushed towards her. "I'll get it!"

Miss Pepperman let out a relieved sigh and began her shaky descent down the ladder. "Oh, thank you, dear! This library truly isn't built for people who need to stand on a chair to get their tableware out of the cupboards!"

Evelyn, who had also hurried over to help, held onto the ladder to stop it from swaying. Once Miss Pepperman stood safely on her two feet again, I climbed up a few rungs and placed the book in its designated spot.

While I did so, Miss Pepperman turned to Evelyn. "While I have you, I wanted to talk to you about the job!"

"What job?"

"This, of course. The library, everything." She waved her hands about in a gesture that seemed to indicate the entire hall. "I was wondering, since you have such a delightful passion for books and I don't have as much time for this job as I would like to, if you would like to work here?"

"Really?"

"You would get paid, of course, and all you would have to do

Never Kiss
your Roommate

is sit here on a few evenings and hand out books to anyone who comes in. It's a doozy, really!"

"That sounds good, Eve," I said, landing back on my feet.

Miss Pepperman lightly touched my shoulder. "Of course I would also ask you, Seth, but Jasper told me that you've joined the drama club and I wouldn't want to keep you from that."

"It's no problem. This is her thing, not mine."

Miss Pepperman turned to Evelyn again. "What do you think, Evelyn? I wouldn't ask if I wasn't in desperate need of some help around here. I don't know if I should say this, but . . ."

Evelyn and I exchanged an intrigued look when Miss Pepperman's rosy cheeks turned even redder. "What is it?"

"Well, I *met* someone," she said—no, *giggled*. "He lives in Gloomswick and I would like to have some evenings off to spend some time with him, you see?"

"Of course," Evelyn said. I bit back a grin. Of course Eve, ever the romantic, was immediately helplessly endeared, probably already envisioning a whole romantic film in her mind, all pastels and hazy lighting and harp music playing in the background. "I would love to work here."

"Fantastic! When would you like to start?"

"Whenever you want me to. I don't have any other afterschool activities."

"How about tomorrow, if that isn't too sudden? The lovely gentleman I'm seeing invited me to his house for a candlelight dinner." She sighed, pressing a hand to her chest. "Isn't that romantic? I feel like I'm sixteen again!"

Evelyn smiled. "I can be here tomorrow."

"Thank you so much, Evelyn. I'll leave you the keys, along with the instructions for the printers and the computers here on my desk. You just have to lock the door and turn the electronics off and that's it! A piece of cake, right?"

"I'm sure I'll manage. Thank you, Miss Pepperman."

"No, thank *you*!" she exclaimed. Then she looked down at her bright red watch. "Oh, but it's time for dinner already! I don't want to keep you two any longer. Go on, off to the Great Hall with you."

"Thanks again!" Evelyn said before we grabbed our things from the table and made our way into the Great Hall.

There, most tables were occupied already, but Evelyn and I managed to find one near the entrance. Jasper and Noelle joined us a moment later. The new seating arrangement was a product of the changed dynamic within our group. Two weeks ago, the idea of the four of us sitting at one table had been unimaginable, but now I only briefly looked up when Noelle sat down on the opposite side. Jasper sank onto the bench next to me. Not that it made a difference.

"*Bonsoir*," Jasper said. "I just saw the blog update. Welcome to the top five, Evelyn!"

Evelyn smiled sheepishly. "Thanks."

"You know, with every update of that ranking I become more convinced that The Watcher might be queer," Jasper mused. "The boy to girl ratio is almost equal now."

I sat up a little straighter at that. "That's an interesting thought. It would for sure limit the number of suspects."

"How so?" Noelle snorted. "I'm queer. So is Jasper. So is Sammy and the majority of the drama club. So are a bunch of people from the cheerleading squad and the basketball team. Besides, anyone could be gay, but still in the closet."

I was less disappointed by that revelation than I was excited.

Never Kiss
your Roommate

Evelyn had also perked up, her fork frozen halfway to her mouth. "You're queer?" I asked.

Noelle shrugged. "I'm bi."

"Hey, me too!"

To my surprise, Noelle leaned over the table to high-five me with a grin. "Nice."

"I'm pansexual, in case anyone cares," Jasper chimed in.

"Which means that he wants to fu—"

Jasper's hand shot forward and clamped over Noelle's mouth at lightning speed. Eyes narrowed, he grumbled, "I swear, if you make one more joke about me being attracted to cookware I will kill you."

Muffled laughter and an amused twinkle in her eyes told me that that was exactly what she had been about to say.

After a second, Jasper pulled his hand back abruptly and wiped it on his pants with an expression of utter disgust. "Did you just fucking lick my ha—of course you did."

"That's to be expected," Noelle said. "Did you not learn *anything* in elementary school?"

While Jasper was busy glaring at her, I lightly nudged Evelyn's foot under the table. This was her chance to come out if she wanted to. I could see her gulping, eyes darting back and forth between Jasper and Noelle, her fingers tightening around her fork. Finally, she gave a small shake of her head.

I shot her a smile that I hoped was comforting and pulled my foot back.

"Hey, do you have any plans this weekend?" Noelle asked, apparently done with her and Jasper's staring contest.

Evelyn shook her head.

"Well, I have a basketball game tomorrow night. You should come. If you want, I mean."

Unlike her inner struggle a few seconds ago, her response to Noelle's question was immediate. "I'll be there."

The corners of Noelle's mouth ticked upward ever so slightly. Looking down at her plate again, she said, "Cool."

"Cool," Evelyn echoed.

"Mon dieu." Jasper chuckled, nudging me with his elbow. "Is it just me or is there some tension in here?"

I was too distracted by his knee pressing against mine under the table to answer and—okay, that was hard to ignore, maybe I did care a *tiny* bit. When a few seconds had passed and Jasper was still looking at me waiting for an answer, sitting so close that I could smell his cologne—because *of course* the pretentious bastard wore cologne, and not a cheap fragrance, either, but one that actually smelled *good*—I abruptly got to my feet.

"I, um . . . I think I forgot something in the library. I'm going to get it and then go back to my room. Good night, guys."

I turned on my heel before anyone could open their mouth to question me, forcing myself to walk at a pace that didn't give away what I was really doing—which was fleeing the scene. Still, with Jasper's gaze burning holes into my back and a sound like sirens ringing in my ears, I couldn't shake the feeling I had already been caught red-handed.

10

Evelyn

The gym had completely transformed since I had been there with Noelle for our self-defense lesson. Where the hall had been empty aside from some equipment standing around, the court was now cleared and the stands were packed. Instead of heavy silence, the air was filled with loud chatter and a tinny voice crackling through the speakers, announcing that there were only ten minutes to go until the game began. The vast majority of the audience was clad in white and navy, Seven Hills' colors, but there were also a few flashes of red here and there where students from the opposing team's school sat.

"I didn't expect this to be such a big deal!" Seth called over the racket, one hand holding onto mine so we didn't lose each other in the crowd.

"Me neither!" I responded.

The players weren't on the court yet, but the cheerleading squad was already busy riling up the crowd from the sidelines, Amelia giving an enthusiastic wave of her pom-pom when she spotted me.

Seth squinted, searching for free seats to sit, when I spotted Jasper in the first row. He beckoned us over and gathered the coat he had draped over the two seats next to him in his lap.

I tugged at Seth's hand. "Over there."

He followed me, somewhat reluctantly, as I made my way towards Jasper. I deliberately left the seat between us free so that Seth had no other choice but to sit there.

"Hey," Jasper said, a broad grin on his face. "Have you talked to Noelle today? How is she?"

"On edge," I replied. Noelle had been like a walking storm cloud all morning, the atmosphere in our room charged like a summer afternoon that promised a thunderstorm. Not like that part was much different any other day. "Is she always like this before her games?"

"No, the day of the first game of the season is always the worst. It's because most of the team went home over the summer holidays and there's a bunch of new players who have no clue what they're doing yet. Noelle worked really hard to get them all into shape."

I nodded, thinking back to all the evenings she had spent in the gym instead of our room over the last few weeks. To keep up the conversation, I asked, "Did you go home over the summer?"

"Yeah, I spent three weeks in Marseilles. Noelle came with."

"She didn't go home to her parents?"

Jasper only shook his head.

Before I could ask why, Seth chimed in. "Do you think they're going to win?"

Never Kiss your Roommate

"Better hope so," Jasper laughed. "Otherwise you'll be screwed, princesse. There's little that Noelle hates more than losing."

"I think I can handle it," I said, but got drowned out by the loud cheers and whistles that suddenly erupted in the crowd around us as Seven Hills' basketball team burst through the doors. Noelle was in the front, wearing the team's blue-and-white uniform, a few curls escaping from her ponytail. A grin more enthusiastic than I had ever seen on her was lighting up her face, her eyes brighter than the neon lights on the ceiling.

When Jasper whooped loudly, she turned to us and gave a short wave.

My hands were already hurting from clapping so loudly, but I didn't stop until the opposing team entered the court and everyone settled down.

While her team got into formation behind her, Noelle walked to the midcourt line to exchange a few words with the other team's captain and the referee. Then, with a whistle and deafening cheers, the game started.

I really didn't know much about the rules of basketball, so most of the time I wasn't quite sure what was going on, but I joined in whenever the others were cheering or booing. Being in the first row felt much more engaging than I had expected; more than once I flinched when the basketball got thrown in our general direction, the floor vibrating beneath my feet as the players darted past.

Towards the end of the first half the teams were tied at twenty-nine points each.

However, I didn't really care about the score—my eyes were mostly trained on Noelle. She was the fastest player by far, always showing up where no one had expected her to and effortlessly stealing the ball from the others. There was a heat in her eyes that I had never seen before, something wild about the way she grinned when her team scored. This was Noelle in her element, I realized. This was Noelle when she *cared*.

Halftime lasted twenty minutes, as Jasper informed me, enough time for us to get snacks and for me to have a quick chat with a breathless Amelia.

Fifteen minutes into the break, Seven Hills' team returned from the locker rooms. Noelle gathered everyone around her and addressed every player individually. Even from here I could tell how fiercely she was speaking, waiting until the person she was talking to nodded before she moved on to the next. I could only imagine what it felt like to have her talk to me like that, intense and in charge. I hated that my heart skipped a beat at the thought.

Finally, the team spread over the court once again, most of them hugging or high-fiving each other before they went to take their positions.

Noelle looked like she was barely able to stand still as she waited for the referee's whistle, bobbing up and down on her toes in a way that reminded me of how eager she had been to try the self-defense trick with me last week. I smiled at her when she sent a quick glance our way, surprised when she smiled back.

A moment later, the second half of the game began. The numbers on the scoreboard continuously climbed higher on each side, until Seven Hills managed to get ahead by six points towards the end.

The game was almost over, and by now I was pretty sure we were going to win. Noelle scored time after time after time, always shouting commands to her team members, always moving, always in control.

That was until she suddenly fell to the ground.

I gasped quietly when she didn't get up right away. From what it looked like, she had jumped to get a better aim at the basket and landed sort of awkwardly on her left foot, which she was now clutching with a pained grimace.

She was only a few feet away from us, close enough for me to hear her harsh breaths. I sat for a few seconds, battling with myself. Then, Seth hissing my name, I got up and ran towards her.

I reached her even before the nurse or any of the teachers could. Noelle was still sitting, her hands clutching her ankle, when I dropped to my knees next to her.

"Hey," I said breathlessly. "Hey, are you okay?"

"What the hell are you doing here?" she ground out between gritted teeth and momentarily looked up from her foot to stare at me instead.

I ignored her question and asked, "Do you want me to help you get off the court?"

"I'm not getting off the court," she hissed. "I need to finish this game. We're winning—"

"I know. But your foot . . ."

"I'm fine to play. Just help me get up." Softly, she added, "Please, Evelyn."

I swallowed hard. "Okay."

Looping my arms around her middle I helped her stand up, but as soon as she put her weight onto her left foot, her leg gave away and she slumped down in my arms, as limp as a marionette with its strings cut, a pained whimper leaving her lips.

Just as I carefully lowered her back onto the ground, a harsh female voice sounded right behind me. "Quick, out of the way, girl. This is *my* job."

I turned my head to see the nurse with her first-aid kit in one hand storming towards us, Mrs. Whitworth a few steps behind her.

Nodding, I went to move away and give them space to tend to Noelle, but her hand suddenly shot forward and clasped mine. "Stay," she said quietly. "Please?"

Hearing the crack in her voice was all it took for me to cave in. I sank to my knees beside her, carefully pulling her head onto my lap.

The nurse sent me an irritated look, but Mrs. Whitworth put a calming hand to her arm and said, "It's all right, Gloria. Let her be."

With Mrs. Whitworth and the nurse crouching on Noelle's other side, I suddenly became acutely aware of how this looked. Noelle's head was in my lap and her hand was still clutching onto mine, her face tilted back just enough for her watery gaze to stay fixed on my face as the nurse felt for injuries. Hundreds of eyes were directed at us and there was murmuring, a threatening buzz like a swarm of wasps that only grew louder the longer I focused on it. I was sure that my heart was pounding loud enough for the entire gym to hear it. Was this too close? Was I giving everything away? Straight girls held each other's hands all the time, right? Could they tell that my palms were sweaty, my breathing labored?

My panicked monologue was interrupted when Noelle inhaled sharply, eyes pressing shut and her hand squeezing mine tight enough to hurt as the nurse pressed into a tender spot.

"Looks like you sprained your ankle," she stated. "Only mildly, but still. You need to get off the court and into the infirmary so I can treat you."

Noelle gritted her teeth, angrily blinking away tears that I

Never Kiss
your Roommate

knew weren't threatening to fall because of the pain she was undoubtedly in, but because she wasn't able to play.

I wanted to say something, anything, to reassure her and stop her hands from shaking, but the words were stuck in my throat. All I could do was watch as the nurse applied ice to the injury and began compressing it with a bandage.

Once she was done, she gave her order, directed at me: "Help me get her off the court."

I carefully lifted Noelle's head off my lap and got up. Noelle was leaning heavily onto me when she was standing, her arm thrown over my shoulders. I tried not to think about the entire school watching me wrap my arm around her waist to steady her, tried not to overthink the placement of my hand, trembling slightly. I was just a girl helping her friend. It was normal. It was allowed.

It felt like ages until we made it to the sidelines and even longer until Noelle was finally sitting on the bench. Instead of going to the infirmary immediately as the nurse told her, she stayed adamant in her will to watch the rest of the game, until Mrs. Whitworth gave her okay.

Even though no one told me to, I sat down next to Noelle, the back of my neck prickling under the gazes of the audience that I was sure were still directed at me. She was incredibly tense for the entire rest of the game, her fingers gripping onto the bench tightly, her jaw set whenever the other team scored. Quiet swears came over her lips every once in a while, but other than that she remained completely silent. Without her, the team was clearly shaken; passes became more imprecise, they lost the ball to the other players more frequently. Still, somehow they managed to stay level with the others.

In the last minute of the game, the teams were tied once again. The other school attacked, desperate to score that one last time, but one of Seven Hills' girls, a tall brunette, managed to get the ball. Within seconds it was in the other half of the court. Then, right before the last few seconds ended, a boy managed to get the ball into the basket.

Noelle let out a relieved sigh as soon as the referee officially ended the game, her shoulders dropping and her teeth releasing her lower lip, which was bloody from all the nervous lip biting. Instead of celebrating on the court, the entire team huddled around the bench to include Noelle, who was already grinning from ear to ear again like she hadn't just sprained her ankle and would spend the night in the infirmary.

The nurse returned to us as the gym emptied, followed by Jasper and Seth. "Come on, now. Let's get you fixed up," she said, shooing the last remaining teammates away.

Noelle reluctantly agreed and let Jasper help her out of the gym. Just before they left through the door, Noelle turned her head to face me one last time.

I couldn't hear her, but I could read her lips well enough to know she said, *Thank you.*

As soon as Jasper and Noelle disappeared in the hallway, Seth turned to me with a raised eyebrow. "That wasn't very subtle now, was it?"

My throat tightened at what that statement implied. In a voice like gravel, I asked, "Was it actually that obvious?"

The smile immediately dropped off his face and made room for a more earnest look. "No, I'm just messing with you. You're fine, Eve, I promise. No one else thought anything of it."

Never Kiss your Roommate

The knot in my chest loosened a little bit at that and I gave a small nod.

"I held Jasper back for you," Seth said, the teasing tone back in his voice. "He wanted to get Noelle off the court, but I told him you'd handle it. Where's my award for wingman of the year?"

"Thanks," I murmured. "How did you know?"

"Know what? That you fancy Noelle?"

"I don't fancy—"

"Pretty much after the first week," he continued like he hadn't even heard my rebuttal. "All those heart eyes you give her at breakfast? The way you acted around her when you were drunk? How your eyes follow her every time she walks by? How you immediately agreed to give her self-defense lessons? Your reaction to her saying she was bi? Your—"

With every sentence, my cheeks turned redder and redder, until I finally said, "Okay, I get it! Jesus, you're awful."

"Awfully good at observing others, you mean," he laughed. "You like her so much it's disgusting to watch, and this was the final piece of evidence. Case closed, Evelyn wants to get laid by Noelle. Boom."

"Seth!" I quickly looked around to make sure no one had heard him. Luckily, the gym was almost deserted by now and the people cleaning up didn't seem to be listening. "It's not like that. I just think she's really pretty and very smart and I like having her around, that's all."

"Eve, you do realize that just sounded like a declaration of love, right? You're head over heels and we both know it."

I gave a noncommittal shrug, tugging at the hem of my jumper. "It's not like it'd change anything. She has a boyfriend. Plus, she still doesn't like me very much, I think."

"How oblivious can someone be?" Seth groaned, gripping both my shoulders, shaking me with every word he said. "She broke up with her boyfriend a few days after the party, it was all over The Chitter Chatter. Since then she's been hanging out with you all the time. She even asked for self-defense lessons. Do you even know what that means?"

"She wants to learn how to fight?"

"No," he groaned, looking about five seconds away from slapping me. "More time with you? Lots of physical contact? The chance at hot locker room make-out sessions?"

"I don't think that's—"

"Oh my God, Evelyn, get your head on straight," he said. "Or in this case, get it on gay. Use your damn gaydar, dumbass."

"What are you doing?" Jasper's voice suddenly appeared out of nowhere. He stood right behind Seth, hands in his pockets and an amused glint in his eyes.

"Founding a cult," Seth immediately said and went to stand next to me, facing Jasper. "Sacrifice one ear and you're in."

Shaking his head, Jasper shifted his attention to me. "What was all of that about? Why do you need to use your gaydar?"

The familiar weight pressed down on my chest again. I was about to lie, make an excuse and hope he bought it, but then I thought back to dinner yesterday, to Noelle and Jasper and Seth talking about their sexualities, how easy it had been for them. I had felt frozen then, my tongue paralyzed with fear, and later that night I had regretted not saying anything. This, I figured, was the universe's way of giving me a second chance, a little nudge in the direction I knew deep down I wanted to go.

Still, the words felt like they were sticking to the back of my throat and I had to painstakingly pry them off one by one. "Well, um . . . I'm kind of . . . I like girls."

I had braced for almost every possible reaction, but a laugh wasn't one of them. "'Course you do," Jasper chuckled. "I've known since you arrived here."

"What? How?"

Jasper shrugged. "You never even tried to hook up with me. In fact, you aren't even remotely interested in me. Do you know how rare that is?"

A disbelieving laugh tumbled from my lips, the air finally reaching my lungs again.

Seth made a strange choking noise that made me look over at him for a split second. "Are you serious?"

"Completely. Advantage of being an androgynous, French god: you're absolutely *everyone's* type, boys or girls. They call me The Confuser because I make everyone question their sexuality."

Seth frowned. "No one ever calls you that."

"No," Jasper admitted. "But that would be cool. So, you like Noelle?"

"No," I replied, at the same time that Seth said, "Yes."

"Interesting."

I felt my cheeks heating up and quickly went on to ask, "How is she?"

"I don't know, really. The nurse kicked me out as soon as I put Noelle down and she's not letting anyone besides Mrs. Whitworth in. She'll probably have to stay there for the night."

"Alone?"

"Yes. But don't worry, princesse," Jasper said. "It's by far not the first time Noelle has ended up in the infirmary overnight.

Knowing her, she'll probably be back on her feet by tomorrow, even if she really shouldn't be."

Before I could reply I suddenly felt a hand on my shoulder, making me jump.

"Oh, I'm sorry, I didn't mean to startle you," Mrs. Whitworth said with an apologetic smile. "Can I talk to you for a moment?"

"Yes. Yes, of course," I hastily said and followed her as she led me out into the hallway where it was a bit quieter. "Is this because I went onto the court without permission?"

"It's not. Don't worry, Evelyn, I'm not angry with you. Quite the opposite, actually."

My shoulders sagged in relief. "Oh."

"I don't know you all that well," she said in her gentle, smooth voice. "But I appreciate empathy and courage, which is what you showed when you raced to help Noelle. You know her well by now, so you must know how . . . difficult she can be, at times. Frankly, I didn't expect the two of you to get along."

"Me either," I said.

"I love all my students and want only the best for them, but Noelle has always been one of those over whom I feel even more protective. She didn't always have it easy. Seeing someone care for her as much as you do . . . it's very special."

I wasn't sure what to say. To hear the headmistress speak about her students with so much warmth in her voice was as unexpected as it was touching.

"I can see how worried you are about Noelle. I want you to take your mind off her tonight. I give you permission to go out into town with Seth and Jasper."

"Really? We're allowed to go out?"

She smiled. "Yes, but only if you return by eleven."

Never Kiss
your Roommate

"Thank you so much, Mrs. Whitworth."

"You're welcome." Her brown eyes glinted cheerfully as she made a shooing motion. "Go ahead. Just don't tell everyone."

"I won't," I said, turning around. "Thanks again!"

"Eleven sharp!" she called after me, but I was already flying through the doors of the gym, towards where Jasper and Seth were still standing, one looking flustered, the other amused.

11

Evelyn

Fifteen minutes later, Jasper, Seth, and I reached Gloomswick. It was even chillier than it had been the other night, but with Jasper striding next to us through the dimly lit alleyways, as confident as if he owned every brick and cobblestone he passed, the houses seemed less like narrow-eyed beasts that might pounce on us at any second and more like gently snoozing giants that nothing could awaken.

Eventually, Jasper led us to a small park that was tucked away behind a tall brick wall and consisted of nothing but two benches, a bunch of apple trees, and a lush meadow that was freckled with wildflowers. Sitting in the tall grass, we shared a bottle of sparkling wine we had gotten at the rundown corner store we had passed on our way. With the fizzy bubbles on my tongue and the starry sky above me, I felt at ease for the first time that day.

Never Kiss
your Roommate

"Evelyn, what are you going to do about Noelle?" Jasper asked. He was lying to my left, arms spread wide and eyes fixed on the sky.

I shrugged, fiddling with the lid of the bottle. "Nothing. I don't even know if she feels the same about me. If she doesn't, it's just going to make things awkward for the rest of the year."

"You're no fun," Jasper said. "I bet you'd stand a pretty good chance."

Normally I would have left it at that, but the alcohol had loosened my tongue and before I could think better of it, I said, "I'm really not good at this stuff, is the thing. I feel like I turn into a blubbering mess every time she's near me. I mean, what am I supposed to say? *You're really pretty and I'm really gay, do you want to date?*"

Seth chuckled. "Brilliant, exactly like that."

Shaking my head, I took another sip from the bottle.

"Hey, Seth," Jasper said. "Are you interested in anyone?"

"Nope," Seth said quickly. "No one."

Jasper and I exchanged a suspicious look. "Are you sure about that?" I poked his side.

"Absolutely, 100 percent sure," Seth insisted.

"You know, maybe I could help you if you tell me their name?" Jasper offered.

"Do I have to spell it out to you in French?" Seth snapped. "I'm not interested in anyone."

Jasper just shrugged, unfazed. "Fine. I'll figure it out eventually."

"Like hell you will." Seth practically ripped the bottle out of my hand.

"He says he doesn't believe in love," I explained.

Propping himself up on his elbow to get a better view at Seth, Jasper asked, "Seriously?"

Seth only gave a shrug.

"Mon dieu, that's dark," Jasper murmured and sank down into the grass again.

In the following silence, the wind whispered in the trees and cars hummed on the roads. The grass was slightly damp beneath me when I let myself sink onto my back, my breath forming little clouds in the crisp night air. I didn't mind. The sparkling wine and the feeling of Jasper's shoulder pressing against mine on one side, Seth's knee knocking against my leg on the other, made me feel warm from the inside out.

With the girls back home, friendship had always felt like something I needed to earn, something that required exertion both to gain and to keep, something that would slip through my fingers like sand if I didn't clutch it hard enough; if I didn't dress and talk and act the way they expected me to. I had gotten good at knowing when to nod and giggle and fawn over the guys they pointed out, good at knowing what to say about the lead actors in the movies we watched even though my eyes had been glued to the actress's face the entire time, good at hiding my phone and my playlists and anything that could give away that I wasn't like them.

My hands had been cramping from struggling to hold onto surface-level friendships, only for them to drop me without a warning, without a second thought.

I had reached Seven Hills with my palms open for the very first time, little crescent moons still imprinted in them from how hard I had dug my nails in all those years. I had had no expectations of it being any other way here, but here I was, lying

Never Kiss your Roommate

between two people who were also wonderfully strange and who *knew* me, and for the first time it didn't hurt a bit.

After a few more minutes of comfortable silence, Jasper quietly said, "Pity that Noelle isn't here right now. Drinking and looking at the stars are probably the two things she loves the most next to basketball."

"She likes stargazing?" I asked.

"Sometimes she spends entire evenings lying in the football field and staring at the sky. She could probably tell you every single constellation up there. Fucking nerd," Jasper snorted, an affectionate undertone and his accent softening the words.

For some reason this unforeseen piece of information made me smile.

"Oh, you're into that, aren't you?"

"Talk dirty to me, Noelle," Seth suddenly moaned, his voice pitched ridiculously high. "Tell me something about the Big Dipper, oh yeah."

Jasper laughed, loudly enough to startle a cat that had been slinking by, prompting it to give an indignant hiss and dart out onto the street. In the same obnoxious pitch, he said, "Did you know that Jupiter is the fastest spinning planet in our solar system, babe?"

"Oh my God, that's so hot." Seth was pretending to breathe heavily, fanning his face with one hand.

Jasper leaned over me to get closer to him and said, his voice a seductive drawl, "Venus is the second brightest planet in our solar system."

"Shit, I think I just came," Seth choked out.

Jasper flopped down on his back again, equally as hysterical.

"You guys are ridiculous, both of you," I said, but couldn't hold back a laugh of my own.

After we had calmed down, I got to my feet, plucking off some of the grass that was sticking to my skirt. "It's almost eleven o'clock. We should head back."

Jasper reluctantly got up before helping Seth off the ground. As we walked up the road, Jasper whispered to Seth, "Do you think there's such a thing as an astronomy kink?"

"Oh, for sure."

"I hate both of you," I said, but didn't duck away when Seth slung an arm around my shoulders.

∘ ∘ ∘

We made it back to the castle right on time, entering through the front door instead of sneaking in through the gym. Mrs. Whitworth awaited us, standing on the stairs with a smile on her face, nodding once before she turned around and went back to the teachers' quarters, her elegant nightgown billowing behind her.

"Do you want us to walk you back to your room?" Seth whispered.

"I think I'll manage."

"This is totally unrelated to anything we talked about," Jasper said, "But just in case you ever need to visit someone in the infirmary, it's the third door on the right when you enter the west wing."

"Ah." I cleared my throat. "Thanks for that completely unrelated information."

I could tell that Seth was holding back a laugh. "Good night, Eve. See you at breakfast."

"Good night," I said and watched as the two of them made their way up the stairs to the boys' wing, Seth a few feet behind Jasper until their tall frames disappeared in the hallway.

Never Kiss
your Roommate

When they were gone, I made my way back to my room, where I brushed my teeth and changed into leggings and a soft jumper. It had been an eventful day and it was past my usual bedtime, so I expected to drift off easily once I went to bed—instead, I found myself lying wide awake. The room felt strange without Noelle. I had gotten so used to having her around at all times that the space now felt empty without her even breathing and the acute awareness of having her a few feet away.

It was absurd, really: in the beginning, I hadn't been able to sleep with her so close to me, and now I apparently couldn't sleep without her.

And then there was the constant fear of having a nightmare, which seemed almost inevitable. There was barely a night I didn't wake up bathed in sweat and with my heart racing, the voices still echoing in my head in a way that reminded me of the first pages of *Wuthering Heights*; I was Mr. Lockwood tossing around in his bed, haunted in dreams by a figure from the past that was begging to be let in, and like Heathcliff being alerted by his screams, Noelle was the one who usually called out my name to wake me.

It had helped to open my eyes and see her on the other side of the room, pulling me back into the present. Tonight, I would wake up alone in the dark again.

When half an hour had passed and I felt no closer to sleep than earlier, I kicked the blanket away and sat up. It was an impulsive decision, but with Jasper's voice echoing in my head, I barely hesitated as I grabbed my keys and stepped out into the hallway.

By now I was used to roaming the castle at night, so I easily found my way around, barely paying any mind to the shadows that loomed in the halls that had scared me so much in the beginning. My fluffy socks made no noise against the stone floor as I crossed the entrance hall and entered the west wing.

To my surprise, I found the third door on the right ajar, a thin finger of light reaching through the crack. It landed on my foot when I took a step closer to peek inside.

The room was one of the smaller ones of the castle, sterile with only a few metal beds and shelves filled with the nurse's equipment. Noelle was sitting on a bed in the center of the room, her back propped against a mountain of pillows, eyes directed at the ceiling.

"Oh thank God," she said when I slipped inside, pushing the pair of headphones down to her neck. "You have no idea how boring it is alone here."

"You've been here only a few hours." I chuckled and came to a stop next to her. "Is it okay if I sit?"

"No." She grinned when I blinked at her in surprise at that response. "I'm sick of being in this bed. Let's go somewhere else."

"But aren't you supposed to rest?"

"I rested. Give me my crutches."

Accepting that arguing wouldn't get me anywhere, I handed her the crutches that were propped against the end of the bed. I stayed close to her when she got up, just in case she needed help, but she got to her feet and headed towards the door in a way that seemed like this was by far not the first time she'd had to use them.

Holding the door for her, I asked, "Where are we going?"

"You'll see. Don't you trust me?"

"Not really."

"Smart girl. Come along now."

The entrance hall was deadly silent except for our steps and the clicking of Noelle's crutches against the floor. She was wearing sweatpants and a big T-shirt now, her hair falling on her shoulders.

When she came to a sudden halt and dropped her crutches to the floor to kneel, I almost ran into her. "Hey!" she quietly said, her voice suddenly three octaves higher than usual. "Hey, come here!"

I wondered for a moment if I had missed something and she had also hit her head, before suddenly, there was a tiny meowing sound. Seconds later, a cat peeked around the corner.

"Come over here, Muffin!" Noelle whispered, reaching out a hand.

It didn't take much convincing for the cat. In the blink of an eye, she darted over to Noelle and pressed her head into her hand.

"Long time no see, pal, where've you been? You've been busy hunting mice in the attic, huh?"

The cat answered with a small meow before going back to purring happily.

"This is Muffin," Noelle said when I sank to my knees next to her. "Mrs. Whitworth's cat."

"I don't think I've ever seen her around before."

"She's usually out here only at night. All the students running around here scare her." Noelle absentmindedly tickled Muffin's chin.

I couldn't decide what was more precious, the copper-furred cat or Noelle, who made little kissy noises at her.

When I reached out and gingerly petted her head, Muffin's eyes opened just a slit wide to look at me as she purred.

"God, I wish I had a cat," Noelle whispered under her breath. She continued petting Muffin for a few more moments before the cat suddenly took off and disappeared around the corner.

With a shrug, Noelle grabbed her crutches and pushed herself up. "So, Mrs. Whitworth told me you were allowed to go out with the boys?" she asked as we crossed the entrance hall. She was whispering even though the clicking of her crutches on the stone was probably loud enough to wake up the entire castle. "How was it and why aren't you drunk? I expected more from you, Greene."

"It was nice," I said. "And we did drink, but tipsy is enough for me after what happened at the Welcome Back Party."

Noelle chuckled. "Pity."

A moment later we made it to the east wing. There, Noelle led the way to the administration office and motioned for me to open the door with her crutch.

I did, surprised to find it unlocked. The office was completely dark, but Noelle found the light switch within seconds.

She pushed her way past me without any explanation and walked around the abandoned desk. "Come here and pick this up for me, will you?"

I went to stand next to her to find her pointing at a large parcel on the floor. Picking it up, I asked, "Are we stealing right now?"

She clicked her tongue. "So much mistrust. This is mine."

She wasn't lying; once I got a closer look at the parcel I saw that it had her name written on it in neat cursive.

"Who sent you this?" I asked as we left the office.

"My mom. She sends me one every month."

Never Kiss your Roommate

Now I really couldn't wait to open it and see what was inside, so I quickly followed her as she led the way to the gym and had me open the door for her.

I blinked into the sudden brightness when she flipped the switch and the ceiling lights flickered to life with a soft whir. Even hours after the game, the hall still smelled faintly of rubber and sweat.

"Why are we here?"

Noelle shrugged. "It's the only quiet place I could think of that doesn't require climbing any stairs."

I nodded, silently following her over to the same bench from where we had watched the last minutes of the game earlier. Where she had been tense and fidgety then, she now seemed completely relaxed as she sank down and took the parcel I handed her. Inside was a huge amount of sweets, but a lot of them were things I didn't know, like tiny plastic bottles filled with some kind of vibrantly colored liquid and a can labeled *Boiled Peanuts.*

"What is all of this?"

"Candy. What else does it look like?"

"Wait," I said, my eyes widening when the realization dawned on me. "You're American!"

Noelle was silent for a long moment, her expression somewhere between shocked and confused. "What?"

"A-am I right?"

"How the hell did you know?"

"The sweets," I explained, pointing at the contents of the parcel. "I don't know most of them, but I think they're American. Plus, you say *candy* instead of sweets, and I noticed that you slip in and out of accents sometimes, especially when you're upset."

"I am upset right now," she said, glaring at me. "I can't believe you found out that easily."

"Why do you want nobody to know?"

Noelle stared darkly at the floor. "I don't want to talk about it. Just let it go and don't tell anyone else, please."

The look on her face stopped me from inquiring any further. The only thing I asked was, "How do you manage to sound so British?"

"Practice. Before I came to the UK, I started learning how to sound all posh and proper. Since I've been here, the American accent has kind of started to fade, so I don't have to consciously suppress it anymore. But I guess that doesn't work as well as I thought it did."

"I wouldn't have thought much of it if I hadn't seen this," I said, pointing at the parcel.

"You really are as much trouble as I thought you'd be."

Knocking my shoulders against hers, I asked, "What's your favorite *candy* then, Miss America?"

She rolled her eyes at me but handed me a small orange package of Reese's Peanut Butter Cups.

While I opened it, she said, "All the different kinds of candy are pretty much the only reason I miss the US."

"Really?"

"Well, that and my mom, of course," Noelle said softly.

My breath hitched in my throat. It was rare that Noelle let herself be as vulnerable as she was right now and even rarer that she offered information of her own without any prompting. "You and your mom are close, aren't you?"

"We are. She's great." Looking up from the parcel, she asked, "Do you want to play truths?"

I hesitated for a moment, taken aback, before I nodded.

"Okay," Noelle said, twisting her whole body to face me. I did

Never Kiss your Roommate

the same, so we were sitting opposite each other on the bench with only the parcel between us. "But if there's a question either of us wants to skip, that's okay."

"Do you want to start?" I asked around a Reese's.

"Sure. Let's start with an easy question. What's your favorite subject?"

"English Lit."

"Disgusting. Your turn."

I chuckled. "What's your favorite season?"

"Winter," Noelle answered promptly. "My birthday is in December. Do you have siblings?"

"No. You?"

She shook her head. "My mom doesn't have time for another child. Hell, she barely has time for me," she said. "Was that your question?"

"No. What's your mom's job?"

Noelle was silent for a moment. I tried to read her expression, but to no avail. It was as if a veil had lowered over her face, translucent enough to just barely make out the silhouette of something moving behind it, but still too opaque to make out what it was. "Pass."

"Oh. Sorry," I said, looking down at my hands. "Why did you break up with Elias?"

This time, Noelle answered without a second of hesitation. "We were never anything serious. After the party, it felt weird to still be with him."

"But . . . didn't you spend almost every night in his room?"

"No. I spent them in Jasper's."

I tried not to show my surprise or, even worse, the strange sense of relief that washed over me at that.

"Okay, my turn. What are your nightmares about?" Noelle seemed to notice the way I tensed and quickly added, "Remember, you can pass."

"No, it's fine. I'm just not sure you want to hear this one. It's a depressing story."

"Trust me," Noelle snorted. "My entire life is a depressing story. I can handle it if you can handle telling."

The thing was, I wasn't sure if I could. I hadn't really talked to anyone besides my parents, and that had been months ago. It was only after a few seconds and with a sandpaper voice that I managed to say, "I was outed at my former school."

In the empty gym, I could clearly hear the hitch in Noelle's breath. I didn't look at her when I continued, "There was this girl, Angelica. She was my best friend. My only friend, really. I knew her for five years and then, at some point, I realized that I liked her." I swallowed hard. "I trusted her with all of my secrets and the thought that this might be any different didn't even occur to me. So one afternoon, when we were hanging out at her house, I told her I had feelings for her."

Closing my eyes for a moment, I could still remember the smell of her room, some kind of sweet perfume and the cigarette she had secretly smoked at the window. After my confession, she had stubbed it out on the windowsill, the quiet crackle the only sound breaking the heavy silence. I waited for five minutes for her to say something or to at least look at me. When she finally did, I realized her smile was gone, replaced by a look of utter disgust, like I was a spider she had just found in the corner of her room and she was about to stomp me dead.

Thinking back on it, the same helpless feeling took a hold of me again; something that felt like swimming in ice water, my limbs growing heavier by the second as the cold seeped through my skin while I realized there was no getting out in time. It was the bone-chilling knowledge that, whatever I said, I couldn't take the words back, could do nothing to restore the image she'd had of me that had shattered the moment I had opened my mouth.

And then she had taken my head and pushed it under.

"She told me to get the hell out and never talk to her again," I said. "The next day, when I went to school, everyone knew."

"Fucking bitch," Noelle hissed, making me look up at her. Her jaw was set, her hands balled into fists where they rested on her thighs. Her eyes were staring at me with so much intensity I had to avert my gaze.

"You could say that," I murmured. "You know, at that time I had barely just come to terms with the fact that I wasn't straight, so I wasn't at all ready for it to be out in the open like that. It already felt terrifying enough to find out that the perception of me that I and everyone else had just wasn't true. I still wasn't sure what all of it meant or how it fit into what I thought to be true about myself; like, would I have to cut all my hair off now so that I fit the stereotypes, or was there something else that was expected of me? Half the time I was still trying to figure out if I was somehow faking it, which I guess is a form of denial as well."

"I went through the same thing when I was figuring out that I'm bi," Noelle said. "It's called compulsory heterosexuality, I think. When all of society expects you to be straight, it makes it even harder to come to terms with the fact that you're not."

I nodded, my words caught in my throat. Under Noelle's steady gaze, I felt tender and raw, a barely healed wound that was still bruised around the edges.

"It's especially fun when you're bi," she said. "Even now I

sometimes still go through these phases where I'm like *Maybe I was just trying to convince myself I'm into girls to make myself more interesting.* Which is just such bullshit. I mean, first of all, there's literally no gain in being a minority, especially when you're already Black. And second of all, no straight person would spend so much fucking time taking *Am I gay?* quizzes."

"You did that too?" I gasped.

"So many times," she laughed, shaking her head. "And if I didn't like the result, I would just go back and pick all the obvious straight answers."

"Oh my God, where were you two years ago?" I asked. The pressure I had felt on my chest a few moments ago had subsided by now. Instead, something warm had settled inside my rib cage.

"It's crazy how you're convinced you're the only one going through these things when in reality there are millions of people who are in the same boat, isn't it?" she asked, running her finger along the grain in the wooden bench. "For me it was Jas who first made me realize that I'm not alone. Not in this, at least."

We were both silent for a moment before she looked up again and said, "Sorry, I didn't want to interrupt your story. What happened then?"

Talking about it felt like pressing my fingers into the wound, the words stiff and clumsy. "After Angelica told everyone, I was the talk of the school. They weren't openly homophobic, but . . . there were a bunch of little things. People would whisper behind my back or write nasty things on the stalls in the girls' bathroom. Guys would tell me to make out with random girls in the hallway for them because they thought it was hot. Some of the girls refused to change in the same locker room as me before

PE." I inhaled shakily. "At some point, I just couldn't take it anymore. I went to my parents and told them about everything."

"How did they react?"

I had to gulp at the memory of them sitting at the kitchen table with me, faces as pale as the wallpaper, my mom white-knuckled as she clutched onto the cup of tea that had gone cold by then, like it was some kind of life raft that would keep her afloat in the flood of awful words that streamed from my mouth.

"They were heartbroken," I said. "Not because I'm lesbian—they didn't care about that at all—but because I had been too afraid to tell them. Dad took me out of school for the last few weeks before the holidays and Mom looked up boarding schools. And that's why I'm here now."

"I'm glad you are," Noelle murmured. "But I also want to punch those assholes for making you go through that."

"Not with your lack of technique," I said, trying my best to make my voice sound light. "We haven't gotten that far in our training yet."

Noelle's expression didn't change. "Is all of that the reason you started taking self-defense lessons?"

"Yes. I took a course that lasted all summer—it was my dad's idea. To make me feel more in control again, not as helpless as I did during those months."

Noelle nodded. Warily, she asked, "So . . . that's what your nightmares are about now? The bullying?"

"Yes. I . . . I keep seeing Angelica looking at me with this disgusted expression and then I'm back in the hallways with everyone staring and talking . . ." I broke off, directing my gaze at my hands again. "There's this feeling of shame that was there even before all of that happened, but it only got really intense when people started looking at me differently and analyzing everything I did. All my bad dreams are *drenched* in that feeling. And it doesn't always go away when I wake up."

"Evelyn." My eyes shot up when I suddenly felt her hand under my chin, gently lifting it to make me look at her. "You have nothing to be ashamed of. Nothing."

I didn't know what it was that made my throat clog up with tears—her words, the touch of her fingers, or the earnest look in her brown eyes, warmer than I had ever seen them. Maybe it was a combination of all three. "I know," I managed to whisper. "It just doesn't always feel like it. When I stare at a pretty girl, for example, I sometimes feel so guilty. Predatory, almost, like I'm doing something I shouldn't be doing."

"I know what that's like," Noelle said, her eyes never leaving my face. "But that feeling and that voice in your head were planted there by our fucked-up society. Don't listen to those losers." She was silent for a moment before her lips curved into the hint of a smile. "If it helps, I for one really don't mind if you stare at me."

With a laugh that sounded dangerously close to breathless, I slapped her hand away. "Shut up."

Noelle only chuckled and handed me a pack of Oreos. "Here, have a cookie. You deserve it."

I shook my head at her but accepted it nevertheless. The following silence was disturbed by nothing but the quiet crinkling of plastic as we passed the Oreos back and forth and the ticking of the clock on the wall.

When the hands were creeping past 1 a.m., I slowly got to my feet. "I think we should go to bed."

Together, we neatly put all the contents back into the parcel.

Never Kiss
your Roommate

When we were done, I helped Noelle get up and handed her the crutches. It was only when we were back in the entrance hall that she spoke again.

"I'm going to have to sleep in the infirmary," she said, her voice echoing from the high walls. "Are you okay on your own tonight?"

I nodded and lifted the parcel. "Do you want me to take this with me to our room?"

"That would be awesome. Just leave it on my desk, or something."

"I still can't believe your mom sends you so many sweets every month."

"What can I say," Noelle grinned. "I like things that are sweet."

I smiled, shifting on my feet. "Thanks for, you know, the talk."

"Thanks for keeping me from dying of boredom," she said. "Text me if you have another nightmare and I'll do my best to drag myself up the stairs to our room."

"I will," I said. "Good night, Noelle."

I was just about to turn around when she suddenly leaned forward and planted a short kiss on my cheek, the touch so light I would've thought I'd imagined it if it hadn't been for her self-satisfied smile as she leaned back. "Sweet dreams."

All I could do was watch as she crossed the hall and disappeared into the west wing, one hand still pressed to the spot her lips had touched.

This was what the opposite of ice water felt like then.

12

Evelyn

October chased off September and brought even gloomier days with it. As the woods surrounding the castle changed, trees ablaze with yellow, orange, and red, the life inside got busier. The drama club was working towards its premiere, meaning that both Seth and Jasper spent most of their free time in the auditorium rehearsing. The basketball team intensified its training for their upcoming game at a school called Westbridge, which, Noelle had explained to me, was the best team in their entire league and had defended its first place for years. She still wasn't allowed to play but attended every practice, watching from the bench with hungry eyes. Meanwhile, I had my first shifts at the library, which were just as easy as Miss Pepperman had promised. Most evenings I could simply curl up with a book in one of the armchairs, only disturbed by the handful of students who came by to research something on one of the computers or needed help finding a book.

Tonight was another one of the slow nights in the library, the only other people being a girl from the student council who was doing research for an essay and a group of year-seven boys who wanted to use the computers. It was nine o'clock when I locked the door behind me and made my way back to my room, my thoughts still caught up in the plot of *Little Women*. I was ripped out of them only when I stopped in front of our door, key in hand and caught off guard by the loud banging sounding from inside.

Still vividly remembering the last time I had opened the door to a strange noise, I gave a loud knock and waited for Noelle to respond before entering.

As I pushed the door open, I wasn't sure what to expect but it was certainly not the sight of Noelle standing on my bed with a hammer in her hand.

"Hey," she said as if nothing unusual was happening. "I didn't think you'd be back this early."

"What are you doing?" I asked, closing the door behind me. "And where are your crutches? You shouldn't put so much weight on your ankle—"

"My ankle is fine. Care to lend me a hand?"

It was only when I climbed next to her onto the bed that I could see what she was trying to nail to the wall. "Fairy lights?"

"Yeah," she said. "Can you hold this for a sec?"

I leaned forward and held the fairy lights up for her, keenly aware of her shoulder pressing against mine. She lifted the hammer and made quick work of fastening them to the wall above my bed. Once she was happy with the results, she tossed the hammer onto the mattress and turned around. As close as we were standing, the pained wince she tried to hide didn't go unnoticed and I instinctively got off the bed, wrapping my arms around her waist to help her get down. As I did, her hands flew up to hold onto my shoulders, her touch as light as if two flower petals had settled there, and refused to let go even as she was standing on her own two feet again.

"You . . . you should really use your crutches," I said, only too aware of the fact that my hands were still on her hips.

Noelle shook her head, her voice lower than before. "They're annoying and impractical."

It took everything in me to step back, making her rose-petal hands drift down from my shoulders. Wordlessly, I picked up her crutches where they were leaning against the wall next to my bed and handed them to her. Against my expectations, she accepted them without protest and used them to get back to her side of the room.

Sitting down at the end of my bed, I asked, "Why the fairy lights?"

"When I used to have really bad nightmares, the worst thing was waking up alone in the dark, so I always left a light on," Noelle said. "Maybe it's stupid but I thought that might help you as well."

For a few seconds, all I could do was stare at her. My voice sounded watery when I choked out, "Not stupid at all. Thank you, Noelle."

Noelle suddenly looked alarmed. "Why are you crying? Did I do something wrong? Do you want me to—"

"No," I said, wiping away the traitorous tears that had spilled out against my will. Looking at the fairy lights and at Noelle's

Never Kiss
your Roommate

worried face, my heart felt like it had grown to twice its size, so big that it filled up my entire chest and all I could get out was, "You did nothing wrong. Thank you."

Her shoulders sagged in relief. "Goddammit, Greene, don't scare me like that."

I released a tearful laugh. "Sorry."

"Are you going to turn them on, then?"

Nodding, I got up to turn off the ceiling light before I switched on the battery pack.

The lights illuminated my half of the room just enough to turn the otherwise threatening shadows into chairs and desks and drawers, each of them glowing comfortingly like tiny stars trapped under our ceiling. A small galaxy just for us.

o o o

Surprisingly, they helped.

I had two nightmares in the following three days and each time those fairy lights were the first thing I saw when my eyes snapped open, reminding me where I was and that the girl who had brought this light to the darkness for me was sleeping only a few feet away from me.

They didn't make my nightmares any less awful, but they made the aftermath more bearable.

It was the fifth night after Noelle had hung them up that something was different. Usually, she was still asleep when I woke up, or at least she didn't say anything; this time, she was the one shaking me awake.

My eyes flew open the instant she gripped my shoulders, my hands reaching up to clasp at her arms.

"Hey," she muttered, her head blocking out the lights as she leaned over me. "You're okay. Just another nightmare."

My chest was still rising and falling rapidly as I let go of her and dropped my head back onto my pillow, blinking as if that would dispel the images burned into the back of my eyelids. "Sorry," I rasped. "Did . . . did I talk in my sleep?"

"You were screaming."

I fisted a hand in the sheets, willing my breath to stop rattling in my throat, my heart to stop pounding, my body to stop feeling like I was going to shake apart under Noelle's steady gaze. Finally, I managed to say, "Sorry for waking you up. You should go back to sleep."

"Don't be stupid. Tonight was worse than usual, wasn't it?"

"Yes," I whispered.

"Then I won't go back to sleep."

"Noelle . . ."

"I want to help you. Is it okay if I do?"

I sat up and, after a moment of hesitation, gave a small nod.

"All right," Noelle said, suddenly unsure. After a few seconds of heavy silence, she asked, "How about you relax and I do your makeup?"

I didn't know what I thought she was going to say, but it wasn't that. For a moment, I wondered if I was somehow still dreaming, but the pounding of my heart, which felt very much alive, proved the opposite.

"Only if you want to."

"I wouldn't have offered if I didn't."

Noelle got up from where she had been perched on the edge of my bed and walked over to the bathroom. I winced when I noticed the limp in her step but didn't have the energy to tell her to use her crutches this time.

Instead, I waited, my arms wrapped around myself, as she rifled through her makeup products in the bathroom. Outside, the wind howled and pressed against the windows, begging to be let in. They creaked quietly in protest but didn't budge.

"What time is it?" I asked when Noelle walked back out.

"Just past twelve," she replied. On her way over, she picked up her phone from her bed and put on a song I immediately recognized. It was by a British indie band I had told her about a week or two ago. Normally, the familiar melody would have made my heartbeat fall back into its steady rhythm; the knowledge that Noelle had not only cared enough to listen but also to remember, however, caused it to leap in a strange staccato I wasn't used to.

After turning on the lamp on my bedside table, Noelle tossed the makeup, some hers and some mine, onto the bed and sat down in front of me.

"Do you want to talk about the dream?" Noelle asked, crossing her legs.

Usually, trying to wake up from my nightmares was like swimming through syrup: it was slow and exhausting and even afterward, when I lay panting in my bed, some of it still clogged up my throat. Noelle had made getting out easier, but sitting in front of her, I could still feel it sticking to my skin. Shaking my head, I said, "I don't think so."

"That's all right," Noelle said, her voice surprisingly soft. While she spoke, she was applying some of my foundation onto a beauty blender. "Is it okay if I touch you?"

Nodding to that question was as natural as breathing.

My eyes slipped shut when her hand came up to cup my cheek, the foundation cool against my skin as she gently dabbed the beauty blender over my face. The longer she worked, the more the nightmare—the stares, the whispers, the laughs—seemed to fade into the distance, the sickening taste slowly leaving my mouth.

"It's a bit of a shame you always wear foundation," Noelle murmured. "You're covering up all your freckles."

I scrunched up my nose, momentarily making her hand still. "I don't like them."

Noelle let out a quiet hum before she continued. Once she was satisfied, she applied a layer of transparent powder to my face.

In the comfortable silence, I focused on the music in the background and the feeling of her fingertips. A few weeks ago, I hadn't been able to imagine being this close to her, much less feeling this relaxed in her presence. I also hadn't imagined her voice to be as soft as it was when she told me to hold still or her touch to be this careful, fingertips so light against my skin it almost seemed like she was afraid I would splinter beneath them.

I knew that, a few weeks ago, I would have felt terribly uncomfortable doing this. I would have overanalyzed every twitch of my face, every flutter of my heartbeat, every tiny change in atmosphere. I would have been rigid, fingers clutched tightly in my lap for fear of accidentally reaching out, of doing anything that could give myself away.

Now, with Noelle, after everything we had talked about in the gym that night, I easily let myself sink into the comfortable silence, and while my heart *was* racing, it wasn't out of fear.

I blinked my eyes open only when her hands left my face and picked up an eyeshadow palette instead. "What color?"

I thought for a moment before I pointed at a shade of peach.

Never Kiss your Roommate

Noelle gave no indication of whether or not she liked my choice, but picked up a smaller eyeshadow brush.

I closed my eyes again without having to be told, waiting for the contact of the brush, but it didn't come.

Instead, Noelle suddenly said, "I'm sorry."

"What for?" I asked, opening my eyes again.

"For the way I treated you when you first came here. I didn't even know you, but I was acting like an asshole."

"Oh," I murmured. "That's okay. You weren't that bad."

"Yeah, I was. You seemed like you were genuinely scared of me."

She wasn't wrong. But looking at her now, with the creases of her pillow still indented in her cheek and the glow of a dozen fairy lights in her eyes, I didn't feel a trace of anxiety. Instead, something about her face made my chest ache. "I'm not anymore."

Noelle's lips—God, I had to stop staring at them—curved into a smile at that. She picked up the brush again and I closed my eyes, glad about the excuse to break eye contact. My skin felt warm everywhere she touched me, tingling where her fingertips rested against my jaw as naturally as if they had always belonged there.

"Hey, Noelle?" I asked when the silence dragged on.

"M-hm."

"When you put up the fairy lights you said you also used to have really bad nightmares. What were they about?"

Just for a split second, Noelle's hand stilled. "That was a while ago. It doesn't matter now."

No matter how hard I tried, I couldn't think of anything that could make her feel this shaky and afraid, to feel the need to leave on a night-light for when she startled awake. Still, I thought it best not to press on.

Noelle, done with the eyeshadow, moved on to my eyebrows. Now able to open my eyes again, I could see the concentrated furrow between her brows, her tongue poking out just slightly between her teeth. It shouldn't have been as endearing as it was.

After mascara and a shiny lip gloss had followed, I asked, "Why are you doing this? Giving me a makeover, I mean?"

"Because that's what I always do," Noelle said. "Whenever I feel like crying, I just cake my face with makeup. My mascara's too expensive for that shit."

"But you're okay with wasting it on me?"

"It's not a waste if it makes you feel better."

"It does," I whispered.

Noelle leaned back slightly to see if my brows were even. I hoped that, in the low light, she didn't notice the way my cheeks heated up under her intent gaze. Next, she picked up some blush. "Smile for me?"

The question in itself made my lips curve upward. Noelle chuckled and gave the apples of my cheeks as well as my nose a generous powdering.

"This is the best part," she then said and picked up a tiny container filled with shimmery powder.

I let out something that sounded embarrassingly close to a giggle when she used her finger to dab a little bit of the shiny highlighter on the tip of my nose.

Smiling, she leaned back to study her finished work. "There, all done."

"Can I see?"

She picked up the little hand mirror next to her and held

Never Kiss your Roommate

it up for me. I almost gasped when I caught a glimpse at my reflection. On most days, I rarely wore more than mascara and foundation, but under Noelle's hands, I had transformed into something dainty and free of imperfection. I wondered briefly if this was how she viewed me, in soft colors and shimmery glitter.

"Do you like it?"

"I do," I said, raising a hand to my cheek. "It looks . . . pretty."

Noelle slowly put the mirror down again. "It does."

"Too bad I have to take it off again."

"I can do it for you," Noelle offered. "I mean, if you want."

My heart stuttered through a few beats. "Only if that's okay for you."

"Sure. I'm gonna get the makeup remover." Noelle slipped off the bed.

I released a long exhale as soon as the bathroom door fell shut behind her, closing my eyes for a moment. This didn't feel real. I was sure at any moment I was going to wake up and realize this couldn't possibly be happening, that there was no way that *Noelle Daniels* was comforting me after a bad dream, not like this, with soft music playing in the background and the room drenched in the glow of the fairy lights above my bed.

But then the door opened and she stepped out with a package of makeup remover wipes in hand and everything shifted into harsh focus again.

Sitting down in front of me, one of her knees pressed against mine, she wordlessly got to work. Her touch was just as gentle as it had been earlier, the palm of her hand warm against my cheek while the other took off my makeup and coaxed my usual self back to the surface.

I felt my eyelids drooping while she did, barely able to hold them open anymore; she had chased the adrenaline from the nightmare right out of me.

"Tired?" Noelle asked, an amused lilt in her voice, when she was finished.

"M-hm."

"Do you think you can sleep now?"

"Yes," I murmured. "Thanks, Elle."

Noelle's eyes widened a little before she smiled, gathering all the makeup products and getting to her feet. I curled up beneath my blanket as soon as she did, barely registering the moment she turned off the music and the lamp next to my bed.

"Sleep well," she whispered.

A moment later, I heard the door to our room opening and then shutting again as she stepped out into the hallway. Under different circumstances, I would have asked where she was going, but any clear thought slipped out of reach as sleep pulled me under.

13
Seth

Drama club rehearsals became my favorite part of the week. Being in the auditorium felt like a safe haven, the stone walls and red velvet seats muffling the noises from outside like we were in the belly of a ship. As soon as the door fell shut, reality slipped away and my head went quiet, all thoughts about schoolwork and my parents disappearing in the distance like a tiny island in the sea. In here, everyone had a purpose, and everything made sense. When things didn't go as planned there were no real consequences; whenever someone felt lost, all we had to do was look into the script and we were back on course. Things were easy and predictable, all of us safe as Jasper steered us towards the vision he had in mind.

I loved watching everything come together—the costumes, the set, the acting—as everyone grew more confident in their roles. Most of all, even though I would have rather died than admit it out loud, I loved watching Jasper. That was another thing about the auditorium: while I avoided his gaze during the day, in here staring at him seemed allowed.

I could have spent days like this, tucked safely behind the control panel and studying Jasper from afar: the way he paced back and forth when he gave his thoughts on a scene, his hands gesturing dramatically, silver rings glittering in the stage lights; the way his face lit up when a line was delivered exactly like he wanted, his grin all teeth and pride; the way he commanded the attention of everyone in the room with just one word or a well-timed clap, a clearing of his throat, or just the sound of his heels as he strode across the stage.

Jasper des Lauriers was the most fascinating person I had ever met, so much so that it almost felt wrong to not direct the spotlight at him the entire time.

Today was different than our usual rehearsals. After going over a few scenes for two hours, Jasper had gotten out several huge pieces of cardboard and said that anyone who wanted could stay and help paint some of the background so that the tower didn't "look as lonely," as he put it.

Now it was almost eleven, which was past bedtime, but we knew that Miss Pepperman was patrolling that night and she would have never punished Jasper or any member of his drama club. Almost everyone had left by now—Sammy, to my surprise, being one of the first to go.

I wasn't sure why I had stayed. Probably for the same reason I had stayed the first time: Jasper had asked. Apparently that was all it took, which was a fact I preferred not to think about too much.

Never Kiss
your Roommate

Now we were kneeling on the stage with cans of paint scattered around. I wasn't sure if it was the stage lights humming above us that made my neck feel warm or the fact that Jasper was sitting right next to me, working on the same piece.

We were both silent for the most part; the only time I spoke was to mutter a quiet *sorry* when I accidentally knocked my elbow against his. The painting itself wasn't very difficult—all we had to do was color in the tree that one of the girls had drawn on the cardboard earlier.

"You don't talk very much, do you?" Jasper asked.

The warmth spread from my neck to my ears. Not the stage lights then. "I don't know."

Jasper chuckled and leaned forward to clean his brush in the cup of water in front of us. I tried to focus on the way the paint tinted the water blue as he swirled the brush, a tornado trapped inside a glass, not on the fact that his arm brushed against mine in the process, making my insides feel similar; a tornado trapped inside a boy.

"Good job with the lights today, by the way. You're getting better every time."

"Thanks," I said.

Silence again. I dipped my brush into the paint and continued working on the leaves.

"Do you maybe want to hang out after this?"

My brush slipped on the cardboard, leaving behind a jagged green line that gave away my shock. Gave away everything, maybe. I couldn't tell by looking at his face, his eyes trained on the traitorous smear of paint before they fixed on me again.

"Like, alone?"

Jasper nodded.

"What about Sammy?" I asked, keeping my voice low so that the others couldn't overhear. "Won't he mind?"

"I suppose he would. If we were still together."

My brain idled for a moment until, finally, his words sank in. "Oh."

"It was more of a friends-with-benefits situation, anyway," Jasper said. "After the thing at the Welcome Back Party the friend part kind of got lost, so neither of us was into the benefits anymore."

I hated the way my heart fluttered at that, stupidly hopeful as if that changed anything. Forcing my voice to stay level, I said, "I'm sorry."

"Don't be," he said. With one hand, he rubbed at his cheek, the motion leaving behind a streak of green paint. "Rehearsals are going to be a bit awkward for a while, but I'm sure it'll be fine in a week or two."

I nodded, unsure what to say. I *always* felt unsure what to say around him, like his mere presence was enough to make me forget every single word I had ever learned. It was bloody stupid.

"So, are you coming back to my room? My roommate won't be back until one."

I finally dared to meet his eyes. They looked less piercing than they usually did, the ice blue melted to clear spring water. Maybe it was the smear of paint on his cheek that gave me the courage to say, "Okay."

Jasper lowered his brush. Raising his voice so that everyone could hear him, he said, "All right, guys, I think that's enough for today! You can leave everything out here to dry. Thank you all so much for helping out—I'll see you all for our next rehearsal on Thursday."

Never Kiss your Roommate

As with every time he spoke, the room immediately sprang into action. While everyone put down their brushes and cleared out of the auditorium, I shakily got to my feet and hurried up the stairs to the control panel. My hands were trembling as I turned off all the lights one by one, the ground beneath my feet rocking a little bit like we truly were on a ship.

Jasper des Lauriers wanted to spend time with me. Alone. In his room.

It felt impossible; he was so far out of my league, a prince and pauper situation but times ten and queer.

But then I looked up again and he was standing by the door, the last one in the room, meeting my eyes with a grin and an "Are you coming?"

And because it was Jasper, I did. I shut off the last light and made my way down the stairs to meet him in the dark, even though the tornado inside me made my head spin.

"Are you tired yet?" Jasper asked when we stepped out into the corridor together.

"Not really," I said. I had been, earlier this evening, before I had gone down to the auditorium, but with Jasper next to me, I couldn't even think of sleeping. "You?"

"Not really."

A smile tugged the corners of my mouth up without my permission.

"How'd you like the scenes we went through today?"

"I loved them," I said honestly. "You're a brilliant writer."

"Merci. Are you into writing too?"

"No, not really. I'm not that good with words."

By now we had reached the stairs that led up to the boys' wing. Moonlight fell through the windows in the entrance hall and cast our shadows onto the steps in front of us. They looked conjoined, lanky limbs melted together into something that wasn't Jasper and Seth but *JasperandSeth*, indistinguishable and inseparable. The sight made something unfamiliar swell in my chest.

"So, what's your thing then?" Jasper asked.

I hesitated for a moment, unsure whether I should be honest or not. Eventually, I said, "True crime. Detective novels. That kind of stuff."

For a moment, I feared he would laugh. Instead, he responded, "Interesting. Do you, like, do research?"

A picture of the current state of my desk, littered in notes and photos relating to the case of JonBenét Ramsey's murder, flashed before my eyes. "Uh . . . a little."

JasperandSeth made it into the boys' wing. Jasper's room was exactly six doors down the hallway from mine; a simple fact, but one that made falling asleep impossible some nights.

"Maybe you should look into the question of who's writing The Chitter Chatter then." Jasper chuckled as he fished his keys out of his pocket and unlocked the door.

"I don't think *I* would be the one who'd solve that if no one else has in two years."

"Nonsense. I think if anyone would, it'd be you," Jasper said. With a sweeping gesture, he added, "Come in."

I hesitantly stepped through the threshold and looked around the room while Jasper shut the door behind me. "Oh wow."

"Don't be bothered by the creative chaos," Jasper said, as if he knew exactly what I was thinking.

"Is that what you call this?" I snorted.

Laughing, he threw his coat onto his bed. "I'll be back in a second. Make yourself comfortable."

I nodded and waited until the bathroom door fell shut behind him before I took in my surroundings.

While one half of the room was plain and organized, the other was swamped in the *creative chaos* Jasper had talked about. His desk was barely visible under the flood of papers, books, and magazines that were scattered across it, most of them covered with neon sticky notes that had Jasper's writing scrawled across them. The wall above his bed was covered in musical theater posters that ranged from *Les Misérables* to *Be More Chill*. Next to his bed was a pile of clothes that seemed bigger than all of my wardrobe and his drawer was covered in a bunch of knick-knacks: a tiny statue of the Eiffel tower, candles, various bottles of nail polish.

The thing that stoked my curiosity the most was a framed picture of him and two older girls standing in front of Seven Hills' entrance. They had the same blue eyes and similarly prominent cheekbones, but a different hair color, a silky black that stood in stark contrast to Jasper's silvery-white hair. For a moment I tried to imagine Jasper with his natural hair color, but it was almost impossible. Judging by the absence of his lip piercing and the shape of his face, still childish and round, the picture must have been taken during his first years at Seven Hills. Looking at their smiling faces—Jasper squished between the two girls, all three of them wearing matching grins—a pang of homesickness ran through me; even though I had talked to my sister only yesterday, I still missed her so much it hurt.

Jasper emerged from the bathroom before I had the chance to study his other pictures. He blinked rapidly as he crossed the room, almost running into his drawer, and let out a string of angry French. Reaching his desk, he grabbed something off it and turned to face me again, now wearing a pair of wide-rimmed black glasses.

For a moment all I could do was stare at him, aware that my mouth was hanging open. "You wear glasses?"

Jasper walked past me and went to sit on his bed, gesturing for me to do the same. While I carefully sank onto the edge of his bed, he said, "Contacts, usually. Without them, I'm as blind as a bat. I don't really wear them in front of others, but you've already seen me hyperventilating with snot on my face, so . . ."

I wasn't sure why, but this new-won knowledge had the same effect on me as the smear of paint on his cheek had. My shoulders relaxed almost imperceptibly and before I could think better of it, I blurted, "You should wear them more often."

"So you're into the nerdy type?" Jasper asked, a broad grin on his face. "Good to know."

"N-no, that's not what I meant—"

"No need to be ashamed, *mignon*," he chuckled. "There's stranger stuff to be into, I can tell you that much."

Before the conversation could progress any further in that direction, I quickly pointed at the picture on his drawer. "So, you have two sisters?"

"Yes, Alice and Catherine. They used to go here, too, but they graduated two years ago."

"Are you guys close?" I asked.

"Yeah, they're great. I just don't see them that often since they moved back to Marseilles."

"Is that where you're from?"

"Yes. My sisters moved back into my parents' house there."

"Are you planning on doing the same?" I inquired.

Jasper absentmindedly flicked a finger against his lip piercing. "I want to go back to Marseilles someday, yes. But I don't want to move back in with my family if I can avoid it."

Never Kiss
your Roommate

"But I thought you and your family were close?"

"My *sisters* and I are," he said. "My parents and I not so much. They still don't know I'm pansexual."

"What?" I asked, staring at him in surprise. Jasper seemed so confident, so sure of himself and his sexuality that the thought he wasn't fully out to everyone hadn't even occurred to me.

He shrugged, lowering his eyes to where his fingers were plucking at his bedsheets. "Why do you think I wanted to go to a boarding school? What happens here, stays here."

"Do you think your parents would . . . react badly?" I carefully asked.

"I honestly have no idea," he said. "I think my dad would probably have a bigger problem with it than my mom. They're both more on the conservative side though, and not really educated about things like this. I would probably have to give them an hour-long explanation of the term *pansexual* first."

"That sucks," I murmured.

We were both silent for a moment before Jasper asked, "What about you? Have you come out to your parents yet?"

"I don't know if you can call it that." I chuckled, scratching at my neck. "Basically, I was watching a movie with my entire family and my sister said something like *Oh my God, Timothée Chalamet is so hot* and I was like *I know, right* . . . and that's how my parents found out."

It had been one of those rare occasions when my parents had agreed to stay in the same room for longer than ten minutes, mainly because we had begged them to. They were sitting on opposite ends of the couch, my sister and I wedged between them like a rampart, though I wasn't quite sure who we were protecting—them or ourselves. Throughout the movie, neither of them really spoke, but with my sister chattering away next to me, the tension had been a bit easier to ignore.

It was only after my accidental coming-out that it fully dissolved. Both of them were smiling, my mom's arm wrapped around my shoulders and my dad's hand ruffling my hair, and afterward, when my sister and I had gone upstairs, I could faintly hear them talking in the living room. That, more than anything, was why I had gone to bed happy that night; not because I had come out, but because I had managed to establish a cease-fire, however brief, between them.

Jasper's surprised laugh ripped me out of my thoughts. "Wow. Well done, Seth, I'm sure that was really smooth."

I had to grin, too, mostly because of the way my name rolled off his tongue.

"What do you want to do?" he asked once he had pulled himself together.

The answer that lay on the tip of my tongue wasn't one I could say out loud, so I kept my mouth shut and gave a noncommittal shrug.

Jasper gestured at the small TV on his desk, in perfect view from where we were sitting. "Do you want to watch anything? *Sherlock*, *Criminal Minds*, any conspiracy theory you haven't looked into yet?"

"Sure," I said. "You decide."

"Mon dieu. A bisexual and a pansexual guy together. How will we ever decide anything?" Jasper joked but got up nevertheless and turned on the TV.

Then he returned to the bed and lay down next to me, his back leaning against the wall. Upon his inviting pat to the mattress beside him, I hesitantly kicked off my shoes and stretched out next to him, leaning back against the headboard.

Never Kiss
your Roommate

Jasper squinted a little as he opened Netflix and selected an episode of *Sherlock*. I already knew all of them by heart, which made it all the more difficult to focus on the screen instead of staring at Jasper.

The entire time I couldn't help but steal quick glances at his profile, at the way the light flickered across his face and tinted his hair blue.

"A shame they didn't have the balls to make Johnlock canon," Jasper said.

I hummed in agreement.

"You know, that's part of why I want to become a director. I want to produce things that are straightforward. No hidden signals that can be read this way or that, or vague allusions in interviews to draw in LGBTQ viewers desperate for any shred of representation. Just something unapologetically queer."

"I would watch everything you make," I said. My voice came out softer than I expected, and it was only when Jasper turned his head to look at me that I realized I was staring again.

"Really?" he asked.

I nodded and looked straight ahead again.

A few minutes passed without either of us saying anything. When I couldn't focus anymore, my eyes drifted down to his hand, which was resting next to mine in the tiny space between us. He had ridiculously long, slender fingers that looked like they were made for playing the piano; silver rings glimmered on two of them and his nails were painted black, and God, why were even his *hands* so attractive? I had never found anyone's hands attractive before.

My mouth went dry when one of them suddenly inched closer, until his pinky finger was brushing against mine in a motion that *couldn't* possibly be accidental, lingered for too long to not be deliberate.

This was confirmed when I finally dared to raise my gaze and locked eyes with him. A smile twitched around his lips, entirely too self-conscious for the Jasper Des Lauriers I had seen striding across the stage only an hour earlier. Then again, none of this was what I had expected from him; I hadn't expected the glasses or *Sherlock* or the surprise in his voice when he asked *Really?*

It was the combination of all three that gave me the courage to put my hand on top of his. Jasper's smile grew and with it the tornado that had been raging inside me since the beginning of rehearsal today, a big confusing whirl that made my hands shake so much I was sure he had to feel it.

Maybe he did and that was the reason he turned his hand over so that our palms were pressed together, fingers interlocking like two pieces of a puzzle that had just been waiting to be assembled, and I was pretty sure that I was a study in scarlet by now, every inch of me burning burning burning. Converting oxygen to carbon dioxide suddenly became an impossible feat. Every atom, every molecule, every cell inside of me was screaming and holy fucking shit, this definitely didn't feel like nothing, this felt like *everything at once*. I was being electrocuted and I was going to die on this bloody bed with his checkered sheets under me and Hugh Jackman watching from the wall and Jasper's hand in mine and ten thousand million volts coursing through my body and—

"Hey, Seth," Jasper murmured, his voice a low rasp. "Do you—"

There was a knock at the door.

There was a fucking knock at the door.

Never Kiss your Roommate

"*Putain*," Jasper said with feeling and scrambled to his feet.

Letting go of his hand felt only a little bit like losing a limb. The ten thousand million volts all drained out of my body at once and left me with a whole lot of nothingness that made me want to sink onto the mattress in a dramatic heap. Instead, I tucked my fingers into the pockets of my pants and scooted back to my initial seat on the edge of the bed, trying to get my heartbeat under control and keep myself from screaming while he crossed the room.

Jasper shot me another plaintive glance before he opened the door. "Hey."

"Oh thank God, you're awake. Can I come in?"

There was a moment of silence. Then, "Of course."

I looked up again to see Noelle stepping past Jasper and into the room, freezing in the doorway when she saw me. Without makeup and wearing sweatpants and a large knitted sweater, she looked like a completely different person from the stompy boots–wearing, asshole-punching girl I knew. Her voice sounded uncharacteristically unsure when she said, "Sorry, am I interrupting something?"

"No," Jasper said, rubbing a hand over his eyes. Gesturing at the screen, he added, "We were just hanging out and watching TV."

Noelle slowly made her way over to the bed. I scooched over to the very end of it to give her enough space as she flopped onto her back, her legs hanging off one side.

Jasper paused the show before he moved towards the bed as well. He sat down on the other end, three thousand light-years away, and reached a hand out to lightly nudge her shoulder. "Is everything okay?"

"Yeah. No. I'm not sure." She groaned and flung an arm over her eyes to block out the light. "It's Evelyn."

I sat up a little bit straighter at that. "What about her? Did something happen?"

"She's okay, don't worry. Has she ever talked to you about her nightmares?"

"Yes."

"Tonight was worse than usual. So I did her makeup."

"You did her makeup?" Jasper incredulously echoed.

"Yes, to help her calm down and make her feel better—I swear it made sense in the moment."

"All right . . . What happened then?"

"Nothing *happened*."

Jasper frowned. "Then why are you here?"

Noelle sat up, looking from Jasper to me and back. "If either of you tells anyone this I'm gonna have to kill you. Do you promise not to?"

We both nodded.

"Okay. Listen, I literally have no idea if it was the fairy lights or the shitty indie music, but I think I might like Evelyn. Like, a lot."

Jasper's face suddenly split into a wide grin. I knew we were both flashing back to the night in the park in Gloomswick, to Evelyn lying in the grass, pink-cheeked and a little bit tipsy as she gushed about her crush on Noelle.

"Praise the Lord, she's finally realized it!" Jasper said, dramatically spreading his arms. "So, did you kiss her or not?"

"No." Even I could hear the regretful tone in her voice. "She was still so shaken after her nightmare, I didn't want to throw her off even more. I really, really wanted to though."

166

Suddenly, I couldn't even be mad that she had interrupted us. There was something terribly endearing about the way Noelle spoke about Evelyn, every syllable softer than the one before.

"Would you look at that, Noelle Daniels is actually a giant softie," Jasper teased, as if reading my mind.

"No, I'm not—"

"Softie."

"No—"

"*Soft.*"

"Jasper, I swear—"

"S-o-f-t-i-e," he spelled with a smirk.

Noelle sent an exasperated look my way, as if expecting me to take her side. I shrugged, just barely holding back a laugh. "That was pretty soft, not gonna lie."

She let out a loud groan and buried her head in her hands. "I hate both of you."

Jasper only grinned. "That's what you said about Evelyn as well. Stop lying, Daniels, we all know you're a puppy acting like a pit bull."

"Shut up," she grumbled, slapping away his hand when he tried to pat her head.

I leaned back against the wall and listened while the two continued bickering. With Noelle between us, the tornado inside me had dwindled into a light breeze that was much easier to ignore. Now that the tension was gone, my eyelids started to get heavier and when Noelle announced that she had to get back to her room to sleep, I went with her.

"Good night, Jasper," I said as I stepped out into the hallway.

Leaning in the threshold, Jasper scratched at his neck. "Good night. Maybe we can do this again sometime?"

"Yeah," I whispered, careful not to wake up any of the neighboring rooms. "I'd like that."

"Okay." Jasper smiled. "Good night. Again."

I turned around with a dumb grin, too happy to even be annoyed when I returned to my room and found Gabe playing something on his laptop, surrounded by empty crisp packets and energy drinks.

Maybe Seven Hills could actually be kind of okay, sometimes.

14
Evelyn

If Noelle was anything, it was persistent.

At least once every day she asked when we could have our next self-defense lesson, only getting more stubborn every time I told her no, that it had only been two weeks since she had sprained her ankle, that I didn't want to risk her getting hurt again.

Of course, it was only a matter of time until I caved in and we both knew it.

It was on Wednesday afternoon, almost a week after the night she had woken me up and done my makeup, that she strode into our room, the door slamming shut behind her, and announced, "Get up, Greene, we're going to the gym."

I blinked at her, slowly shutting my book. "Says who?"

"Me," Noelle said with a grin. "I just went to see the nurse. She says my ankle is all better now and I'm allowed to start training again today. So, no more excuses. Teach me how to deck someone."

Rationally, I wasn't sure if it was a good idea. Before, I had been nervous around her; now, my heart was doing backflips in my chest every time she so much as looked at me. When I closed my eyes I could still feel her fingertips against my skin, her breath warm against my cheek, sweet like a promise. I had been so close then, just seconds away from reaching out and pulling her into a kiss, just to see if her lips were as soft as they looked in the hazy glow of the fairy lights. Even now, sitting on the other end of the room, I felt something tugging at my very core like there was a magnet inside my rib cage and another one in her hand, insistently drawing me closer.

I knew that, if I wanted things to stay the way they were, I had to say no.

The problem was that if *I* was anything, it was weak for Noelle Daniels.

"Okay," I said. "But only if you promise to tell me as soon as something hurts and that you won't take it too far."

"Promise," she immediately said.

And that was how, ten minutes later, I found myself standing in the empty gymnasium again, the scent of rubber and maple wood familiar by now. This time, I barely hesitated before I met Noelle on the blue gym mats.

"What are we doing today?"

"I think it's best if we start with something easy," I said. "I'm going to show you how you can keep someone at a distance, for situations like the thing at the party."

Even while I was speaking, Noelle was already getting into fighting stance. "Cool. What do I have to do?"

"Just step a little closer to me."

Noelle did as I said, until she was only inches from touching me, the tips of her sneakers almost pressing against mine. Her eyes were locked with mine, searching my face. Under their inquiring gaze, I did the opposite of what I really wanted: I lifted my arm and blocked her with a forearm to her chest, stopping her from getting any closer.

"This is what you have to do," I said softly. "And if that doesn't work just slide your arm farther up so it's pressing against your attacker's neck."

Noelle swallowed. "Okay, sounds easy. Can I try?"

Nodding, I dropped my arm.

Noelle pressed hers against my chest and then very slowly moved it to my neck, the entire time watching me carefully to make sure she wasn't hurting me. She wasn't. If anything, being this close to her made my head spin in a way that was everything but bad.

Forcing myself to take a step back, I said, "Good. Um . . . are you up for something more serious?"

"*Up-For-Something-Serious* is my middle name."

A nervous chuckle slipped past my lips. "Can you put your hands around my neck?"

Noelle's eyes widened almost comically at that. "Are you sure? I don't want to hurt you."

"You won't."

She didn't seem convinced but stepped closer and carefully placed her hands on my neck.

I inhaled sharply as soon as she touched me, fingertips featherlight against my skin.

"A little tighter." I hoped she didn't notice that my voice was seconds away from cracking. "Pretend you're choking me."

"Kinky," Noelle said, breathing a laugh that sounded just as shaky as I felt. A moment later, her grip tightened a little bit, just enough for me to feel her fingers around my neck.

"What you want to do," I said, "Is lift one arm, twist your body at a 90-degree angle, and crouch down while simultaneously slamming your arm down. That way you get your attacker's hands off your neck and trap them with your other arm. This will allow you to strike them in the face with your elbow."

While I explained, I slowly went through the motions. First I raised one arm, twisted, squatted, and brought my arm down. Her hands lost their grip on my neck immediately and I easily caught them with my left hand, pressing them against my chest while I lifted my other arm and stopped inches before my elbow could actually make contact with her face.

"Whoa." Noelle stared in wonder at where her hands were immobilized before she looked back up at me. "That was sick."

Letting go of her, I took a step back. "Do you want to try?"

Noelle nodded.

"Is . . . is it okay if I touch your neck?"

She cleared her throat, the sound loud in the quiet. "Yeah."

It was only then that I fully understood what I had gotten myself into. My heartbeat stuttered as I reached out and put my hands on her neck, carefully brushing her hair out of the way. Her skin was warm and smooth like velvet; her pulse thrummed under my fingertips, matching the violent pounding of my heart.

Only a breath away from her, the world narrowed down to the curve of her lips and her eyes, dark as they burned into mine.

In the silence, the only sound was my blood rushing in my ears and my shaky breathing. Then, my voice, barely above a whisper. "Are you going to be mad if I kiss you?"

Noelle tilted her head a little and smiled in a way that made me feel like I was burning up. "I'm going to be so fucking mad if you don't."

I couldn't breathe and I was lost, and then my hands moved to her cheeks and my mouth was on hers and I was *found*.

The first thing I realized was that Noelle tasted like sugar and cherries.

The second was that, for someone who liked to act like nothing mattered to them, Noelle kissed like nothing in the world mattered more, like she had a point to prove or a score to settle, like this was a battle to win mountains and kingdoms and she was the last soldier standing.

The third realization came when I felt her smiling against my lips, my thumb moving to rest on the dimple in her cheek: I suddenly couldn't remember why I had ever thought that wanting this was wrong.

My eyes slowly fluttered open to see Noelle with her eyes still closed. When she opened them, her pupils were blown wide, her eyes dark and hooded.

"I should have done this weeks ago," she muttered, the rasp in her voice sending a shiver down my spine. A heartbeat later her hands grabbed onto my hips and pushed me up against the wall.

Where the first kiss had been like a drizzle in July, this one was a hurricane.

This time, her lips were hot and demanding as they crashed onto mine, her hands sure and steadying where they rested on my waist. My fingers moved to tangle in her curls to anchor myself, just enough to keep me from losing myself in the waves of heat rolling off her. I was trapped between her and the wall at my back, but I didn't mind that in the slightest; without it, I probably would have slid to the floor right there, nothing but a puddle of endorphins and the looping thought of *finally finally finally*.

By the time we separated, both of us were out of breath. Eyes still closed, I let out a disbelieving laugh, which mixed with Noelle's shaky exhale. Without the demanding hum of the magnet, everything was so quiet.

I blinked into the light only when Noelle lifted one hand off my waist to brush off my face some stray strands of hair that had slipped out of my braid. "Was that your first kiss?"

"Yes."

Noelle closed her eyes and rested her forehead against mine with a soft chuckle. "Was it like in your romance books?"

"So much better," I breathed.

A slow, satisfied grin spread across her face before her lips brushed over mine again, the touch so light it sent a tingle all the way down to my toes.

"You're a natural," she whispered.

My cheeks hurt from smiling so wide. "But there's always room for improvement, right?"

"Oh, definitely." This close, her face was like the sun, and the hand still on my waist made me feel like I had swallowed all its light. "I'll have you know I'm an incredible tutor."

"So, there'll be more of this to come?"

"Of course. I mean . . . if *you* want it too."

"*Yes*," I said, way too quickly and with way too much force.

"Good," she whispered and leaned in for another kiss. It lasted too short for my liking and was interrupted by her pulling back to glance at the clock on the wall. "Shit, I have basketball practice in, like, ten minutes."

Never Kiss your Roommate

Expecting her to let go of me, I leaned back against the wall to steady myself. Instead, she suddenly cupped my face with both hands and studied me, her intent gaze making the blood rush to my cheeks. "What is it?"

"Nothing," she laughed. "You just have my lipstick all over your face."

I rubbed over my lips with the back of my hand, staring down at the dark red streaks on my skin before I looked up at her again. "What are you looking so smug for?" I asked, unable to hold back a laugh.

Noelle took a step back, burying her hands in her pockets, and said, "I'm not." The smirk twitching around her lips just proved my point, but the first basketball players stormed into the room before I could point that out.

"Hey, Daniels!" One of the boys jogged over to us and slung an arm around her from behind. "Heard you're training with us today again?"

Noelle shrugged his arm off but didn't look unfriendly when she turned around to him. I was still busy catching my breath, wiping my hand over my mouth again in a quick gesture I hoped went unnoticed. "Yeah, I am. Still gotta whip you all into shape for the Westbridge game."

Another player strolled up to us. "Hey, Captain," she said, pointing at the blue gym mats at our feet. "What's all this?"

"I, uh . . . showed her some self-defense tactics," I quickly said.

Noelle nodded, scratching at her neck. I hoped I was the only one who noticed the disheveled state of her hair. "Yep. So . . . see you after practice?"

"Okay," I breathed, "See you later."

The magnet immediately gave an indignant pull when I

walked away from her. Dizzily, I wondered if it would always be this way from now on, a constant hum trying to draw me back to her that only ever ceased when her hands were on me. For some reason, the thought wasn't as terrifying as it maybe ought to be.

I turned around once more only when I was at the door to find her standing in the center of the room, absentmindedly dribbling a basketball with one hand while the other players were shouting and running around her. It was when she met my eyes and her lips quirked into a private smile meant for no one but me that realization set in: I had kissed a girl. Not only that: I had kissed *Noelle Daniels* and *she had kissed me back*. Oh God.

15

Evelyn

Living with Noelle turned out to be a blessing and a curse all at once. The best thing about it: she was always within reach. The worst thing about it: *she was always within reach.*

While it had been hard to stay away from her before, now it was simply impossible. It was the knowledge that I could kiss her anytime she allowed me to that made it so difficult to focus on anything else. She was the first thing I saw when I woke up, the last thing I saw when I fell asleep, and the entire time in between she was pretty much the only thing on my mind.

The worst thing was that I couldn't get anything done for the life of me. As hard as I tried, in the end I always seemed to end up in her arms again, too far gone to even care that there was a stack of unfinished homework on my desk.

One morning we missed breakfast: Noelle had been getting

ready for class, with her eyes half-closed and features soft in the hazy morning light, and I had truly meant to only steal a quick good morning kiss, but that little peck escalated into a proper make-out session that had left me breathless.

We almost came late to class as a result, slipping into our seats only seconds before Miss Pepperman entered the classroom. Between Noelle's Cheshire-cat grin and my glowing red cheeks, it had been no surprise that Seth immediately figured out what happened and promptly informed Jasper as well.

Other than them, no one knew yet. I wasn't sure where we were standing now; all I knew was that I liked getting kisses and being held and the way she whispered my name into my hair when she stumbled into the bathroom in the mornings. For now, that seemed like a good place to start.

o o o

My brain was so occupied with all things Noelle that I barely paid attention in class, especially the ones I had had little interest in from the start. When I got called on twice in math and was unable to answer, I realized that I needed to do something to catch up.

The easy answer was to ask Noelle since she was brilliant (and somehow much more attentive than me) in class, but as she rendered me absolutely useless, I decided I needed to get help elsewhere. Seth also wasn't an option; the drama club's play would premiere in two days, so he spent most of his free time in the auditorium.

My last resort was Amelia. Surprisingly, she had eagerly agreed to meet me in my room on Friday afternoon and, a little

Never Kiss
your Roommate

less surprisingly, showed up five minutes earlier than we had arranged. Now we were both sitting cross-legged on my bed with our books and a flurry of notes on the mattress between us while we pored over polynomial functions together.

Amelia was good at explaining and more patient than I had expected, calmly going over everything again when I admitted that I hadn't understood it the first time and smiling encouragingly when I tried to solve a problem myself.

"Well done!" she exclaimed when I got the solution. "See, it's not as difficult as it seems, is it?"

I made a face. "Amy, this alone took me twenty minutes. I can't spend that long on one question in an exam."

Brushing a strand of copper hair behind her ear, she tapped her pen—a fancy fountain pen that had her name engraved on it—on my notepad. "All it takes is a little bit of practice. It gets easier after a few times."

"I guess," I said, "But there are much more fun things you could do in your free time, aren't there?"

"Fun, maybe, but not as important in the long run. *Business before pleasure* is what my parents always say."

Setting my notepad down on the bed, I asked, "Don't you get tired of only ever doing what everyone expects from you?"

Amelia's gray eyes, which were fixed on the page of notes in her lap, suddenly took on the tint of storm clouds. "Does it matter? Doing that has helped me get this far."

"I think that's how people get burnt out," I tentatively said. When she didn't look at me, I put my hand on top of hers and gave it a light squeeze. "You know it's okay for you to do what *you* want every once in a while, right? You deserve to enjoy yourself. You deserve to be *happy*."

There were a few heartbeats during which all she did was stare at where my hand was resting on top of hers, her entire body rigid. Then, she shoved her notes to the side and abruptly got to her feet. "I need to use the bathroom."

I didn't get to respond before the door slammed shut behind her and the lock clicked. Sometimes it was hard to remember that Amelia was a seventeen-year-old like me. Especially in moments like this, where it was so clear that *she* was the main reason she was stuck in this cage of high expectations she had built for herself, I couldn't help but feel sorry for her. I felt like even if someone handed her the key on a silver platter, she would have still preferred to stay behind bars.

While she was gone, I picked up my phone from my bedside table and opened The Chitter Chatter, which, thanks to the awful internet connection in our room, took a while to load. The last update had been posted yesterday evening and detailed that Sammy, Jasper's ex, seemed to be seeing Aiden from the drama club now.

Amelia stepped out of the bathroom again before I could finish the article. Straightening her skirt—she was one of the only people I knew who wore her uniform long after classes were over—she asked, "What are you doing?"

"I was just seeing if there was anything new on The Chitter Chatter."

Amelia wrinkled her nose and sat down on my bed again. "I will never understand what everyone finds so interesting about that poorly written gossip blog."

"It's the mystery around The Watcher's identity that's so intriguing, I guess." I leaned forward a little. "Surely, you've thought about it as well, haven't you? Who do you think it is?"

Never Kiss
your Roommate

"I think it is someone with way too much time on their hands who should be directing their attention to things that actually matter, and also an incredibly bitter person who likes causing anarchy in our community." She made a meaningful pause. "I'm sure you can think of someone who seems to hate everyone here and would not be opposed to taking their own issues out on others."

I stared at her for a few seconds, uncomprehending, before I understood what she was trying to say. Lowering my voice even though there was no one else around, I said, "You think Noelle would . . . ?"

"I would not put it past her," Amelia said. "After all, it started as soon as she arrived here two years ago."

Frowning, I tapped my pencil against the paper. I couldn't align the image I had of Noelle with the one of The Watcher, but before I could tell Amelia that, the door opened.

"Hey, Evelyn, I—"

Noelle paused in her tracks when her eyes landed on Amelia, one of her eyebrows lifting. Bracing a hand against the door frame, she said, "What the hell are you doing here, Amanda?"

"She's helping me with maths," I explained.

Meanwhile, Amelia twisted around to glare at Noelle over her shoulder. They were like two cats getting their claws out every time one dared to step into the other's territory, always hissing threateningly at the other like they were ready to scratch each other's eyes out if the other came within reach.

Noelle's shoulders only relaxed a little bit when I offered her a smile. "Don't mind me," she said, flopping onto her bed before grabbing a pair of headphones as well as a stack of files from her bedside table. "I'll just be over here doing . . . basketball captain stuff."

I nodded and looked down at my notes again. To Amelia, I said, "I think I get the polynomial functions thing now. Thanks for explaining everything to me again."

"Of course. Is there anything else you need—" She was interrupted by loud rustling as Noelle grabbed a bag of gummy bears and opened it exaggeratedly slowly. I bit my lip to hold back a laugh when Amelia closed her eyes for a moment, waiting until the noise was over. "Anything else you need help with?"

"I don't think so."

"Are you certain? We could get more into exponential functions if you want . . ."

"I'm sure. My head is exploding already," I said. "But if anything comes up I'll definitely come back to you on that."

"All right," she said, gathering her things. "I will see you at dinner."

The door had barely fallen shut behind her when Noelle tossed her headphones onto her bed and got up, locking the door, which was something she always did, before she finally headed towards me.

"Can I?" she asked.

I nodded, breath catching in my throat when she climbed onto the bed and straddled my lap. Wrapping my arms around her, I tipped my head back to look at her. "Hey."

The kiss she pressed to my lips was unexpectedly soft, sugary sweet from the artificial strawberry flavor of the gummy bears she had just eaten. I doubted I could ever get used to this—every time her mouth found mine it drew a quiet gasp from me, like my body was surprised at every tiny bit of affection it received.

"Maths schoolwork? Really?" Noelle leaned back slightly. "I could have helped you with that."

"I know." My voice came out sounding embarrassingly breathy after just one kiss. "But then we just would've ended up like this again."

I felt her chuckle more than I heard it. "You say it like it's a bad thing."

"It is if I fail."

"You won't fail," she said. "You're too smart for that."

I only gave a quiet hum and tipped my chin back. She got the message and, with an affectionate laugh, leaned in for another kiss that made my head feel even fuzzier. Noelle had the ability to wipe my brain of any comprehensible thought within seconds; it should have been alarming, but with her weight in my lap and her fingers gently tracing the shell of my ear, I could feel nothing but a giddy sense of wonder.

"You taste like sweets," I dumbly informed her when she pulled back.

"You're sweet," she murmured. When I let out a surprised laugh, she leaned back, a horrified expression on her face. "Shit, forget that I said that. Who am I becoming?"

Before I could respond, the silence was interrupted by a sound that made both of us jump. There was a short drum solo, followed by an electric guitar and then a smoky female voice. On top of me, Noelle noticeably tensed.

"Sorry, that's my phone," she said, a confused furrow between her brows, and got up.

I watched her cross the room to fetch it, immediately feeling cold without her on top of me. Over the past weeks, I had noticed that Noelle had different ringtones for different people: Jasper's was the French national anthem and the one time Seth had called her, her phone had played the opening theme of BBC's *Sherlock*. This one I had never heard before.

Noelle's eyes darted over to me for a second before she pressed the phone to her ear and said, "Hi, Mom."

Those two words were enough to cut through the pleasant fog in my head. I suddenly felt like I was intruding and I was about to get up and get my earphones so she could have more privacy when Noelle made a strange choking noise.

"What?" With the hand that wasn't holding the phone, she gripped tightly onto the edge of her desk. "Two days ago? I thought you were in Boston right now?"

A pause. Then, "And you're . . . you're sure it was him?" Noelle asked. Her voice sounded strangled, like there was an invisible pair of hands wrapped around her throat. "Did he try to get to you?"

She was silent for a few endless seconds. Her eyes looked over at me, but I didn't feel like she *saw* me. It was like she was staring right through me, gaze empty, at something I couldn't view. All I could perceive was a prickling sense of danger that made the hairs at the back of my neck stand up.

"So no one knows where he went after that?" She closed her eyes, her face ashen. "No, I—I'm fine, Mom. Thank you for telling me. I . . . I need to go now."

She listened for a few more seconds, the faraway look still in her eyes when she lowered the phone. I sat frozen, unsure what to do. Finally, I got to my feet and said, "Hey. Is everything okay?"

Noelle's mouth opened and closed again, like she was choking on the words, unable to get them out. When she spoke, her voice was as thin and fragile as old paper. "I'm sorry, I . . . I think I need a moment."

"Okay. Is there anything I can—"

"No," she cut me off. "I just . . . sorry, I can't do this right now."

Before I could react, she was already pushing past me and stumbling out of the door. I winced when it fell shut, the sound harsh and final. My feet were urging me to follow her, but my head was smart enough to know that wasn't what she wanted. Instead, I stayed in the too-quiet, too-empty room and tried to ignore the cold that washed over me as soon as she was gone.

o o o

I had expected Noelle to return to our room after an hour, maybe two. Now four hours had passed and there was still no sign of her. She had missed dinner and so had I, seeing as the dread in my stomach left no room for any appetite. Now the castle was cloaked in ink-blue night and since bedtime was less than an hour away, the noise in the girls' wing had quieted down to soft murmurs and scattered footsteps.

My first instinct after she had left was to grab a book and slip under the covers. It was what I always did when I felt like things were spiraling out of my control—I had read on the train to Seven Hills and after the confrontation with Noelle on my second day here; I had read the day after the party when I had been terrified of Noelle's reaction; and even now I read every time I felt homesick.

At my old school, jumping headfirst into fiction had been the only thing that had stopped me from cracking; things had been horrible, but at least I had known that once class was over, I could spend the rest of the day in another reality where nothing could hurt me, where obstacles made the hero stronger, where villains got what they deserved, and where pain was always followed by a happy ending.

However, with Noelle's last words still hanging in the air, escaping into the pages now seemed like a cowardly thing to do.

Instead, I paced around the room, trying to come up with an answer as to where she could've gone. I had already asked Jasper if she was with him, then I checked the gym, the common room, the Great Hall, and even the library, even though I knew she wouldn't voluntarily set foot in there.

With a sigh, I stopped in front of her desk, looking at it as if I would find the answers to any of my questions within the mess on top of it. My eyes landed on her stack of magazines that kept piling higher every week, the glossy pages tattered in places from the number of times Noelle had flipped through them. It was the first time I really looked at them, so it was only then I noticed the little sticky notes that were marking some of the pages.

Out of sheer curiosity, I picked one up and flipped to one of the tagged pages to see the article headline: "Crystal Danell: The Queen of R&B is Back with Another Album."

The photo beneath the title showed a woman, presumably Crystal Danell, strutting down a sidewalk, one hand lifted to wave at the camera. She wore classy black high heels and a pink pantsuit that was shockingly bright against her warm brown skin, her hair framing her face like a soft cloud.

Looking at her face, my heart skipped a beat. Not just because it was beautiful, but because that smile on it was so *familiar*. I knew the sly glimmer in her eyes, knew that curl of her lips; after all, I had felt a duplicate of it against my mouth only a few hours earlier.

Crystal Danell's features were sharper, with a stronger jaw-line and more prominent cheekbones, and her hair was much

Never Kiss your Roommate

curlier, but there was absolutely no doubt that she looked eerily similar to Noelle.

With a sense of detached wonder, I picked up the next magazine. This time, Crystal was on the cover, along with a man I didn't know and the headline "Who's Crystal Danell's New Lover?"

After I had a look at two more magazines, it became clear to me that the only thing Noelle had been reading over the last few months were things featuring articles about Crystal, even if they were only a few sentences long.

The more I read, the more pieces I found to put the puzzle together: Crystal Danell was an R&B star who seemed to be pretty famous in the US, had been nominated for a Grammy, and was involved in a lot of charity work. She had also been dating an actor I didn't know for a while last year but then broke up with him and was working on a fashion line of her own.

When the magazines became repetitive, I decided to do my own research and, since reception was terrible in our room and even loading The Chitter Chatter took ages, decided to go down to the library. Muffin was the only living soul I encountered on my way there. She watched me warily for a moment before she stalked off around the next corner, slinking back into the shadows from which she had emerged.

Finally, I reached the library, my heart rate spiking at the obnoxiously loud jingling of the keys when I unlocked the door. I froze, one hand on the door handle as I listened for any steps coming my way, but when nothing happened, I soundlessly slipped inside.

The light vanished as soon as the door fell shut behind me, leaving me in pitch-black darkness. My own breathing seemed deafening in the thick silence, the creaking of the wooden floor-boards beneath my shoes ringing out like screams. The tall shadows surrounding me swallowed the shine of my phone's flashlight, the light never quite reaching the back of the room. In the darkness, the shelves seemed to come alive, closing in on me as I passed between them, and I had to slap a hand over my mouth to stop myself from crying out when I bumped into one of them. By the time I reached the computers, my breathing was ragged and my heart pounding so loudly I could hear nothing else over it.

The computer needed ages to turn on and when it did, its humming was so loud I feared the entire castle could hear it. After casting a few paranoid glances over my shoulder, I went on the internet and searched for Crystal Danell. The first pages all said exactly the same things I had read in the magazines, nothing new or particularly interesting, so I decided to search for more specific things that answered what I was looking for: I typed in *Crystal Danell's daughter.*

The first site that popped up seemed to be a fan page of sorts, showcasing mostly photos of Crystal. I scrolled down without seeing anything relevant to my search and I was just about to click off the site when a small picture in the upper-right cor-ner made my breathing hitch. There was Crystal, a few years younger, along with a girl that had to be around thirteen. They were in what seemed to be a shopping center, Crystal carrying a few shopping bags with one hand while the other was resting protectively on the little girl's back.

Seeing them next to each other was the final piece of evidence.

Even four years younger, in denim overalls and pigtails, Noelle was clearly recognizable. The only real difference was the

Never Kiss your Roommate

expression on her face: her smile was wide and infectious, her eyes shining up at her mom like she had hung the moon for her. It was an expression that I had seen only in short flickers, and even then, it had been nowhere as bright as the one on young Noelle's face.

The picture was captioned: *Crystal going shopping with her daughter Ashley.*

Ashley?

I stared blankly at the page, blinking a few times as if that would change what I was reading on the screen.

Ashley. Ashley Danell.

For a moment I tried to think of Noelle as Ashley, but I couldn't align the name of a complete stranger with the girl that I felt I knew so well.

It was then I realized that maybe I didn't know her all that well.

With a sudden sense of panic, I reached out and shut the computer screen off, the chair screeching loudly in the silence when I got to my feet and raced towards the door. I only slowed down my steps once I was outside, numbly making my way towards the entrance hall.

Here in the hallway, I could see a bit better than in the library, the high windows letting in the faint glow of the moon and—the stars. Jasper's voice echoed in my head again: *Sometimes she spends entire evenings lying in the football field and staring at the sky. She could probably tell you every single constellation up there.*

How hadn't I thought of this before? With my heart picking up its pace again, I spun around and sprinted back the way I'd come, past the library to the door at the very end of the hallway.

When I had been to the gym earlier to look for her, I hadn't noticed, but now as I flew across the hall I saw that the emergency exit was propped open with a brick, just like the last time we had snuck out.

A shiver ran down my spine as I stepped outside into the crisp October night. In front of me, the football field stretched out, deserted save for the dark figure sitting in the grass close to the center mark.

The wind tore at her clothes and her hair, but she didn't seem to care, chin tilted to look up at the sky above. When I neared her, I could see the glint of a cigarette as she lifted it to her lips, followed by delicate wisps of smoke escaping from her nostrils, rising into the night air before the wind carried them off.

Drenched in moonlight, Noelle looked like a statue. She reacted like one, too, when I sat down in the grass next to her; her eyes kept staring blindly at a spot somewhere in the sky, her features as unmoving as marble. Beautiful, but impossible to get through to.

"Hey," I softly said.

Her answer was so quiet I almost didn't hear it. "Hey."

"Do you . . . do you want to talk about what happened?"

Noelle looked to the side, lifting the cigarette to her lips again. She took her time taking a drag and exhaling. Finally, she said in a voice that was all gravel stones, "Sorry. I know you don't like it when I smoke."

"I don't care whether you're smoking right now or not. I care about whether or not you're all right."

"I'm fine," she murmured.

"You don't seem fine."

Silence. The wind carried over the distant sound of a train

Never Kiss
your Roommate

passing through Gloomswick in the valley below. When I glanced at Noelle again, her face looked like she wished she could be in one of the carriages, rushing through the night to somewhere else, someplace far away from here.

"Noelle," I whispered. "You can talk to me. What did your mom tell you? Who's *he*?"

A muscle twitched in her cheek: the first crack in the marble. "I don't want to talk about it. Drop it, Evelyn."

"No," I said, surprising even myself with how firm my voice was. "I know that it might be . . . difficult to talk about, but whatever it is, you don't have to deal with it alone."

In a jerky motion, Noelle plucked the cigarette from her lips and snuffed it out in the grass next to her. It went out with an angry sizzle: crack number two. "You don't know anything."

"Yes, I do. I know that Crystal Danell is your mother. And I know that Noelle isn't your real name."

At that, her head whipped around and she finally looked at me. "How?"

The look in her eyes, guarded and blazing with fury, was the same one with which she had fixed me on my first day at Seven Hills. For a split second, I felt the way I had then, small and pathetic, chilled to the bone by the wind and her stare.

However, this time I didn't look away. "Your magazines," I said. "I'm sorry if you didn't want me to look at them. I didn't think anything of it."

Noelle was silent for a long moment. Then, she said, "Okay."

"Okay?"

"I don't mind you looking at my magazines or searching things on the internet. I'm glad that's out of the way then." She lifted a hand to rub at her temple. "That's the least fucked-up part."

I gulped, directing my gaze down at my hands. "Were you going to tell me?"

"Maybe."

"What about the rest then?" I pressed. "Why did you take an alias? Was it just so that the press couldn't find you here?"

Noelle shook her head, her jaw clenched and her hands balled to fists where they were resting in the grass. "You don't need to know about that."

"But what if I want to?" I asked, blinking angrily to keep myself from crying. "I told you about everything that happened to me."

The final crack. The marble splintered and gave way to just Noelle, wide-eyed and fragile as the wind tore at her hair. She wasn't a statue; she was a paper doll trying not to get carried off by the breeze. "Why does it even matter?" she asked. Something in my chest clenched at the way her voice shook, edging on desperate. "You don't have to know everything about me to *know* me."

"Not everything. But today Amelia told me she thinks you're The Watcher and I couldn't even defend you because I don't know enough about you to be sure." I swallowed hard, fighting down the lump in my throat. "I hate that."

Noelle flinched like she had been physically punched in the face. "I hate that too. I don't want you to feel that way. But this is something I won't talk to you about."

"Why?" I whispered. "Why won't you let me in?"

"Because it fucking hurts," she said. Her voice cracked halfway through. "It's not . . . I can barely *think* about it. I wish I could be like you and face it, but I can't. I know that's cowardly and not fair to you, but I—" She broke off, drawing in a shaky breath. "I've always been better at running away, I think."

Never Kiss
your Roommate

All the frustration seeped out of me at once when I saw that her eyes were glistening with tears and when a particularly strong gust of wind made her tremble even more, I couldn't help but scoot closer to her. She melted into me the moment I wrapped my arms around her, her hands clutching at my sweater.

"I'm sorry if I made it sound like you have to tell me everything," I murmured into her hair after a few heartbeats. "You don't, especially not when it's something triggering. That was stupid of me to say."

Noelle's voice was small and slightly muffled. "It's okay. I'm sorry for getting so angry."

I closed my eyes for a moment and simply breathed in her familiar scent—night air and smoke and the coconut shampoo she used—and I was glad I hadn't stayed in our room with a book.

"Hey, Evelyn?"

"Yeah?"

She lifted her head from my shoulder but didn't look at me, her eyes trained on where her fingers were interlaced with mine in her lap. "I want to get better at this whole opening up thing. I promise I'll try. Because I . . . I want this to be something serious."

My breath caught in my throat. "Like, girlfriends?"

"Yeah." She finally met my gaze, lips curved into a small smile. This close, I could see the lighter dots in her warm brown iris, little specks of gold that looked like the stars she loved looking at so much. I was sure that if I stared long enough, I could find an entire galaxy in her eyes. "Like girlfriends."

"Okay," I breathed.

I had no idea who leaned in first, but only a heartbeat later, her mouth was on mine. At that moment, it didn't matter that she tasted like smoke or that I could feel the tracks of dried tears when I cupped her face. All that mattered was that she was okay and I was holding her and—oh my God, I had a *girlfriend*.

"So, what do we do now?" Noelle asked, leaning her forehead against mine. "Are you okay with making this public or . . . ?"

"Maybe not right away?" I quietly said. "It's just . . . after everything that happened at my last school, I would prefer to keep this to ourselves. Just until I've gotten a bit more used to it."

Noelle nodded and, in a voice like honey, said, "Okay. Whatever makes you most comfortable."

"Thank you," I whispered. Her words and the kiss had left me feeling warmed from the inside, but as another gust of wind took hold of us, both of us shivered. "We should go inside. You're going to catch a cold from staying out here for so long."

To my surprise, Noelle got up without complaint. Her fingers were icy when I slipped my hand into hers, prompting me to make a little detour to the kitchen when we went back inside. There, I managed to make a cup of tea without waking everyone in the castle up and even found some leftover dessert from dinner that I brought back to our room.

Noelle waited on her bed, wrapped in two blankets and wearing one of my woolen sweaters over her shirt. The sheer feeling of *fondness* that settled in my chest at the sight only grew when she smiled at me and held the mug of tea to her cheek to feel its warmth.

On the floor in front of her bed lay one of the magazines I had looked through, still open to one of the pages about Crystal Danell.

I closed it and placed it back on her desk, facedown.

16

Seth

On Sunday, Jasper was the one who seemed to have swallowed a tornado. It didn't have anything to do with me though; it was the day of the play.

The play. Last night I had lain awake thinking about what would happen afterward, when I wouldn't have rehearsals as an excuse to hang out with him anymore, to see him several times a week, if only from afar. The thought was one of the bad ones I sometimes had, the ones that were like bees or wasps or hornets, something stingy in any case, that kept buzzing around my head so loudly I couldn't focus on anything else.

Now, in Jasper's presence, the buzzing had momentarily stopped. We were in the backstage area of the auditorium, leaning against one of the tables filled with props while the other members bustled around us, each in varying stages of panic. It was a tiny room that was stuffed with racks of old costumes, the air thick with the smell of dust and hairspray. By hanging up a few dark bedsheets, the left-hand side had been converted into a changing room where the actors could get into outfits while next to it, people were crowding in front of the mirror.

Jasper's fingers were drumming against the table, his face a dark cloud as he asked, "We only have fifteen minutes left, where the hell is Gina?"

"Still searching for her wig," I said.

"She still hasn't found it? Mon dieu, this is awful," Jasper said, more to himself than to me, and nervously glanced at his watch for what felt like the twentieth time in only the last two minutes.

"Don't worry, she'll find it," I said with much more confidence than I was actually feeling. "I think Alissa said she had it a few minutes ago."

"There's so much that could go wrong though. What if someone forgets their lines? Or what if there's a blackout? God, we'd have no lights, no sound . . ."

"When was the last blackout around here?"

He paused and lifted a hand to run his fingers through his hair. "I don't know, a year ago, maybe?"

"So how likely is it there will be one during the play?"

"You're right," he muttered. "Still, something could happen. Why the hell am I doing this? Jesus, I should have never agreed to do this."

"Jasper." I turned around to face him and waited until his eyes—a stormy ocean today, all seafoam and crashing waves— met mine. "This is what you *do*. Queer media for queer people, right? Today you can make that happen. It's going to be good. Hell, it's going to be bloody *brilliant*."

He opened his mouth, probably to list a few more ways his play could be ruined, but was interrupted as Miss Pepperman suddenly stuck her head through the door. "Oh, there you two are! I've been looking everywhere . . . I couldn't let the show start without wishing you good luck, now, could I?" she chirped.

Jasper's face lit up considerably as she made her way towards us. "Thank you, Miss Pepperman."

She clapped her hands, looking from Jasper to me and back. "Are you nervous? Thrilled? Anxious?"

"*Excited* probably describes it best," Jasper answered.

Liar, I mouthed. He pretended he didn't see it.

"I can tell! You have worked so hard on this, so many hours of work leading up to just these forty minutes on stage . . ." She sighed dreamily. Then she suddenly turned to me. "And you, Seth? Are you also excited?"

I gave a small shrug. "I'm excited to see it come together, but I'm only doing the lights, so . . ."

"What do you mean, you're *only* doing the lights? That's a great deal of responsibility to take on! One wrong button and the entire stage is plunged into darkness!"

I gulped, a horrible vision of Jasper's disappointed face making the buzz in my head louder again.

"Nothing like that is going to happen," Jasper quickly interjected. "Seth is always perfect."

"Of course he is. You boys are such bright kids, so ahead of your time!"

"Thank you, Miss Pepperman. You should really get back to the auditorium now, to get a good seat and all . . ."

"Yes, yes, of course! I can't wait for the play to begin. Break a leg, boys!" she exclaimed, before scurrying out of the room.

The smile vanished from Jasper's face as soon as she was gone. "Oh God, this has to be good, she's expecting so much—"

"You could never disappoint her," I said, trying to sound comforting even though my own heart was racing now. "You could put a little hamster in a wheel on stage and start yodeling and she would think it was art."

Jasper's shoulders lost some of their tension at that. "You have a vivid imagination, mignon," he laughed. "Maybe *you* should be writing plays."

"Hold on, I've been wanting to ask this for weeks. Why do you keep calling me a minion?"

He stared at me for a moment as if he wasn't sure if I was joking or not. Then, he did the thing I least expected: he burst out laughing. "I'm not calling you a minion, idiot," he snorted. "It's French. It's like calling someone cute."

"Y-you've been calling me *cute* this entire time?"

"Yes. Like right now. You're really cute when you blush."

I looked away, raking a shaky hand through my hair. "Don't . . . don't do things like that. You can't just keep teasing everyone like it's a game."

"It isn't a game," he said, a frown replacing the smug grin. "And I don't talk to everyone like that."

I forgot how to breathe for a moment, suddenly overly aware of how close we were. At some point during our exchange, he had stepped closer; now he was standing right in front of me, near enough for me to touch him if I only raised my arm in the slightest. Just the thought of it brought back the ten-thousand-million-volt feeling I had felt on Thursday. "What do you—"

"Guys, I found it!"

I slowly closed my mouth, looking at Gina as she waved her

Never Kiss
your Roommate

wig in victory. I couldn't trust my hands to stay at my sides, so I stuffed them into the pockets of my trousers, nails digging into my palms.

"And you're also wearing your costume, perfect!" Jasper said, spinning around to take in the room. Nothing about him suggested that he felt even a single millivolt. "Is everyone else ready?"

Affirmative murmurs sounded from all around us, reminding me that we weren't alone, even though the last few minutes had felt like they'd taken place in another realm outside of this reality, some kind of fucked-up parallel universe situation that had decided to spit me back out right here, sweating and flushed.

"Perfect," Jasper said. Then he turned to me again. "Good luck out there."

My throat felt tight. "Thanks. You too."

I was about to push past him to head out the door when his hand suddenly caught my wrist. It was all I could do to stop myself from fainting when he suddenly leaned down a little and whispered into my ear. "I'm not playing any games with you, Seth Williams. You'll see."

Holy fucking shit. Aware of Gina eyeing us curiously, I tried to keep a blank face despite the blush creeping up my neck, my hands trembling in their polyester prisons. Jasper lingered a few more seconds before he stepped back, reached out to straighten my tie, and turned on his heel.

My heart felt like it was trying to hammer its way out of my chest as I left the backstage area and entered the auditorium. The room I had grown to love for its comfort and quiet had transformed from a safe haven into a bustling harbor, the high-pitched laughter and layered chatter as obnoxious as the screeching of seagulls. The rows before me were packed with students and teachers whose eyes followed me as I hurried up the stairs to the control panel.

I was suddenly immensely grateful that I didn't have to get onto the stage with the others. If this was already making me nervous, I couldn't imagine what the actors felt like now with only two minutes left until the play began. Letting my eyes roam the auditorium, I spotted Amelia's copper hair and, in the row in front of her, Evelyn and Noelle. Noelle had her arm draped casually across the back of Evelyn's seat while Evelyn leaned closer and whispered something in her ear; even when they tried to be subtle, it was still so obvious that, even in the sea of people, they were only gravitating towards each other.

I turned back to the task at hand and went over the entire control panel, checking if everything was working.

The curtains opened and revealed the stage just as I was done. I quickly switched the big ceiling light off and turned a single spotlight on, which I directed at the center of the stage.

Into the light stepped Jasper. With his silver hair illuminated like a halo, he looked like he couldn't possibly be a man of flesh and blood, much less the same seventeen-year-old who had almost run into his dresser in front of me a few days ago.

The expression that spread across his face as his eyes drifted over the crowd in front of him didn't hold even a hint of the nerves he had practically been shaking with only a few minutes earlier.

"*Bienvenue*, everyone. Welcome to this year's play," he said. His voice was deep and smooth through the speakers on the walls, impossibly attractive with the noticeable French accent. "It's a pleasure to have so many of you here tonight to watch

Never Kiss your Roommate

what the drama club and I have been working on for the past months. I would like to thank everyone who had a part in the process and supported us along the way."

Claps, more whistles. Jasper drank them all in like they were water and he had been thirsty for ages.

"Some words about the play: This is not your typical fairy tale adaptation but something completely different. I know that some of you might not like it, but truth be told, I don't care. The reason I wrote this was mainly to set a sign for the kids like me. For the kids who are struggling, who are uncertain, who are hiding, who are hurt. For the kids who are different than most people and who don't have it easy." He was silent for a moment, letting his words sink in before he continued. "I want to show you that it's okay. That you, no matter who you are, are not alone, no matter how hopeless things might seem sometimes. That whatever makes you different isn't something you need to be ashamed of, but something to be embraced, to be celebrated. That, if no one has told you yet, I see you—you are valid and so loved. So, this play . . . well, it's honestly just really fucking gay."

While the audience broke out in a mix of laughter and yells, I could see him mouthing something along the lines of *Sorry for swearing* at Mrs. Whitworth. I was grinning so wide it hurt.

With my eyes fixed on his face, time seemed frozen for a few moments. I only got ripped out of my daze when Jasper's eyes suddenly met mine with a questioning look. Too late I realized that he had continued talking, probably saying the play would begin now, which was my cue to turn all the stage lights on.

Cheeks flaming red, I rushed to light up the rest of the stage.

Jasper gave me a small smile and jumped off the stage to take his seat in the front row.

Even as Sammy appeared in his tower and the play began, I was still screaming on the inside. This was possibly the most embarrassing thing I had ever done, missing my cue because I had been too busy *staring* at Jasper. I was just glad that no one but him seemed to have noticed.

It was only after a few minutes that I got a little calmer and focused on the play unraveling before my eyes, relieved that everything else was going well so far. The sound was good, the actors were at their best tonight, the audience was responsive to all the little jokes, and I managed not to mess up again.

Soon the first scene, an introduction showing Rapunzel and his mother sitting together and talking in the tower, was over and the prince entered the stage. He witnessed the way the witch climbed up to Rapunzel and when she was gone, he did the same. In true fairy-tale fashion, they of course fell in love with each other right away.

After a bunch of queer jokes and them getting to know each other better, Rapunzel's mother started to realize that something was going on and eventually caught the prince climbing the tower. However, instead of making the prince go blind and sending Rapunzel off to a place where he couldn't be found like in the original fairy tale, she decided to go see the royal couple.

She told them about Rapunzel and their son. The king, wishing for a grandchild to take the throne in the future, wasn't happy at all with the news. To convince the prince to stop seeing Rapunzel, he sent a young girl from the village to the tower at the time that the prince usually came to visit, making the prince believe that Rapunzel was in love with her and not him.

Heartbroken that the prince no longer came to see him, Rapunzel agreed when his mother asked him to move to the

Never Kiss
your Roommate

other side of the kingdom. In Rapunzel's absence, the prince found out about the king's ploy. When he arrived at the tower and Rapunzel didn't react, he tried to climb the façade himself and fell.

After hearing about the prince's near death, Rapunzel ran away from his mother to go see him and the two made up.

Eventually, the people of the land and even the queen and king, as well as Rapunzel's mother, who had realized that their closed mindedness had only brought their children harm, gathered around the tower to celebrate their wedding. The play ended with Rapunzel and the prince kissing as a pride flag was waved from the tower.

The grin on Jasper's face as the curtains opened again to reveal all the members of the drama club was brighter than all of my spotlights combined. Noelle was standing up on her seat and whistling loudly while Evelyn clapped like her life depended on it. Miss Pepperman was crying through a pack of tissues Mrs. Whitworth had handed her halfway through the play. I, for the first time in a while, thought of my parents and wished just for a second that they would have been here to witness this.

In the midst of the thundering applause, Jasper briefly met my eyes, making my veins crackle with static. A moment later, he bowed along with the rest of the drama club and the curtains fell shut.

o o o

It took about an hour until everyone had left the auditorium and we had cleared the stage of props. Jasper and I were the last ones left. I half wished, half dreaded he would ask me why I was still there, but he didn't. He probably knew anyway; I felt like the answer was written all over my face, seeping out of every pore and filling the air between us as we silently shut the lights off.

Once we were done and the auditorium lay before us, dark and quiet, the stage naked without the cardboard trees and the tower, he asked, "Would you mind helping me with these?"

I nodded immediately, stepping closer to the boxes filled with costumes that needed to get stored away in the basement. There was no way I couldn't with the way he looked, practically glowing with happiness, the tension long gone from his body.

"Merci." He threw me a grin over his shoulder and picked up two boxes, leaving the other two for me.

It was late in the evening by now, so barely anyone was still around. It felt good to be alone with him again, just *JasperandSeth*. With him, the bees and wasps and hornets transformed into butterflies and relocated to my stomach, where they fluttered every time our elbows knocked together in a way that was accidentally not an accident.

Jasper only hesitated a tiny bit as we made our way down the stairs to the basement, passing the same spot where he had hyperventilated the night of the party. With some fumbling around in the dark, he unlocked the door and strode inside, turning on the fluorescent ceiling light. It came to life with a few flickers, its crackling and humming accompanying the noise of our footsteps as we crossed the room, which still looked exactly the same as we had left it after the party.

Jasper unceremoniously dumped his boxes on the table right next to where the skeleton was still leaning against the damp brick wall. The king's costume spilled onto the ground as he did; he leaned down to get it, but I beat him to it. Jasper blinked at

Never Kiss your Roommate

me when I, after a second of hesitation, gently set the crown down on top of his silver hair. I wasn't sure why I had done it, but I was glad I had when he gave a breathy laugh and a tiny curtsy.

He looked like he wanted to say something, but in the end, he just grabbed the red cloak and draped it around the skeleton's shoulders before balancing the crown on top of the skull. A chill ran down my spine as I studied it; with clothes on, it suddenly looked startlingly alive, so much so that I could have sworn it winked at me when I turned to follow Jasper.

Both of us released a relieved breath when we left the basement, but it was only once we were back in the boys' wing that Jasper asked, "So, how'd you like it? The play, I mean?"

"It was so much better than I expected. I can't believe no one messed up even once."

"God, I know," Jasper laughed, running a hand through his hair. "I didn't expect it to go so well. Did you see Miss Pepperman? She was crying almost the entire time."

"I did," I said. Then, after taking a deep breath, I said what had been burning on my tongue ever since the play had ended. "Hey, Jasper? I'm sorry for what I did with the lights in the beginning."

Jasper came to a halt, turning to fully look at me. I hesitantly stopped in my tracks. "What are you talking about?"

"In the beginning, before the play started, I missed my cue to turn the stage lights on. Sorry about that."

"Jesus, Seth, who cares? No one even noticed," he chuckled.

"Still," I reluctantly said. "That was my job and I messed up, just because I was distracted."

"Distracted by what?"

It probably wasn't the smartest thing to say out loud, but then again, neither was anything else I said when he was around. "You. I was . . . looking at you."

Jasper's eyes widened a little in surprise. "Oh."

I waited for him to say something else, anything that could make this less awkward, but he seemed to be just as at a loss as I was.

"Fuck," I muttered, running a hand over my face. "Sorry, I shouldn't have said that. That was weird. I'm making this weird."

"No, you're not," Jasper said. "Stop apologizing for everything."

"Sorry."

It was hard to make it out in the dimly lit hallway, but I was pretty sure that the look on Jasper's face was somewhere between wanting to strangle me and wanting to laugh. "Seth. Stop it."

I was just getting more and more nervous the longer he looked at me. "I can't. I'm just really sorry for messing up the lights for such a stupid reason when we went over everything so many times–"

"*Seth.*"

"Sorry, I—"

The next thing I knew was that his lips were crashing onto mine.

The first few seconds were clumsy and desperate and felt like falling without ever hitting the ground. Then Jasper gripped my face with both hands and lined it up, made it better, and *oh*. This was what the tornado inside me felt like when it was released then, catapulting both of us into the eye of the storm in a tangle of limbs and frantic hands.

Jasper pulled back just long enough to rasp, "Is this okay?"

"So fucking okay," I breathed before I pushed his back against the wall.

And shit, I had stopped believing in God when I was thirteen, but kissing Jasper felt like a religious experience. There was something holy in the way I could feel his lashes tickling my cheek, slender fingers resting at the base of my neck like they belonged there, my gasp when his fingers tugged at my hair like a breathless prayer.

By the time Jasper broke the kiss, my lips were tingling. I couldn't quite hold back a delirious laugh when my eyes fell on the picture of one of Seven Hills' founders that hung on the wall right next to us, staring us down with a disapproving frown.

Jasper smiled at the sound and carefully took my hand that had been clutching his shoulder, my breath catching in my throat when he dropped a featherlight kiss onto each knuckle, the gesture unexpectedly gentle after the demanding kiss a few seconds earlier. "You need to stop being so hard on yourself, Seth. You're . . . you light everything up."

I blinked at him for a few seconds, my brain too fuzzy to make sense of anything he was saying. Still in a haze, I murmured, "Well, yes, that's kind of what you do when you're the lighting guy."

I could feel Jasper's chuckle vibrating through my own body where we were still pressed against each other. "No, that's not what I mean. *Tu es mon soleil.*"

"What does that mean?"

"You are my sun."

For a moment all I could do was stare at him. Then, a nervous little laugh made it past my lips. "I think I might have to get a French dictionary."

Before he could respond, heavy steps sounded through the hallway, making us jump apart immediately. Señor Garcia, our Spanish teacher, stared at us for a few seconds before he grumbled, "I don't even want to know. Go to your room, both of you. Your *own* rooms, please."

"Yes, Sir," I muttered, while Jasper, the smug bastard, apologized in Spanish.

Shaking his head, Señor Garcia headed down the hallway.

As soon as he was out of sight, I said, "We . . . we should really go."

Jasper nodded, albeit reluctantly. To my surprise, he firmly grabbed my hand as we made our way to our rooms, only letting go once we were standing right in front of my door.

"Night, Jas," I whispered.

"Good night." He leaned down to press a kiss to my cheek, just barely grazing the corner of my mouth, before he turned around and sauntered towards his own room at the end of the corridor.

In utter disbelief I leaned against the door and watched him go, raising a hand to touch my lips. He looked back once more as he stepped inside, making my heartbeat stumble in a way that was utterly terrifying, until the door fell shut behind him and I was left alone to try to understand what had just happened.

Falling asleep that night was almost impossible. For hours I tossed and turned, replaying the evening in my head, until sleep finally had mercy on me and pulled me under.

○   ○   ○

Jasper and I were back in the basement. He was wearing the same outfit he had worn earlier, black pants and a billowing white shirt that sometimes slipped down to reveal a sliver of his collarbone. Around his shoulders was the red velvet cloak and atop his silver hair sat the golden plastic crown, wobbling precariously as he swung himself onto a table.

"Well?" he asked, leaning back on his hands, an easy grin on his lips. "Are you going to just stand there?"

Laughing, I stepped closer to him, until I was standing between his spread legs and he had to tilt his head a little to look up at me. "Are you sure that this is the best place to do this? Bit dark down here. And damp. And spider-y."

"Don't tell me you're afraid of the basement, mon soleil," Jasper chuckled. His hands were resting on my waist, slender fingers slipping under my shirt, cool against my skin. "It's just you and me. Isn't this what you've been wanting for so long?"

I nodded, but couldn't help but cast a glance over my shoulder to make sure no one else was there. Oddly enough, the skeleton wasn't where it had been earlier, but before I could wonder where it might have gone, one of Jasper's hands traveled upward, sliding up my back until it tangled in my hair.

"Hey." His voice was low, raspy. I swallowed thickly and turned my head to face him again, finding him looking up at me with the hint of a smile tugging at his lips and a flush on his cheeks, the plastic crown sparkling in the dim light. "Stop worrying. You always think too much."

"Sorry," I said. "It's just all new. And . . . scary, kind of."

"Don't be scared," he whispered. His hand tugged a little at my hair, pulling my face closer to his until I could feel his breath on my lips. In the half-light, his eyes were glowing like embers. Meanwhile, I was already burning up. "Just kiss me."

I didn't need to be told twice. Carefully cupping his chin in one hand, I leaned down and brushed my lips against his, unable to hold back a disbelieving smile when his legs wrapped around my waist, pulling me even closer. There was a soft clinking sound as the crown slipped off his head and went clattering to the ground, but neither of us cared.

I paused only when he suddenly laughed. It was a startlingly loud, throaty sound unlike anything I had ever heard from him that sent a shiver down my spine, this time not a pleasant one.

"What's so funny?" I murmured, slowly leaning back. It was when my eyes fluttered open that the blood in my veins truly froze.

It happened quickly. One moment he was simply grinning up at me, eyes wide and vacant. Then, as if in slow motion, the skin began to peel off his face. Creamy white gave way to tissue and muscle, red and gory enough to make me feel sick, until finally the skull appeared. All the while I was trying to back away, but his legs were still wrapped around my waist like a vice, bony heels digging into my lower back, keeping me in place.

The skeleton laughed again, a hollow noise that made my hairs stand on end, and said, "Oh, Seth. You don't really think he likes you, right? You, of all people?"

With my tongue paralyzed by fear, all I managed to whisper was, "But . . . he kissed me first."

"Aw. He kissed you first?" it mocked. Jasper's smooth accent had morphed into one that sounded more like mine, thick and Northern. "You seriously think that meant anything?"

"I . . . I don't know, I—"

The skeleton leaned forward, to the point that I could make out the cobwebs glittering in the empty space behind its eyes. Inside its chest, below Jasper's shirt still hanging off its shoulders, the fairy lights' battery pack clattered against its ribs. "Don't be ridiculous. I thought you knew better than this by now. Just look at them!"

It jerked its chin at something behind me. I turned my head as much as possible to see what it was talking about, only for my breath to catch in my throat when I spotted my parents. They were standing in the middle of the room, a few feet apart, as if there was

210

a physical barrier between them that kept them from coming any closer to each other.

"I asked you to do one simple thing for me! One thing, but of course that was too much to ask of you, wasn't it? You forgot it like you forget everything, because you only ever care about yourself!" Mom screamed. She was wearing her work clothes, her eyes red and swollen.

"I only care about myself?" Dad yelled back. He was staring at her with a stoic expression, but even from afar I could see the vein pulsing in his neck, the one that always popped out when he was angry. "Who went out every night this week? I stayed here every night, I . . . I cooked and I cleaned and I tucked in the kids . . . I told them you had business meetings when they wouldn't stop asking where you are. You know, if you can't stand being around us, then bloody leave!"

"Fine!" Mom yelled. "I'll leave!"

"No!" For a split second, I thought that I had cried out; then, I spotted the silhouette that had broken out of the shadows. It was me, a few inches shorter and at least five years younger, my round little face swollen with tears, frantic red patches covering my neck. Clutching Mom's sleeve, the young me begged, "Mom, please don't leave, you have to—"

"Seth, this has nothing to do with you." Dad's jaw was set, the vein in his neck pulsing pulsing pulsing. "Go back to bed. And tell your sister to stay in her room as well."

Younger me stared up at my mom, eyes watery, waiting for her to object. When all she did was give a curt nod, he abruptly turned around and disappeared into the shadows again.

"Great, now look at what you've done!" Dad exclaimed as soon as he was gone.

"What I've done? You *started this!*"

"Because you're being *selfish!*"

"And you're not being *fair!*"

"You're *unreliable!*"

"You're *controlling!*"

"You're—"

"You see?" the skeleton quietly said, directing my attention back to it. "That's what happens, sooner or later. Love like you dream of doesn't exist. Never has, never will. Sooner or later, everything goes to shit. It's best to accept it now. Keeps you from getting hurt, hm?"

I swallowed, trying to drown out the sound of my parents still going on in the background, every inch of me shaking with the familiar anxious tremor I had felt a thousand times before. In the corner, little me cowered under one of the tables, wetly gasping for air as tears poured down his cheeks. In his hand, he was clutching the brown paper bag he had learned to breathe into when he got like this.

"In fact, now that I think about it . . ." the skeleton mused, grinning at me when I met its empty eyes again. "It's better not to have a heart at all. Don't you agree, Seth?"

Before I could react, one of its bony hands darted forward, the skull's cackling echoing from the low basement ceiling as its fingers reached straight into my chest, sharp pain erupting as they closed around my heart and pulled—

∘ ∘ ∘

And then I woke up with a gasp, the skeleton's laughter still echoing in my head. On instinct, my hand frantically moved

212

to press against my chest, until I could feel my heart pounding under my palm, a panicked drumming that calmed only after a few shaky inhales.

I was alive. I was safe. I was okay, mostly, at least.

And I was also sure that I wouldn't fall asleep again after that nightmare my brain, the bloody horror movie producer, had come up with. *Fucking hell.*

17

Evelyn

On Monday, I found myself sitting between Noelle and Seth in class. Other teachers might have reprimanded Jasper and Noelle for swapping tables, from their initial seats in the front of the room to the ones next to us in the back, but Miss Pepperman had smiled only when she had entered the class and noticed our new seating arrangement.

Now, a few seconds after the bell had rung to end the lesson, she was standing in front of the blackboard, her hands fluttering nervously at her sides. "Please wait a moment before you storm out, I still need to give you your homework!"

Everyone who had already started to get up slowly sank back onto their chairs.

"Don't worry, it's not much! Maybe it will even be fun!"

Next to me, Noelle snorted. Seth looked equally as

unenthusiastic, though he had been in a strange mood all morning. He was sitting next to Jasper but was adamantly avoiding his eyes, somehow even more fidgety than he usually was. The entire time he was clicking his pen, tapping his foot, thrumming his fingers against the table, raising his gaze only to glance at the clock every other minute.

At breakfast, Seth, known among the cafeteria workers for always coming back for seconds, hadn't even been able to eat anything. By now I was honestly worried he was ill.

"I prepared some questions about *Wuthering Heights* that I want you to go over with a partner so that you can take turns answering and asking questions," Miss Pepperman explained as she handed out some worksheets. "But not with just *any* partner, of course. I assigned you one that I am sure will be a good match for you!"

I inevitably tensed a little. Most people in my class seemed nice enough, but then there were also those to whom I'd never spoken and whom I knew only from articles on The Chitter Chatter.

"All right, so we have Chelsea and Halima . . . Elina and Jasper . . . Eric and Lily . . . Seth and Amelia . . . Lauren and Samar . . . Evelyn and Noelle . . ."

Noelle knocked her foot against mine under the table but didn't look up from where she was scribbling on her notepad, a smile matching mine tugging at her lips. To my left, Jasper was grimacing, clearly not too happy; Seth looked about ready to slam his head against the desk.

"Come on, it could be worse. Amelia isn't even that bad," I whispered to him.

He sent me a blank stare. "Would you like to swap?"

"No, thank you," I chuckled. "I think I prefer a lovely afternoon with my girlfriend over an awkward one with her."

"I thought so," he muttered miserably, momentarily glancing over at Jasper.

Since yesterday, after Jasper's play, something seemed different between them and I couldn't help but wonder if what I was thinking was true. I was pretty sure that he didn't want me to talk about that right here in front of Jasper and Noelle though, so I swallowed down every question I had for now.

Squeezing his hand, I said, "I'm sure it will be fine."

Seth grabbed his bag without a response, leaving the classroom without waiting for any of us.

Jasper looked like he was about to head after him, but Elina, who was one of the members of Amelia's cheerleading team, suddenly appeared next to him.

"Hey!" she said. "Is it okay if we revise now? Like, right now? I have cheerleading practice later today . . ."

Jasper stared after Seth for a few more seconds. Then he directed his attention at her and said, only sounding a little bit strained, "Sure, no problem. What do you think, we could grab a coffee at the vending machine downstairs and see if there's a seat in the common room?"

"Awesome! See, I'm not that good at English Lit, so I'm glad I got paired with you . . ."

Jasper was barely listening. Waving good-bye to Noelle and me, he followed Elina into the hallway, heading in the direction opposite to the one Seth had darted.

"That was weird," Noelle commented as soon as he was out of earshot, swinging her bag over her shoulder.

"Do you think they . . . ?"

"I sure as hell hope so," she laughed, stepping out the door after me. "Anyway, about that homework. Is it okay if we do that later this evening? I scheduled two hours of extra basketball practice today."

"Sure, that's fine. I have to work in the library later, so we could do it there?"

"Perfect." She sent a quick glance down the hallway before hooking a finger through the strap of my bag to pull me into a short kiss. It wasn't much more than a peck, really, but it was enough to make my heartbeat stutter.

"Perfect," I echoed, unable to hold back a grin, and watched her disappear down the stairs.

o o o

Seeing as everyone else was busy, I for once had time to catch up on some reading, so the next two hours flew by like minutes. At around five o'clock, I left my room to go down to the library, but I hadn't even made it downstairs yet when my phone suddenly vibrated.

When I finally managed to fish it out of the depths of my bag, my mom's caller ID flashed on the display. "Hey, Mom!"

"Hi, sweetie!" she exclaimed, so loud I had to hold the phone away from my ear. "You haven't called in so long, I thought I'd check in on you!"

"I was going to call you later today," I said. "There was just so much going on these last few days, so I kept forgetting—"

"But everything's okay? You're doing well?"

"I'm doing really well," I said, involuntarily smiling as I crossed the entrance hall at a leisurely pace. Around this time, most students were hanging out in the common room or busy with extracurriculars, so no one was there to overhear me.

"That's so good to hear! Your dad and I were a bit worried after you said you had some problems with your roommate in the beginning."

"I wasn't worried," my dad's gruff voice interjected in the background.

Already having suspected that I was on speaker and he was hanging about somewhere near, I laughed, "Hey, Dad. It was a bit difficult, but we've sorted it out. Everything's really good right now."

"I forgot to ask you last time, but are there any, you know . . . *nice girls* at your school?" Mom asked.

In the background, I could hear Dad chuckling. Looking over my shoulder to make sure no one was near, I said, "I actually may or may not have a girlfriend."

This time, I was prepared for my mother's delighted squeak and held the phone at a safe distance from my ear. "Evelyn, that's lovely! What's her name?"

"Noelle."

"Wait—I thought that was your roommate you didn't get along with?"

"I told you, there was a lot going on," I laughed.

"Will we get to meet her?" my dad asked, his voice a bit distant as he was still hovering around in the background. I could vividly imagine them standing in the kitchen at home, my mom probably still in the blouse she wore to work and my dad with his cup of afternoon tea in hand. The image made my throat feel a little tighter. Usually, it was easy to push my homesickness to the side. It was only during our calls that I was overcome with this acute feeling of *longing*, a bittersweet taste in my mouth every time I hung up.

"I suppose you'll see her when you come here for the Winter Banquet in December."

"We're really looking forward to it," Mom said. Even through the phone, I could tell that she was holding back tears just by the slight quiver in her voice. "We miss you a lot, sweetheart."

Before I could respond, a quiet sob suddenly sounded from the room to my right. Halting in my steps, I rushed to say, "I miss you too. I have to go now, but I'll talk to you soon!"

Pocketing my phone again, I carefully pressed closer to the door, slightly ajar, which made it easy for me to peek inside. My eyes widened in surprise when they fell on Amelia.

"Hey, are you all right?"

A stupid question. She was standing by the window in the empty classroom, frantically wiping at her eyes with her sleeve as I neared her from behind.

"Amy." I gently put a hand on her shoulder, urging her to turn around. "What happened?"

"Leave me alone," she sobbed and twisted out of my grip.

Her voice was sharp, but I was far too used to crying in empty classrooms after school hours to simply leave her here like this. "Hey," I softly said. "Talk to me. Maybe I can help?"

At that, she only began to cry even harder, shoulders shaking like the leaves on the tree behind the window, desperately clinging to the branches so as not to be carried off by the wind. "There is nothing you can do. Please just go."

"I'm not leaving you here like this," I said and hoisted myself onto the windowsill next to her. Her eyes were swollen and red, cheeks wet with tears, so I rummaged in my bag until I found a pack of tissues. "Here. What's going on?"

She accepted the tissue with trembling hands. "If I say, you have to promise not to—"

Before she could finish, the door suddenly flew open and Seth poked his head inside. "Oh, here you are. I thought we wanted to meet in the common room to do that stupid assignment—shit, is everything all right?"

Amelia hastily wiped her eyes dry with the tissue. "I am fine."

"You don't look like it," Seth remarked and came to a halt next to us. "What's wrong?"

"She was just about to say." I gave Amelia's shoulder a light squeeze. "Go ahead. We won't tell anyone."

Amelia was silent for a long moment. Then, avoiding my eyes, she muttered, "It's my last English essay. I got a C."

Seth and I exchanged an incredulous look.

"You're . . . you're crying because you got a C in English Lit?" I asked. "Hey, that's not that bad. At least you—"

"No, it *is* bad." I knew I had said the wrong thing when tears welled up in her eyes again. "It is terrible. Everything is terrible."

Before I could think better of it, I hopped off the windowsill and pulled her into a tight hug. At first, she stiffened, but then, with a muffled sob, she went boneless in my arms. Her fingers clutched my shoulders, every inch of her trembling while I held her and rubbed soothing circles on her back with one hand. Behind her, Seth awkwardly patted her shoulder. Neither of us really knew what to say, so we just stayed like that until, after what felt like ages, Amelia pulled back with a sniffle.

Never Kiss your Roommate

"Sorry," she said, turning to look at Seth. "I don't want to waste your time. We should get started with our homework."

He lifted an eyebrow, staring down at her in disbelief. "Are you sure? If you want to go to your room and be on your own or something, that's okay too. We can still work on it tomorrow."

"No." She resolutely wiped the last tears away and raised her chin. "I feel better. Let's get this over with."

Seth looked too tired to argue and slumped onto the chair next to him with a shrug. "Fine."

I glanced at the clock on the wall, wincing when I realized that I was running late for my library shift. Still, I was reluctant to leave them here like this. "Are you going to be okay on your own?"

Both gave an unconvincing nod. Next to each other, both pale-faced and bleary-eyed, they made a pitiful picture.

"Okay . . ." Looking at Seth, I said, "I'll be in the library if you feel like hanging out later."

"Yeah, maybe," he mumbled.

After giving Amelia another short hug, I hurried outside and down the corridor to the library. On my way there, I straightened my shirt with one hand; there was a wet spot near my collar where Amelia had pressed her face, but it wasn't too noticeable.

I had just entered the library and made myself comfortable at one of the desks when Noelle trudged inside. She was wearing sweatpants and a hoodie, her hair still wet from showering and even curlier than usual.

"Hey," she said as she set down the two mugs she had been carrying and slumped onto the chair next to me. "I figured we might need some caffeine if this is going to take longer. At least, I will."

I grimaced as I took a few sips. Whereas Jasper's coffee was basically just milk and sugar, hers was nearly black. Next to me, Noelle put her arms onto the table and rested her head on top of them.

"Rough practice?"

"Yeah," she said, muffled by her arms. "It was hell today. If I have to tell one more stubborn white boy to pass to his team-mates instead of trying to score himself, I'm going to scream."

Chuckling, I reached out and massaged her shoulders, draw-ing a contented sigh out of her.

"Don't you think you're pushing yourself a bit too hard?" I murmured. "You've had practice every other day this week."

She shook her head, hissing through her teeth when my fingers met an especially tender spot in her right shoulder. "It's necessary. We're playing against Westbridge next week-end. Mrs. Whitworth told me that it's been twenty years since Seven Hills last beat them. *Twenty years.*"

"You want to impress Mrs. Whitworth?" It was more of a gen-tly put statement than a question.

"I guess," Noelle muttered. "She's given me so many chances. I want to show her that she was right to believe in me, you know? And, aside from maths, it sure as hell isn't going to happen through my marks, so this is my best shot." She was silent for a moment, before she added, "Also, I hate their basketball team. I want to see those pretentious fuckers go down."

"She adores you either way," I said. "You know that, right?"

Noelle only hummed. Under my hands, the tension in her neck and shoulders slowly melted away, her eyes slipping closed. Like most afternoons, there was no one else in the library, so for a few seconds, the only sounds were the quiet humming of the

Never Kiss
your Roommate

old radiators and the clicking of the tree branches against the windows. The sun was already starting to set, spilling light the color of honey onto the wooden floor and our desk.

After a few moments of comfortable silence, Noelle said, "Hey . . . when we have away games, there are usually a few free seats on the bus. Would you maybe like to come with?"

"I would love that," I whispered and, seeing as no one was around, dropped a short kiss onto her shoulder. Then, I let go of her and pulled Miss Pepperman's worksheet closer to us. "Come on, let's do this. The sooner we start, the sooner we finish."

Noelle only groaned, her head still resting against the table. "Evelyn, I don't think you understand. I feel like a bus ran me over. This is too much."

"What about this: you revise with me and in return you get a kiss after every correct answer. Deal?"

Noelle's head shot up so quickly I feared she got whiplash. "Deal. But only if I also get one for every wrong answer *you* give."

"Okay." Ignoring the blush painting my cheeks pink, I picked up the page with all the questions we were supposed to answer and cleared my throat. "First question. What was Emily Brontë's pen name?"

"Easy. Ellis Bell," Noelle smugly said.

"Correct."

Noelle scribbled the answer onto her worksheet before she reached out and pulled me into a coffee-flavored kiss.

When she leaned back, her expression was significantly brighter than before. "Okay, your turn. Please feel free to give a wrong answer," she said. "When was *Wuthering Heights* published? Uh, I mean *first* published, sorry."

"Oh no, I'm bad with dates. I think . . . in the eighteenth century?"

Noelle shook her head, grinning at me. "Close, but not the correct answer. It was published in the nineteenth century—1847, to be precise."

With Noelle already cupping my cheek and pulling me in again, I couldn't even be mad.

Slightly out of breath, I said, "Elle, we're never going to finish all the questions if you keep doing this."

"Hey, this was your idea. You can't just promise things like that and chicken out later."

With a breathless chuckle, I picked the next question. "Okay. What is Edgar Linton doing when he's introduced for the first time?"

"I don't know . . . running after Catherine? He's always just running after Catherine."

"No," I said. "He's weeping over a puppy. Next question."

"How are Ha . . . Hareton and Catherine related?"

"Catherine is Hareton's aunt."

"Correct," she said. There was a frustrated edge to her voice and somehow I was pretty sure it wasn't because I got the answer right. It was then I realized this was the first time I was hearing her read something out loud.

"Who is the main narrator of the book?" I asked.

"God, what was his name . . . Lock . . . Lockwood?"

"Yes, well done!"

I had intended for it to be just a short peck, but Noelle grabbed my face before I could back away and I was too far gone to do anything but kiss her back. My mistake in suggesting this game began to dawn on me; it was like one of those drinking games

Never Kiss your Roommate

where the longer it went, the drunker you got, leading to you getting even worse at the game and in turn drinking even more. I hadn't stood a chance to begin with.

This time, it was Noelle who pulled back. A little haltingly, she read, "In what region of England is the story set?"

"Gloucestershire, I think?"

"Oh babe, you're lacking concentration. I feel like you're really not taking this seriously," Noelle teased. "It's set in Yorkshire."

"Oh, I'm so sorry," I laughed.

Against my lips, she whispered, "I'm not."

After Noelle got the next question wrong (she was too busy playing with my fingers to really listen), it was her turn to read the next one for me.

However, instead she suddenly asked, "Hey . . . can I tell you something?"

I nodded, leaning back a little to get rid of the kiss-induced fog in my head.

Noelle's expression was much more serious now, her fingers nervously fidgeting, so I gently clasped her hands with mine. "You don't have to tell me if you don't want to, you know?"

"No," she said. "I told you I would try to be more open with you."

I gave her an encouraging smile. "Okay. I'm all ears."

"So . . . you probably noticed how I read in a . . . weird way?" she asked in an uncertain voice.

"It's not *weird*."

"You know what I mean, all the pauses and words I skip and stuff."

I silently looked at her, willing her to go on.

"I'm dyslexic."

"I kind of assumed that already."

"Really?"

"Yes." I reached out to tuck a curl behind her ear. "Why were you so nervous about telling me?"

"I don't know, it's stupid really," she said, her eyes fixed on a dent in the table. "I guess I didn't want you to think I'm dumb or anything."

"Why would I think that?"

"I don't know." Noelle shrugged. "It's just that I still have problems reading out loud and sometimes in quiet, too, and my spelling and grammar and all of that are shit."

"Is that why you never read out loud in class?"

"Yeah. And it's also why I was acting like a dick when you went through my notes during your first week here. I didn't want you to find out that way. Do you remember that?"

"Oh my God, *that* was the reason?" I asked. "Jesus, I thought you were hiding something much worse."

"Like what?"

"Like notes for The Chitter Chatter."

Noelle blinked a few times like she wasn't sure she had heard me right. Then, she burst out laughing. "You really thought I was The Watcher?"

Now that I said it out loud, I felt stupid. "Well, what did you expect when you acted all mean and mysterious?"

"Evelyn, have you ever seen me voluntarily read a book or set foot in this library? Does it seem like I have the patience or the vocabulary to regularly write blog entries?"

"I don't know," I chuckled. Desperate to change the subject, I picked up the worksheet again. "Let's do a few more questions."

She agreed, and soon we were back to quietly asking and answering and exchanging short kisses.

That was until someone suddenly cleared their throat behind us. With my heart feeling like it was being dropped from the castle's highest tower, I immediately lowered my hands that had been tangled in Noelle's hair. No one ever came here on a regular day, which was the only reason I hadn't been concerned about kissing Noelle here.

Looking over my shoulder, I let out a sigh of relief when I saw that it was just Seth.

"Hey," he said, awkwardly stuffing his hands into his pockets. "Can I come in or . . . ?"

I quickly shuffled back a little in my seat. "Of course!"

"Thanks," Seth muttered and sat down at our table. He was as pale as when I had left him with Amelia, dark circles under his eyes and his hair sticking up in every direction. His shoulders looked tense, his fingers nervously making fists and then loosening them again.

"Are you okay?" I asked.

He raked a hand through his hair. "I'm not sure."

"Have you finally eaten something?"

"Don't feel like it."

Noelle frowned and picked up her bag, rummaging through it until she found a chocolate bar that she tossed onto the desk in front of Seth. "There. Eat something. You look like you're about to faint."

Seth stared at her and then at the chocolate bar, as if it was something completely alien. Eventually, he picked it up and started unwrapping it with shaky hands.

I watched him carefully, making sure he ate the entire thing. "Did you have anything to drink?"

"I drank like four cups of coffee. I thought the caffeine would make it better because I didn't really sleep all night, but now I feel like my heart is going to explode," he said, pressing a hand to his chest.

"Jesus, Seth." I handed him my water bottle. "What happened?"

Seth took a few sips before going back to fidgeting nervously. "After the play, when everyone was gone, Jasper and I, uh, brought some boxes to the basement and then on our way to our rooms he . . . he kissed me."

Noelle tilted her head. "And why is that such a bad thing?"

"It's not a bad thing. I mean it wasn't, it felt really, really good—like *insanely* good—but then I went to my room and I couldn't sleep all night and I had this really fucked-up nightmare and I kept thinking about him and what if this was just a one-time thing?" Seth said, almost stumbling over his words in his hurry to get them out.

"Why would you think that?" I asked. "I mean, he obviously really, really likes you, everyone can see that—"

"But what if he doesn't like me *like that*?" Seth answered with a panicked look in his eyes. "You saw him after the play was over. What if this was just an adrenaline thing?"

"Seth, you're overreacting. You just need to stop thinking so much."

He snorted, dropping his head. "Yeah, tell that to my bloody brain."

"Did he say anything to you at all after the kiss?" Noelle asked.

"He . . . he called me his sun."

"His *son*?!"

"What? No, his *sun*. As in sunshine."

"Ah." Noelle grinned. "Such a charmer."

"That doesn't sound like he wasn't taking it seriously to me," I said.

"I don't know. I'm probably just thinking too much into it again," Seth muttered and rubbed a hand over his eyes. "I'd just really like to know where we stand right now."

Teasingly, I said, "I thought you didn't believe in love."

"I don't." Seth frowned. "This isn't about love, it's ... attraction. It's just chemistry: hormones and neurotransmitters and—"

"I get it, you're too cool to have feelings," I laughed.

"This has nothing to do with being cool, it's *science*—"

"It's depressing!"

"Whatever it is, I can't blame you," Noelle threw in. "He's pretty attractive, isn't he?"

"God, *so* attractive," Seth said with a miserable look on his face.

"I think it's the French accent," Noelle mused.

"*Right*? How is that even allowed?"

"He's all right," I murmured.

At that, Seth cracked a grin for the first time that day. However, it crumbled when footsteps suddenly neared us and Jasper sauntered into the room, wearing his glasses—which was something he had only recently started doing—and a long dark coat over his school uniform.

"Salut," he said. Stepping behind Seth, he bent down to press a kiss to his cheek. "Is everything okay? You disappeared so quickly after class."

"Yeah," Seth breathed. It had taken all but one sign of affection from Jasper to bring the color back into his cheeks. "Yeah, I'm fine."

"I noticed you didn't eat anything at breakfast and I didn't see you at lunch either," Jasper said. "So I asked Mrs. Whitworth if we could leave the castle tonight to have dinner in town and she said yes. Of course we don't have to do that if you don't want to though. It was just—"

"I'd love that," Seth interrupted.

"Perfect," Jasper said and slipped his hand into Seth's.

And just like that, Seth was back to his usual self, as if Jasper's fingers intertwined with his were enough to stop the frantic buzzing that I knew was going on inside his head.

o o o

Unsurprisingly, we were even less productive now that Jasper and Seth had joined, so we didn't finish our task in time for dinner and had to take the worksheet up to our room with us after we left the Great Hall.

Noelle pulled me through the door by my hand, locking the door behind us before she led me over to her bed; I sank down on one end, she on the other, our notes and my copy of *Wuthering Heights* lying between us on the sheets.

This time, we went through the questions efficiently and without interruptions, both of us wanting to get it over with now that night was quickly falling.

"Good job!" I said when Noelle had answered the last of the questions. "See, that wasn't even that bad, was it?"

"It was all right," she acquiesced as she shut the book. Meeting my eyes again, she asked, "I still don't really get it though. What do you like so much about reading?"

I thought about it for a moment, my chin propped in one hand. "I don't know, I . . . I like that it's an escape. And I like that in almost every story, there's a lesson to be learned, you know? There have been books that have completely altered the

Never Kiss
your Roommate

way I see the world, like, through fiction, I've come a little bit closer to understanding reality. And especially with these older books, I just love how they're written. I know you find the language off-putting, but once you've grown accustomed to it, it's so pleasant. There's this flow to it, and the phrasing is so . . . I don't know how to describe it, but it's so delicate." I broke off, my cheeks heating up when I noticed that Noelle's eyes had glazed over. "Sorry, that was a really boring ramble, wasn't it?"

"No, it wasn't," she said, her voice surprisingly earnest. "I like hearing you talk. Go on."

"I . . . really?"

She gave a nod, shifting a little closer to me.

And so I did. I told her about the book that had made me fall in love with reading, then the one that had shown me good people could do horrible things, and the one that had taught me being yourself mattered more than anything else. I told her about my favorite authors, my favorite genres, my favorite bookstore all the way back home, about how reading allowed me to get out of my head no matter what was going on in my life.

"So, kind of like basketball, right?" Noelle asked at one point.

"Yeah," I said, unable to hold back a smile. "Kind of like that."

I stopped talking only when she leaned forward and captured my lips in a slow kiss that stole the breath from my throat. "Is this your way of shutting me up?" I asked, leaning into the hand that was cradling my cheek.

"What? No, I just . . . I love your mind."

What was I supposed to do other than kiss her again? My hands moved to her waist of their own accord, fingers curling into the soft fabric when her teeth nipped at my bottom lip and *oh.*

"Noelle," I whispered, and somehow my voice must have carried the heat that was simmering in the pit of my stomach, the same one that had begun earlier in the library, because Noelle's eyes suddenly widened a little. "Do you want to—"

"Yes," she immediately said. "But only if you're sure that this is what you want."

I gave a nod, but Noelle caught my chin in one hand. "Words, love."

And God, something about that pet name and her voice, soft yet insistent, laced with something that I could only describe as *wanting*, made my skin prickle. "Yes," I breathed. "I want this."

The smile on Noelle's face grew at that. I watched with an anticipatory flutter as she swept the papers off the bed before setting *Wuthering Heights* down on her nightstand so gently it made something in my chest ache.

She was just as careful when she grabbed onto my waist and pulled me on top of her so I was straddling her lap, my arms looped around her neck. For a few seconds, all I could do was stare at her; with her chin tilted up to look at me, her eyes shining with warmth, and the golden glow of the lamp on her bedside table catching in her curls, she looked so beautiful I forgot how to breathe for a moment. It didn't help that her fingers had slipped under the hem of my shirt, gently tracing my lower back, the touch so light it sent a pleasant shiver down my spine.

"I've never done anything like this before," I whispered.

"I know. I've never done it with a girl before either," she murmured, her voice sounding surprisingly nervous. "I guess we'll just have to figure it out together, hm?"

"Yeah," I breathed and leaned down to kiss her again, just to ground myself.

Never Kiss
your Roommate

"Can this come off?" Noelle asked when she leaned back, tapping my tie.

I nodded, still a little breathless after the kiss, and watched as her nimble fingers quickly undid the knot. Meeting my eyes again, she tugged at the collar of my sweater. "And this?"

"Uh-huh," I said, raising my arms so she could get it over my head, unable to hold back a breathless chuckle when she tossed it somewhere behind her without looking where it landed.

"Lots of layers to this uniform," she commented, lifting her gaze to grin at me. I could have kissed her again just because of that attempt to make me feel less nervous. A moment later, her voice was almost achingly soft again. "How about this?" she asked, tapping the button at the top of the white dress shirt I had worn underneath.

With the way she was looking at me, there wasn't a single thing I wouldn't have done for her. "Yeah," I whispered. "Go ahead."

I wasn't sure if I was imagining it or if her hands really were trembling just a little bit as she slowly undid one button after another, until I could shrug the shirt off. Left in only my bra, I suppressed the urge to cross my arms in front of my chest.

Noelle seemed like she could tell I was getting nervous again because she gently pulled me down for another kiss, sweet and unrushed. Somehow, the familiar territory gave me the courage to reach behind me and unclasp the last item of clothing, letting it fall to the mattress just as she opened her eyes again.

In the silence, I could hear her breath catching in her throat. "Look at you," she muttered, reaching out to trail a finger from my shoulder down to my collarbone, a whisper of a touch that was that much more intense against my naked skin. "You're so beautiful."

I swallowed thickly, my heart pattering in time with the rain thrumming against the window, heat lapping at my body everywhere she touched. Tugging at her shirt, I softly asked, "What about you?"

At that, Noelle leaned back with a grin and unceremoniously pulled it over her head before moving on to the shirt underneath, not a trace of self-consciousness in any of her movements. Meanwhile, I suddenly found it very hard to breathe as I watched the silhouettes my hands had spent so much time memorizing through cotton and wool get revealed.

I wasn't going to survive this. Noelle was going to be the death of me, but it would be the sweetest one I could ever have wished for.

When she was undressed and there was no fabric left between us, she looked at me again and leaned forward, carefully lowering me onto my back, the pillows cool against my overheating skin. She was the one straddling me now, a pipe dream pressed against me, one hand splayed across my rib cage. Her hair tickled my face when she leaned down, her lips brushing against my jaw as she whispered, "You're shaking."

I didn't respond for fear of the noise that would leave my mouth if I opened it. Instead, I tilted my head, silently asking for an actual kiss, but Noelle only smiled, gently brushing the hair out of my face with one hand while she was holding herself up with the other. Basketball practice had paid off; the sight of the muscles straining in her arm only made my head spin more.

"Still sure you're okay with this?" she asked.

"Noelle," I said, my voice coming out breathier than even I had expected, enough to make her eyes widen almost unnoticeably. "I think I'm going to die if you don't touch me soon."

The concerned expression on her face morphed into a

Never Kiss
your Roommate

disbelieving grin at that. A moment later, she dipped her head again, pressing soft kisses to my neck before moving lower, warm hands slipping under the hem of my skirt. I tangled my fingers in her hair and closed my eyes, unable to keep them open any longer.

Before, I had always been a little scared when I had imagined my first time, and even when I had thought about how it would be with Noelle, I had still felt shaky with nerves.

Reality was so different from anything I had expected.

It wasn't scary. It was soft and careful and a little clumsy, but never awkward or painful. It was nervous chuckles and quiet reassurances, breathless smiles and uncertain hands learning their way across uncharted territory. It was *Noelle*, who accepted my trust like it was a treasure and gave me hers with the same earnestness, who gently directed me when I didn't know what to do, who called me *love* and *beautiful* and whispered my name like it was a prayer.

That was really what it felt like, I dizzily thought between kisses: worship in its purest form, like we had carved out a space in heaven that was just for us, that began and ended with this bed, built from the sound of Noelle's shaky breaths and the reverent look in her eyes as she watched me come apart beneath her.

For years, I had feared what it meant to want this, had dragged the thought around like a ball and chain. Now, with Noelle tracing shapes onto my arm and hiding her grin against my shoulder, my skin still tingling everywhere she had touched, the weight was finally gone; she had coaxed the guilt right out of me, taken me apart and put me back together without leaving a single crack for it to ever creep back in, and it hadn't hurt a bit.

18

Seth

The road through the woods always felt scary the few times I'd walked with Evelyn. The pair of us jumped at every snapping branch, every little sound coming from the woods, and usually dashed down the hill as quickly as possible to put the looming trees behind us. Internally, I cursed myself every time for watching so many true crime documentaries that made it that much easier to imagine faces and silhouettes in the shadows as we made our way through the woods.

Now as I walked hand in hand with Jasper, the only thing making me nervous was him. He was a picture in black and white, the only color the blue of his eyes that flashed whenever he stepped into the light of a streetlamp. With his long black coat and the shadows dancing across his face, he looked as mysterious and intimidating as the protagonists of the crime novels on my bedside table.

That was until he offered me a bright smile and asked, "Is there any place you'd like to eat at?"

"I don't know," I said. "I've only been to town, like, three times so far. I had dinner at Giovanni's with Eve once, I really liked it there."

"Giovanni's it is then."

We were silent for a moment. In the distance, the town came into view.

Jasper asked, "Can I ask you something?"

"What is it?"

"Why were you acting so strange all day? You barely looked at me during class and ran off immediately afterward, and now you're so quiet."

I was silent for a moment, feeling his gaze boring into my cheek. I couldn't really explain my nightmare to him; it seemed bloody stupid now that I looked back at it. Still, I decided to go with most of the truth. "After we, you know, kissed last night, I kind of panicked. I couldn't sleep all night because my brain kept replaying the whole thing and going down this spiral of thinking that maybe it was just a one-time thing and you don't actually like me like that."

Jasper had slowed his steps during my explanation. Now he came to a complete stop. "Are you serious?"

I swallowed hard. "Yes?"

"Mon dieu," Jasper said. "I'm sorry, I should have made that clearer. This isn't like what I had with Sammy. It's not a pastime. I like you, Seth. So much."

His words punched all the air out of my lungs. My voice came out almost inaudible when I asked, "Really?"

"Yes." A furrow appeared between his brows. "Why is that so hard for you to believe?"

"I don't know. You're you. And I'm me. And I'm not like Sammy or the other people you've been with, I think. I'm . . . a bit strange."

"I like strange."

I breathed a nervous laugh. "Fucking hell. If you had said that last night, I maybe wouldn't be running on one hour of sleep on our first actual date."

Jasper's smile widened. "For what it's worth, those dark circles under your eyes are strangely attractive."

"Guess I'm never going back to sleep."

Jasper chuckled, a low sound that was ridiculously charming, and tugged me closer by my hand. "I still prefer it when you're emotionally stable and don't seem like you might faint any second."

"Noted," I murmured.

A moment later, Jasper caught my chin in his hand and his lips found mine, soft and unrushed. It was different from last night's frenzied kiss but felt just as head-spinningly, earth-shatteringly amazing, to the point where we had to stop kissing because I couldn't stop grinning. *Attraction.* That was what I had settled on in the hours leading up to dawn last night.

"Come on," Jasper laughed. "Let's go somewhere warm."

I wouldn't have minded staying like that, with Jasper's hair glowing in the light of the streetlamp and my fingers clutching the lapels of his coat, but a chilly gust of wind and the promise of food made me reluctantly let go of him.

With Jasper's hand tugging me along, the remainder of the walk seemed to pass by within seconds. He only let go once we were standing in front of Giovanni's, and only to hold the door open for me.

My stomach rumbled when I stepped inside and was met with the delicious smell of Italian food, reminding me that I had barely eaten anything all day.

"Ah, *bambini*, long time no see!" Giovanni's voice boomed. "A table for two, yes?"

"That would be perfect," Jasper answered.

My ears felt a little bit warm as we followed the larger-than-life man to the back of the restaurant; I blamed it on the difference in temperature after having been outside when in reality it was Jasper's hand resting on my lower back like it was the most natural thing in the world.

The table Giovanni led us to was right next to the window, a bit secluded from the rest of the patrons. While we got out of our coats and sat down, he fished a lighter out of his pocket and lit the candle in the middle of the table. "I'm just going to make it a little more romantic for you boys."

When Jasper stilled in surprise, Giovanni tapped his cheek and said, "I've got an eye for these things."

"Last time you thought I was on a date with Evelyn," I pointed out.

There was a lot of moustache happening on his face, so it was hard to read his expression, but I was pretty sure he was grinning. Ignoring my objection, he clapped a hand on my shoulder, hard enough for my entire body to jerk forward. "A drink on the house for you two! What would you like? Coke? Sprite?"

Once we had both ordered, Giovanni turned around to tend

to a family of four that had just entered the restaurant. I shivered at the cold blast of air they brought in with them and tugged the sleeves of my sweater down to my knuckles.

"It's so cold this year."

Jasper nodded. "I read that it might even snow next month. Maybe we'll have a white Christmas."

"Shit, it's not even that long until Christmas," I said. At Seven Hills, the weeks seemed to blur into each other, the change in seasons mostly perceived from behind the windows of the castle. I couldn't believe it had been two months since Evelyn and I had arrived at the beginning of September, but at the same time I felt like I had known Jasper and Noelle for much longer than that.

"I'm so excited for the Winter Banquet," Jasper said, closing his eyes like he was envisioning it. "All the food and the dancing, seeing everyone dressed up . . . Are your parents coming?"

I scratched at my neck. "I have no idea. They're still in the middle of settling their divorce, so . . ."

"Shit." Jasper's eyes widened. "I forgot that that's the reason you're here."

"It's fine," I said, plucking at the tablecloth just to have something to do with my hands. My mind flashed back to the nightmare, to Mom and Dad screaming at each other, their voices ringing from the walls of the basement, but I quickly pushed the thought away. "It's been a bloody long time coming."

"Why did they split up?" Jasper broke off. "Sorry, is that inappropriate to ask?"

"No, it's okay," I said. "There wasn't really one specific reason. They just . . . fell out of love, I guess, but waited way too long to end things. Over the last few years, they could barely

Never Kiss your Roommate

stand being in the same room and there was so much *yelling*, you know, every day, over nothing. We would be having dinner together and suddenly one of them would explode and then they wouldn't talk to each other for days. It was like sitting on a powder keg for years and just waiting for that final match to blow everything up for good."

Jasper's eyes were unusually serious, his head tilted as he listened attentively. "I can imagine how exhausting that must be. Aren't you kind of glad you could finally get away from all of that?"

"I don't know, I . . . I was glad when they told me they were filing for a divorce and looking for separate places, but I wasn't prepared for them to send me to the middle of bloody nowhere without asking me first, you know?"

He nodded. "Do you still wish you could go home now?"

I thought about it for a moment before I slowly said, "A month ago, I would've packed my bags right away if I'd had the chance. But now I've got you and Evelyn and Noelle. I wouldn't change that for anything. And besides, I haven't spoken to my parents since I came here, so . . ."

"Not even once?" Jasper asked, eyebrows lifting in surprise.

"No. At first I didn't because I was pissed they'd sent me here against my will. Then I just kind of forgot." I shrugged. "I wouldn't know what to talk to them about now. I've never been that close to them to begin with, but now it'd be proper awkward." Even though my tone was light, my stomach churned with guilt at the thought of the over fifty text messages I had ignored.

Jasper reached across the table to squeeze my hand before the feeling could take over. "For what it's worth, I'm glad they sent you here."

"Yeah, me too," I murmured, unable to keep myself from grinning when instead of letting go, Jasper's hand stayed on top of mine.

His nails were painted silver today, matching the rings on his fingers and the lip piercing that glinted in the candlelight. Looking at him with his hair tousled from the wind, a flush on his cheeks from the heat inside the restaurant and the sleeves of his sweater pushed up to his elbows, I suddenly couldn't remember why I had ever found him intimidating.

Both of us jumped when Giovanni suddenly appeared at our table again. "Pizza salami and penne all'arrabbiata for you boys. *Buon appetito!*"

"*Grazie,*" Jasper replied. I was disgustingly endeared by his attempt to imitate an Italian accent and had to consciously force myself to stop staring and focus on my food instead.

However, it was only a few seconds before a strange choking noise made me look up again. Jasper was staring down at his pasta with a fearful expression, his face two shades redder than it had been a moment ago.

"Everything okay?" I inquired.

"Uh-huh. Good pasta."

I went back to my pizza, which tasted just as good as the last time I had been here. Jasper continued eating as well and for a moment the only sound was the soft music and the chattering of the other patrons. That was until Jasper suddenly slammed his fist down on the table.

"Putain!" he choked out.

"What is it?"

"The pasta." He blinked rapidly, fanning his face with one hand. "It's so spicy, oh my God."

Never Kiss your Roommate

Curious if it really was that bad, I reached across the table and tried it as well. Almost immediately, my mouth began to tingle. "Oh wow. Are you sure you can eat that?"

Even though he looked like every inch of his body revolted against it, Jasper nodded and brought the next fork of steaming pasta to his mouth. "I'm okay."

"Really? You're turning red."

"It's—" He broke off, coughing uncontrollably. In a cracking voice, he wheezed, "It's fine."

By now, I couldn't hold back a laugh. "Jas, you're literally crying. Just stop eating."

Jasper lifted a hand to his face to find it wet with tears. A string of French fell from his lips before he reached for his glass and gulped down half of it in one swig.

"Excuse me," I said, waving Giovanni to our table. "Could we have some milk? Oh, and do you have ice cream?"

Giovanni looked from Jasper to me—and started laughing out loud. "Oh, bambino, I knew this was going to go like this."

A moment later, he reappeared with a bowl of chocolate ice cream and a glass of milk that Jasper downed right away.

"Are you all right?" I asked.

"Yes," Jasper rasped, his face slowly returning to its normal color. "It's just my pride that's bruised."

Wheezing, I leaned back in my chair. "Mate, this was the funniest thing I've seen in *weeks*."

"*Mate*?" he asked miserably. "This really diminished my sex appeal that much, huh?"

"No, it didn't."

I wasn't lying. I treasured each of these moments when his perfect appearance gave way to this version of him that only few people got to see. Like the way he had looked at me when I helped him during his panic attack; or the smudge of paint on his cheek; or him stumbling through his room searching for his glasses; or his nerves before the play. They didn't make me want him any less; on the contrary, with each of them, I liked him a little more. I supposed that this was the thing that all those romance books Evelyn read were talking about—true affection was to like someone not *despite* their flaws, but *because* of them.

Attraction, I corrected myself. *Attraction, nothing more.*

We left Giovanni's a few moments later. On some unspoken agreement, we made our way to the park we'd been to with Evelyn last time we were in town together, only stopping at the same little shop as last time to buy a cheap bottle of wine with the loose change from the restaurant.

"Comes in handy that you're eighteen, old man." Jasper chuckled as he opened the bottle.

"Shut up."

"God." Jasper grimaced after his first two sips. He was propped up on one elbow in the grass, facing me. "This tastes horrible. My French parents would be appalled."

Laughing, I took the bottle out of his grasp. It really did taste like it cost exactly three pounds, flat and acidic.

"You know," Jasper suddenly said. "I was thinking that I could come out to my parents when they come here for the Winter Banquet. If they actually come for once, that is."

"That sounds good," I said. "Why wouldn't they come?"

Jasper shrugged. In the dark, his eyes were bottomless pools with depths the light of the streetlamps behind the wall a few feet away couldn't reach. "There's always something stopping them. They're both surgeons, so they don't have a ton of time. My sisters will definitely be there though, so I can at least introduce you to some of my family."

I almost choked on the sip of three-pound wine at that. "You want your family to meet me?"

He sat up at that. "Would you not want that?"

"N-no . . . I mean, *yes*, I would love that, I just didn't think you'd want that."

"Why not?"

"I don't know," I said, plucking at the grass with my fingers instead of looking at him. "I just . . . didn't think this was that serious to you."

There was a moment of silence. A heartbeat later, Jasper's hand curled around my chin and gently made me look at him. "How many times do I have to tell you I like you until you believe me?" he asked. "I want to be with you. *Actually* be with you, not like the thing I had with Sammy. Which is terrifying because I've felt that way only one other time and that ended in flames."

"Why?"

"It was back in France." His voice was so quiet I could barely hear it over the whispering of the leaves. "This girl and I had been dating for almost a year when I found out she was cheating on me with one of my best friends. After that, I didn't want to get into anything serious."

"I'm sorry that happened." Jasper's hand was still cradling my chin; I turned my head to press a kiss to the inside of his wrist. Over his surprised inhale, I whispered, "I promise I won't be like them. I won't hurt you."

"I know you won't." Jasper's lips curved into a small smile. I matched it when he pulled me in for a kiss, his warm hands sliding from my chin to the back of my neck.

Normally, I wouldn't have said it out loud, but the wine and his kiss loosened my tongue. "I'm scared too."

Jasper pulled back slightly, his hands in my hair a steadying anchor. "Why?"

Because no one's ever made my heart race like this. Because the things that Evelyn finds comforting—soul mates and destiny and red threads tying people together for eternity—terrify me. Because I know nothing like this can ever last and in the end we'll crash and burn. Out loud, I only said, "I've never really been in a relationship before."

"That's okay," Jasper murmured. "We'll figure it out together."

I smiled. "Sounds good."

I leaned forward at the same time that Jasper lay back in the grass, making me topple on top of him in an ungraceful heap, but his arms wrapped around me before I could get up.

"Is this okay or am I too heavy?" I asked. "I don't want to hold you down and make you feel claustrophobic or anything."

Jasper shook his head, his hair fanned out in the grass like a halo. "This is perfect."

Splaying a hand on his chest, I leaned in again. It *was* perfect; his heart beating sure and steady beneath my palm, speeding up when my mouth met his; his lips, soft and generous, the wine somehow tasting more expensive on them; the scent of night air on his neck; the grass I plucked out of his hair when we got up to head back to the castle; his laughter when we raced up the stairs, both a little tipsy.

The only thing that wasn't perfect was the fact that we had

to split in the hallway and go to our separate rooms, but at that point, I was so blissed-out that my grin stayed firmly in place even upon seeing Gabe.

Things were so fucking good. All I had to do was stop thinking so much.

19

Evelyn

The day of Noelle's away game saw us leaving the castle in the early hours of the morning. The sun was just coming up behind the hills, bleeding orange into the deep blue sky and reflecting in the windows of the bus, which was bigger than I had expected, painted blue with Seven Hills' school emblem taking up one side. Fog was draped over the surrounding hills like a blanket and the air tasted like morning dew and winter; November had arrived and was lulling the world beyond the castle walls to sleep.

Noelle and I were standing with the rest of the basketball team, our breaths forming white puffs in the chilly morning air as we waited for everyone to arrive while a few feet away from us, the cheerleading squad was already getting onto the bus in a single file.

I jumped when I suddenly felt a hand on my shoulder. "Hey!" Amelia said. She was standing behind me with a smile, cheeks rosy from the cold. "I did not know you were coming with. Any particular reason?"

Next to me, Noelle looked like she was holding back a grin. "Oh, you know, team spirit," I lied.

"I see! Would you like to sit with me on the bus?"

"I think I'm going to sit with Noelle," I said. "But maybe we can sit together on the way back?"

Amelia's smile crumbled. "Oh. Yes, that's fine with me."

"Cool," I said and watched as she turned around and got on the bus.

A small nudge from Noelle got me moving as well. Together, we found two free seats in the back while Amelia sat down next to Elina in the front, adamantly avoiding my gaze when I passed her.

Noelle let me take the window seat before she sat down next to me. While I had to stifle a yawn, she seemed wide awake, incessantly moving around and bobbing her leg until I put a hand on her knee.

"Sorry."

"It'll be fine," I assured her. "You trained so much for this."

Noelle didn't look convinced as she looked over her shoulder at Mrs. Whitworth, who was coming along since it was the first away game of the season and was sitting next to Miss Pepperman, who had dressed all in blue to match the occasion.

The bus was almost completely full now and the bus driver was about to close the doors when a silver mop of hair poked inside.

"Apologies for being late," Jasper told the driver, his eyes raking over the rows of seats until they found us. Seth was close behind him as he strode down the aisle, both wearing matching grins.

"What are you doing here?" Noelle asked, a broad smile on her face when Jasper and Seth squeezed into the row behind us.

"What's a fan club with only one member?" Seth said, ruffling my hair.

Noelle raised an eyebrow. "Since when are you guys interested in basketball?"

"We aren't," Jasper snorted. "We just thought it would be fun to cheer you on, Daniels. Plus, who else is going to hold back Evelyn when she tries to storm onto the court again?"

"That's not going to happen," I objected. "She gave me her word to be careful."

Jasper shook his head. "Noelle doesn't know the word *careful*."

I silently disagreed, the memory of her gentle fingertips from the other night still on my skin, but didn't say anything.

"Shut up, Frenchie," Noelle said without any heat. "Believe it or not, I'd prefer to sleep in my own room instead of in the infirmary."

"Me too," I threw in.

Seth chuckled. Then, he said, "Hey, Eve, did you see the new update on The Chitter Chatter?"

"The one about you two?"

A few days ago, The Watcher had posted an entry about Seth and Jasper being together. I had read it several times, so I could recite it by memory by now:

> Seven Hills' golden boy and that one tech
> nerd are apparently now a thing. It's not like

we didn't all know that Jasper was going to
find a new boy toy soon, looking at his dating
history and the fact that there's always someone desperate enough to try to throw themselves at him, but I think no one expected
that someone to be Seth Williams. But don't
worry, @everyone that just had their hopes
of getting a piece of the infamous Jasper
Des Lauriers crushed: I'm sure he'll be on
the market again soon. After all, no one ever
manages to keep Jasper's interest for long.

I had been afraid, afterward, that anyone might give them
trouble for it, but nothing like that happened; instead, they
received smiles every time they walked down the hallway holding hands.

"No, the update of the *Hottest Students* ranking," Seth ripped
me out of my thoughts.

"I haven't seen that yet. Why, anything interesting?"

Seth and Jasper exchanged an amused glance. "You're in first
place."

"No way," I gasped. "Really?"

Noelle cocked her head. "Why so surprised? Have you never
looked into a mirror?"

"Seriously, princesse, have a little more confidence!" Jasper
said. "You and Seth are selling yourselves too short. He's in
fourth place now."

"You are?"

Seth rubbed at his neck, a sure sign that he was flustered.
"Apparently. But I honestly think it's just because The Watcher

bases the ranking on how they like certain people, not really their looks."

"You sound like you have an idea who The Watcher might be," Noelle commented, leaning a little closer. "Do you know anything we don't?"

"I have my theories," was all that Seth said, crossing his arms before his chest with a smug grin.

Jasper looked at him with an amused flicker in his eyes. "I don't take it you want to share them with us just yet?"

"No, not yet. I don't feel like I have all the evidence I need to draw a definitive conclusion yet."

Noelle raised an eyebrow and turned around in her seat again, just as the bus started moving. After a few moments of driving through the woods, past shivering trees desperately trying to cling onto their red and orange dresses, Noelle picked up her backpack and ruffled through it. She made a triumphant little noise when she found her headphones and plugged them in.

"Do you want to listen to something?" she asked me.

"Sure."

Noelle handed me the second earbud and scrolled through her music library, her face lighting up a little as she selected a song. I recognized it almost immediately as the ringtone that had sounded when her mom had called her the other night. The song was catchy and Crystal's voice was incredible, warm but rough at the same time, emotional and composed all at once.

"She's an amazing singer," I said. Luckily everyone else around us was loud enough to drown our voices out completely.

Noelle nodded, her eyes alight with something that was half pride, half longing. "I know. I always loved it when she would sing to me as a child."

Never Kiss
your Roommate

"It must be so cool to have a singer for a mom."

She shook her head. "Not always. After she got her record deal, she barely had any time for me."

"Oh." After a moment of hesitation, I asked, "What about your dad?"

"What about him?"

"You never really talk about him."

"There's not much to talk about. He got my mom pregnant when she was still in college and then split. Never called or anything. The only time we heard from him again was when Mom had her breakthrough, but she was smart enough to know he was only out for money."

"How did she get famous, anyway?" I asked.

"She had to drop out of college when she got pregnant and started working a bunch of small jobs. Wherever she went she was singing, so naturally she was singing while cleaning tables in a diner as well." Now the lilt in her voice was definitely pride. "It just so happened that this one guy who she later found out worked for a record label was having dinner there. He heard her and was pretty impressed. He asked for her number and a few weeks later my mom got an invitation to record a demo track. After that, it all went pretty quickly."

"Wow," I muttered. "I thought that kind of stuff only happens in movies."

"Right?" Noelle chuckled. "It was insane how quickly everything changed after that. Before, we were living in Brooklyn, in a tiny apartment with water damage and then all of a sudden we moved into a fucking penthouse in Manhattan and there were bodyguards following us everywhere."

"Coming to Seven Hills was a pretty big downgrade then, huh?" I laughed.

Noelle shook her head, suddenly serious. "No. It was the best decision I ever could have made."

Smiling, I linked my pinky fingers with hers where it was resting between us on the seat, concealed by her body. "I think so too."

About half an hour later, Westbridge came into view. It wasn't a castle like Seven Hills, but probably just as old, with a weathered brick façade and a tall iron gate that opened for us. Noelle was the first one to jump out of the bus, quickly followed by the rest of the team and the cheerleaders. Seth, Jasper, and I trailed after them at a more leisurely pace.

○ ○ ○

One of Westbridge's players waited for us inside the entrance hall of the old building and asked for the players to follow him to the changing rooms. While the rest of the team hurried after him, Noelle hung back for a moment.

"Good luck," I said and pulled her into a quick hug.

"Thank you. I'm glad you're here," she whispered before she let go of me.

Ruffling her hair, Jasper said, "*Bonne chance*, Daniels. I'd say break a leg, but I'm afraid you'd take that too literally."

"I sprained my ankle *one time* and this is what I get," Noelle huffed. "See you after the game."

With that she turned around, jogging after the rest of the team as they disappeared down the hallway. Seth, Jasper, and I followed Mrs. Whitworth and Miss Pepperman to the stand, where we managed to find seats in one of the first rows.

The game went by in a blur. At first it seemed like Westbridge

Never Kiss
your Roommate

were well on their way to winning, but as the minutes ticked by, Seven Hills slowly but surely gained the upper hand.

"Seven Hills takes the lead again, thanks to another three-pointer by Noelle Daniels," the nasal-sounding announcer said. "Come on, Westbridge, we've got two minutes left to turn this thing around!"

Jasper, Seth, and I cheered loudly, despite the dirty looks from everyone around us. Noelle grinned over at us and reached up to tighten her ponytail.

At this point, I wasn't even actively watching the game anymore. My eyes stayed glued on her the entire time, watching as she sprinted across the court and shouted commands, a smirk on her face as she stole the ball from Westbridge's players and scored point after point.

I only looked up at the scoreboard when the buzzer went off again, this time for Westbridge.

"And Westbridge catches up! Come on, guys, one more point and we—"

Even before he could finish his sentence, the crowd suddenly went wild. Noelle had snatched the ball from one of Westbridge's players who had been in the middle of attempting another attack on Seven Hills and had somehow made him stumble over his own two feet.

Now she was charging towards their half of the court until she reached the defense line. I still had no clue how basketball worked, but it looked like she was in a good position to score; a little far away but I was sure that she could've done it.

However, instead of doing it herself, she suddenly passed to a guy a few feet ahead of her. He looked a little startled at suddenly getting the ball because, like me, he had probably expected her to try to score on her own. Finally, a grin spread on his face and he threw the ball.

The buzzer got completely drowned out by the outrage that broke out around us as he scored. A few seconds later, the buzzer sounded another time, this time signaling the end of the game.

"They did it!" Jasper yelled over the noise.

Seth answered, but I was barely listening to them. Down on the court, the basketball team was tangled in a victorious huddle; they were jumping and cheering, arm in arm, one of the cheerleaders running towards her boyfriend, who met her in a victorious kiss.

I tore my eyes away from them and searched for Noelle instead, only to find her already looking up at me, jerking her head towards the door while holding up ten fingers.

A moment later, the basketball team and the cheerleaders left the court and headed for the locker rooms. I waited for exactly ten minutes, then I got up.

"Where are you going?" Seth asked, looking up at me with a puzzled look on his face.

"I, uh . . . have to use the restroom," I lied. "I'll meet you at the bus."

Jasper raised a brow at me, clearly knowing what was going on, but didn't say anything.

Finding the locker rooms wasn't as hard as I had feared; there were some signs pointing me in the right direction and the heavy stench of sweat and deodorant in the air was unmistakable.

Peeking my head through the door labeled *Guests: Girls*, I was met with the sight of an empty changing room, misty with the humidity from the showers around the corner, and then Noelle, now wearing sweatpants and a hoodie that her wet hair was dripping onto.

Never Kiss your Roommate

Before I could even say anything, she was already crashing into me, winding her arms around my neck.

"We won against fucking Westbridge!" she laughed, her voice slightly muffled against my shoulder. "Did you see their stupid faces? Holy shit. The last time Seven Hills won against them was in *2001!*"

Wrapping my arms around her, I pressed a kiss to her temple. "You were amazing."

Noelle pulled back, her eyes bright with victory. "Can I kiss you?"

"You don't always have to ask," I softly said.

"Yeah, I do," she murmured before she pushed me up against the lockers and kissed me with so much force my legs went weak.

Noelle was rougher than usual, all her caution thrown overboard as she pressed up against me, teeth biting at my lip and her hands firmly holding me in place. My hands found their way to her hips, pulling her even closer, until I could feel her heart racing against mine. For a few moments, my world narrowed down to nothing but her lips and her hands and the feeling of her eyelashes tickling my cheek—that was until I heard the door opening. My eyes fluttered open just in time to see it fall shut again, followed by the sound of footsteps sprinting away.

Noelle's head whipped around immediately. "Shit. Did you see who that was?"

The humidity in the room suddenly felt stifling, like there wasn't enough oxygen to fill my lungs, just barely enough to whisper, "No."

Noelle turned back to me. "Hey, don't worry," she said, brushing a strand of hair behind my ear. "It was probably just one of those Westbridge losers. I'm sure they didn't even think much of it."

"Probably," I murmured.

Noelle reluctantly let go of me and grabbed her bag. "Come on, we should go."

I nodded, quickly fixing my hair in one of the mirrors before I followed her outside, still feeling a little shaky.

Almost everyone was on the bus already, except for a few boys who were still stowing away their things. Mrs. Whitworth and Miss Pepperman were waiting for us when we arrived, both wearing bright smiles.

"Well done, Noelle!" Mrs. Whitworth exclaimed. To my surprise, she pulled Noelle into a tight hug, which she returned after a second of shock. "I'm so proud of you."

When Noelle stepped back, her eyes were shining. "Thank you, Mrs. Whitworth."

"What talent!" Miss Pepperman chirped. "Those boys can only dream of playing like you!"

Noelle laughed, a little bit flustered. A moment later, Mrs. Whitworth shooed us onto the bus. While Noelle sat with her teammates, I slid into the seat next to Amelia. "Hey!"

Amelia didn't look at me. "Hello."

"Good game, huh?"

She nodded.

"Is everything okay?" I inquired.

"Of course," she said. "I'm just tired."

I had a feeling she was still a little cross because I hadn't sat with her on the way here, but didn't say anything. While she closed her eyes, I glanced over my shoulder at Noelle. She was laughing with the rest of the team, still buzzing with energy.

Never Kiss your Roommate

When our eyes met, her smile softened around the edges, became something only ever reserved for me.

In the row in front of her, Jasper had his eyes closed and was resting his head on Seth's shoulder, their hands intertwined while Seth flipped through a well-loved copy of *Dr. Jekyll and Mr. Hyde*. I tried to push away the pang of jealousy that ran through me at the sight. After all, it had been my decision to keep what Noelle and I had a secret. I had been paralyzed by the fear that the nightmares I still had—though much less frequent—would become a reality once again, and keeping our relationship to myself felt safe in the same way that never flying on a plane for fear of it crashing did—I was aware that I was missing out, but the looming dread of the unpredictable persisted.

In my mind, my feelings for Noelle were like spring water, pure and healing, gentle but insistent in the way they kept rushing onward. As long as no one knew about them, they couldn't be poisoned, couldn't be turned into a weapon that destroyed the confidence and the self-acceptance I had spent the last months painstakingly piecing back together, one tiny fragment at a time.

It seemed stupid now to be afraid to hold her hand in public while Jasper and Seth and so many others at our school did it without thinking twice, without repercussions.

If I was honest with myself, I felt like it was pretty obvious something was going on between us anyway, so when I thought back to the sound of the door opening in the locker room a few minutes earlier, I suddenly didn't feel any fear.

The dam holding the stream back had been dying to break for a while now. I wanted to hold her hand and hug her and not make up excuses to be present at her games. I wanted to put my head on her shoulder in public like Jasper did and be comfortable enough to fall asleep. I wanted to run onto the court like the cheerleader earlier and kiss her when she won, spin her around like in a romantic comedy, show the whole world how proud of her I was, regardless of what anyone might have said.

I wasn't ashamed of us. I wasn't ashamed of *me*. I had the privilege to live in a space where I could express myself without fear of danger; maybe it was time to step out of the glass closet I had locked myself in once and for all.

20

Evelyn

Noelle Daniels caught with yet another hookup.

These words were the first thing I read when I woke up on Sunday morning. Below them was a photo that showed the girls' locker room at Westbridge, shot through a tiny crack in the door. It was blurry, as if the photographer had already been in the process of turning, but Noelle was still clearly recognizable, eyes bright with triumph and an uncharacteristically soft smile on her lips.

I, on the other hand, wasn't; a black box had been edited in to conceal my entire body, so it wasn't clear who Noelle was pushing against the lockers.

Below it was an article, shorter than most others, but even snider in tone.

If you've been following The Chitter Chatter for a while (or have a set of working eyes), you might know that Noelle Daniels is what some might call a slut. To me, it seems like none of her relationships have ever been anything serious. It's always a few weeks of snogging at parties and then she drops them like nothing's ever happened. Honestly, I have started to doubt if Noelle Daniels is even capable of truly loving someone other than herself.

Now, she's found her next victim. I think I'll let you figure this one out yourselves, but one thing is for sure: the person deserves much better than Noelle.

(Thank you to the anonymous submitter for this photo.)

Before I could even process these words, which stood in such stark contrast to the picture that it made my head spin, the door burst open and Noelle rushed inside. "Evelyn! Have you looked outside?"

I lowered the phone as she crossed the room, a gust of cold air following her. She had left for her morning run while I had still been fast asleep; now she stood next to my bed with her hair in a ponytail and a flush on her cheeks.

"What is it?"

"See for yourself," she said, icy fingers grabbing my hand to pull me to my feet.

My eyes widened when I saw what had caused the bright grin

Never Kiss your Roommate

on her face. Overnight, the landscape around Seven Hills had transformed into a Christmas postcard. Behind the ice flowers glittering on the window, I could see the dusting of snow that covered the hills and trees, a perfectly even blanket that was marred only by Noelle's footprints that led around the castle.

Glancing over my shoulder at Noelle, who was beaming like it was her birthday, I remembered how she had told me that winter was her favorite season. Now, pressing her palms against the glass and breathing against it to be able to look outside, she truly did look like this was the best thing that had ever happened to her.

"I can't believe you went for a run in this cold," I said, unable to hide the slightest bit of concern from my voice.

"It was so nice! At least until I couldn't feel my toes anymore. And my fingers. And the tip of my nose."

Chuckling, I stepped closer to drop a kiss onto said nose, only for her to tilt her head and lean in for a real kiss. Her lips were so cold I felt like mine were going numb with it, making me let go of her after only a few seconds. "You're freezing. Go have a shower."

"Stop fussing, I'm fine." She leaned in again and I closed my eyes, certain she was going for another kiss. Instead, she wrapped her arms around me and slid her ice-cold hands under my shirt.

I stumbled back with a yelp. "Noelle! Shower, now."

"You're worse than my mom and Jasper combined," she huffed, but for once did as I said, grabbing a few clothes and disappearing in the bathroom while I got dressed. When I joined her, Noelle was already doing her makeup and offered me a smile in the fogged-up mirror.

Wrapping my arms around her from behind, I asked, "Hey . . . have you read the last update on The Chitter Chatter?"

"The one about me?"

"Yes."

"I have," she said with a shrug.

I rested my chin on her shoulder. "Does it not bother you?"

"Not really. The Watcher didn't reveal your identity, so it's all good. I'm used to them talking shit about me." I didn't reply, only watched as she applied highlighter to the corners of her eyes and the tip of her nose. The sight made me think back to that night in my bed, her smile when she had done the same to me, her voice as soft as her touch as she murmured *This is the best part.*

"They're wrong," I said, my outburst sudden enough to make Noelle jump.

"Who's wrong about what?"

"The Watcher. You're not a slut. And you're not incapable of loving others," I said. "You love *so much.* I don't understand how they can't see it."

Noelle was silent for a moment. Then, with a quiet sigh, she put down her brush and met my eyes in the mirror again. "Evelyn . . . I know it's not true. *You* know it's not true. I don't care what anyone else thinks."

I was silent for a moment before I put my hands on her waist, urging her to turn around. "I've been thinking. I don't want to hide this anymore, Elle."

Her eyes widened a little as understanding washed over her face. "Are you sure? You don't have to feel this way just because you're scared of what The Watcher might know. Outing someone is too far, even for them."

"I'm sure," I said. "This isn't some kind of dirty little secret that no one must ever know about. It was stupid of me to treat it like that in the first place."

"But you had your reasons," she murmured. "There's no shame in being in the closet if it's for your own well-being. There's no shame in being in the closet, *period*."

"I know," I said. "But I can't let what happened in the past hold me back forever, right? That would mean they won. And in doing this we're taking the power away from The Watcher. We're doing it on our own terms." I paused, suddenly unsure. "Unless you don't want anyone to know?"

"Bullshit," Noelle immediately said. "Of course I want that. Not being able to kiss you whenever I want *sucks*."

"So we're doing this?" I asked, my heart leaping at the thought.

"Of course we're fucking doing this."

My chuckle got lost in her mouth when her lips captured mine, soft and reassuring. She pulled back for a heartbeat to whisper, "I'm proud of you," and somehow those four words were enough to loosen the knot in my chest for good.

When we left the room ten minutes later, the grin was still firmly in place on both our faces. Noelle's hand in mine felt like it belonged there, so much so that I wondered how I had ever gone without it. My steps were lighter now that I no longer had to suppress the urge to reach out, like an itch I couldn't scratch, and even though there was an anticipatory flutter in my chest, it was nothing like the anxiety I would have felt two months ago.

Control was the key, I realized. For the first time, I was owning my narrative, without fear or restraint, and now there was nothing anyone could do to weaponize it. And besides, this time I wasn't alone. Noelle's hand held onto mine firmly, unapologetically, her boots hitting the floor with the determination of a soldier charging into battle. With her next to me, my back immediately straightened, chin raised, as if fear wasn't even an option.

The reactions were all the same. In the entrance hall, we attracted some curious glances and whispers, but no one paused to look at us or met our eyes with anything different than a smile. I wasn't surprised. With Noelle staring people down like she was practically challenging them to say something stupid to her face, I wouldn't have dared to act up either.

Jasper and Seth all but cheered when we neared their table, prompting Noelle to give an exaggerated bow before she tugged me onto the bench next to her, her left hand staying intertwined with mine all throughout breakfast.

This was how easy it could be then.

o o o

As it was a Sunday and none of us had any schoolwork to do, we spent most of the afternoon outside. After a walk through the Christmas-postcard woods that Mrs. Whitworth had encouraged all the students to visit after lunch, we made our way back to the castle. The snow crunched beneath our boots, glistening in the afternoon sun, the air crisp and cold enough to make all of us pink-cheeked. I hadn't prepared for such a cold winter when I had packed my bags in September, but Noelle had found a pair of mittens in her drawer; now each of us was wearing one while we walked holding hands, keeping the other tucked safely inside the pockets of our coats. No one really spoke much, all of us too busy marveling at the icicles hanging off the trees and the

Never Kiss your Roommate

autumn leaves encrusted in snow. It seemed like the world had been laid to sleep, dozing beneath the blanket of white that had settled, quiet and peaceful.

That was until a snowball suddenly came towards us at the speed of light, too fast for any of us to duck, and hit Seth right in the head. He made a soft sound of surprise, rubbing his temple.

"Okay, who the fuck threw that?" Jasper asked, dramatically twisting around to spot the perpetrator.

Noelle hid her grin behind her hand when a bunch of year-eight students took off running. I had to laugh when she bent down and gathered some snow in her hands, quickly and expertly forming a snowball. She aimed it right at Jasper, and it definitely would've hit him if he hadn't stepped aside to dodge it in the last second, making it fly right at the person standing behind him.

Amelia shrieked as the snowball hit her right on the forehead, one hand flying up to touch the skin as if she expected to find blood there.

"Sorry, Amanda!" Noelle shouted, clearly looking not sorry at all.

Amelia didn't respond. Instead, she stomped inside without more than a glare, slamming the door behind her.

"Good job, Noelle," Seth commented, earning himself a snowball to the chest.

Jasper was already crouching down to form another. Gracefully rising to stand, he declared, "Oh, this means war."

Noelle looked far too excited as it hit her shoulder, giving her an excuse to immediately throw another one at Jasper.

Within seconds, a vicious snowball fight broke out, with Jasper and Seth battling Noelle and me. I was terrible at aiming and kept missing Jasper and Seth, but Noelle was good enough for the both of us.

We probably would have gone on until the sun went down if Miss Pepperman hadn't appeared at the top of the steps to tell us to get inside if we wanted some hot chocolate.

Noelle didn't need to be told twice and immediately dragged me inside after her, Jasper and Seth in tow. After we got ourselves some steaming hot chocolate from the Great Hall, we made our way to the common room.

It was one of the largest rooms of the castle, located on the first floor of the west wing. Students of all ages lazed around on worn-down leather couches and clunky armchairs, playing board games or poring over books. Every once in a while, a teacher would poke their head through the door to make sure that there was no chaos, sometimes sitting down to help with schoolwork or simply chat with the older students.

We managed to hunt down a couch and two armchairs close to the crackling fireplace—the heat it emanated, along with the hot chocolate trickling down my throat, quickly thawed my freezing limbs. With the chill draining out of my body and Noelle's arm around my shoulders, it was so easy to close my eyes and simply relax into the feeling of *warmth*, lulled by the chatter all around us and my friends' quiet conversation.

I probably could have fallen asleep like that, if Seth hadn't suddenly murmured, "Is it just me or are people staring at us?"

"They've been staring all day," Noelle replied, not even bothering to open her eyes.

Meanwhile I suddenly felt a pit in my stomach. People *had* been looking at us all day, but not like this, not like there was something to be genuinely shocked by.

Never Kiss
your Roommate

My neck tingled as I felt more than a few eyes on me. Some girls from the year below us were staring in our direction, whispering to each other and not even looking away when I met their eyes. A little farther to the left, two guys were laughing, one of them pointing at us. Even some of the younger students were grinning at us, gawking so obviously that there was no doubt about it—wherever I looked, people looked back at me.

Jasper swearing in French was what interrupted my frantic search for a hint as to what was going on, his phone in one hand. Seth, who was sitting in the armchair next to him and could therefore see what Jasper was reading, paled a little.

"What is it?" I asked.

"It's um . . . it's The Chitter Chatter," he said. "There was an update fifteen minutes ago."

"What does it say then?" Noelle sighed.

After exchanging an unsure glance with Seth, Jasper hesitantly handed her the phone. Leaning over her shoulder, I read:

Well, that didn't take very long. Evelyn and Noelle solved the little guessing game I gave you losers themselves before any of you truly had to use your gray matter.

Remember how all of us thought Noelle would rip that sweet girl to pieces when she first arrived here? How we were honestly scared for her well-being? How we thought she wouldn't last more than a few weeks with Noelle as her roommate?

Funny how the tables have turned, huh? I'm not sure for how long exactly they've been getting it on, but that's beside the point. Their little fling is nothing compared to the real big secret Noelle has been hiding from us.

Or should I say: That Ashley has been hiding from us?

Yes, you read that right. Her real name is Ashley Danell, born and raised in New York, daughter to the semifamous R&B singer Crystal Danell. If you had to look up who that is, then welcome to the club. Danell is quite a big number in the US, but apparently too mediocre to make it all the way to Europe. Just like her daughter, she's probably just popular because of good looks and a decent amount of charisma.

At least now we know why it seems like Noelle thinks she's better than everyone else here, hm? I wonder what it was that made her change her name? Bets are now on . . .

Noelle took longer than me to read it. My lungs felt like all the air was being crushed out of them as I studied the succession of emotions on her face, vague curiosity turning into amusement turning into shock turning into something that simply looked . . . numb. By the time she handed the phone back to Jasper her hands were shaking, eyes glassy.

"What does this mean?" Jasper asked. He had the same wide-eyed look I was sure I was wearing.

Noelle shook her head, tongue clamped down by panic. Her empty mug clattered to the floor as she got up, but she didn't

Never Kiss
your Roommate

pause, didn't look like she noticed at all. Ignoring Seth's questioning gaze, I picked it up and hurried after her.

I caught up with her in the girls' wing, almost at our door. "Noelle," I said, reaching for her sleeve. "What's going on?"

When she turned around it was with tears welling in her eyes, a guttural sob tearing free from her throat. Pressing a hand to her mouth, she shook her head.

"Hey," I said, gently taking hold of her shoulders. "Talk to me. How bad is this?"

"Bad," she choked out. "Really, really bad."

I fought down the wave of panic that threatened to crash over me. "Is there something I can do?" I broke off when I realized how little I knew about this, that I truly had no idea what her real name being revealed meant, or if there was anything that could be done now, so I added, "Someone I can call?"

"No," she whispered.

"What about your mom?" I frantically asked.

"No, she . . . She's in the middle of touring." She leaned her back against the wall, drawing in a shaky breath as she blinked away the tears. "I'm probably being overdramatic. I'm sure it's not a big deal."

"It is a big deal if you almost have a panic attack." I was silent for a few moments, just watching her as she tried to calm down, her chest rising and falling with every ragged breath. There were a million questions I wanted to ask, but looking at her, I knew that she wouldn't answer any of them. Instead I said, "I want to help you. Is it okay if I do?"

Noelle stilled. Inhaled, exhaled, slower this time. Then her eyes met mine, finally looking *at* me and not through, and she nodded.

"How about you relax," I slowly said, taking her hand, "And I do your makeup?"

Noelle looked confused at hearing her own words echoed back to her before her eyes lit up with understanding and something in her shoulders seemed to loosen a little. Her voice was raspy when she murmured a shaky "Okay," her hand gripping onto mine hard enough to hurt.

I didn't say anything and I didn't pull away. Instead, I let her fingernails imprint little half moons into the palm of my hand and led her into our room, where I gently pushed her down onto the bed and got to work.

Noelle didn't say another word that night.

21

Seth

Over the next week, I watched Noelle unravel. After the article about her mother came out, she was different—subdued, almost. She didn't talk much when I was around, didn't eat a lot, constantly looked over her shoulder in the corridors, paranoid, like she expected the shadows in the alcoves to pounce on her or the ceiling to crumble over her head.

"She's like she was when she first arrived here," Jasper told me one evening.

"Do you know why?"

"No. She doesn't talk to me about this stuff."

Evelyn didn't know what was going on either. Even she found Noelle hard to get through to; she had told me that she sometimes woke up to Noelle having nightmares now instead of the other way around. What they were about, she never told Evelyn.

Instead, she spent most of her time in the gym, either training with the basketball team or having self-defense lessons, which she asked for almost every other day. I didn't tell Evelyn what it looked like because I was sure she had realized it, too, by now—Noelle seemed like she was preparing for battle.

While Evelyn and Jasper tried to get through to her, I focused not on *what* was going on with her but the *why*. Or rather, the *who*. By now I had a pretty good idea of who The Watcher was. I had suspected it from the beginning, but the recent updates on The Chitter Chatter had affirmed my little theory.

On Friday, I decided to finally do something about it; before class, I grabbed Amelia by the sleeve and tugged her into one of the quieter alcoves.

"What do you want, Seth?" she sighed, sending a pointed glance at the watch on her wrist. "Class begins in less than ten minutes."

Tightening my grip on her sleeve, I said, "It's you, isn't it?"

"Seth, I do not have time for this right now. What are you talking about?"

"Don't play dumb when we both know you aren't," I said, narrowing my eyes at her. "You're The Watcher. Am I right?"

"I . . . what?"

"You heard me." I took a step closer; she took a step back but didn't get far with the wall at her back. "You're the person who writes The Chitter Chatter. It makes sense because it started a year after you arrived here. And being on the student council and the cheerleading team, you find out a lot about other people around here."

Amelia shook her head, but the flicker of fear in her steel-gray eyes betrayed her. "That is ridiculous, I would never—"

Never Kiss your Roommate

"You fancy Evelyn, right?" I cut her off. "That's why you were crying the other day. She told me that before we found you, she was speaking to her parents about Noelle on the phone. You heard her. And that's also why she's been climbing in the *Hottest Students* ranking."

By now, all the color had drained from her face. "Seth, I—"

I ignored her interjection and continued. "Then you put me higher because I was there to comfort you as well. Jasper is just there because you know everyone finds him attractive. Same with Noelle. Or maybe you fancied her as well at some point? Doesn't matter. Then last week you saw Evelyn and Noelle in the locker room at Westbridge. I still have no idea where the hell you got it from, but you were hurt, so you wanted to get back at Noelle by releasing that information about her mom. Am I right?"

Amelia only gaped at me, eyes bulging as she struggled to find words. I had been fishing with my dad once when I was thirteen; she reminded me of the trout we had caught, fresh out of the water, thrashing around on the land. Then, I had felt so much pity I had begged my dad to throw the fish back into the lake in tears. Looking at Amelia, all I felt was a grim sense of satisfaction.

"I do not—I am not like that," she finally managed to stutter, clutching her books tighter to her chest. "I do not fancy Evelyn."

I couldn't hold back a disbelieving laugh. "*That* is your biggest concern? Not the fact that you've been cyberbullying the entire school for the last two years?"

Amelia shook her head. Her face was pale, her expression impenetrable. "Please . . ." she said. "Meet me after the class is over. I will explain everything to you, I swear it."

I considered her for a moment. Taking in her trembling hands and shuffling feet, I felt like I already had all the information I needed. Still, it couldn't hurt to hear her side of the story. "Fine. I'll meet you in the room we found you last time."

She nodded before abruptly turning around and hurrying towards our classroom. I followed her at a more leisurely pace and sat down in my familiar seat between Evelyn and Jasper, who didn't notice the anxious glance Amelia threw my way.

The next hours seemed to crawl by at a snail's pace. I was buzzing with curiosity about what it was she had to say and couldn't help but look her way all throughout class; whereas her hand was constantly raised on every other day, she was unusually quiet today, her face pale as she stared down at her notepad, mechanically scribbling things down every now and then. When the bell rang, Amelia was the first one to get up and bolt out of the room. I stayed behind for a moment, slowly putting away my things before I swung my backpack over my shoulder and headed to the classroom where Evelyn and I had found her crying almost two weeks ago.

Amelia was already there, leaning against the windowsill like she had been last time. Only this time she wasn't crying and she also wasn't shaking like she had been this morning. Instead, there was a look of quiet determination on her face that I didn't know what to make of.

"So." I pulled the door shut behind me. "What do you have to say for yourself?"

"Nothing," she quietly said.

"Nothing?" I echoed, lifting an eyebrow as I came to a halt in front of her, my hands in my pockets. "Come on, Amelia, at least *try* to convince me. Do you have any excuse? An alibi

Never Kiss your Roommate

for what you've been up to whenever a new entry was posted? Anything?"

Amelia pushed herself away from the window and walked towards me, meeting me in the center of the room. "I do have an alibi."

Studying her, I felt like Sherlock when he first met Irene Adler; I could read absolutely nothing from the look on her face.

"Sure you do," I snorted. "What is it?"

Amelia took a step closer. Inhaled a shaky breath. Said, "You."

I saw her hands reaching out for me, her face leaning closer, but my brain refused to believe what was happening until her mouth was on mine.

Her kiss was closemouthed and firm, lips pressing against mine without moving, her hands hovering just above my shoulders without actually touching me. I could feel her sticky lip gloss against my mouth, hear her breathing shakily through her nose, smell her perfume, a sickeningly sweet, flowery scent that reminded me of the bouquets of white lilies people had at funerals.

I pushed her away, forceful enough to send her stumbling, but it already felt too late.

Suddenly, *I* was the trout. How hadn't I realized before that she was in her element again? Now I was the one gasping for breath, sickness coiling in my stomach as I furiously rubbed the back of my hand over my mouth, as if that could make it undone.

"Why . . . Why the hell did you do that?" I choked out. "I'm with Jasper. You—you *know* that."

"I do," she whispered.

I tried to make sense of anything that had just happened, but her face was like a house that had all its windows shuttered.

When I came up with nothing, I abruptly turned around and stormed into the hallway, desperate to leave the situation and her face and the overwhelming scent of her perfume behind.

Jasper. I had to tell Jasper.

However, before I even made it to the boys' wing, I was distracted by the commotion going on in the entrance hall.

A day after the article about Crystal Danell had been posted on The Chitter Chatter, it had been picked up by a bigger local news outlet. As a result, several news teams had turned up at Seven Hills over the past few days, swarming around the front yard and filming the outside, stopping students in their tracks when they entered and left.

So far, none of them had dared to come inside. Now, a camera team of three stood at the bottom of the stairs, blocked by Mrs. Whitworth, who was standing on the bottom step with her hands on her hips.

The warm smile she usually wore was replaced by a furious glare, her voice shaking with anger as she said, ". . . but to try to invade the privacy of a seventeen-year-old like this? This isn't journalism, this is a *disgrace*. You should be ashamed, every one of you!"

The two male cameramen shuffled around in embarrassment. The female reporter, on the other hand, wasn't ready to accept defeat. "Please, Mrs. Whitworth, just a few questions. Being the headmistress, surely you knew about her real identity? Did Crystal ever come here to visit Ashley? Did—"

"No comment."

"But—"

"No buts," Mrs. Whitworth coldly said. "I will not allow you to make a spectacle of my students. This is private property—I

Never Kiss your Roommate

will more than gladly call the police if you do not leave within the next two minutes. Have I made myself clear?"

At that, the reporter finally lowered the hand that was waving the microphone under Mrs. Whitworth's nose. "Come on, guys," she sighed and shuffled away with the two cameramen in tow. "We'll try again later."

I shot them a dark look as I passed by them. When I reached the staircase, Mrs. Whitworth was still glaring after them, breathing heavily, her hand clutching the banister. "Looks like I'll have to call the police," she murmured. "Unbelievable. *Unbelievable.*"

I briefly debated whether I should tell her how brilliantly she had handled the situation, but then I remembered why I was going to the boys' wing in the first place: *Jasper.*

On the way to his room, I ran a hand through my hair a few times and made sure that my tie was straight, rubbing my hand over my lips once again, still slightly sticky with Amelia's lip gloss. Then I lifted my hand to knock at his door.

There was music sounding from inside, loud enough to make the floorboards beneath my feet vibrate, a dark melody with sultry French vocals. I knocked again, thinking that maybe he hadn't heard it over the loud chorus. Again, nothing.

A few guys from my class came down the hallway, murmuring to each other as they passed me. I suddenly felt the same self-consciousness that had followed me everywhere during my first weeks here. I looked like a loser, standing in front of my boyfriend's door and not being let in.

Two more knocks and the music inside quieted down all of a sudden. Heavy steps neared the door before it finally swung open.

I stepped forward, ready to slip past him into the room, but the look on his face stopped me.

Jasper was clad in only his black pants and the white shirt of his school uniform, which was partly unbuttoned, the sleeves rolled up to his elbows. Through the hair that was falling into his eyes, I could see them staring back at me, dark and unreadable in the dim light in the corridor.

"Hey," I said. "Is everything—"

Jasper cut me off before I could finish my sentence. "You're really going to ask me if everything is okay right now?" he asked, every word articulated sharply and laced with venom.

I blinked. "I just came to talk to you about—"

"Amelia?" Usually, every one of Jasper's sentences was drenched in amusement, like he was in on an inside joke that everyone else didn't know. Now, the dry laugh he let out didn't hold a shred of humor. "Don't bother. I already know what I need to know."

I swallowed as realization hit me. "It's already on The Chitter Chatter."

He nodded. His hand was gripping onto the door frame so tightly his knuckles turned white, his gaze as steely as the rings on his fingers.

"Jasper, I . . . I didn't mean for it to happen," I murmured. Even as I was saying it, I knew that it wasn't enough. "And I came here right away to tell you, I swear—"

He shook his head. "I just don't understand how you could do it after I told you what happened. After you *knew* that this was exactly what I was afraid of."

My eyes stung as I remembered that night in the park: *I promise I won't be like them. I won't hurt you.*

I know you won't.

"Please, Jas," I whispered. "I promise it's not like that. Just let me in and we can talk about everything—"

"I've already let you in too many times." He gave another throaty laugh, a terrible sound that made the hairs on the back of my neck stand on end. "I guess you really were serious when you said you didn't believe in love, huh? Stupid of me to think that had changed."

The look on his face was like my father's when he had stared at my mother and asked for an explanation for her behavior. There was a similar vein in his neck, blood rushing rushing rushing, and I suddenly felt like I had slipped out of time, out of place. I knew that I had to say something, anything to explain this to him, but the only thing my brain supplied was a steady stream of *I fucked up I fucked up I fucked up and now I can't fix it.*

Jasper studied me, waiting. I wanted to do what I had done during my parents' arguments as a kid—turn around and hide away in my room to cry—but I couldn't do that because now *I* was the one on the other side of the battlefield, even though I had no idea how I had gotten here. The thought of it made me feel sick.

When a few seconds had passed and I didn't say anything, Jasper gave a nod, the jerky motion betraying the disinterested look on his face, and said, "All right. I think it's best if you go now."

"Jasper, wait—"

On instinct, I reached out to grab his sleeve, but he immediately ripped his arm out of my grasp. "Don't touch me," he said, voice alarmingly quiet. "I don't want anything to do with you, Williams."

Before I could utter a word, the door slammed shut. A second later, the music rose again, now even louder than before.

I turned around in a trance. The corridor before me was blurry and I almost bumped into someone as I walked back to my room, too focused on watching my shadow on the wall next to me. It was no longer *JasperandSeth*. Just a single shadow person with strangely long legs and slouchy posture, walking like the world was resting on his shoulders. Not in a cool, heroic Atlas way. Atlas was strong. Without Jasper, Shadow Seth looked pathetic.

I wasn't Sherlock Holmes or Hercule Poirot or even bloody Miss Marple. I was the kind of unimportant side character who would be found dead at the beginning of the novel, the talk of the town when the detective arrived. *Have you heard about the body they found? Young lad walked into the trap with open eyes. A right idiot, him.*

When I made it to my room, Gabe wasn't there for once and couldn't witness me crumbling onto the bed. I pulled out my phone, unsurprised to see a new notification from The Chitter Chatter.

Seth cheats on Jasper with Amelia Campbell.

I wanted to climb out of my skin and throw the useless bag of bones into the basement next to the skeleton. It had been right all along. *Love like you dream of doesn't exist. Never has, never will. Sooner or later, everything goes to shit. It's best to accept it now.* I thought I had accepted it, but the crushing weight on my chest suggested something else.

My subconscious had tried to warn me. I should have paid closer attention, should have known that it was in my DNA to

Never Kiss
your Roommate

mess things up. I wasn't better than my parents. I was exactly the fucking same.

With that thought playing in my head like a broken record, I, for the first time since I had come here, clicked onto my father's messages. There were over fifty, all different stages of exasperation. The last one, which I had received two days ago, read: *Hi, Seth. I know you're probably not going to respond, but I wanted to let you know that I finished moving. I'm renting a little apartment a few blocks away from our old house. It's not huge, but there's a spare room here for you if you want it. You don't have to decide right now. Just please for once let me know if you read this. Love, Dad.*

Staring down at it, I had to choke down a hysterical laugh. This was what I had wanted all along: to go home. The knowledge tasted of bitter irony. There was a ringing in my ears that got louder and louder, a shrill, high-pitched tone that bored itself into my skull. Belatedly, I realized that it was the sound of dialing, my phone pressed to my ear even though I hadn't consciously lifted it there.

"Hello? Seth?"

After not hearing Dad's voice for over two months, my throat constricted at the sound. He was silent for a moment. I could tell that he was listening, probably trying to at least hear my breathing.

When I finally spoke, my voice came out sounding robotic. "Hi, Dad."

"Seth! Jesus Christ, I didn't think I'd get to hear your voice again anytime soon." He let out a chuckle that sounded uncharacteristically nervous.

"Yeah. Sorry I didn't respond. Or call," I numbly said.

"I'm just glad you're speaking to me now. How are you? Is everything okay?"

"I'm fine," I ground out, even though my eyes were burning and my stomach felt sick and I couldn't get rid of the smell of Amelia's perfume that clung to my clothes and wouldn't go away. "I . . . I saw your text about your new apartment. I'm glad you found one."

"Oh, yes! It wasn't easy and it's not that great, it has water damage and stuff, but other than that it's . . . it's good!"

I nodded even though he couldn't see, blindly staring at the opposite wall, gray bricks all blurring together.

On the other end of the line, Dad cleared his throat. "So . . . were you calling to let me know you want to come back to Manchester?"

Speaking was difficult when you were choking on funeral flowers. All I got out was a shaky, "Yes."

"Okay! Okay, that's great, you're more than welcome here. What do you say, I'll call your headmistress and we can get you moved back here in time for Christmas?"

"Can I . . . can I come now? Like, right now?"

"*Right now*? Seth, did something happen?"

Yes. I ruined everything and it's all my fault. Stop sounding so bloody sympathetic. Yell at me for being such a horrible son. Tell me to stay here, tell me I can't come. Out loud, I only whispered, "Please, Dad. I want to come home."

"Of course you can come home," he muttered. "I'll call the school and let them know."

I pressed my eyes shut, exhaling shakily into the silence of the room. Through the walls, I could still hear the music from Jasper's room, my heart rattling around in my rib cage at every

Never Kiss your Roommate

beat. I wished it would stop. I wished the skeleton would come back and pluck it right out, for real this time.

"Thanks, Dad."

"Of course," he softly said. "I'll pick you up at the station tomorrow, all right? We can talk about everything then."

"Okay," I said even though it wasn't and hung up.

I got up and left the room in the same mechanical manner I had made the call, my legs carrying me to Evelyn's room seemingly without my doing. Standing in front of her door, I also heard music, but it wasn't dark or taunting, but some light and calming study sounds that immediately ceased when I knocked.

"Hey," Evelyn said. The look on her face, somewhere between pity and confusion, told me she had already read the update on The Chitter Chatter. Tugging me inside, she said, "Here, sit down. Do you want something to drink? You look pale."

"No thanks," I rasped. Instead of sitting down on her bed like she gestured for me to do, I hovered by the door. *Do it quick, like a Band-Aid.* "I just came to tell you that I'm leaving."

Evelyn froze. "What?"

"I talked to my dad. He offered to let me come home. I'm leaving tomorrow."

"Wait . . . you called your dad?"

"Yeah."

"But . . . but what about us?" Evelyn asked, an incredulous frown on her face. "What about Jasper? Are you really just going to leave like this?"

"Yeah. I think he'll appreciate it."

"Seth, you know that's not true. I know you didn't kiss Amelia. You can explain everything to him—"

I shook my head, the lump in my throat growing with every

passing second. "No. You didn't see the way he looked at me. He's not going to listen to anything I say."

"But everything can be fixed by talking if you truly love each other—"

"This isn't one of your bloody romance novels," I snapped. The words came out harsher than intended, enough to make her wince. *Nice going, Seth. Hurt everyone else who matters as well, just push them all away.* "Nothing's ever that perfect. I don't love him. And he most definitely doesn't love me anymore, if he ever did."

"But—"

"Evelyn." I gently took hold of her shoulders, trying my best to soften my voice when I lied, "It's okay. I'm not sad about it."

"I don't believe you," she whispered, twisting so that my hands fell away, useless. "And I also don't believe that you didn't feel anything for him. Do you want to know what I think?" She raised her gaze, looking me straight in the eye even though there were tears clinging to her lashes and her hands were trembling. "I think the problem isn't really that you don't believe in love. It's that you don't believe that you deserve it."

Her words felt like a punch to the gut, and I took a stumbling step back like there truly had been an impact, all the air knocked out of my lungs.

"I have to go pack my things," I said, barely hearing myself speak as I turned on my heel and let my legs carry me into the hallway. "I'll get on the first train tomorrow."

The door fell shut behind me before she could respond.

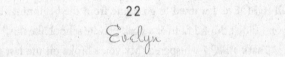

22
Evelyn

Seth departed early the next morning. He had cleared his room while it was still dark outside and now stood in the front yard with his suitcases in hand, the picture identical to when we had first arrived, except his eyes had been brighter then and instead of rain, his coat was now sprinkled with snow. We had been scared to set foot out of the front door at first, but there were no reporters in sight anymore, all of them scared away after Mrs. Whitworth had called the police last night.

"Are you sure you want to do this?" I asked. "Maybe if you wait a day or two he will talk to you, maybe—"

"I'm sure," he said. His voice sounded hoarse, like he had spent a period of time screaming at the top of his lungs. He didn't seem as angry as he had last night when he had come to my room; instead, he seemed defeated, which was somehow even worse. Running a shaky hand through his hair, he raised his eyes to one of the windows. Jasper's face was indecipherable as he stared down at us, ignoring Noelle, who was still trying to convince him to go downstairs and at least say good-bye. Gulping, Seth looked down at his feet again. "He made it clear that he doesn't want anything to do with me. I don't think anything I say could change that."

I feared that if I opened my mouth, the tears I was fighting to hold back would spill, so I only nodded.

Seth seemed to notice and took a step closer to me. "Hey. It's all right, Eve. I wanted to go home from the beginning. I told you I didn't think I fit in at a posh private school like this."

"That's a lie," I whispered. My voice broke on the last word and with it the dam that had been holding my tears at bay. They were hot on my cheeks in the winter air; I didn't bother to wipe them away. "You will always fit in here."

Seth was silent for a moment, looking like he was about to cry as well. Then, he murmured, "Come here."

My feet moved of their own accord and I all but crashed into him, burying my face against his chest as he wrapped his arms around me. I could hear his shallow breaths as his fingers buried themselves in my coat, and I suddenly didn't know who was clinging onto whom, who was holding whom up.

Seth had been my first and best friend at Seven Hills, probably the only real friend I had ever had before. To me, that day we had met on the train with our matching Agatha Christie copies had always seemed a little bit like fate; to see him go now felt like the earth spun the wrong direction all of a sudden, like the sky was falling, like something at the core of the universe was profoundly, terribly *wrong*.

He let go of me only when an angry pair of boots came our way, the thin layer of snow and gravel crunching beneath them. Seth's eyes lit up as he turned around, probably expecting Jasper, but I knew just from the sound of the footsteps that it was Noelle.

The irritated expression left her face when she came to a halt next to us and saw the tears on my cheeks and Seth's pale face. "Hey," she said. "I tried to talk to him, but he's being a stubborn dumbass."

"It's okay," Seth said. "He has every right to feel this way."

"This is just all so fucking stupid. It's The Chitter Chatter we're talking about here. This just gives The Watcher the satisfaction they wanted when they planned this."

Seth stayed silent for a moment, looking up at the window once again before he said, "I have to go now. My train leaves in a few minutes."

"Are you sure you don't want us to walk you to the station?" I asked.

"No, that's all right." He tried for a smile but failed miserably. "You guys have classes soon. I'll be fine."

Digging into my bag, I procured four timeworn paperback books. "Something to read for your journey," I said. "Miss Pepperman wanted to get rid of a bunch of old library books. I saved every book with the word *murder* on the back cover for you. I was going to give them to you on Christmas, but . . ."

I hadn't expected this to be the thing that would make him tear up. "Thanks, Eve," he said, carefully storing them away in his bag before he rubbed his hand over his eyes.

"Promise to stay in touch, okay?" I whispered.

"Of course," he earnestly said. Then he turned to Noelle, who, to both our surprise, met him in a hug.

"This sucks," she said against his shoulder. "Are you sure you don't want to stay? Who else is going to solve the case of The Chitter Chatter?"

Seth stilled. "I, uh . . . might have already done that."

"What?" Noelle and I said in unison. She stepped back with a frown. "And you didn't tell us anything?"

"I thought it was pretty clear by now." He paused, considering, then he said, "If you really want to find out more about The Chitter Chatter . . . you should ask Amelia."

Before either of us could reply, Seth looked up at the window once more, but Jasper's silhouette had disappeared. With a nod, more to himself than to us, he picked up his bags and turned around.

Noelle and I watched, dumbfounded, as he disappeared down the road we had walked together the first time, when the trees still had leaves and we hadn't known a thing about life at Seven Hills. A moment later, he was gone; the only evidence he had ever been there were his footprints in the snow. By noon, they would disappear as well.

◦ ◦ ◦

After Seth's departure, the day seemed to stretch endlessly. Throughout class, my eyes kept wandering back to his empty seat, the room silent when a question was asked that I knew Seth would have been able to answer without a beat. At lunch, it was quieter at our table than usual, none of us speaking much as we pushed our food back and forth on our plates. In the afternoon, Noelle and I sat alone in the common room facing two empty armchairs.

Never Kiss
your Roommate

"I have to go to basketball practice," Noelle said at four o'clock. "Are you going to be okay on your own?"

I offered her a strained smile. "I'll be fine. Have fun at practice."

She got up, but paused once more to press a short kiss to my forehead. I closed my eyes, soaking in the simple comfort for a few seconds. Over the last few days we had gotten good at replacing the hard conversations we both knew we ought to be having—the ones about her mom and her real name and the news reporters that had swarmed the premises—with physical affection. Later tonight, I wanted to try to get her to talk to me again, but for now it was easier to simply lean into the touch and nod when she tucked a strand of hair behind my ear and said, "I'll see you later."

Once she had disappeared through the door, I opened my book again, hoping it would be enough to distract me. It wasn't, but before I could think too much about Seth, Jasper suddenly sank onto the couch next to me.

"Hey, you," I said, closing my book.

"Hey," he rasped. With dark circles under his eyes and his lips bitten raw, he looked no better than Seth had this morning. "Have you heard from him yet?"

"He's still on a train. The first one was delayed."

Jasper nodded silently and ran a hand over his face. After clearing his throat, he said, "I'm sorry if this is strange, but . . . I want to talk to Amelia about what happened, but I don't want to go alone. I know that you're closer with her, so . . . Would you come with me?"

I sat up a little at that. "Did Noelle tell you what Seth said about her?"

He shook his head.

"He seemed certain that she is The Watcher."

"But that would mean that she . . ."

"Probably planted a camera somewhere before she kissed Seth," I said.

Jasper gulped before he got to his feet. There was something jerky about his motions, devoid of any of the grace he usually moved with. "Only one way to find out."

Gathering my things, I followed him. We quickly made our way to the girls' wing, uncaring of the stares that a few of them shot Jasper's way as I led him to Amelia's room.

After taking a deep breath, I raised a hand and loudly knocked at the door a few times. Next to me, Jasper nervously fiddled with his lip piercing, both of us listening as steps sounded from inside the room.

I was expecting Amelia, only to be taken aback when a girl that was around three years younger than us opened the door. Looking up at us with wide eyes, she asked, "Can I help you?"

"Uh . . . yes, actually," Jasper said. "We are looking for Amelia. Is she here?"

"Not right now. I think she's in a meeting with the student council. I don't know when she'll be back."

Jasper and I exchanged a quick glance.

"Do you mind if we come in and wait here for her?" I asked.

She looked uncertain, but eventually said, "Okay. I was just about to leave anyway. Just don't touch anything, please."

"Of course not," Jasper assured her before she left.

My heart was beating in my throat as I stepped through the door. Everything was in order, just like every other time I had been here. With all her books neatly stacked on top of each other on her desk, her bed looking like a hotel employee had

Never Kiss
your Roommate

just made it, and not a single piece of clothing lying around, it almost gave the impression that no one was even actually living here, like this was a film set or a showroom at IKEA.

As there weren't many things lying around anywhere, the camera on her desk was even more obvious.

Nudging Jasper with my elbow, I walked up to it. It was only a small device, nothing professional, and as I turned it on, there were only three files on it. Jasper's breath hitched in his throat when he leaned over my shoulder and saw what I was looking at.

The first thing on the camera was a video. It began with a hand in front of the lens, making it impossible to see what was going on. When it lifted, the upper half of Amelia's face came into the frame, her eyes staring at the camera for a moment, a furrow between her brows. She reached out once more and the camera shook a little as she adjusted it, then she stepped away.

The camera was now filming the center of the room, a frame that was all too familiar from the video that had been posted on The Chitter Chatter. Jasper inhaled sharply when only seconds later, Seth entered and Amelia stepped into the shot to greet him.

There was no audio, so it was impossible to know what they were saying. The only thing giving any information about the progression of the conversation was Seth's changing facial expression, first wary, then a little confused. By the time Amelia stepped closer to him and leaned in for the kiss, the only emotions written all over his face were shock and disbelief.

Jasper tensed as the snippet that had been posted on The Chitter Chatter began, showing the two of them kiss. Only that this time it didn't cut off right in the middle, but we could see Seth pushing Amelia away and taking a step back, wiping a hand over his mouth. A moment later, he bolted out of the room while Amelia fetched the camera and turned it off.

A choked noise from behind me made me spin around. Jasper looked like he had seen a ghost as he whispered, "Oh God. If I had known it was like this, I wouldn't—*fuck*, I should have listened to him."

"You couldn't have known," I gently said. "It *looked* real."

"Yes, but I know *him*. I should've known that he wouldn't do something like that."

"It's too late to undo it now," I murmured. "Don't beat yourself up about it."

Jasper was still staring blankly into space, breathing heavily. Then he suddenly marched towards her desk, but I immediately grabbed his arm.

"Let me destroy it," he said, trying to shake me off. "Who knows what else she's planning to film with this?"

"All our evidence that Amelia is The Watcher is on that camera," I reminded him, adamantly holding onto his arm. Subconsciously, I had gotten into fighting stance, slightly crouched with my feet planted firmly on the ground. "Besides, if you wreck it, she'll know we were here right away. Maybe we can use this information against her."

Jasper stared down at where my fingers were clutching his arm in surprise before finally taking a step away from the desk. "You're right. Sorry."

I picked the camera up myself, finding the memory card and pocketing it. Then, I gently took him by the arm and said, "Come on, let's get out of here."

He silently followed me outside.

"I'm going to hide this in my room," I said, holding up the memory card. "Noelle should be back by now too. We can talk about everything together."

Jasper nodded and together we made our way to my room. Once there, I quickly fished my keys out of my backpack, but froze when I tried to turn them in the lock. The door was already unlocked.

With a strange feeling in the pit of my stomach, I pushed it open, only to see that the room was empty, Noelle nowhere to be seen.

"Elle?" I shouted, stepping through the threshold and looking around. "Are you here?"

I didn't get a reply. Opening the door to the bathroom, I checked if she was in there, but the bathroom was just as deserted.

A lump formed in my throat as I turned around to look at Jasper. He was still standing by the door, hands in his pockets and looking at me questioningly.

"Something's happened," I said. It wasn't a suspicion or an idea; it was a feeling of *knowing* that something wasn't right that had overcome me the second I had found the door unlocked. Noelle, paranoid and on edge as she was, always turned the key twice in the lock to make sure it was locked and often walked over to the door just to double-check that no one would get in. She wouldn't have left it open without a good reason, especially not now, after reporters had circled the castle like vultures for several days and could return at any moment.

Now that I looked around, I also got the terrible sense that someone had been rummaging through the room; some of her drawers were pulled open, items of clothing scattered around where they hadn't been when I had left the room this morning. The duffel bag she always took to basketball practice lay at the foot of the bed.

Behind me, Jasper asked, "What are you talking about?"

"I . . . I think Noelle is gone."

"What? Where would she go?"

"I don't know," I whispered, slowly spinning around. "But something's not right."

Jasper frowned. "What makes you think that? She probably just went to the gym, or back to the common room or something."

"No," I firmly said. "She always makes sure that the door is locked, you know that. It was open. Did she text you anything?"

While Jasper obediently pulled out his phone and checked for any texts, I walked over to my desk where mine was charging. Not a single message. When I tried to phone her, there were a few bone-chilling seconds of the phone dialing before it went straight to voicemail.

I was just about to turn around again when my eyes landed on the history essay that I had only started writing yesterday. My heart skipped a beat. Something had been added beneath the few sentences that I had written last night; it was Noelle's writing, hasty and hard to read.

I had to leave. I had no choice. His name is Kyle Turner.

"Jasper," I said.

Something in my voice must've sounded strange, seeing as he was by my side in a matter of seconds, leaning over my shoulder to see.

"Who's Kyle Turner?" I whispered.

Jasper shook his head; in his eyes, I saw the same helpless confusion that I felt. "I don't know."

"Oh God," I choked out, taking a step back from the desk, as if that would make the note and its sinister meaning vanish. "What if he's the reason why she's here? Why she took on an alias and seemed so scared when The Chitter Chatter revealed her real name?"

"But how would that guy, presuming he . . . took her or something, even get in here? Teachers are patrolling the entrance hall to make sure no other reporters come in here. Someone would've noticed a stranger roaming around school," Jasper said. "Besides, how would he get her out of here without attracting anyone's attention? I'm pretty sure Noelle wouldn't just go with him. She'd probably scream her lungs out and put up a fight."

"But what if she couldn't?" I asked. Tears were stinging in my eyes for the second time that day. "Maybe he had something against her. We don't know a thing about him or their relationship. If she really was hiding from him here, he must have some kind of power over her."

Jasper lifted his hand to his mouth, nervously chewing on his thumbnail. "What are we going to do now?"

"We . . . we need to get help," I said, trying to pull myself together, shake off the fear that was digging its icy fingers into my skin. "We should tell Mrs. Whitworth or the police."

"I don't think the police can do anything yet. Noelle has barely been missing an hour, she could be anywhere. They won't act on just our suspicion and this little note. And if we tell Mrs. Whitworth, she'll just tell us to wait until the police find her." He was silent for a moment. "If we don't tell her anything, we'll be able to go out and try to find Noelle on our own, but if we go to Whitworth, she'll make sure we stay put."

"But how are we even going to try to find her?" I frantically asked. "We don't have any clue besides his name, and it isn't even unique. There are thousands of Kyle Turners."

Jasper was silent for a few seconds before he took a deep breath and turned to look at me. "I think I know who could help us. We should call Seth."

"Okay," I quickly said. "Do you want to, or—"

"Maybe it's best if you talk to him."

I nodded. My hands were shaking a little as I dialed his number and put the phone on speaker, waiting for him to answer. I was already fearing he wouldn't pick up when the beeping on the other end of the line finally stopped.

"Evelyn?" Seth asked in a voice that was probably supposed to sound cheerful. "It's barely been a few hours. Missing me so much already?"

"Seth," I quietly said. "I need your help."

"With what?" Seth immediately sounded much more alert. "Is everything all right?"

"It's Noelle. She's . . . she's gone," I whispered. Fear slid its hands up to my throat, wrapped around it, squeezing tighter with every image that entered my mind. Noelle unconscious. Noelle hurt. Noelle in danger, alone, even though she was supposed to be here with me right now, safe.

"Are you sure? What happened?" Seth asked incredulously over the loud sound of a train driving past him.

Noelle, who had spent the last few days terrified and who hadn't told me why. Noelle, who maybe would be here now if I had pressed more, if I had made her talk to me that night on the football field or any night after that, if I hadn't been so easily distracted with a kiss here or a touch there, so desperate to believe everything was going to be fine. *This isn't one of your bloody romance novels*, Seth's voice echoed in my head again. *Nothing's ever that perfect.*

After waiting a few seconds for me to answer, Jasper gently took the phone out of my hand and wrapped an arm around me, his touch feeling like the only thing holding me together as I started to shake in earnest. His voice was almost timid when he spoke. "Seth? It's me."

There was silence for a moment, only interrupted by an announcement about a delayed train in the distance.

One of Jasper's hands, the one that wasn't holding me, gripped tightly onto the phone. "Noelle has gone missing. We think she may have been kidnapped," he said.

"I . . . what?" Seth asked. "Jasper, if this is some kind of joke—"

"It's not," Jasper insistently said.

"Did you call the police yet?"

"No, we . . . we feel like it might be better if we try looking for her ourselves first."

"Who's *we*? You and Evelyn?"

"Well, we don't really know what to do, but you . . . I mean, you know so much about these things. Could you . . . is there any way that you can come back here and help us? Please?"

Silence, again. Then, "I'm still waiting for my delayed train to Manchester, but I can take the next one back to Seven Hills. I haven't gotten very far yet because of the bloody weather, so I'll try to be there within the next hour."

"Thank you," Jasper breathed.

"I have to go now," Seth said. "The train back will be here in a few minutes and I'm on the wrong platform."

"Okay."

There were a few seconds of silence, both waiting for the other to say something, Seth's labored breaths sounding in time with Jasper's.

Finally, Seth hung up and the line went dead.

23
Evelyn

Night was pressing against the windows of the castle by the time Seth knocked at the door to my room, hair disheveled and his cheeks red from the cold, rasping an uncertain "Hi."

"Hi," Jasper breathed and stepped aside to let him in.

Seth hesitantly brushed past him, carrying the chill inside with him. His eyes softened when they landed on me and he crossed the room in a few long strides, sinking down next to me on the edge of my bed.

"Thanks for coming back," I whispered, trying my best to return the smile he gave me.

"Of course," he quietly said. Then, he pointed at the piece of paper in my hands. "Is that the note she left?"

I handed it to him with a nod. Over the past hour, I had read it so many times that by now the words were engraved in the back of my eyelids.

I had to leave.

There was no surprise in the statement. It sounded resigned, like there had never been a chance for her to stay here in the first place.

I had no choice.

The hint of an apology; *I'm sorry I had to go. I wish I could have stayed.*

His name is Kyle Turner.

This was the sentence that I stumbled over every time. To me, it seemed like it contradicted the first line. It was too much information to come from a girl who had already given up. Instead, it seemed like a plea to use this knowledge to help, to look for her, but at the same time it was only a bread crumb and the forest remained as infinite and impenetrable as it would have been without it.

"We thought it'd be better if we go out and look for her ourselves first," Jasper said, sounding as uncertain as I felt. "The police don't go out looking right away, right?"

"No, it's kind of a complicated procedure." Like every time he talked about these things, Seth's voice was unbelievably calm. "They'll ask for a detailed report first and then they'll assess what risk level she is, but I'm not too sure where they would put her if they see the note—she's a Black, queer, teenage girl, but it looks like she went willingly and with someone she seems to know, so . . . I don't know. Does she have a history of running away?"

"No, but a history of hiding," Jasper said. "In the first few weeks of her being here, we constantly had to go looking for

Never Kiss your Roommate

her. She was always in the attic with Mrs. Whitworth's cat, or somewhere outside where she could see the stars."

"Police will probably tear up the entire castle before they search anywhere else then," Seth said. "Until they decide to send out search teams, a few hours will probably have passed, and we've already lost at least the one hour it took me to get back."

We were all silent for a moment. Then, Seth asked, "Did you google him already?"

"Yes." Jasper leaned against my desk. "But there are tens of thousands of results."

"And no one here saw him?"

Jasper shook his head. "I asked around, but no one noticed anything out of the ordinary. It's like she just disappeared into thin—"

Before he could finish his sentence, the phone in my lap suddenly vibrated, making all of us jump. The call was from a number I didn't know. I answered immediately, even though my stomach swooped as I did, and put it on speaker.

At the other end of the line, everything was silent.

"Hello?" I quietly asked. "Noelle?"

There was some rustling, a muffled male voice. Then, "Evelyn." Hearing her voice, even though it was hoarse and shaky, felt like getting my first breath of air after being underwater for too long.

"Elle, are you okay? Are you hurt? Do you—"

"I'm fine," she quickly said. *She's lying*, Jasper mouthed. "Listen, I . . . I don't have a lot of time. I'm just calling to let you know that I . . . I'm so grateful for the time I got to spend with you." She paused. "No matter what happens, I'll always remember."

"Noelle, I—"

"Remember that time we talked about *Wuthering Heights* in

Philline Harms

303

the library? I even read the book because you asked me to. You couldn't remember that it was actually set in Yorkshire."

"I remember," I whispered. My heart felt like it was lodged in my throat, pounding frantically.

"That was funny," she rasped. The male voice said something else and her breathing hitched. "Evelyn, I don't know if I'll be able to talk to you or . . . or see you again. But I want you to know that I'll be all right. Please don't try to look for me. Don't do anything stupid. Just . . . can you promise me that you'll be fine?"

It was only then that I realized what she was doing. She wasn't calling to tell us how to help her; she was calling to say good-bye. The tears I had been able to keep at bay until then finally spilled. "I can't," I sobbed. "I don't think I will be. Please, tell me what to do to help—"

"There's nothing you could do." Noelle inhaled shakily. "Just . . . just know that if I could have, I would've stayed. I really wish I could've."

"N-no," I said. "Noelle, I won't accept that. I'll find a way, I promise. This isn't—"

Before I could finish my sentence, the line went dead. I was left staring at my phone, my shoulders shaking as tears kept pouring down my cheeks, dripping down my chin and onto the black screen. This might have been the last time I would hear Noelle's voice. The same voice that had told me not to be ashamed of who I was, that had woken me up from nightmares, that had whispered against my lips and neck and wrist.

The same voice that had told me she used to have bad dreams every night, too, that had shaken as she had spoken to her mother on the phone, *You're sure it was him?*, the voice that had promised she would try to open up to me, just not about this one thing, *I've always been better at running away.*

I was pulled back into the present when Seth suddenly said, "I think I've got him."

"What?" I whispered. Looking up, I saw him sitting next to me with his phone in hand, the other at his mouth as he nervously chewed on his thumbnail.

"God, we're lucky. The bloody idiot let her call from a landline."

Jasper sank down on the mattress next to him with a frown. "What does that mean?"

"With a mobile phone, it would've been pretty much impossible for us to legally track him, but this was so simple. Ever heard of reverse phone number search? All I had to do was google the phone number and, because it wasn't listed as private, this address came up."

I leaned over to see what he had pulled up on the screen. It was a website with the slogan *Find out who called you, right now, online and for free* at the top and a box below it in which Seth had typed the number Noelle had called from.

"*Miller's Holiday Rental*," Jasper read. "*49 Green Lane* in ... *merde*, this is only two hours away!"

The relief that washed over me at that was almost tangible. "Let's go then. Seth, you can drive, right?"

"Well, yes, but I don't have a car."

"I can get us one," Jasper said, suddenly getting to his feet. "I'll meet you in the courtyard in ten." He was out of the door before either of us could respond.

"Jesus," Seth murmured, running a hand over his face. "This is a shit idea."

Ten minutes later, Seth and I were standing in the same spot where we had said good-bye earlier that day. None of this felt real. Shivering in the night air, I desperately wanted to believe that any moment I was going to wake up from this nightmare and find Noelle sitting at the edge of the bed, surrounded by fairy lights and with a grin on her lips when I told her about the ridiculous dream I'd had.

A few feet away from me, Seth was pacing back and forth, glancing down at his watch every other second. I knew that, in his head, he was probably rattling off all the statistics on missing person cases he had ever read. I was glad I didn't know them.

Both of us jumped when Jasper stormed out of the castle, triumphantly waving a set of keys.

"Where'd you get those from?" Seth asked.

"Gina," Jasper curtly responded, already rushing towards the car park at the back of the building. Seth and I jogged after him, the freshly fallen snow crunching beneath our boots. I pulled my coat tighter around myself and clutched Noelle's favorite sweater, which she had left in our room, closer to my chest.

Like most cars in the car park, Gina's was sleek and shiny, dark enough to blend in with the night. Seth gulped when Jasper pressed the key into his hand but got into the driver's seat without hesitation. Jasper's shock of bright hair disappeared in the backseat, so I rounded the car and slid onto the passenger seat on the left.

"Better buckle up," Seth said, his hands clutching tightly onto the steering wheel. "This might be one hell of a ride."

Then, we were driving. The engine roared loudly, headlights cutting through the dark, but there was no sign that anyone in the castle noticed our departure and soon, Seven Hills was swallowed by the woods in the distance. Behind the windows, shadows and lights blurred together as we darted through the night like an arrow let loose.

Seth was driving at a hazardous speed. Under different

Never Kiss
your Roommate

circumstances, I probably would have asked him to slow down, but with Noelle's strained voice still ringing in my ears, I was glad every time the number on the speedometer rose.

Once we made it out of the woods, Seth pushed his phone into my hands. I was glad for the distraction that navigating gave me and tried to focus only on the map on the display, not on the gruesome possibilities my brain supplied every time I thought about Noelle. Her sweater was bundled up in my lap, soft cotton that smelled faintly of cigarette smoke and vanilla perfume.

Jasper gave a reassuring squeeze to my shoulder when he noticed me tensing up, even though he looked just as pale as me.

Thanks to Seth's style of driving and the lack of traffic around us, the drive didn't take two hours.

In my mind, I had expected a seedy cabin in the woods; instead, the small house at the end of the road looked unexpectedly inviting. Flowerpots stood on the steps leading up to the door and a friendly sign welcomed us to *Miller's Holiday Rental*. It was only the yellow curtains drawn shut that made its appearance seem sinister.

"Do you think they're still here?" I asked.

Seth looked less than convinced as he turned off the engine. Just by the look on his face, I could tell he had also noticed the glaring absence of another car.

"Let's find out," Jasper muttered. After taking a deep breath, he opened his door and got out onto the street.

Seth wordlessly followed him. I got out last, softly shutting the door before I walked up to the others.

"What are we supposed to do?" Jasper asked, gesturing at the front door. "Are we just supposed to knock and hide in the bushes to see if someone comes out?"

Seth shot him a bewildered stare. "Are you taking the piss right now?"

"Do you have a better idea?"

"Not really," Seth admitted.

"All right. I'll do it then."

Neither of us was convinced this was a good idea. Still, Seth and I hid behind the bushes at a safe distance from the door and watched as Jasper climbed up the front steps, his walk uncharacteristically uncertain. He took a deep breath before he raised a hand and gave three loud knocks, immediately turning around and darting towards us.

We waited with labored breaths for someone to step out, Jasper panting next to me. Only when five minutes had passed and nothing had happened, I got up from my crouching position behind the bushes. "This is stupid. If they were really in there, this man wouldn't just come out."

"You're right," Seth said.

"Maybe we should split up?" Jasper said. "Go around the house and see if there's anything there. If anything happens, yell for help."

Seth shook his head. "Jas, splitting up is how people get *killed*. Also, I think it's pretty obvious there's no one here. There isn't even a car. In fact . . ."

He turned around and walked over to the front door. I couldn't see what he was doing as he crouched down by the doormat, his back to us, but a moment later, he turned around with a key glinting in his hand. "He put the key back for the owner of this rental to find. They're not here anymore."

His words snubbed out the last little glimmer of hope that had still been flickering in my chest. I wordlessly turned around and

Never Kiss
your Roommate

went back to the car, back into the passenger seat. A moment later, Seth and Jasper got in as well.

"We're not going to find her, are we?" I asked, voice shaky. "She could be anywhere by now."

"I'm sorry," Seth said. He had chewed on his lip so much that it was bitten raw by now. "I really thought this was it. It's just . . . in the novels, there's always some kind of clue, a witness. Something more than this."

"It's not your fault," I murmured. "It was dumb to think we could solve this ourselves."

Seth shook his head, frustrated. "For someone who has spent so much time watching true crime cases, you would think I had a better grasp of what to actually do when something like this happens."

"Stop," Jasper suddenly said, making both of us turn around in our seats. "I know you like to talk down about yourself, Seth, but now's not the time for that. You already brought us this far. Somewhere in that brilliant brain of yours there must be another idea."

Seth looked down at his hands, swallowing. I could practically see the wheels spinning in his head as he thought thought thought until suddenly, he turned to me and asked, "Evelyn . . . on the phone, Noelle was suddenly talking about *Wuthering Heights*. Do you remember what she asked you?"

"She asked if I remembered the afternoon when we studied in the library together."

"Right. And then?"

"She . . . she talked about how I couldn't remember where it was set." My chest constricted when I thought back to that afternoon, of her smile against my lips and the warmth I had felt then, with the rain pattering against the windows and her hands cupping my face. Quietly, I added, "I thought it was set in Gloucestershire when it's actually set in Yorkshire."

Seth's eyes widened. "Noelle couldn't care less about classic literature. She was trying to give us a clue."

"You think she's being taken to Yorkshire or Gloucestershire?" Jasper asked. He was leaning forward, his arms braced on the back of our seats.

"Gloucestershire," Seth said, already getting out his phone. "She said something like *Remember when you didn't know it was set in Yorkshire.* She wouldn't say the name of the place out loud in front of him, that would be stupid. She knew that only Evelyn knew what the other place is."

My heart started racing as I watched him type, the flame in my chest rekindled. "But Gloucestershire is still big. Do you have any idea where—"

"Gloucestershire Airport." Seth held up his phone. "I've heard of it before. It's used for private aircraft; chartering private jets or helicopters, that kind of thing. If he wants to get her as far as possible as quickly as possible, that's where he would take her."

"Are you sure?" I asked.

"No." He put the car in reverse. "But it's the only idea I have."

"Jesus," Jasper breathed. "You're brilliant."

A moment later, we were racing through the night again. Gloucestershire wasn't too far, only roughly ninety minutes. At Seth's speed, I was sure we could make it in seventy. Still, they were seventy minutes of wondering and worrying. None of us talked much, the silence disturbed only by the monotone directions that Seth's mobile gave.

That was until I almost jumped out of my skin when my own

Never Kiss your Roommate

phone suddenly rang. I held my breath, only to deflate when I saw it was Amelia.

"Evelyn?" her voice crackled through the speaker. Both Seth's and Jasper's expressions darkened immediately. "My roommate told me you were looking for me earlier. I just came by your room to talk to you, but you weren't there. It is the middle of the week and bedtime started ten minutes ago. Where on earth are you?"

"In the car," I said, distracted when the robotic voice told Seth to take the next exit towards Gloucestershire Airport. "Noelle is gone. We're getting her back."

"I . . . what? Are you in danger?"

"Not yet," Seth murmured.

"Jesus. Shall I—"

I ended the call before she could finish her sentence. We didn't have time for this; ahead of us, the airport was already coming into view. With his jaw set and his hands clutching the steering wheel, Seth pulled into the car park—and abruptly slammed onto the brakes.

As the airport's operation hours were long over, the car park, which was surrounded by woods, was deserted. The only other vehicle was a black rental car with tinted windows that was parked right beneath a streetlight.

Seth swallowed hard before he neared it at a snail's pace, coming to a stop right behind it. All three of us were holding our breaths, waiting for something to happen, but there was nothing. The engine of our car was still running, but other than that there was complete silence.

Seth was the first one to shake off the initial shock. "Quick, we need to get out and check if Noelle's in that car. We don't have time to wait."

"One second," Jasper said and reached into the space between his seat and the door. I sucked in a sharp breath when I saw what he was holding. The knife glittered menacingly in the lights on the dashboard as he held it out for Seth. "Here, take it. Just to be safe."

"Is that a bloody *kitchen knife*?" Seth asked, sounding close to hysterics.

"Well, it's not bloody yet," Jasper said. When both of us only stared blankly at him, he muttered, "Sorry, bad joke. I went by the kitchen after I went to Gina's room. Just so we're not completely defenseless."

"Jesus, Jas, you don't seriously expect me to—"

"Fine," Jasper said. "Then I'll take it. Let's go."

A nervous shiver ran down my spine as he got out of the car, followed by Seth. I hesitated for a moment before I stepped outside as well, watching as Seth put a hand on the passenger door, blinking in disbelief when it swung open just like that.

Seth stood frozen for a moment before his head disappeared inside the car. A moment later, he stuck his hands inside . . . and then he suddenly reemerged, lifting Noelle out of her seat and carefully setting her down on her feet.

Her arms and legs were bound with ropes and she was still wearing the clothes she had worn to basketball practice. With my heart almost leaping out of my chest, I ran up to her as Seth made quick work of untying her, holding onto her waist to steady her, but before I could reach them, Jasper let out a yell.

I turned around to a man I didn't know charging towards us, practically flying across the empty car park, eyes blazing with fury.

Seth was done untying her the second Kyle reached them.

Never Kiss
your Roommate

He shoved Seth out of the way with enough force to make him fall to the ground before he grabbed Noelle and tried to get her back inside the car. I was almost by their side, but Noelle reacted before I could even do anything: with one of her hands balled to a fist, she swung and hit Kyle right in the nose.

He let go of her, stumbling back with one hand pressed to his face, just as Jasper reached them. He jumped onto Kyle, holding him to the ground with his entire weight while one of his hands held the knife above Kyle's chest.

Noelle stared down at them in shock, shaking her right hand.

"Elle!" I shouted.

Her head whipped around immediately. A second later, I was crashing into her, holding her tight enough to feel her heart racing, the same frantic rhythm that was drumming in my chest.

"That punch was terrible," I choked out, muffled against her shoulder. "What did I tell you about your thumb?"

Noelle chuckled tearfully. "I'm sorry, Coach, it won't happen ag—"

An agonized scream cut through the silence before she could finish.

All the air was knocked out of my lungs, my smile crumbling when I let go of Noelle and saw what was happening. Suddenly, Jasper was the one on the ground, pinned down by Kyle, who was crouching over him. But the scream hadn't been his. It was Seth's, his eyes wide in horror as he stared at the knife, now in Kyle's hand and pressed against Jasper's throat.

24

Seth

Just for a few seconds, time seemed to stop.

My eyes darted around, taking in the details of the freeze-frame before me. Jasper, on his back, his hands pressed against the ground, his skin as white as the snow beneath him. The light of the streetlamp reflecting off the knife that dug into his skin just below his Adam's apple, not hard enough to draw blood, but surely enough for him to feel it. His wide eyes staring up at the man holding him down, neither a stormy sea nor a quiet pond, but a bottomless black as the pupils swallowed his irises.

This was what it felt like then. The climax in all those stories I had read, the big showdown between the detective and the killer when just for a brief moment all hope seemed lost. The difference was that while reading, I always knew that things

Never Kiss
your Roommate

were going to be all right in the end, that the resolution was right around the corner, could count the pages left.

The reality felt like drowning with no land in sight. Looking at Jasper, I could feel the water trickling down my throat, one drop at a time, a steady *drip drip drip* that slowly filled my lungs. I tore my eyes away from his face and stared at the man holding him down instead.

Can you describe the culprit?

Name: Kyle Turner. Age: at least two years older than us. Clothing: baggy jeans and a dark brown jumper, remarkably unremarkable. Hair: almost chin length, a dirty blond the same color as the unkempt beard. Eyes: blue. Wide. Paranoid as he twisted his head from side to side to see if any of us were making a move. No one did.

"You bastards," he ground out. Accent: American. "I didn't want to hurt anyone! Why did you have to come and ruin everything?"

In the silence, Jasper's ragged breaths sounded deafening.

Finally, Noelle took a shaky step forward, ignoring Evelyn's hand that grabbed onto her arm to stop her. "Kyle, please . . . let him go. You don't have to do this."

"I do, Ash. I came all this way for you. I won't let them take you." His gaze wandered to Evelyn and me. "You two. On your fucking knees. Hands where I can see them. *Now!*"

Evelyn and I exchanged a quick look before we both sank onto our knees, hands raised.

"Ashley, pick up those ropes. I want you to tie the boy and the girl up," he said, jerking his chin to indicate Evelyn and me. "Come on, quick!"

Noelle shook her head, her voice nothing but a whisper when she said, "Please don't make me do this."

"Darling, our jet is almost ready. Don't stall now." Kyle's eyes were soft as he looked at her, even as he pressed the knife harder against Jasper's throat.

A stifled little noise made it past Jasper's lips. His chest was rising and falling rapidly in time with his shallow breathing, his eyes screwed shut as he forced himself to stay still.

My mind flashed back to him hyperventilating on the stairs at the Welcome Back Party a million light-years ago, to the way he had crumbled in the closet, gasping for breath. Now he lay stock-still as the man's knee pressed against his chest, holding him down with his entire weight.

I was kneeling close enough to be able to touch him if I reached out; Kyle was still looking at Noelle, so I dared to lower one of my hands and stretched it out, lightly brushing my knuckles against Jasper's wrist.

His eyes immediately found mine, wide with panic, his cold fingers clutching mine as he tried his best to breathe evenly.

I pulled my hand back and put it up again before Kyle could see but couldn't tear my eyes from Jasper's face.

"It's okay," Evelyn said, but her voice sounded shaky. "Elle, it's all right. Do what he says."

Everything fell silent again. Then, somewhere to my right, I could hear steps as Noelle walked up to the car. They returned, slowly, reluctantly.

I looked up to see Noelle standing a few feet away from us, holding the ropes that Kyle had used previously to tie her up. I had no idea how the hell we had gotten to this point.

"Go on," he impatiently said. "Start with the girl. Hands behind her back."

Noelle swallowed hard, her gaze never leaving Evelyn as she

Never Kiss your Roommate

went to kneel behind her. Her hands were gentle as she took Eve's hands and guided them behind her back, meeting not even a little bit of resistance; even though she had taken months of self-defense lessons, she was helpless to Noelle.

"I'm so sorry," Noelle whispered. Tears were shining in her eyes and she was shaking in her thin top and sweatpants, the wind tugging at her hair. "This is all my fault."

Evelyn shook her head. "No, it's not. None of it is."

Noelle didn't say anything and continued loosely wrapping the rope around her wrists. My eyes darted around the empty car park, but there was no one near, not a single soul to help us. The only sounds were the wind in the trees and the distant hum of cars on the road, so quiet they might as well have been in my imagination.

"Tighter," Kyle ordered.

After a moment of hesitation, Noelle tightened it a little.

"Tighter, Ashley," Kyle said again. Jasper made a quiet choking noise as the blade dug in hard enough to constrict his breathing. "We don't have time for games."

"I will never forgive you if you do this," Noelle whispered. "Never. Please, Kyle, he's . . . he's my best friend." Noelle's voice broke on the last word.

"I'm sorry, Ash," Kyle said. The fact that he actually sounded sincere was almost as terrifying as my observation that the hand holding the knife to Jasper's throat had started to shake uncontrollably. "It's their fault. If they hadn't come here, none of this would be happening. Now please do as I say."

Noelle looked at him for a few more seconds before she pulled the rope tight enough that Evelyn inhaled sharply. Then she tied it off with a knot.

"Turn around and let me see your hands," Kyle barked, directed at Evelyn.

She did as he said, twisting so he could see the way her wrists were tied.

Kyle gave a short nod and gestured for Noelle to go on.

After lingering behind Evelyn for a few more seconds and giving a short squeeze to her hands, Noelle got up and walked over to me. My body stiffened as I felt her hands on me, but I let her put my hands behind my back without trying to struggle.

A lump formed in my throat as the rope tightened until my hands were completely immobilized. The *drip drip drip* increased. I was sure my lungs were filled at least halfway by now. I couldn't fucking *breathe*.

Hours away, my dad was probably still waiting at the station to pick me up. And Mom—fuck, I hadn't talked to her in months. What if I never got the chance to now? She probably thought I hated her. I didn't. I wasn't even angry anymore. Kneeling there, I suddenly would have given everything just to be curled up in front of the TV again with her hands running through my hair while I made fun of her shitty rom-coms.

Why had we ever thought this would be a good idea in the first place? Why hadn't we just stayed in the castle and called the police? Why had we—

"Good," Kyle said when Noelle was done. I flexed my hands against the rope but found no give. *Drip drip drip*. After checking the way I was tied, Kyle ordered, "Now, Ashley, I want you to be a good girl and get into the car. Go on."

Noelle shook her head, trembling as the wind took a hold of her. "No. I'm not leaving them here."

Through gritted teeth, Kyle said, "Yes, you are."

Then, in the blink of an eye, he suddenly got to his feet, the knife still in his hand, and charged towards Noelle. He had probably expected Jasper to be too shaken to get up right away, but Jasper scrambled to his feet as soon as Kyle let go of him and sprinted after him. He had almost reached him when Kyle suddenly whirled around.

From where I was kneeling, I couldn't see what happened. It was only when Jasper stumbled backward, turning ever so slightly, that I could see it.

Blood.

There was so much blood.

It was on his hands and on his chest, already soaking the white cotton of his shirt, a quickly spreading, ruby-red patch beneath the school emblem, so much darker than the fake blood they used in films.

Over the rushing in my ears I could make out Noelle's scream, but not a single sound left my mouth. All I could do was stare at Jasper as he stood there, blinking down at the red on his fingers in disbelief.

It was the sound of sirens that startled me into turning my head. Kyle stilled, his face pale in shock as he looked at the quickly approaching police car and the ambulance that was right behind it.

Swearing, he turned on his heel and ran towards Noelle, but before he could get very far, two uniformed officers had already gotten out of the car and jumped him, wrestling him to the ground. While one of them pinned Kyle to the ground, the other made quick work of putting him into handcuffs.

It all went so quickly that I barely had enough time to register what had just happened; one second Kyle was chasing after

Noelle, the next he was flat on his stomach in the middle of the car park, his cheek pressed against the asphalt.

He started struggling and screaming Noelle's name only as the officers hauled him to his feet, but he had no chance of getting anywhere. I could hear the two men saying something, but I wasn't paying any attention to them.

Jasper was still frozen in shock, looking at the scene before him, his face strangely blank. He stood in a spot where neither the light of the streetlamps nor the ambulance's headlights could reach him, his back turned to the paramedics getting out of the vehicle. None of them noticed him as he shook in the wind, shrouded in darkness.

I jumped when I suddenly felt hands untying the rope around my wrists.

It was a third officer, a woman looking down at me with a worried expression. "You all right there? Are you—"

I didn't wait for her to finish whatever she wanted to say but lurched to my feet the moment my hands were free. She shouted something after me, but I didn't care, already running towards Jasper. "Jas!"

He turned slowly, blinking at me. One of his hands was still pressed against his chest, fingers smeared with red. "Seth," he rasped, "I think I'm going to—"

That was all he got out before his legs suddenly gave away. Somehow I managed to catch him before he hit the ground, my arms wrapped around his middle.

Unable to hold him up for long, I lowered him to the ground so that he was lying on his back. "Jasper?" I whispered, pulling his head onto my lap. "Jas, open your eyes. You're okay, just look at me. Look at me—"

He didn't react in the slightest. His eyes were shut, his entire body limp in my arms. By now a large part of his shirt was tinted crimson, the color shockingly bright against his pale skin. The flickering light of the police car painted his face in a ghostly blue glow, illuminating the thin sheen of sweat on his face.

Dark spots danced before my eyes as I stared down at him, motionless and unresponsive, his skin hot beneath my fingertips despite the freezing temperature. "No," I whispered. "Jasper, please—"

A man's voice interrupted my senseless stammering. "Let go of him, please. Let us help him."

I looked up to see two paramedics towering above me. "N-no, you don't understand, he's my—"

A hand on my arm interrupted me. "Come on, Seth, let them do their job," Mrs. Whitworth said. When had she gotten here? "There's nothing you can do right now."

Swallowing, I lowered Jasper's head to the ground and got up. Mrs. Whitworth wrapped an arm around me and pulled me against her side as soon as I was standing, like she was fearing I was going to follow Jasper's lead and pass out.

She led me only a few steps away, to where Noelle and Evelyn were sitting next to each other on the curb.

I felt like I was in a trance as I sat down, only now realizing that my pants were wet where I had been kneeling in the snow. "I'm going to need to do a quick checkup on you guys," the female paramedic announced, coming to a stop right before me. "Can you tell me your names?"

Like a robot, I went through the motions of telling her everything that had happened and did what she said, following the light of her flashlight with my eyes when she asked me to, answering her questions about whether I was hurting some-where or not, letting her wrap a blanket around my shoulders when she noticed I was shaking.

Halfway through her examination, the paramedics put Jasper onto a stretcher and carried him inside the ambulance.

He was gone before I could even ask if I could come along.

○ ○ ○

I had been to the hospital only once before, when I had broken my arm in PE in primary school. Even then, I had hated the smell of antiseptics and the glare of the ceiling lights against the mint green linoleum floor, and was glad when I could finally go home with my cast on and a cool story to tell.

Today, the feeling was no different. I had been sitting in the uncomfortable plastic chair next to the bed for going on two hours now, watching the seconds tick by on the clock. Next to me was Mrs. Whitworth; while Evelyn and Noelle had been taken to the police department to give a statement, she had taken me to the hospital. Wearing no makeup and sitting hunched over in her chair, she looked no better than I felt.

When I had asked her who had called the police and where she had come from, she explained to me that Amelia had been the one to notify her after she'd called Evelyn. She had heard the directions my phone gave in the background while I was driving, thus being able to tell the police where we were. I supposed that, though a lot of this was her fault, we also had to thank her, but that paradox was too complicated to think about now, so I pushed the thought away.

Instead, I looked up and asked the nurse, "When is he going to wake up?"

"As I said," she said, an impatient edge to her voice as she repeated the same answer she had given me every other time I had asked over the previous two hours, "I don't know that. You'll just have to wait and be patient."

I directed my eyes at the bed in front of me again. Jasper was wearing a hospital gown that had slipped down a little, revealing parts of the bandage that was covering the cut on his chest. In the harsh light of the ceiling lamp, he looked even paler than usual, his skin thin enough to show his veins and almost as white as the pillowcase on which his head was resting. Every once in a while, he would stir a little, but mostly his breathing was steady.

The doctor who had been here about an hour ago had told me it hadn't been as bad as it looked. Jasper hadn't passed out from blood loss—which, it turned out, hadn't been as severe as it had seemed—but from the extreme anxiety his claustrophobia had caused mixed with lack of sleep over the last forty-eight hours. He had been awake for a few minutes during the ride to the hospital but had been unconscious again as his wound had gotten stitched. Now it was just a matter of time until he woke up, though I had been warned that because he had been close to having a panic attack and wouldn't stay still for the paramedics, he had been given a tranquilizer that perhaps hadn't completely worn off yet.

"I'm going to get some coffee from the cafeteria downstairs," Mrs. Whitworth said, offering me a tired smile as she got to her feet. "Can I get you anything?"

"No, thank you," I quietly answered.

Mrs. Whitworth nodded and turned around, her heels clicking on the linoleum floor as she walked out of the room. Then, silence fell once again.

I leaned forward and reached for Jasper's hand. Earlier, I had taken off each of his rings. They were lying on his bedside table now; the sight of the silver, stained with blood in places, made my stomach twist.

I was just examining the way his nail polish had chipped off when Jasper's fingers suddenly twitched in my grasp. With a start, I looked up, just in time to see his eyes fluttering open. They blinked into the bright light for a moment before they slowly took in the room. Finally, they landed on me.

"Seth?" Jasper rasped. "What happened?"

"You're in the hospital," I said, my throat a little tight. "Kyle cut you with his knife, remember?"

It took a few seconds for Jasper to fully comprehend my words. "Oh." He looked down at his chest. The hand that I wasn't holding came up to lightly touch the bandage, but he dropped it immediately, grimacing slightly in pain. Then, he suddenly jolted and scrambled to sit up. "What about Noelle and Evelyn? Are they . . . are they all right?"

I gently pushed him down onto the mattress again. "They're fine. They're just at the police department giving their statements."

He nodded, slowly. Due to the sedative, all of his movements seemed a little delayed, his gaze a little spaced out. Then, suddenly, his eyes became focused again, fixing me intently. "I'm so sorry, Seth. I saw the rest of the video. I never wanted to—"

"Shh, it's okay," I said, squeezing his hand. "We don't have to talk about it right now."

"No, I . . . I want to." He tried to prop himself up on his elbows but immediately fell back against the pillows, wincing in pain. "I should've known you wouldn't kiss her. I should've known."

Never Kiss your Roommate

"It was bad timing," I objected. "I don't know what I would've done if I had been in your place."

"You probably wouldn't have *broken up* right away."

"No, probably not," I said, only sounding a little bit like I was holding back tears. "But it doesn't matter now. I'm just glad you're okay."

"Me too." He gulped. "Will you forgive me?"

"I already have," I softly said. "And I'm sorry too. For leaving right away and not trying harder to explain everything to you."

"It's oka—"

"Wait, I'm not finished," I cut him off, my eyes trained on where our fingers lay intertwined on the coarse hospital sheets. "You remember how I said I didn't believe in love?"

He gave an uncertain nod.

"That was a lie." I forced myself to look up at him again. "My perception of love *was* a little bit screwed—I guess seeing your parents fight every day kind of messes with your head like that, but . . . I did believe in it. I just didn't believe that *I* would ever get to receive it, and especially not from someone like you."

"We already talked about this," Jasper muttered, squeezing my hand a little tighter. "I *told* you I liked you, no matter how strange you think you are—"

"I know. It just . . . never fully sank in. There was always this voice in my head that told me sooner or later everything would go to shit and you'd realize you didn't actually like me like that." Even as I said it, the images of skeletons and cobwebs and dark basement corners seemed to fade away. *Bet you didn't expect this, did you, you stupid fucking skull.* Quietly, I continued, "It only really clicked when I saw how hurt you were after you'd read the article. And at that point I felt like it was already too late; in my mind, it just proved that I didn't deserve to be with you because sooner or later I'd fuck it up anyway."

"But you didn't," Jasper said. "Amelia did, mostly. And our lack of communication, but that was mutual. We were both overdramatic idiots."

"I guess," I murmured. Smiling felt strange after hours of self-loathing and anxiety, and that was without the bloody near-death experience. "So . . . are we going to try again? With more communication and less crippling self-doubt this time?"

Jasper swallowed, like he still couldn't truly believe it. "Really? You'd want that?"

"Of course," I whispered. "I like you. Like, *proper* like you. Like you so much I sometimes can't think around you and I feel like I'm being electrocuted or like I swallowed a tornado or the bloody sun or . . . yeah. Something like that." I broke off, cheeks flushed as I prayed that Jasper was so high off his ass from his medicine that he wouldn't remember this one bit.

Jasper let out a quiet laugh, only wincing a little bit as he did. In a terrible imitation of my accent—which, to my horror, I found endearing rather than insulting—he said, "I *proper like you* too. And I would love to try again. And again and again and again, if that's what it takes to get it into your thick head that I'm serious about this."

"Okay," I breathed. "But only if you promise not to get yourself almost killed again. And to stay far away from kitchen knives. And sharp objects in general."

"I'll try." He yawned quietly, turning his head a little farther so his cheek was squished into his pillow. "I don't like being in the middle of one of your detective cases very much, I think."

"Me neither," I said. "You scared me so much, asshole. If I

326

hadn't believed in love earlier, I for sure would've when I saw you lying there. I've never been that bloody terrified in my entire life. If things had turned out any worse than they did . . . I honestly don't know what I would've done."

A tired grin appeared on Jasper's face at that, and even though it was nowhere as radiant as it usually was, it was still enough for my heart to skip a beat. For once, the sensation didn't scare me a bit. "Ah, yes. Nothing like some light stabbing to turn a man into a hopeless romantic."

"Shut up." I chuckled, pinching his arm. In a more serious voice, I added, "You did so well when he was on top of you though. I can't imagine how scary that was, especially with your claustrophobia."

"I tried to do what you taught me." His words were slightly slurred by now, the French accent getting thicker with every syllable. "Twelve deep breaths, over and over."

Somehow, his words, along with the achingly vulnerable look on his face, made me feel similar to the way I had felt when I'd held his hand for the first time, except this time it wasn't a hundred thousand million volts, but a pleasant buzz that made me feel warm all over. When I noticed that his eyelids were already starting to slip shut again, but he was still trying to keep them open, I lifted his hand to my mouth and pressed a short kiss to his knuckles. "Go back to sleep, Jas. You're safe now."

He stirred a little underneath the covers, forcing his eyes to open again. "Will you still be here when I wake up?"

"Of course," I murmured. "I'm not going anywhere."

"Okay. *Bonne nuit, je t'aime,*" Jasper whispered, almost inaudible, and relaxed into the mattress, his hand staying in mine even as he let the waves of sleep pull him under. As I studied his peaceful face, the echo of his words still hanging in the air, I, for the first time in hours, felt like I could breathe again; the *drip drip drip* had finally stopped.

25

No one uttered a word during the drive to the police station.

Huddled in the backseat next to me, Noelle looked ashen and tired, her head leaning against the window while her eyes stared out into the night, dark and unseeing. Earlier, while we had waited for a second police car to arrive, I had helped her pull the sweater I had brought over her head, but her teeth were still chattering, every inch of her shaking. Her sleeve had ridden up enough to reveal the faint rope burns on her arms.

Wordlessly, I guided her hand to my mouth and pressed a soft kiss to her wrist. I half expected her to pull her hand away; instead, she gave a short squeeze to my fingers and shifted so her head was resting against my shoulder.

With her curls tickling my cheek and her breathing growing

more even in my ear, I closed my eyes and took my first deep breath in hours.

I opened them again only when the car rocked to a stop. One of the officers led us inside the building and into a narrow corridor with doors on each side and a row of uncomfortable chairs where Noelle and I were told to wait. When he disappeared around the corner, we were finally alone together.

Still, for a few long moments, neither of us said anything, both of us blinking into the harsh fluorescent light, disoriented. There were so many questions, I didn't know where to start, or if now was even the right time to say anything.

In the end, Noelle was the one who spoke first. Staring down at her hands, she murmured, "I met him at a friend's party when I was fifteen."

"Noelle," I whispered. "We don't have to talk about it now."

"Yes, we do," she firmly said. "I should have told you long ago."

Shutting my mouth, I nodded for her to go on.

"Kyle was really popular; everyone kind of knew his name and a lot of the girls I knew were crushing on him. He was nineteen then, four years older than me. It . . . it felt good when he spent the whole evening with me and gave me the most attention out of everyone." She swallowed audibly, her hands clasped tightly in her lap. "After that party, we started hanging out almost every day and after just two weeks he asked me to be his girlfriend. He was really sweet, always buying me flowers and taking me to fancy places and stuff. It was nice to be desired like that. So I said yes.

"I didn't tell my mom about him because I knew she wouldn't have liked the big age gap between us. At that time she was recording her third album and spent pretty much every minute

330

at the studio, so she didn't even notice. Whenever she asked me where I was spending the night, I just told her I was with a friend."

Her eyes were glazed as she stared at the white wall in front of us.

"After only a few weeks he began talking about moving in together in the future, marrying, even having children." I inhaled sharply through my teeth. Noelle looked over at me for a brief second. "A major red flag, I know. At the time, I didn't take it seriously—he was dramatic like that, so I just laughed every time the topic came up. The second red flag in hindsight was that I was suddenly spending all my free time with him. Whenever I wanted to leave, he asked me to stay longer, spend the night at his, even skip classes. After a while he started asking me where I was going every time I left, wanted to know exactly who I was meeting or talking to. One time I caught him going through my phone, but he just laughed it off and made a joke out of it, said something like *Just making sure you're not cheating*, and I dropped the subject. Without me noticing, he restricted any kind of contact with my friends, especially male ones, and even classmates, until he was pretty much the only person I had to talk to." She shook her head and murmured, her voice hoarse. "I was so dumb back then."

"No, you weren't," I quietly said. "You were just young."

"So young," she whispered. "I was fifteen and everything had gone so fast. When he eventually tried to go past just making out, I refused. I was scared to go there."

My fingers dug harder into the armrest of my chair. I had an idea what would come next and I wasn't sure I could stomach hearing it from her mouth, but she continued.

"One night we were at a party together. He got me drunk." She stopped, forcing herself to take a deep breath. "I can't remember everything that happened that night. I know that I asked him to take me home and that he brought me to his apartment instead."

Even though it wasn't like me, the strain in her voice made me wish I had gotten my knuckles bloody earlier.

"When I woke up the next day, I felt dirty and ashamed and suddenly uncomfortable being around him. But I had no one to talk to about it since I hadn't spoken to my friends in over three months and I was set on not telling my mom anything about him. In the end, I decided to meet his best friend, the one who had hosted the party where we had first met. He knew Kyle better than anyone else, so I was convinced he could tell me that he wasn't like that, that it was okay, that it was a normal thing and I didn't have to worry.

"What I hadn't thought of was that Kyle was still going through my phone. He found my text asking his best friend to meet me and confronted me about it, telling me I wasn't allowed to see him. That was how our first actual fight started. I told him I was sick of him being so controlling; he hit me. Then he locked me in his apartment."

She was silent for a moment. I wanted to say something, but none of the words I knew seemed big enough to encompass the sheer dread that had overcome me. I suddenly felt so cold I was sure my breath ought to be forming clouds by now; the way Noelle was describing it—matter of factly and numb, like she was talking about a TV show and not her own past—made my insides freeze.

"I climbed out of his window and took a cab home," she continued. "In the meantime, he had gone to his former best friend's

Never Kiss your Roommate

house and beat him up to the point that he had to go to the hospital." By now, her fingers were clenched so tightly her knuckles were showing. "I told my mom about everything that happened the second I got home. I cried and she listened and then she hugged me and we went to the police. We got a restraining order against Kyle that prohibited him from coming anywhere near me, but I still didn't feel safe. A week later, my mom sent me to Seven Hills under a new name." She gulped. "I thought that was it. But then, earlier today . . . or I guess, yesterday now, I got a call from him. I had blocked his number, but he used a burner phone. He had found out my location because of the information from The Chitter Chatter that was spread in the news. He told me that he had a hit on my mom. I believed him because she didn't pick up when I tried to call her and because of the talk I had with her a while ago."

"Was it the call I overheard?"

"Yeah. Mom told me that he had shown up at the meet and greet at one of her concerts and had tried to threaten her before security kicked him out. Knowing that, it seemed plausible." She looked away, rubbing a hand over her eyes. My heart sank at the thought; Noelle, who always beamed when a new package from her mom arrived, who collected magazines about her, and who had played me her music with so much pride, had been terrified enough for her mother to put herself in such danger, to go and meet the man from whom she had fled to the other end of the world. "I left the castle while on a video call with him so he could make sure I wasn't talking to anyone—all I managed was the note you found, which I had to write while still staring into the phone so he wouldn't suspect anything—and got into his car in the woods. He took me to this holiday rental where he had lived the last few days and had all his stuff and then took me to the airport. He wanted to take a private jet to fucking *Switzerland.*"

"How . . . how did you convince him to let you call me?" I asked.

"He knew that we were together from The Chitter Chatter. I told him I wanted to say good-bye to you before we left for the airport so I could *let go of the past and be all his,* or some shit," she snorted, but there wasn't a trace of humor in her voice. "The fucker was delusional enough to believe me."

Meeting her eyes again, I tried for a shaky smile. "That hint you gave about *Wuthering Heights* was really smart."

She pulled her sleeves over her knuckles, her eyes looking a little clearer, not as far away as they had a few moments ago. "I knew you would like that."

I was silent for a moment, the only sound filling the hallway the humming of the ceiling lights and the clicking of computer keyboards from behind the closed doors. Finally, I murmured, "But after everything he did . . . How is this okay? How can you stand it when I touch you?"

"You have never been like him," she softly said. "You know . . . before I met you I always thought love was something violent, that it was about taking something from the other. But you never tried to take. You just gave so much, more than I sometimes felt I even deserved. You showed me the difference between being in love and thinking love was the same thing as fear and all its symptoms—the heart racing and the shaking and the willingness to give up all of yourself to make the other person happy. You showed me that it doesn't—shouldn't—hurt."

I swallowed hard. Warmth was pooling behind my eyes, but I

Never Kiss
your Roommate

was determined not to let the tears spill. If Noelle could tell her entire story without crying, I could keep it together now. "What about the others? Elias?"

"It was . . . I'm not sure how to explain it," she murmured. "I think it was an attempt to regain control over my sexuality—if I put myself out there and behaved overly sexual on my own terms, no one else could try to take anything from me without my permission. Didn't really work out though. I still had this obsessive need for control whenever I was with someone and always dropped them before things could get serious." Her lips curved into a faint smile. "Until you came around and somehow smashed all the walls I'd spent so much time building."

Warmth flooded my veins at that, thawing the frost that had coated my insides. Before I could think better of it, I reached across and intertwined my fingers with hers. "Thank you for letting me in," I whispered. "You're the strongest person I know. Truly."

Noelle's smile widened and reached her eyes, lit up her face, lit up the entire *hallway*. Her voice was like honey when she muttered, "Come here."

A heartbeat later, her hands caught my face and the world fell away. With her lips on mine, I, for the first time since I had found her hasty note, didn't feel like I was trapped in a fever dream. In the kiss was everything we hadn't gotten to say yet: *I'm sorry, I missed you, I'm so glad you're okay. I thought I'd lost you. I can't lose you.*

"There aren't any other things I should know about, are there?" I breathlessly asked when I pulled back, my forehead still resting against hers and our hands lying intertwined on the armrest between us.

"Just one," she said, her voice as sure as her fingers where they curled around the back of my neck. "I love you."

Oh. There they were; the three words I had read so many times, had heard in films, had imagined over and over again someone saying to me. However, nothing had been able to prepare me for the feeling of hearing them in Noelle's voice, spoken like a promise, with her eyes wide and earnest and her lips a breath away. "I love you too," I said, dangerously close to crying once again, but this time for an entirely different reason. "Though that's not really a secret anymore, is it?"

"Secrets are overrated anyway," Noelle whispered and kissed me again. And again and again and again, until I felt dizzy from it and the only thought my endorphin-flooded brain could produce was a frenzied *Thank you* to the universe.

For years, I had been so in love with the *idea* of love—the perfect kind, the one that was pressed between two spines and flickered across silver screens—I had lost sight of what it really meant. Now, I understood that, in reality, it didn't have to be perfect or dramatic or shiny enough for everyone else to see. It was the fairy lights in our room and the sweater I had brought her and the sweets she only ever shared with me. It was Noelle remembering my favorite band and listening when I talked about my books and asking for consent every time she kissed me. It was the racing of my heart when her team won and being unable to sit still when she got hurt and knowing where to find her when she had fled into the sea of stars that one night. More than everything, it was shakily laying yourself bare over and over again and trusting the other would be gentle with the scars they found.

The love I had stumbled into wasn't a delicate rose garden.

Never Kiss
your Roommate

It was a buzzing field of wildflowers where thistles and thorns sometimes hid beneath the surface instead of lying in plain sight but once you knew your way around, it was so much better than soft petals and straight paths, better than fiction, better than I had ever dared to dream. It wasn't perfect; it was real, and it was ours, and that made all the difference. I was only pulled out of my daze when the door next to us suddenly opened and a woman stepped out. "Ashley Danell and Evelyn Greene, if you'd please follow me inside?"

Noelle breathed a quiet sigh and reluctantly let go of me. When she leaned back, the smile was still on her face and though she looked drained, her chin was raised high. "Let's get this fucker behind bars."

I took her smile and her words and my newfound knowledge and tucked them into my pocket for safekeeping as the woman ushered us into the room. Somehow, our conversation in the flickering neon lights of the stuffy police department seemed like the beginning of a new chapter—a new book, even. And God, I already knew I was going to love this one.

26

Evelyn

Before we knew it, we'd stumbled into December. Suddenly, the halls were decked with holly, and branches of mistletoe hung from the arched doorways, much to the delight of the younger students, who screeched each time they found themselves beneath one of them. The weather was freezing now, a chill creeping in through the old windows, but the fire crackling in the common room and the cups of tea and hot chocolate that were given out in the Great Hall each afternoon helped combat the cold.

It had been almost two weeks since what we only referred to as *that night*, and since then, a few things had happened.

One: our parents were notified about what had happened, leading to a bunch of panicked phone calls and lectures. The longest conversation had been between Elle and her mom. To

338

Never Kiss your Roommate

all our relief, Crystal was perfectly fine and, as the police told us later, had at no point been in any danger, as Kyle admitted that the alleged hitman had never existed.

Which brought me to number two: Kyle was now behind bars and probably would not be free again any time soon. The knowledge had visibly lifted a weight from Elle's shoulders; she was still shaken, quieter at times, but she didn't have nightmares anymore and didn't constantly look over her shoulder when she roamed the castle.

Three: Jasper had returned from the hospital. Right after, he had still seemed a little bit rattled, but after a few days of being nursed by Seth, who barely spent a second apart from him, he was doing much better and was willing to tell anyone who would listen about his heroic near death—the whole thing had gotten a bit dramatized in hindsight.

Four: Mrs. Whitworth had allowed us to take a few days off classes. When we came back, Elle, much to Miss Pepperman's delight, started reading out loud in class because *if I can survive a fucking kidnapping, I can survive pronouncing a few words wrong.*

Five: Elle had pushed our beds together so they formed one queen-sized bed. Its pros: we could now sleep in one bed at night without having to worry about falling off the mattress. Its cons: getting out of bed was a challenge that neither of us felt like facing most of the time, resulting in both of us lying around doing nothing except kissing and talking and kissing some more.

The sixth change came in the form of the little head presently bumping against my cheek to wake me up. Blinking my eyes open, I was met with the curious gaze of the pitch-black kitten that was perched on the mattress next to me.

Cookie was a few months old and from the same pet shelter from which Mrs. Whitworth had adopted Muffin. It had taken some begging on my part, but after a few days, I convinced her that another cat in the castle surely wouldn't make a big difference and that the tiny kitten could serve as not only an early birthday present but also a therapy animal for Elle.

Scratching at Cookie's fur, I wasn't sure what was more adorable: her or Elle, who was lying next to me with her face nuzzled into the crook of my neck. After a glance at my phone that told me it was past noon already, I reached a hand out to lightly caress her cheek and whispered, "Elle. Wake up."

The only reply was some incoherent muttering that was muffled against my neck.

Accepting that that approach wouldn't work, I lifted Cookie and gently set her down on Elle's stomach. As expected, the kitten gave a small meow and pawed at Elle's hand, prompting her to crack open an eye. "You two," she murmured, voice still hoarse from sleep, "Always conspiring against me."

I smiled back at her. "You love us."

She only hummed and stretched a little, not unlike the cat huddled between us.

"We should get up," I said, poking her cheek. "The Winter Banquet is today."

"And?"

"You wouldn't want to miss out on all the food, do you? Just think of all the cakes and desserts . . ."

One corner of her mouth quirked up. "Good argument, but you're gonna have to bring a bit more to the table than that, Greene. As far as I'm concerned, the sweetest thing in this entire castle is lying right next to me."

340

Immediately, I felt my cheeks heating up. A few months ago, I hadn't understood the women in the novels who would blush and faint at the slightest sign of affection. Now, after having experienced Elle's flirting firsthand, I sometimes felt like I was in need of some smelling salts as well.

To hide how flustered I was, I reached out and put my hands over Cookie's ears, whispering, "Not in front of the child."

Elle laughed, a sound that made my knees go just as weak as her words, and gently set Cookie down on the floor before swinging her feet over the edge as well. "Let's get ready then. We still have to see Mrs. Whitworth before the banquet."

I yawned one more time before I followed her into the bathroom. We got ready in comfortable silence, for the most part—at least until I reached for my foundation to cover the faint splatter of freckles on my nose.

"Don't." Elle lightly clasped my wrist. "I love all eighteen of them."

All it took were seven words from her to render me completely useless. I stared at her, my hands frozen halfway to my face and my mouth agape, until she leaned forward to press a kiss to the tip of my nose. "Time is ticking, love."

Mental note: find out if I can buy smelling salts online.

We stepped out into the corridor a few minutes later. Elle didn't lock the door; instead, she left it slightly ajar so that Cookie could wander around the castle if she felt like it.

Mrs. Whitworth's office was in one of the towers, overseeing the premises. I climbed the stairs in front of Elle—while I was wearing a knee-length, light pink dress, she had slipped into a tight-fitting, sparkly red evening gown that she had to gather in her hands so as not to step on it.

Jasper and Seth were waiting in front of the door, both dressed in suits. Whereas Seth was wearing a classic black-and-white three-piece, Jasper had gone for a more extravagant suit in a wine-red color.

"Salut," he said when we stopped in front of them. "You two look beautiful."

I gestured at Jasper's fingernails, which for once, weren't painted black or silver but the color of his suit, "You too! I love the nails."

"Thanks, princesse. Seth painted them."

"He only had to use half a bottle of nail polish remover to clean them up afterward," Seth laughed.

Jasper only smiled.

"What has you grinning like that, Frenchie?" Elle asked, poking his arm. "Do you have something to tell?"

"Well . . ." he said, clearing his throat. "I had a phone call with my parents earlier. I finally came out to them."

Elle and I gasped in unison. "That's amazing!" she said, getting onto her tiptoes to pull him into a hug. "Did they understand the whole pansexuality thing?"

"Not at all," he laughed. "But they understood that I have a boyfriend, so that's something."

"They invited us to come to Marseilles in spring," Seth threw in, a broad grin on his face.

Elle finally let go of Jasper. "That's awesome. I'm so proud of you, Jas, honestly."

"Aw," Jasper cooed, patting her head. "Soft Ashley is here to stay, huh?"

That was another thing that had changed. Since our return to the castle, Elle had stripped off her alias and reclaimed her real

Never Kiss your Roommate

name. When I had asked her what she wanted me to call her, she told me to keep calling her by the nickname I had given her; *Noelle* represented the years of hiding and living in fear, but *Elle* was something else, a reminder that there had been light even during the darkest time in her life that was only reserved for the two of us.

Before Elle could object, the door behind the boys opened and Mrs. Whitworth stepped out. "Thank you so much for coming before all the festivities start," she said, the strained smile on her face immediately making all four of us sober. "Please, come inside, have a seat."

My stomach dropped when she stepped aside to let us pass and I saw what was going on inside: on one of the couches in Mrs. Whitworth's office sat Amelia, framed by her parents.

Amelia's mother was a red-haired woman with sharp facial features and a penetrating gaze that followed us as we squeezed onto the couch on the opposite side of the room. Her father, clad in a custom-tailored suit and with his graying hair combed back neatly, looked just as harsh, every inch of him radiating control and authority.

Between them, Amelia seemed small and lost, a little girl among two unmoving statues. She was sitting with her back straight and her fingers clenched tightly in her lap, not a single wrinkle in her skirt or a hair out of place. Surely she would've seemed just as cold and collected as her parents had she not been shaking like a leaf in the wind, her eyes darting across the floor without ever meeting mine.

Mrs. Whitworth shut the door and cleared her throat before she hurried to sit behind her desk. Breaking the tense silence, she said, "Mr. and Mrs. Campbell, these are the students affected by the recent events. Ashley Danell, Evelyn Greene, Seth Willams, and Jasper Des Lauriers."

Mrs. Campbell only nodded curtly while her husband said, "Pleasure to meet you." He didn't sound pleased in the slightest.

"Mr. and Mrs. Campbell came to talk to you before the Winter Banquet begins," Mrs. Whitworth told us. "I hope you don't mind."

I shook my head wordlessly while the others muttered quiet affirmations.

"Very well," Mr. Campbell said. "You see, we are in a bit of a difficult situation here. We know all about what our daughter has been up to over the last few years. She has confessed about her internet blog and about the part she played in endangering the lives of some of you."

During the few seconds it took him to speak these sentences, Amelia noticeably shrank into herself, wilting like the flowers on Mrs. Whitworth's desk.

Mrs. Campbell gave a brusque nod. "We want to apologize for the harm that she has caused. If we had known that she was behind all this, we would have put a stop to it immediately. Sadly, we did not, so now we are here, in a situation that I believe none of us want to be in."

"Mr. and Mrs. Campbell told me they would take Amelia out of Seven Hills as a consequence," Mrs. Whitworth said, her voice smooth and quiet. "But I think that, seeing as you four are the students most affected, you should be the ones to decide. I'm aware that it's a difficult situation for you, and a lot of pressure, but I'm confident that you're able to make the best, most nuanced decision."

For a moment, everything was silent. I swallowed hard,

Never Kiss your Roommate

looking at Amelia's pale face and the way her nails were digging into the palms of her hands to stop them from trembling. While the four of us were sitting on a couch together, Elle's hand on my thigh on one side and Seth leaning into me on the other, she looked utterly forlorn. Finally, I asked, "Could we have a word with Amelia for a moment, please? Alone?"

Mrs. Whitworth nodded, immediately getting out of her chair. "Yes, that sounds like a good idea. Mr. and Mrs. Campbell, if you would follow me outside?"

Amelia's parents got up reluctantly, clearly not happy about this turn of events, but left the room without uttering any complaints.

Amelia let out a breath she probably had been holding the moment the door fell shut behind them. Then she slowly looked up at us, the look in her eyes that of a convict awaiting their turn to step up to the gallows.

"Amelia . . ." I said. "Can you tell us why you did it? Why did you write the blog?"

She was silent for so long I was starting to think she wouldn't answer. Finally, she whispered, "Because I was sick of being quiet. I . . . you've seen my parents." Her voice shook so much I was afraid it was going to break. "With them, there was never any room to express my opinions, no one who heard me. But on that blog, I could say anything and people would listen."

Elle huffed.

Amelia's eyes shot up to look at her. "I know it is not an excuse," she said. "The things I wrote were unacceptable. I just . . . I was so angry, all the time. Most of it was directed at me, but it was easier to take it out on everyone else, make others feel the same shame I felt, make them feel helpless. I hated myself, so I hated on others. And in the end, that just made everything worse."

"I still don't understand why you directed so much of that anger at her though," Jasper interjected, gesturing at Elle. "You always seemed to dislike her, but as time went on, you downright hated her. Why is that?"

Elle sat up a little straighter, clearly interested in hearing that answer.

Amelia looked even more embarrassed now, unable to hold Elle's gaze. "In the beginning, it was just jealousy, I think. You always seemed so confident and in charge. Like you were not afraid of anything. I hated that because . . ." Her throat bobbed as she swallowed. "Because I knew I could never be like that."

Elle shook her head. "I was never like that. Never will be. No one is scared of nothing."

"Maybe," Amelia softly said. "Either way, everything got worse when Evelyn arrived here."

"Because you liked her," Seth simply stated.

I could feel my jaw dropping as I stared at Amelia. At first, it didn't make sense—I didn't want it to. But then I thought back to the afternoon we had spent studying, to her crying in the empty classroom, to her face when I hadn't sat with her on the bus. The entire time I had only had eyes for Elle. How could I have been so blind?

"I am sorry, Evelyn," Amelia said, her features softening when she locked eyes with me. "I know that it was wrong to lash out at No—*Ashley* when I realized I could not have you."

"Speaking of *that* article," Elle cut in. "How the fuck did you find out about my real name?"

Amelia's shoulders went up in a helpless shrug. "I was in the

Never Kiss your Roommate

library to post another article and when I turned on one of the computers, it was open to this website with pictures of your mom. There was a photo of you when you were younger and below it was your name. Whoever used the computer before me hadn't turned it off properly."

"Me," I whispered, nausea washing over me at the memory. "That was me. When I googled your mom after finding her name in your magazines."

Elle's head whipped around to stare at me.

Before she could even open her mouth, I said, "I'm sorry. God, I'm so sorry, Elle, this was all my fault—"

"Shut up," she said, but there wasn't any heat in her voice. "It wasn't just you. It was a chain reaction of shitty events. If the news hadn't spread the information about my location, Kyle wouldn't have known where to find me. If Amelia hadn't posted it on The Chitter Chatter, it wouldn't have been picked up by other news outlets. If I didn't have my magazines lying around, you wouldn't have found out about my mom. I could go on."

Despite her words, I still felt guilt pooling in my stomach. Elle, who could read my face like an open book by now, noticed. Grabbing my hand, she said, "Stop blaming yourself. It doesn't matter now. All of us are okay."

I turned back to Amelia, who was staring at her feet, hunched over like there was a weight on her shoulders that grew with every passing second. Suddenly, I couldn't find it in me to be angry with her. Because studying her, all I saw was myself a few months ago; a girl who was insecure, lonely, and full of disgust for herself, who cried while she practiced saying the words *Mom, Dad, I think I'm lesbian* in the mirror, who didn't feel like there was a single person in the world who she could talk to. Who knows what would have happened if I hadn't had my parents and my new friends? If the ice water had become more and more paralyzing, no one there to help me get out? Maybe I would have turned my hatred outward as well.

"I'm sorry, Amy," I said after a moment of silence, hoping she could tell I was being sincere. "If I had known, I would have tried to help you come to terms with everything you were feeling. I know how hard it can be, especially when you have no one to talk to about it."

Amelia looked up at me, her eyes widening a little in surprise. "Thank you."

"One more thing," Jasper said. "Is that the reason why you tricked Seth into kissing you and put it on your blog? To hide your feelings for Evelyn? Or . . . or did you want to suppress them?"

"Both, I think," she softly said. "Seth had been so kind to me when he and Evelyn had found me crying, and he was the only boy I could bring myself to kiss. I knew I could never like him or any other boy like that, but I felt like I had to at least pretend. Because somehow I felt like everyone could tell I liked Evelyn." Her voice sounded like it was about to break the longer she spoke. "I was . . . I was terrified of anyone finding out. Especially my parents."

"It's okay, Amelia," Seth said. "I understand."

"No," she whispered, tears pooling in her eyes. "It is not okay. I almost ruined your relationship. I nearly got all of you *killed*. I do not deserve sympathy."

"You're also the reason the police found us," I pointed out. "Who knows what would have happened otherwise."

Before she could answer, the door suddenly opened and

Never Kiss your Roommate

Mrs. Whitworth poked her head through the door, Mr. and Mrs. Campbell looking impatient behind her.

"Are you finished yet?" she asked.

The four of us exchanged a glance and it was at that moment and without a single word uttered that I knew we were all on the same side.

"Yes," Elle said. Her voice was clear and firm, without a trace of doubt. "Amelia should stay at Seven Hills." Amelia's shoulders, as well as her parents', sagged in relief.

Her mother gave a nod before turning to Amelia. Sternly, she said, "You're lucky. Do not disappoint us again."

Amelia gave a weak nod.

"Mr. and Mrs. Campbell, why don't you go ahead and find yourselves a seat in the Great Hall," Mrs. Whitworth said, a small furrow between her brows. "Amelia will be downstairs shortly."

Without so much as another glance at us, the two strode out into the hallway.

o o o

Amelia exhaled a shaky breath as soon as the door fell shut behind them, her eyes fluttering closed for a moment.

"No offense," Elle snorted. "But your parents are assholes."

Not even Mrs. Whitworth bothered to object. Instead, she offered us a small smile, one hand lightly rubbing Amelia's shoulder in a reassuring gesture. "Well done, you four. Now, get out of here and have fun, all right? The Winter Banquet is starting and I imagine you've had enough hardship for at least ten years. Go ahead!"

We didn't need to be told twice and immediately filed out of the room, but Amelia grabbed onto my arm before I could run off. "Why did you do that?" she asked in a thin voice. "Why did you not let them expel me?"

"Because I want you to be here," I said, gesturing at our surroundings. "I want you to be out of your parents' reach, in a safe space where you can be yourself. It's what everyone deserves."

Amelia's mouth opened and closed a few times before she managed to whisper, "Thank you."

"It's all right. No one here knows that it was you who wrote The Chitter Chatter. You can start over." I squeezed the hand that was still on my arm. "I'm always here if you need to talk. Now go and grab a pretty girl to dance with."

Amelia let out an incredulous laugh. Then, without another word, she turned around and hurried down the stairs.

An arm slung around my waist the moment she was out of sight. "We really are some nice fucking people," Elle muttered before pulling me down the stairs and towards the Great Hall.

However, we had barely made it to the entrance hall when the doors suddenly burst open and heavy steps made their way towards us.

I looked over to see who had entered, only to blink in confusion.

"Giovanni?" Seth shouted. "What are you doing here?"

The giant man steered towards us with a laugh. Even though he was wearing a suit and had his hair combed back, he looked out of place between the students and parents bustling around the hall. "Ah, bambini!" he hollered, frantically trying to straighten his tie. "How nice to see all of you alive, eh? Maria told me what happened!"

"Are you here for her?" I asked.

"Yes! Have you seen her?"

"Actually, we have no idea who—" Seth began, but got cut off by Giovanni.

"Ah, *bellissima*, there you are!"

I turned my head just in time to see Miss Pepperman coming down the hallway. Her face lit up as soon as she saw Giovanni, and she hurried towards him faster than I would've thought she could move.

"Oh my, there you are! I was already thinking you forgot!" she exclaimed, throwing her arms around him.

Giovanni shook his head. "Of course not! The restaurant . . . there was so much to do, so many guests, I just couldn't leave and then I looked at the clock and it was already six! I came here as fast as possible!"

Miss Pepperman let out a youthful giggle as he pressed a kiss to her cheek and turned to look at us. Standing next to each other, they were like a caricature, Giovanni huge and heavyset next to the tiny librarian. "Children, I didn't realize you knew my Gio! Why did you never say anything?"

Giovanni nodded, resting his hands on his hips. "Yes! Didn't I tell you to say hello to Maria for me when you came to the restaurant?"

"Wait, so y-you . . . you are Maria?" I stammered. "And he's the mysterious guy living in town that you've been seeing all along?"

"Why, of course! We've been together for a few months now!"

"Oh my God," Seth said, turning to stare at me. "How did we not see this coming?"

"Shall we go inside then?" Miss Pepperman chirped, pointing at the door to the Great Hall. "The food is already waiting."

Giovanni linked arms with her, only turning around once more to grin at Jasper and say, "Better hope it's nothing spicy, eh, bambino?"

While Jasper scowled, Seth burst out laughing. Together, we followed after the odd couple, the whir of voices growing louder the closer we came. A heavenly scent wafted through the festively decorated halls—cinnamon and cloves, chocolate and pine—and by the time we stepped through the arches of the Great Hall, I couldn't restrain a giddy smile. The ceiling lights had been dimmed and replaced by hundreds of candles that were scattered across the tables, their soft golden glow flickering across the faces of the guests.

However, I couldn't fully take everything in before my eyes landed on a pair in the back of the room. With a quiet gasp, I grabbed onto Elle's hand and tugged her with me as I hurried towards them.

"Mom! Dad!"

They didn't have the chance to say anything before I crashed into them.

"There, there," Dad said, his rumbling laughter vibrating against me when he tightly wrapped his arms around me. I took a deep breath and buried my face against his shoulder, inhaling the familiar smell of *home*.

"Oh, it's so good to see you," Mom murmured when I moved on to hug her. "And how pretty you look in that dress! All grown up."

I stepped back and intertwined my hand with Elle's again, who was standing rooted in place, an endearingly nervous look on her face. "Mom, Dad," I said, my voice giddy with excitement. "This is Elle."

"The girlfriend, hm?" Mom asked. In the dim light, her eyes were shining with warmth.

"The girlfriend that almost got kidnapped," Dad grumbled, shaking her hand. "I couldn't believe it when Evelyn told me. Damn stupid of her and the boys to get themselves into danger like that."

Elle looked like she tried to bite her tongue, but eventually still blurted, "Dumb, but also really brave. If it weren't for them, I probably wouldn't be here right now."

Dad leveled her with a gruff stare. "Careful with the things you say and the people you disagree with, Ashley. I still haven't decided whether I think you're good enough for my daughter or not."

Elle's eyes widened a little. "I'm sorry, Mr. Greene, I didn't mean to disrespect y—"

She broke off when he suddenly cracked up laughing. "Don't look so shocked, I was just joking! After everything Lynnie told us about you, I couldn't get myself to dislike you even if I tried."

"Dad!" I said. "Not funny."

Elle shrugged, scratching at her neck. "A little funny."

A high-pitched beeping sounded through the room before the interaction could get any more awkward. The source of the noise was the microphone that Mrs. Whitworth, who had changed into an elegant pantsuit, was holding as she stepped onto a little makeshift podium.

The room came into motion as everyone scurried to sit down at the long tables. Elle spotted Jasper and Seth, who were saving seats for us, sitting with two girls who had to be Jasper's older sisters.

Once the last murmurs had died down, Mrs. Whitworth

began. "Good evening, everyone! It is a pleasure to welcome all of you to Seven Hills' annual Winter Banquet. As always, a few introductory words from me before we get to what all of you are probably here for: the food."

Loud claps and hoots from the students mixed with the chuckles of the parents.

Mrs. Whitworth waited with a patient smile for the room to quiet. "I would like to thank the teachers for their wonderful work this year. I couldn't wish for better colleagues, even in turbulent times like the past few weeks. However, it isn't just the teachers who amaze me; above all, it's the students who have made this year so special." She paused, her eyes drifting over the rows of tables before her. "I would like to take the time to honor two students who have stood out this year. One of them is Jasper Des Lauriers."

After a split second of surprise, Jasper stood up and gave a little bow.

"The play you have written and directed with the drama club this year is the perfect embodiment of all that this school tries to be: tolerant, open, and diverse. I want to thank you for reminding all of us that this is what truly matters."

Jasper's *thank you* got drowned out by the applause around me. Elle and I clapped the loudest, only matched by his sisters.

Seth was the only one who was silent: his eyes were fixed on Jasper, a small smile playing around his lips. Jasper noticed, too, and after a split second of hesitation, leaned over and grabbed Seth's chin to pull him into a short kiss.

Seth's cheeks were flaming red when Jasper let go of him, but he was beaming even wider than before.

Mrs. Whitworth cleared her throat, directing the attention

Never Kiss your Roommate

back to her. "The second extraordinary student is the person who has managed to score a win against Westbridge and get the basketball team to first place in the league for the first time in years. Seven Hills' first female team captain, Ashley Danell!"

Elle's grin was all teeth as she pumped her fist in the air. "Hell yeah!"

Chuckling, I pressed a kiss to her cheek. Pride settled into my stomach; not only for her, but also because a few months ago I wouldn't have thought it possible to sit here with a girl's arm around me and kiss her, in front of my parents, in front of the whole school, and not feel a sliver of fear.

"Well done, Ashley!" Mrs. Whitworth shouted over the loud clapping and the basketball team's cheering. "Now I don't want to bore all of you any longer. Let's eat!"

The doors to the kitchen slammed open the moment her sentence ended, and into the Great Hall strutted all of Seven Hills' cooks and kitchen staff, carrying dishes and pots filled to the brim with copious amounts of food.

Noticing Seth's incredulous expression, I nudged his leg under the table. "This *posh private boarding school* didn't turn out all that bad, did it?"

He shook his head. "Ask me again in a few months when I'm failing my GCSEs because I was too caught up in solving the mystery around The Chitter Chatter and a bloody kidnapping to retain anything we did in class."

"Seth, we both know you're going to do better than all of us combined," I laughed. "And if not, we'll just all have to stay here another year, won't we?"

"I like the sound of that," he said, clinking his glass against mine before both of us dug into the food.

In the quiet that settled over the hall once everyone was busy eating, Elle's gasp was clearly audible.

I looked up in surprise, but before I could ask what was going on, Elle was already on her feet, sending her chair scraping across the stone floor. My eyes followed her as she darted across the room until they landed on the woman who had appeared in the doorway.

With high heels and a black evening gown, Crystal Danell looked like she had stepped right out of one of the magazines that were stacked on Elle's desk. However, one thing was different. In all the photos of her, she had worn a small, professional smile, ready for the camera and the press. Now, as Elle flung herself into her arms, there was a genuine, bright grin on her face, though it quickly disappeared as she buried her face in her daughter's curls.

In the startled silence that followed, it was easy to make out what they were saying.

"I didn't think you'd come," Elle muttered, sounding a little choked up, though I was pretty sure that Jasper, Seth, and I were the only ones to notice. "Aren't you in the middle of your tour?"

"I am." Crystal Danell's voice was smoky and warm, much like when she was singing. "But I canceled the photoshoots and interviews I had scheduled today. Did you really think I wouldn't try everything to see you after everything that happened, baby?"

Elle took a step back; from where I was sitting I couldn't see her face, but I was pretty sure it displayed a similar expression to her mom's affectionate smile. "I missed you so much."

Some murmurs began to arise. Looking around, I realized that most of the other students seemed either surprised or disbelieving as they heard her soft tone, soaked in real emotion for once. They knew the stone-cold girl who would snarl at people in the hallways or the vicious team captain who yelled at her teammates on the basketball court, not the girl who turned on the fairy lights every night and talked to our kitten in a baby voice. I wondered if they understood what this meant, if they felt as honored as I had to finally be let in.

"I missed you, too, sweetie," Crystal said, reaching out to stroke Elle's hair in a gesture that was so gentle it made something in my own stomach twist.

"Come on, let's get you a seat!" Elle said, grabbing her hand despite all the eyes that were on her. "You need to meet Evelyn and my friends . . ."

I stood, suddenly taken by the same nerves that Elle had probably felt a few moments earlier.

"Mom," she said when they reached us, slinging an arm around my waist. "This is Evelyn. My girlfriend."

"So I finally get to meet you! Hi, I'm Crystal," she said and pulled me into an unexpected hug.

After a startled moment of hesitation, I wrapped my arms around her in turn. When I opened my eyes, I found Elle beaming at me. "I'm so glad you could come," I murmured.

"Me too. It's about time I finally got the chance to come here." She then suddenly turned to me. "Jasper, hi! Ashley told me so much about you."

Jasper's ears had gone a little red, his hands nervously clasped in front of him. "Hi, Miss Danell."

"Oh, it's just Crystal," she chuckled.

When Elle appeared with another chair, Crystal sat down with us and quickly got into a conversation with my parents.

I was sure that after Giovanni and now Crystal, nothing could surprise me anymore. That was, until another pair entered through the archway and Seth's fork clattered onto his plate.

"Your parents?" Jasper asked, wide-eyed as the two neared our table.

Seth gave a nod, slowly getting to his feet like he couldn't believe what he was seeing. "Sorry we're late," the man said in the same thick Northern accent I had grown so used to, offering Seth a startlingly familiar grin. He was just as tall and lanky as his son, his movements a little bit clumsy as he gestured at the brown-haired, green-eyed woman next to him. "We underestimated how slow traffic is with all the snow up here."

Seth was still blinking at them like he was sure any moment they would evaporate into thin air. "You . . . you drove the entire way here? Together?"

The woman gave a small nod, nerves written all over her face, which was just as much of an open book as Seth's. "We couldn't miss out on this now, could we?"

Seth gulped, still frozen in place. Then, he suddenly stepped forward without another word and pulled her into his arms, his quiet "I missed you" muffled into her hair.

I wasn't aware of the tears pooling in my eyes until Elle handed me a tissue, wrapping an arm around me when I chuckled tearfully, thinking back to the countless times I had caught Seth staring down at the messages on his phone, always so bad at pretending they didn't affect him. On the other side of the table, Jasper quickly wiped a hand over his eyes before he stood and went to introduce himself.

They were interrupted when Miss Pepperman stepped onto the podium and tapped against the microphone to get everybody's attention. "Hello everyone!" she chirped. "I hope you

Never Kiss
your Roommate

have all eaten well because, oh my, I am bursting! But enough sitting around! The dance floor in the entrance hall is now open. Have fun!"

The second she finished her sentence, some people jumped to their feet and headed out the door, where loud music was starting to play.

"Do you want to?" Elle asked.

"*Yes*," I immediately said, my heart leaping at the idea.

Elle only stopped once more to tap Crystal on the shoulder. "Mom? Will you still be here when I come back?"

"Of course, baby," Crystal responded, squeezing her daughter's hand. "My flight is scheduled in two days. I'm staying in a hotel in town."

Elle nodded, clearly relieved, before she turned around and pulled me towards the door.

I gasped when we stepped out into the entrance hall. Dozens of couples in sparkling dresses and fancy suits were twirling across the floor, drenched in the golden glow of the chandelier overhead. Fairy lights were wrapped around the railings of the stairs and draped across the arched doorways, shining like the stars I could just barely make out behind the windows. It was like I had stepped into a ballroom like the ones in Jane Austen's novels, except I didn't have to spend the evening courting the person I had set my eyes on but walked in with her hand already firmly in mine.

"A little corny, isn't it?" Elle said with a teasing grin that told me she knew exactly what I was thinking.

I shook my head, still utterly starstruck, and whispered, "It's *romantic*."

Elle hummed and lowered into a small curtsy. In an

exaggerated Regency-era British accent, she asked, "May I have this dance then?"

"Yes," I breathed, trying and failing to hold back a giddy smile. "You may."

The next thing I knew, Elle was pulling me onto the dance floor, her hands on my waist and her eyes shining brighter than all the stars in the sky. Looking over her shoulder, I saw Jasper and Seth whirling around in a tangle of limbs, both of them laughing as they tried to figure out the steps. Close to them was Sammy, Jasper's ex-boyfriend; he smiled at Jasper as he twirled by with his arms around Aiden from the drama club, not a trace of hostility on either of their faces. Miss Pepperman and Giovanni were swaying in the corner, offbeat but beaming at each other.

Finally, on the outskirts of the crowd, I spotted Amelia. She was standing with Elina, the girl from our class who was on the cheerleading squad as well. She was grinning at Amelia, tugging at her hand until Amelia breathed a nervous laugh and let herself be pulled onto the dance floor, timidly placing her hands on the other girl's waist.

"Elle," I whispered, jerking my head in Amelia's direction.

She turned us around a little so she could see, whistling through her teeth. "Who would've thought."

"Looks like everyone's getting their happy ending after all," I softly said.

Elle smiled in a way that made my heart feel like it was too big for my chest and pulled me closer until I could see every little speck in her warm brown eyes, open and unguarded—and God, I was so in love with her I felt it in every cell of my body, all the way down to my toes.

In a sudden moment of clarity, I thought if I could have shown my younger self any glimpse into the future it would have been this one; I would have wiped her tears away, kissed her on the forehead, and told her *Look how much better it'll get. You'll find people you won't have to hide from, and you'll fall in love. With her, and with yourself too. Just hold on a little longer.*

She probably would have never believed it then, just like I wouldn't have believed it if anyone had told me on my first day here that the girl sitting in the windowsill with a cigarette between her fingers and thunderstorm eyes would end up becoming *this* to me.

Now, I leaned in, every touch as natural as breathing, and pressed my lips to the dimple in her cheek, just because a few months ago I wouldn't have known it was there and because I *could*.

"About time."

The End

ACKNOWLEDGMENTS

I started writing this book when I had just turned sixteen, barely just out to my parents and still very much struggling with my sexuality. Had someone told little closeted me then that roughly four years later this silly little story I was working on every day after school would end up as an unapologetically queer novel people could buy in bookstores, I would have never believed them.

Since its beginning—a rough, *rough* beginning—on Wattpad, this book has been touched by so many incredible people without whom this story wouldn't be what it is now.

I want to thank the amazing team at Wattpad for taking a chance on this story: Ryan LaPlante, who stumbled upon the first draft and somehow saw potential in it. The Wattpad Stars team, especially Irina Pintea and Emma Szalai, who helped me so much on my writing journey. Carmen Ho, who had to wade through the massive manuscript it was at the time it entered the Paid Program, and somehow still showed it so much love. The Wattpad Books team: Robyn Cole, who witnessed me making a fool on the phone when I was offered this publishing deal; I-Yana Tucker, my wonderful talent manager, who got up early to get on calls with me on the other side of the world and replied to all my panicked emails at lightning speed, making this whole process way less scary with her supportive older sister energy; Jada Parada-Hemmings, who worked hard to make me seem like a real author; Hannah Drennan, who designed the absolute cover of my dreams; Rebecca Sands, whose amazing first notes pushed the first draft from a Wattpad story to something that actually felt like a real novel; Jen Hale, who's my personal hero simply because of her talent for catching all those pesky little errors and inconsistencies all while leaving the funniest, sweetest in-line comments; and last but not least Deanna McFadden, my incredible editor who was so gentle with me throughout the most draining editing stages and who taught me lessons about writing that I'll always treasure. Thanks to all of you, I always knew this book was going to be in good hands, and especially the fact that it was mostly a collaboration of so many inspirational women makes me so happy!

Thank you to my family for always believing in me, for never making me feel anything less than unconditionally loved, for letting me ramble about my edits at the dinner table, and for supplying me with tea and chocolate. I didn't let you read any of this for the longest time because I wanted you to be able to hold it while you do; I hope that, even though you might not understand all the gay jokes in this, you liked what you read. *Michel und Ylvie: das hier ist wahrscheinlich das Einzige, was ihr von dem Buch lest, aber das ist okay. Ich hab' euch lieb!*

To my friends, Elise, Lorena, Merle, Linda, Louisa, and of course Vera, the first person I knew in real life who read this story: thank you for cheering me on from the sidelines, for listening to my Snapchat rants, and for getting me out of my head when I needed it. I couldn't ask for better friends.

To all my other friends, the ones who live on the other end of the world but still feel so close, especially Grey, Alicia, Akriti, and the entire Discord channel: thank you for reading over stuff when I wasn't sure if it was stupid, for sending me some vaguely threatening but mostly wholesome memes, for vibing with me on Snapchat, and for the Discord love spams. I'm so grateful to have met each one of you and can't wait to see the things you'll do. Of course, also a thank-you to Stella, who, with her fan art and singing, stays carrying the fandom!

Last, but definitely not least, I want to thank you, my readers. Whether you read this book when I was posting irregular updates back in 2017 or you've just heard about it for the first time this week, thank you for spending time with these characters, for all the comments and messages over the years and, through the love you showed Evelyn, Seth, Noelle, and Jasper, for also making me love myself a bit more when I needed it the most. Without you, none of this would have ever been possible, and for that I'm forever grateful.

ABOUT THE AUTHOR

Philline Harms has been writing from the age of eleven and since joining Wattpad in 2016 her stories have garnered over five million reads. When she's not working on a story, Philline can be found curled up with a book, spending time with her friends, or crafting obscurely specific Spotify playlists. Philline is currently a university student residing in Germany.

Want more? Why not try . . .

Can Emma and Vivian stay together
even when summer is over?

Want more? Why not try . . .

Sometimes the last thing you're looking for
is the one thing you need the most . . .

Want more? Why not try . . .

From the outside, Everest has it all, but
there's only one girl who can see him
for who he truly is

Want more? Why not try . . .

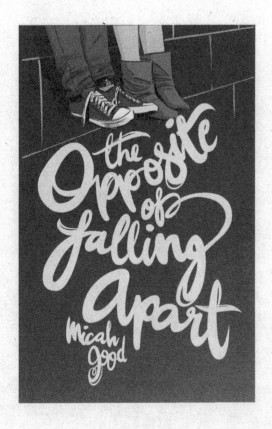

Can Jonas and Brennan help each other
to stop living in the past and start
dreaming about the future?

Want more? Why not try . . .

Can Amelia hide her dark past from
bad boy Aiden?

Want more? Why not try . . .

Can Johnny and Alison find the strength to battle the monsters lurking in the shadows of their magical boarding school?

wattpad

Where stories live.

Discover millions of stories created by diverse writers from around the globe.

Download the app or visit www.wattpad.com today.

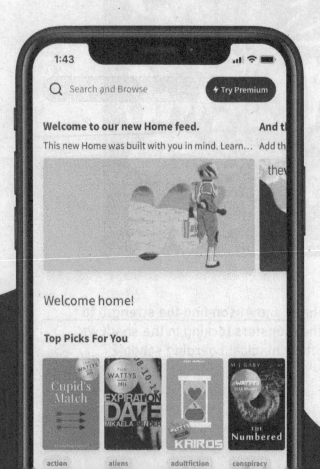